No Turning Back

Roger Rees

Roger J Rees is Emeritus Professor of Disability Research in the School of Medicine at Flinders University, Adelaide. He was educated at the London School of Economics, Monash University and the University of New England. He has taught in Australia at the University of Canberra and Flinders University.

He has held teaching fellowship positions at Arizona State University, the Bureau of Child Research University of Kansas, the brain trauma unit at New York University and at the Medical Research Centre (MRC) Cambridge University.

His principal research interests have been in the neurosciences with a focus on rehabilitation from brain injury. He has run a trauma rehabilitation program for people with brain injury, neurological disorders and those diagnosed with HIV.

He travelled in Ethiopia and walked with the Hamar tribe as part of his preparation for *No Turning Back*. This is his first book of fiction.

Also by Roger Rees

Parents as Language Therapists

DELSC (Developmental Language Skills Curriculum) Volumes:
1 Orientation Skills 2. Receptive Language 3. Expressive Language

Plateaus and Summits Transition to Employment for
People with Brain Injury

Locked In State, in; Science at its Sharpest
(edited by Robyn Williams)

Re-writing the Script – Influence of Context on Behaviour
(including rewriting the script video for television)

The Art of the Possible
Review of the Royal Rehabilitation Centre Sydney

Interrupted Lives: Rehabilitation and Learning following Brain Injury

Out of Calamity – Stories of Trauma Survivors
(Preface by Dr Norman Swan)

Roger Rees has also written a number of broadcast scripts
for the ABC Science Show and published many articles
in journals and newspapers.

ROGER REES

NO
TURNING
BACK

HYBRID
PUBLISHERS

Published by Hybrid Publishers

Melbourne Victoria Australia

www.hybridpublishers.com.au

First published 2017

National Library of Australia Cataloguing-in-Publication entry (pbk)

Creator: Rees, Roger J., author.

Title: No Turning Back / Roger Rees.

ISBN: 9781925272802 (paperback)

Subjects: Anthropologists – Australia – Fiction
Physicians – Ethiopia – Fiction
HIV-positive persons – Fiction.

Cover design: Gittus Graphics

Typeset in Minion Pro

In childhood you own little more than your secret places, the thoughts in your head.

Tim Winton, *Island Home*

... once a choice has been made it cannot be reversed; every event has its inevitable consequence; the clock goes on ticking.

David Malouf, *The Writing Life*

And here, in Age, I feel the need
Of some Divining Colander
To hold the best of all since done
And let the rest slip through.

Rosemary Dobson, *Rosemary Dobson Collected*

for Max Kemp

1: Travelling

Map of Ethiopia

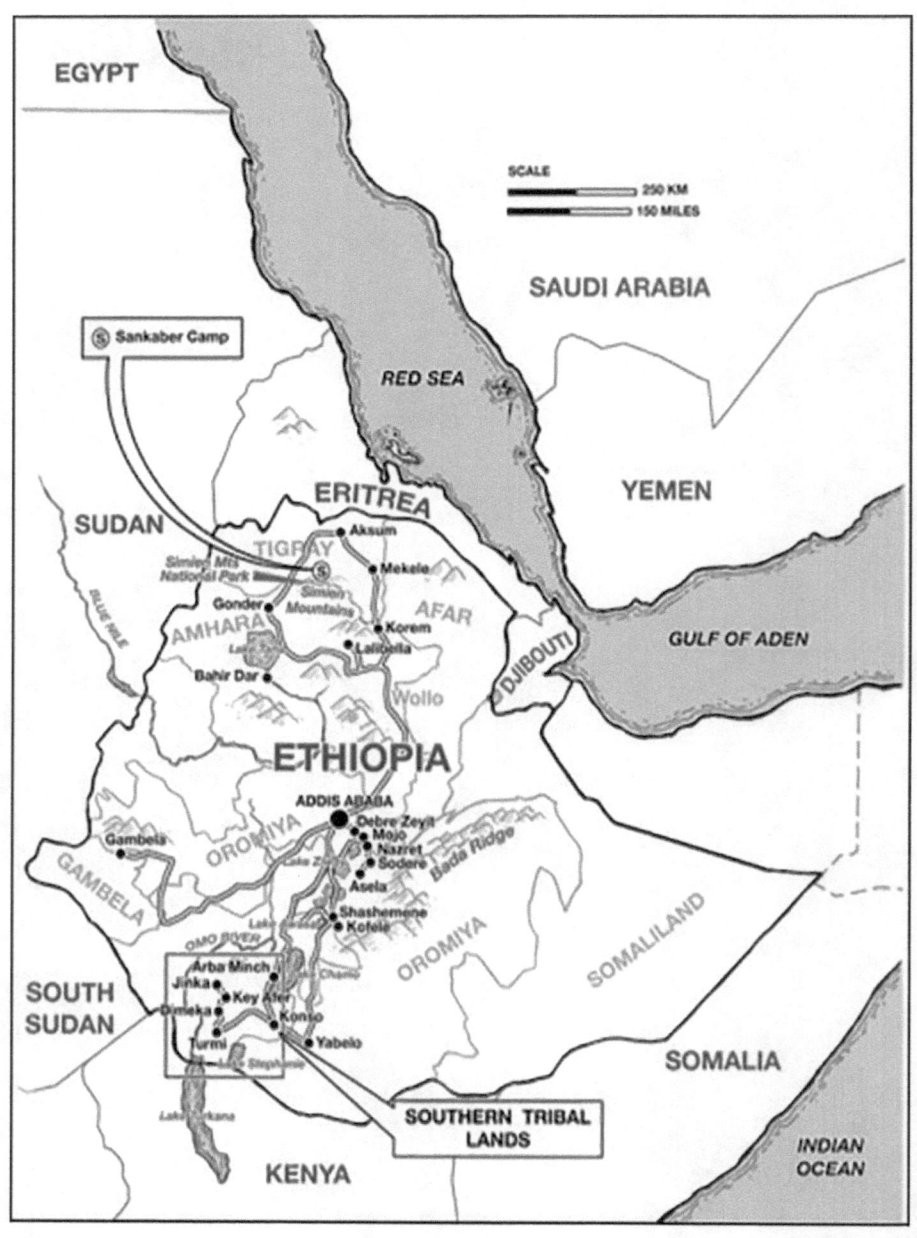

Addis Ababa, 1985

IT WAS A TIME of tumult. The second great Ethiopian famine of the twentieth century was ending. Detritus of human and animal corpses were everywhere, and in the countryside death's pallor was on every face.

Slowly, very slowly, food distribution was beginning to reach isolated villages, but only after a million people had died. Unrest and anger, accompanied by a sense of hopelessness, was felt in every village and small town.

Spend a few weeks with me and you will learn what famine does to people and how we can make sure this never happens again, wrote the Ethiopian anthropologist Zeno Wolde to his visiting students, among whom were the young Australian anthropologist Louise Davitt and her British colleague Carmen Smith. They had just flown into Addis Ababa from Heathrow Airport to begin a month's fieldwork with Zeno.

Louise, originally from country South Australia, was twenty-three: confident, blonde, tall, slim and adventurous. Carmen, a twenty-four-year-old Lancastrian, was short, dark-haired and rather plump. As an independent, working-class girl, she was well read and had a passion for fun and travel. They were both writers ... Louise was a poet and brilliantly observant; Carmen was a chronicler of travel and history with, like Louise, impeccable research talents. They had met nine months before at London University, where both were enrolled in a postgraduate doctoral program. Within a week of introducing themselves they were friends.

They were picked up at the airport by Abebe, Zeno's Addis University driver, in an old diesel Nissan Patrol 4WD. He greeted them with smiles and enthusiasm. '*Selam* (Hello), *selam, merhaba,* welcome!' he exclaimed as he shook hands with Louise and Carmen.

Abebe drove from the airport along hectic, crumbling roads. They saw beggars in rags alongside smart, brightly dressed men and women; lone barefoot children skipping through the dust and gravel thrown up by heavy trucks; well-groomed children walking hand in hand with parents; laden donkey carts alongside chauffeur-driven Mercedes; men driving scrawny goats beside six-axle trucks carrying cattle and produce to the city market. AK47-armed Derg soldiers were on every corner. As much as possible, pedestrians avoided them and wove their way among lorries, taxis and cars of every size, age, make, condition and colour. Throngs of people surged around temporary market stalls at roadside intersections. Petrol and diesel fumes filled the still, clammy air.

It was late afternoon, and the shops and roadside stalls were full of people bartering for food, fabrics and fuel: a conglomerate of humanity, some barely existing, others clearly enjoying the pleasures of the city. The two women saw starving people with cerebral palsy, handicapped people begging and limping along, while others sauntered into the few palatial restaurants to be welcomed at the door by uniformed maître d's. These first visions caught Louise's attention and heightened her emotions, especially when a gaunt, crippled boy begged at their car window as they stopped at an intersection. She felt helpless and realised how a traveller's heart could harden when faced with such profuse distress.

In the city centre, they drove past the limestone St George's Cathedral, Addis Ababa's famous Orthodox Coptic church, with bold notices inviting worshippers to *Meet your God*. Louise stared as hundreds of worshippers kissed its perimeter walls, seeking blessings and answers to prayers.

'They come every day, looking for cures for sickness, and confirmation of riches in heaven,' said Abebe. 'Cathedral's locked at the

4

moment for a priest's prayer service, but there is still much to see in the grounds. If you like, I'll stop, so you can take a closer look.'

He parked the 4WD in a side street. Louise and Carmen climbed down, tired, but keen to observe the rituals and customs of Addis Ababa's faithful. The Coptic worshippers ignored them. People repeatedly kissed walls, stained with a million previous kisses, or knelt in devotion on adjacent paths and grass – anywhere they could find a space. They bought cheap amulets of St George with images of him and his lance on a fat white horse, and endlessly repeated an Old Testament mantra in Amharic: *God is our heavenly Father and we will obey him.* Hundreds, of all ages, stood or knelt. Abebe told Louise they were waiting for a sign that the Second Coming was near. Did these people really believe in the Second Coming? All this intensity, this level of devotion, was so unexpected – not what Louise had imagined or read about. She stood and watched these people, in their pleading and prayer.

Amid their mutterings, Louise thought of the once-a-week sedate Anglican worshippers at her home church in the Adelaide Hills, with people dressed in their Sunday best, thanking the vicar for his oft-repeated sermon about St Paul on the road to Damascus. Incredulous at what they were observing, Louise and Carmen walked away past street vendors and climbed back into the 4WD.

'Nothing much will come of their prayers, but they'll be back again tomorrow,' Abebe said, as if to confirm his scepticism. 'They are here every day; it's been like this forever.'

They drove the last mile to the university campus, entering via high, imposing black wrought-iron gates; the university name was printed in metre-high letters on an adjacent stone wall. Once inside, they drove down a wide avenue of palm trees with well-tended flower beds, shrubs and lawns on either side. Beyond were pictur-esque features of the old formal Selassie buildings, set alongside hibiscus and bougainvillea. Further along the driveway and its many tangential paths, students sat in animated conversation; young men and women embraced in the shelter of pepper trees, while others stretched out, enjoying late afternoon sunshine.

'Campus is a good place to be, very different from in the city,' said Abebe. Louise and Carmen had to agree. This was an oasis compared to their first experiences of Addis Ababa. The 4WD swung past two-storey stone administration buildings and pulled up outside a prefab student accommodation block.

After introductions to other students, Carmen and Louise unpacked in a small, sparsely furnished bedroom with two single beds. At 5.30 pm it was still too early to go to bed, despite their tiredness from the long flight. Louise was buoyant, just as she had been when she first arrived in London. She was anxious to explore the campus. She put on close-fitting grey tracksuit pants with the Australian gold and green stripes on the legs and asked Carmen to go with her, but she declined, saying she needed to rest. 'Louise, you never stop. Even now, when we haven't slept for a day, you're in your conquer-all, find-out-about-everything mood!'

'I'll just stretch my legs; I won't be long, no more than half an hour.'

'Enjoy yourself.'

The campus was vast and sprawling. It would be easy to get lost, Louise thought, as she followed signs pointing to the Department of Ethiopian Studies. She stood for a moment in order to get her bearings, unsure of which way to go. Ethiopia's heritage was everywhere. She sensed the spectre of another time in this land as she saw more distant pillars at buildings' entrances, stone-lined pathways and monuments: symbols of the Ras dynasty, and of the old Emperor Haile Selassie, 'Elect of God'. She imagined him feeding his pet lions that apparently used to roam freely in adjacent grounds. Ethiopian life had changed irrevocably since the Emperor's demise in 1974.

The campus was quiet except for the city traffic beyond the perimeter walls. Sighting further signs pointing to *Ethiopian Studies,* she strode on. Soon she was in front of a flight of wide stone steps leading to heavy, engraved double doors at the department entrance.

Feeling weary, her mood changed. She looked at the imposing

stairway, then turned and walked slowly back the way she had come.

As she walked, she regained her usual confidence and decided to capture the effects of these first hours in Ethiopia in her notebook: the cool evening air in this high plateau city, the well-maintained Haile Selassie-endowed buildings, the contrasting shacks and poverty, the teeming people, uniformed Derg soldiers, the beggars and worshippers. As she walked she also recalled some of the finer points of articles in journals about Ethiopia and realised she needed to explore the creative lives of some of Ethiopia's writers because, she believed, good literature reflected the lives and spirit of the people. Writers such as Abbe Gubennya and Mengistu Lemma, she had been told, held a mirror up to their society. She would read their work. She pushed on and arrived back at the hostel in time to join Carmen for an evening meal.

In London Louise was usually up by seven, but here everyone was afoot as soon as it was light. Each morning she was wakened by loud music and the cacophonous sounds of traffic. Abebe called on the first two mornings to take them on short tours of the city. On the first morning Louise watched the hazy sun as it broke free of the rooftops, causing shadows and splashes of bright light. People were already at work: hundreds of them, walking along with well-dressed children, presumably on their way to school. Some people sat on the kerbside, others sprawled on pavements around buildings and shacks. Abebe parked in a side street adjacent to an entrance to Addis Ababa's huge Mercato Market.

They walked down the crumbling lane to the market entrance. Since Louise knew only a few words of Amharic, the comfort of Carmen's company strengthened her resolve to communicate with stallholders. Carmen had spent six months in Kenya, but Louise had never been to Africa before and, despite her gap year in Italy, had rarely left the reassuring noises and patterns of Adelaide and London.

Stepping round street vendors, they entered the market. Abebe advised that it would be safest if, at least on this first visit, he accompanied them. While the rest of Addis Ababa symbolised a country establishing a fresh identity under the Derg, the timeless, noisy and vigorous Mercato Market remained unchanged. Louise was surprised at the labyrinth of streets and alleyways, the blacksmiths' forges spewing smoke and flames, and the tanners sitting with piles of hides and fresh skins hung up to dry, still crusted with blood. There were men cutting rocks and others trimming vegetables, while aromas of spicy beef curries, fruit, vegetables and flowers, along with the smells of donkeys and goats, wafted over the stalls.

For the next hour, the three of them picked their way between stalls amidst the din of bartering chatter. The market's tumult could be exhausting, but Louise felt joyous at the sight of the chaos and obvious vitality. Abebe suggested they stop for coffee. They sat alongside other customers eating spicy meats wrapped in *injera*, smelling the scent of incense burning. Everyone had warned them about the risks of wandering in Mercato but, in reality, walking alongside the noisy throng, they felt quite safe.

They left the market exhilarated; the taste and smell of coffee still with them along with the sights and sounds of Ethiopians plying their trades.

Ayzore – 'Be Strong'

AFTER THREE DAYS of meeting fellow students and touring Addis Ababa, it was time to prepare for the first field trip. Louise and Carmen registered for the one-day pre-fieldwork course titled *Anthropology and Health*, introduced themselves to the department registrar and collected handouts giving general information about Addis Ababa and Ethiopian life. Louise read: *Other than religion, it is agriculture and pastoralism that fill the days of well over 80 per cent of the country's eighty million people. Literacy levels are still well below 50 per cent. Women are highly respected in Ethiopian society, but the same cannot be said for gays and lesbians. Homosexuality is not acceptable ...*

She continued reading: *Medical anthropology that we promote is concerned with the relationship between Ethiopian cultural factors, and the nature and extent of health and disease ... especially in isolated rural regions.*

In the refectory she found her colleagues skim-reading the notes and discussing Ethiopia's different cultural and language groups.

'These notes are detailed,' said Rosalind, an English researcher from Manchester.

'It'll take a few days, at least, to absorb all this,' replied Carmen.

'Yes, and there's so much more to learn in the field,' said Rick, an American anthropologist from Baltimore's Johns Hopkins University, who had previously completed fieldwork in Ethiopia.

Louise listened as Rick told Bassam, who had just arrived from Jordan, about the major and minor Amharic and Oromo dialects which varied from valley to valley.

'How long will it take us to learn to speak some Amharic when we are with village people?' asked Horst, a tall, open-faced, blond student from Hamburg.

'That depends on who you meet, and whether you can quickly establish trust. Most village people are very isolated. You'll learn to communicate if you watch them closely, that's my experience,' advised Rick.

'So we get the best results if we stay in the background, observing rather than asking too many questions too soon?' asked Louise.

'Yes, slow, steady and quietly persistent – that's the strategy,' said Rick. 'Anyway, Dr Wolde will give you excellent advice. He's a great teacher who knows the fieldwork sites better than anyone. You'll be in good hands.'

'Is Dr Wolde the author of these notes?' asked Carmen.

'Yes, he's the author, and our fieldwork supervisor. I met him when he visited my uni – that's why I grabbed the opportunity when this trip became available.'

'What did you like about him?' Louise asked.

'He's a good communicator and a brilliant researcher.'

Carmen said, 'Just listen to his introduction: *The people in isolated valleys have little experience of centralised government and essentially live in a conglomeration of hundreds of independent small towns and villages, each sharing the running of their own affairs among its men folk, according to title, age and occupation.* I wonder what role women play in these villages?'

Louise knew from her readings that village women had significant domestic responsibilities. 'Okay, here's a reference to women's roles,' she said, reading from the notes: *Women are largely responsible for the organisation of agricultural routines … and the many markets which help to bind villages and local regions …'*

'I can't understand all this information,' said Bassam, who was struggling with the handouts written in English.

'Don't worry,' said Louise, 'we're all struggling to get the picture, but by the time we return I'm sure you'll have as much Ethiopian

wisdom and understanding as the rest of us – we're no different.'
They all laughed, Bassam included.

'Zeno Wolde will expect us to have read his handouts so we have some framework for our initial fieldwork experience,' said Rick. 'He will support us. He won't let you fail.' Rick directed this last remark to the apprehensive Bassam.

Louise had read about Ethiopian village life before leaving London. She was careful, though, not to express her knowledge too openly, especially among students she did not really know.

In their room that evening, Louise said to Carmen, 'In a few days we'll be in the field and with people whose language we don't understand.'

'You mean we'll be thrown in at the deep end?'

'Probably, but I don't mind. According to Rick, we just need to merge with village people, appreciate their customs,' said Louise. 'And it's the women we have to get to know. I'm sure they are the bedrock of Ethiopia's society, but also the most oppressed.'

'Isn't that always the case everywhere? Louise, you amaze me. You walk around the city, read Wolde's notes, recognise the influence of the saints or *kiddus* as you call them and, in a few hours, you provide a rationale as to why you want to spend time with people in the Southern Tribal Lands. How do you do it?'

'Thanks, Carmen, but like everyone else I'm on a steep learning curve.'

'Don't I know it! Now, what do you understand by *doomfata*, or *Fekkare Iyesus* or *debtera* or even *azmari*?' They both laughed.

Louise shared her concerns that the fieldwork would be demanding. Yet, she envisaged they would be at ease when they met village people and agreed with Carmen that no matter how well prepared they were, there would be pitfalls.

'Yes,' said Carmen, 'I suppose there are always pitfalls – like catching giardia or even malaria.'

'Are you afraid of catching a disease?'

'Maybe, but I guess I'm not as confident as you about staying

11

healthy in remote regions. There are plenty of people who have taken every precaution and still get malaria or cholera.'

Louise reminded Carmen of the Amharic expression *Ayzore*, which means 'Be strong!' It is a call of encouragement to Ethiopian women when they are in labour. And it's also a call of encouragement when people walk from village to village over steep and rocky ground, just like, thought Louise, her grandmother's advice that hardship could be endured.

'My dad's advice was to not get above yourself and things will be okay,' said Carmen. 'He's a true Lancastrian, a foreman in a foundry, and that's not getting above yourself.'

Louise remembered the hollow faces of women in photographs her London University supervisor Mike Boetcher had shown her – colour photos of mothers and babies waiting to be seen at a makeshift Médecins Sans Frontières clinic in Jinka, Southern Ethiopia, and of Ethiopians from Tigray and Amhara fleeing the famine-ravaged north; of decorated Hamar and Banna women at their open markets, Mursi women wearing lip plates, and aerial photos showing the vast Omo river valley. What strategies could she use to stop hunger for the Ethiopian peasants? How could she be practical?

'You know,' she said to Carmen, 'it dawned on me a couple of days ago that anthropologists have to be like poets, and need to be accurate as well as compassionate about the people they describe.'

'I like that ... give me an example.'

'What about Sylvia Plath's poem 'The Mirror' – the first few lines tell us how we should proceed in the field.'

'What does she say?'

'Essentially she recommends we should be truthful and have no preconceptions about what we observe and record – don't let love or dislike cloud your observations.

'Yes, being truthful is important,' said Carmen. 'Louise, you are the only person who thinks that poets can contribute to scientific enquiry! Where do you get all these ideas from and what makes you so fearless?'

Early Life – South Australia

AFTER LOUISE DAVITT was born in 1962, her mother Monica sang lullabies as she rocked her infant daughter. Family members said the child inherited her mother's temperament – gentleness, blended with steel. Louise's father Gerald sang Mozart's 'Cradle Song: Sleep my Princess Oh Sleep', and his daughter's eyes would shine. As she grew older, he was impressed by her capacity to make decisions with calm, intelligent deliberation.

Louise and her older brothers, Geoff and Alex, spent school holidays on their paternal grandparents' barley and sheep grazing property near Crystal Brook in South Australia's mid-north. The children loved the creeks and birds and the ancient gnarled eucalypts. After winter rains the land was green, but in summer it baked to brown and yellow. Their grandparents had worked hard all their lives, solely to make ends meet; they never expected to be rich, and taught their son and grandchildren that hardship was a great leveller. Louise's grandmother Margaret was a lifelong member of a local book club, while her grandfather Max supported the local football. They played tennis on their homemade tarmac court and regularly entertained friends in their battered hundred-year-old farmhouse. Often life was challenging but troubles never struck root for Louise's grandmother.

Drought, low incomes, Margaret's miscarriages and a stillbirth had affected the grandparents' lives, yet Margaret Davitt could appraise and put into perspective the truth of what happened. In any situation, she was the family's sounding board, observing events and asking, 'Is this event good, bad or of no consequence? And where could it lead? And what effect would it have on the grandchildren, now and later?'

Margaret liked to play games of questions and answers. 'I learn from listening to the stillness in life,' she would say, 'and then I enquire.' Louise loved talking with her grandmother. She remembered how Margaret had once told her that she owed her health and resilience to the salubrity of fresh winter winds and summer's hot breezes that prevailed in Crystal Brook.

'Fortitude in the face of adversity, that's your grandmother,' her father often said. Louise knew how her grandmother's ideals were distilled in memorable phrases:

> *Nothing to fear in life.*
> *Hardship can be endured.*
> *Everyone has talent.*
> *True love is everlasting.*

Her grandmother's motto was to enjoy life and be happy in the moment. 'Laugh much, and when you experience difficulty, pause, and think carefully before you make a decision.' She told Louise that life's journey was rarely straightforward, and she recognised that Louise was keen to travel and meet different people.

Louise's father, ever tethered to practical matters, was no romantic. He too advised her how important it was to be able to adapt to setbacks, which were part of life's merry-go-round.

On her grandparents' farm, Louise ran through tall barley, walked for miles, gathered blackberries and native peaches called quandongs, fished for tiddlers in creeks, watched small trout twist and dive in the farm dam, climbed trees, built dens and learnt how summer's burnt landscape would always recover by the next spring.

Since puberty, Louise's features were admired: her broad brow, fine nose and full lips; her expressive, deep-set blue eyes; thick honey-blonde, shoulder-length hair; and her tall athletic body with long muscular legs. But she never flaunted her looks.

As a teenager with many friends, swimming and surfing at an Adelaide suburban bayside beach was a favourite pastime. They spent long days at the beach, their skin turning nut-brown. And it wasn't long before she experienced young love. She knew the facts of life, had casual boyfriends but never slept with them, though occasionally she thought she would like to. At sixteen, her mother arranged for her to be prescribed the pill. Louise fell in love with a classmate friend, Luke, but they didn't make love. However, with Rob Hardy things changed.

Rob was a first-year medical student whom she met while in her final year at high school. In the dunes at sunrise, below a cobalt sky, they experimented with and enjoyed their intimacy. Rob glowed in her company. They became a close couple. They sailed together across the Spencer Gulf in a friend's racing yacht. Once they sky-dived above Strathalbyn: a gift from Louise to Rob on his birthday. Her family wondered if Rob and Louise would ever part. Her mother, observing them, said, 'I think they'll always be together.' The two teased each other openly.

'Your hair's like a spiky echidna,' she told him one evening at a family dinner after they had spent an afternoon at the beach. Rob laughed, and joked that this was the price he had to pay for spending so much time with Louise at the beach.

Alone together on an early summer evening, nestled in their dune resting-place, Louise stepped out of her shorts, knickers and t-shirt and raced Rob into the surf. Initially uncertain, Rob threw off his clothes and together they plunged into the lapping waves. Rob was excited at her desire. He held her by her waist; they kissed with salty lips and clung to each other. Louise arched back against him and Rob felt himself pushing into her amid the breaking waves.

Slowly they parted and swam out to deeper water, kissed again and held each other's hands as they floated on the rolling waves, and waited for the waning of the day.

'We'll be like this forever,' Rob whispered in her ear.

15

'Yes, I know we will. If ever I go away,' Louise said with a distant look, 'I will always think of you, I promise you that.'

About to complete her first degree, Louise sat at her desk in a brightly decorated study-bedroom as a late-spring drizzle glazed her windows. The conclusion of this preparatory stage of her career was in sight. Focused, she had adopted her father's adage: 'Fortune favours the prepared mind'. Passion blended with intellect, her ideas gathered momentum. University staff and fieldwork supervisors were struck by the rousing quality of her seminar presentations and essays. Characteristically, she wrote, *People die in their houses and in the bush amid cocoons of silence …*

After four years she graduated with first-class honours in anthropology. The next step was to enrol for postgraduate studies in the joint schools of African Studies and Tropical Medicine in London, learn some Amharic and begin fieldwork studies in Ethiopia. 'So here I am ready to leave,' she murmured. She was excited but wondered what lay ahead, who she would meet, and where travel would take her.

Set now for London and separation from family and friends, there were farewells. It was going to be difficult to say goodbye to Rob. She'd known and loved him for nearly five years. At times they talked about doing great things together, travelling, having children and a family life. Rob always thought of Louise as his partner, an unusual, beautiful young woman. And now she was going abroad on an indefinite stay. He wondered whether Louise would forget their beautiful times together, the range of their common interests, the welcoming and love from each of their families. 'To give all this up, for what?'

'I'll write to you,' she said again as they embraced in the airport departure lounge.

Rob watched her ascend the aircraft steps, stop at the top, turn and wave then disappear. On the flight Louise's thoughts were pulled in two directions, sadness at leaving, but also excitement and determination.

Louise was a keen letter writer. Her first November in London in 1984 had been surprisingly wet. Louise praised the grey clouds and the water that flowed from old leaf-filled gutters. She wrote home to her parents and her Adelaide boyfriend Rob about … *steady rain and kettle drum sounds that herald advancing thunder across London. They excite me.* She continued: *The thunder can roar across London's squares and often the torrential rain seems to me as if it could knock down buildings. And it's fun when, as I ride, my wet hair becomes horizontal in the surging winds that often accompany the rain.* She concluded: *And you know, the mist when the rain ceases hangs over the river, like it's all part of London life.*

Her letters helped her family, Rob and other friends feel they were in London with her.

Meeting Zeno Wolde

THE FIRST GLIMPSE Louise had of the group leader Dr Zeno Wolde was in a draughty portable hut on the Addis University campus adjacent to the Ethiopian Studies building. As she sat waiting for the instructions, maps and timelines for the field trip in the Lower Omo Valley, a striking athletic man walked in. Louise was surprised; she hadn't expected someone so startlingly sensuous, so unacademic and riveting. He introduced himself with a friendly confidence and air of authority. His language was clear and he appeared to have boundless energy, like a replenished mountain stream bubbling along before them.

'What do you think?' Louise whispered to Carmen before Zeno began his talk about what he expected of them.

'Every one of us,' Zeno began, 'every one of us, I'm sure, has been moved by the history, geography and culture of rural Ethiopia – attracted here in one way or another, by watching film and television, by photos, or by reading books and research reports. Ask yourselves what has brought you here. Share your answers with me and your colleagues.'

Louise glanced at Carmen and was about to say something when Zeno asked again, 'Why have you come to Ethiopia? Are you here because Ethiopia is considered to be the cradle of civilisation, or are you here because, at this time, Ethiopia is considered one of the poorest countries in the world and you want to see what poverty is like?'

No one responded. Zeno carried on. 'Or is it our history that you want to explore and the fact that we are the only African country that has not been colonised? Or have you been provoked to try and understand the nature and extent of Ethiopia's disastrous famines in 1974 and again in 1984, when over a million people starved to death?'

A deep hush enveloped the room. Zeno appeared despondent when he spoke about the famines. In one of his essays, part of which was in his introductory notes, he had suggested that decisions that people didn't make, and events that *didn't* happen – like improved education and agricultural practice – were largely responsible for the famines. Louise recalled reading that Zeno had hiked across the country and lived with peasant people and knew their history.

'Don't be frightened to ask questions. Interaction is essential. That's what we're here for.'

They were unsure how to respond. Zeno noticed Louise looking at him. He looked at her, a head-to-toe gaze. He liked what he saw and found himself face-to-face with a young woman of allure. Louise was conscious of his gaze.

Because of Zeno's interested stare she floundered a little. 'This is a general question,' she said nervously. But then, encouraged by his smile, her self-assurance returned. 'What are your priorities for us and on which particular areas will we focus?'

'Okay, that's a good question,' he said, looking directly at Louise. He explained that while his overall fieldwork priorities were in the far south in the Omo Valley, he would begin by taking them to rarely visited settlements in a valley below the Bada Ridge to the south-east of Addis Ababa. He wanted to provide a contrast with the nomadic tribes of the south. As he spoke, he pointed to places on a large wall map.

'Your priorities are to observe and record conditions that influence the physical and emotional health of isolated rural populations. Respect and enjoy these people. Remember, being among them is a privilege. That thinking will reward you. Think of yourselves as explorers. In your notebooks, record images, ideas, and if possible snatches of dialogue to paint unique pictures. Make sure your notebooks are always within reach. Record small details about people's homes, the landscape around their homes, what they are wearing, what they eat and drink, and relationships between men, women and children. Record whether you think a village is holding together, or because of the famine is about to unravel. Find out about the origins of the village. Listen to the people. Be patient. Date your notes. And above all, try to think of yourselves as cameras and help readers to feel as if they are there with you. To begin with, observe a whole village, then focus on detail, and generate life from that detail. I want you to shake up people's perceptions of Ethiopian rural life. My notes and references should help. Are there any questions?'

'Wow, what a performance,' Carmen whispered to Louise. 'What are we supposed to ask him after that? He reminds me of Brutus in Julius Caesar imploring from the pulpit … *Countrymen and lovers! hear me for my cause, and be silent, that you may hear … awake your senses.*'

'That's brilliant, Carmen.'

'Thanks, the quote just came to me. It seemed appropriate. We used to have to learn chunks of Shakespeare like that in my high school English classes.'

'You've caught his mood and high expectations for us.'

'I don't know if I will fulfil his expectations, but I like him,' said Carmen.

No one asked Zeno a question. They remained in awe of his zeal for promoting the uniqueness and value of Ethiopian rural life – *people of another world,* he had called them.

Zeno smiled and continued, expecting the students to adopt his enthusiasm and commitment. 'We will drive south-east from Addis to Mojo and then Nazret. Then we'll take a track to Sodere, so that you can see the settlements in the Awash River Valley. If reports of the roads to Asela and to Kofele are satisfactory, we'll explore the villages below the Bada Ridge.'

These names and places were just dots on a map to the students.

A yawning gap existed between Zeno's life experiences and those of the bright but inexperienced students. He didn't expect them to bridge it in a few short weeks but wanted them to become involved with village people. He wondered whether any of them had the passion and commitment he expected.

'Our goal is to reach Jinka, the main town in the lower Omo. We'll stay there and, if time permits, we'll visit the small Hamar towns of Turmi and possibly Dimeka, on the border of the Hamar and Banna tribes. There you'll experience the tribal markets.' Zeno's face lit up with enthusiasm. 'You will find all these places on the maps in your fieldwork packs. We'll be away for three weeks.'

Louise hoped that Zeno Wolde would support her, introduce her to significant people and help find references for her writing, so she could return to London and Adelaide as an ambassador for some of the poorest but most resilient people in Africa.

She recalled that *Ambassador*, in its original English definition, was: *a messenger sent on a mission to represent a country or people.* Was this what Zeno Wolde expected of his students? Would Louise Davitt, Carmen Smith or even Bassam Hashoud become messengers in their writing and advocacy?

Driving South

IT WOULD TAKE six or seven hours to reach their campsite just south of Sodore. Five people in the first 4WD were Abebe the driver and camp cook, Louise, Carmen, Horst from Hamburg, and Zeno. Degu, a part-time driver, drove the second 4WD containing four more students. The loaded vehicles moved at varying speeds as they wound through early morning Addis traffic. Abebe sounded the horn continually to avoid donkeys, horses, goats, pedestrians and other vehicles.

Then they reached the open road and dusty plains which sloped away to gaunt etched hills above Debre Zeyit. Even farmers less than a hundred miles from Addis struggled to harvest meagre, shrivelled crops. Louise stared at the barren and often stony landscape, noticing every bend in the road, every small child herding goats, every field and distant village. Although she'd read about rural Ethiopia, she now realised the scale of the country could be overwhelming. The riddle of Ethiopia's splendour, harshness, deprivation and opportunity was before her.

'And here we are, less than two hours drive from Addis, and we see all this,' she said to Carmen.

'It's bad enough when you read about famine in the papers, but when you come face to face with drought and such obvious poverty,' Carmen said, 'that really brings it home to you. It's like being reminded of Dimbleby's BBC documentary at Korem in Tigray all over again. Remember that?'

'Yes, most people who saw the film thought starvation just

happened in a faraway country.' Louise was realistic.

As they drove they watched the early morning sun glow on hillsides and nearby mountains, on the narrow dusty roads in need of repair, on fields with acacia bushes, stunted trees and savannah grass. They saw smoke from distant villages rising in columns. Zeno told them stories in clear accented English, punctuated with Oromo and Amharic names of places and people. Louise, Carmen and Horst listened, captivated by his zest as, with a flourish of his hands, he related the life and history of the landscape and its people.

Louise whispered to Carmen, 'If you wanted to choose an Ethiopian tour guide, no one could be better than Zeno Wolde. Aren't we lucky?'

They gazed at fields with heaped stones, thorn bushes, drooping crops and distant farm workers harvesting maize and sorghum. Louise stared, trying to absorb the glare, the delight and also the harshness of a farmer's day. She wondered whether they would continue farming as their forebears had done, and just accept drought, either surviving their short harsh life or dying where they worked.

Or perhaps change would come to this place, where the sun rises slowly and the morning mists and brief drizzle dampen village gardens.

A Roadside Stop

AFTER NEARLY THREE hour's driving, Zeno called a halt. 'Okay, Abebe, pull over and stop at that gravel space just ahead.'

Minutes later, the second 4WD pulled up. They were glad to stretch their legs and have a break. Everyone gathered around Zeno. He suggested the students find seats on the rocks next to the vehicles. If they needed to relieve themselves then the bush behind them was appropriate.

They sat on rocks, their feet apart on the gravel for balance. Water bottles were passed round. Zeno placed himself in the middle of the group. He wore a necklace with a beautifully carved dark wooden cross which seemed out of place for a man who presented such an animist and radical view of his country. In this roadside setting, as in the lecture theatre, he was a natural one-man show. He quickly altered topics in a conversation as his stream of thought was diverted by the landscape, or by a student's grimace or smile. Given the cross he was wearing, they were not surprised when he told them that it was impossible to avoid religion here. 'Ethiopia,' he said, 'was originally an ancient kingdom with Christianity in its Coptic form as the official religion.'

In this isolated roadside stop, looking towards the light and shadow of the wooded valley below, they listened intently. Zeno didn't expect they would be quiet for long. The blonde Australian woman would be sure to ask questions.

'Ethiopian people, even remote, poor people, are very religious, but they also know how to enjoy themselves,' he said. 'Enjoyment can also be a religion, you'll see.'

Carmen chewed her lip, and in her Lancashire accent, spoke up. 'Tell us how religion can be enjoyed?'

He paused before replying. 'I want to tell you that although I am not religious, I respect those who are, especially as their beliefs have often helped them to survive difficult lives. And their beliefs, particularly Ethiopia's Coptic Christian beliefs, have existed here since earliest times, and at least since the tenth century.'

Carmen nodded but Louise knew she was an atheist and was still holding to her scepticism.

'Although there are Muslim villages here, as in Afar, generally the villages of this region and, of course in the north in Amhara and Tigray, are places of passionate Christianity with many religious festivals and happy occasions. People believe that when there is suffering, as in the famines, eventually their God will relieve them and plentiful times will return. This attitude is at the core of their optimism.'

'Were they still optimistic during the recent famine?' asked Horst.

Zeno shrugged, eyes narrowing. 'During the famine, of course not, but you'll find proof on this trip that when the famine ended, the Ethiopian people quickly recovered their spirit. Pessimism is the real enemy; it can rot and destroy the fabric of village life.'

Louise felt her face flush with admiration for Zeno's passion. She watched the way he gestured as if his whole body spoke about the famine and its aftermath.

Zeno talked about his long embrace of Ethiopia's people, extolling one tribe, one family group, one small farm after another, alluding to different cultures, dress, language and history. The students listened intently.

'You'll no doubt face scenes that could be unpleasant. Poverty, by Western standards, is everywhere in Ethiopia, particularly out here. You will have to cope with seeing many unpleasant scenes. Ethiopia's rural poor are very poor. Many people think they're just backward, but these are outstanding people who make significant contributions to their community. Try and think like that. There is much to see and admire – village people will welcome you.'

'Dr Wolde,' Louise said, 'it has taken you years to identify closely with the native people of Ethiopia, so what do you expect of us on this short visit?'

He looked at her warily. 'My best advice is, spend time with these people, accept them as equals and note their traditions. Tradition is important for them. They have much to teach us. And their lives won't change quickly, especially in isolated villages.'

Zeno explained how tribal elders, steeped in tradition, did not contemplate changes to their way of life. 'But,' he said, 'some younger people are on the move, mostly to try and get work in the cities. Movement of people signals change, however minor. Ultimately they will judge what's best for their community.' Then he added, 'Especially now the famine is almost over.'

The group remained sitting on the rocks, chatting among themselves, with a slight breeze rustling leaves. Zeno emphasised how they needed to live among village families, share with them and chronicle their lives. Louise thought about her Australian Aboriginal friend Mandy Watson and how through her dot paintings and Dreamtime stories she was able to recall the lives of her ancestors.

At this point, as the morning sun began to warm them, Zeno said they should continue their journey. They rose, stretched their legs and climbed back into the vehicles.

2: Aboriginal Influence

Mandy Watson

MEMORIES HAVE A place in one's thinking. Louise's time, when she was thirteen, with her Aboriginal friend Mandy Watson in South Australia's town of Crystal Brook was no exception. Louise remembered the day she first saw Mandy at the town football oval one Saturday afternoon. She was a lively, dark-skinned girl about her own age with shiny brown eyes, who was wearing a bright-coloured dress and seemed to chat with everyone. Louise was intrigued. Mandy skipped along like an excited cockatoo. She was tough, fleeting, rarely in one place or with one friend for long.

Later Louise heard she was known as flippant and a school truant. Mandy didn't share the conservative country town's views about the separateness of Aboriginal Australians which, even in early 1970s, was still practised. Mandy's spirited and often mischievous behaviour led many of her teachers to dislike her. In turn, she took little notice of their advice and direction. During the week when Louise first met Mandy, her brothers Geoff and Alex were staying at the family home at Stirling in the Adelaide Hills.

The sight of Mandy walking jauntily round the oval and the flash of her smile made Louise want to get to know the girl. So she left her grandfather's car that was parked facing the peeling white oval railings, fastened her anorak tight and headed into the cold breeze. The girls smiled as they came face to face.

'What's your name?'

'Louise.'

'I like that. Mine's Mandy. Where do you go to school?'

'At Stirling, in the Adelaide Hills.'

'Are you here on holiday then?'

'Yes, we always come here for holidays.' Gaining confidence, Louise asked, 'Do you go to school in Crystal Brook?'

'Nah, haven't been to school for weeks. No one can make me go. It's boring.'

'What do you do when you don't go to school?'

'Hang about, meet boys, do some painting.' She paused. 'Most of all I look for wild animals and collect lizards and frogs. Collecting stuff's good.' Noticing Louise's expression, she added, 'But I don't keep everything, not live things, I let them go again.'

Louise imagined meeting Mandy's friends, walking and camping in the bush and patting the soft fur of a joey, or koala. Then with the quick smile which always lit up her face whenever something excited her, she said, 'I like wild animals. Can you show me some?'

'Sure – do you want to find some this afternoon? Now?'

'Yes, if we can, but I'll tell my granddad what I'm doing.'

'Okay!'

The girls walked back to Louise's grandfather's station wagon. 'This is Mandy,' Louise said proudly to her grandfather, who was standing with his footy friends on the edge of the oval. 'Is it okay if I go for a walk with Mandy?'

'Oh, hello.'

Her grandfather looked surprised, then said, 'Yes, but be back at the clubhouse when the game's over and we can have some of your grandmother's goodies.' Louise knew that Grandfather Max Davitt had definite routines that he didn't like to change. Talking with his mates on Saturday afternoon at the footy was one of them.

The girls wandered away. Mandy suggested they search for lizards in a paddock at the edge of the oval.

'You're Aboriginal, aren't you?' Louise asked suddenly. She had little idea about Aboriginal Australians, except that they were black and mostly lived in the desert. Meeting Mandy was exciting.

Mandy smiled. 'Yep, and proud of it.'

'Have you always lived here?'

'Not always. Mum and Grandma come from up north at Oodnadatta.'

'Did you live there?'

'To begin with, and then mostly with Grandma.'

'When did you come here?'

'Last year, when Grandma got sick.'

Louise wanted to ask where her mother and father were and who she lived with in Crystal Brook, but didn't. She was dazed.

'Go on,' Mandy said warmly, 'ask me all you like and then I'll ask you where you really come from.'

'Okay, what does your grandma do?'

Mandy looked puzzled. 'Grandma paints about the Dreaming. It's a while since I've talked about Grandma's painting. None of the other kids at the school are interested. I can show you some if you like.'

'I'd like that.' Louise was intrigued. She wasn't sure how you could paint dreams.

'See that pond over there, that's where we'll find frogs. Sometimes I wade out and then my boots get sucked down in the mud and I put my head under the water to see what's there. But I don't stay under long.'

'That's amazing.'

At four-thirty, when the siren went for the end of the match, the girls were half a mile away, searching for frogs at the edge of the small pond. Louise didn't hear or didn't want to hear the siren. As she trailed her hand through the water her fingers snagged on slimy knots of weed. In the depths light shimmered and the scent of eucalyptus and wild honeysuckle hung over the water. Feeling a feathery breeze on her cheek and seeing clouds scudding across the sky, she was captivated. She would have ignored even a trumpet call.

'There's one,' said Mandy, expertly catching a small frog and nestling it in the palm of her hand. 'Here, want to hold it?'

Louise held out an open hand and Mandy gently transferred the minute frog.

'Grandma paints frog Dreaming; how they find and go to water-holes. I'm learning how to paint frogs and lizards so catching them I know what they look and feel like.'

Louise wasn't at all sure what catching frogs and lizards had to do with painting, let alone Dreaming, but Mandy was persuasive.

'Don't squeeze the frog – you need to hold it properly. You'll soon learn.'

At this point, with the cold and sticky frog in her hand, Louise was aware that the football siren had gone long ago, and it was a good fifteen minutes' run back to the oval. 'I have to go,' she said handing the frog back to Mandy.

'Okay, I'll come with you; we'll put froggy back in the pond.'

Light rain began to fall, dimpling the water's surface. The girls ran back across the field, dodging low-hanging boughs. When they reached the pavilion they climbed quickly up its wide timber steps.

Louise thought her grandparents might be worried. It was out of character for her to be late. 'This is my friend Mandy.'

Louise's grandmother held out a hand and Mandy grasped it, but did not look her in the eye.

'Don't be shy,' Margaret said.

After an awkward silence Louise noticed a transformation in Mandy, from the confident effervescent girl searching for frogs to the hesitant girl in the pavilion.

'When will I see you again?'

'I don't mind, whenever,' replied the subdued Mandy.

'What about next Monday? Will you be around then?'

'Yeah. I'll be around.'

'How about two – two o'clock. I'll get a lift here.'

Louise did not want to lose contact with her, especially as she was someone very different from her schoolfriends, someone who found delight in ponds and frogs and weeds. And she was someone who didn't live with her parents.

'I'll be here,' Mandy said as Louise climbed into the back seat of the station wagon.

◈

When they reached the farm, Margaret asked, 'What did you think of Mandy?'

'I liked her. I'd like to meet her again. Could we go on Monday?'

'Alright. I'll drive you into town. I'll drop you off at the oval. If you have a good time with her, you can invite her back to the farm.' Margaret Davitt was urbane and considered by her friends to be a most lovable person who, though tough, was always welcoming, irrespective of whether a person was a white Anglo-Saxon or Aboriginal. In her community she was deemed to be radical in the way she respected Aboriginal culture.

Louise was overjoyed. 'I love you.'

Margaret's tanned face creased in delight. 'And I love you, Louise. Now, tell me about Mandy and why you like her.'

'She's different. She's daring and knows all about frogs and lizards and she cares about them.'

Dot Painting – 'You'll soon learn'

ON THE MONDAY, after an early lunch, Margaret Davitt drove Louise to the town oval. Mandy was already standing there, holding a canvas satchel. Louise and Margaret got out of the car. 'Hi Mandy, this is my grandmother.'

'Yes, I remember. I've brought something to show you.'

'That's great.' Louise moved close to Mandy.

'You girls enjoy youselves. I'll be back here at four o'clock.' Margaret climbed into her car, waved and drove away.

'She's nice,' said Mandy.

'Yes, she's special.' Louise watched her grandmother's car disappear in a cloud of dust between waving roadside gum trees.

'My grandma in Oodnadatta is special too.' Mandy rummaged in her satchel. 'I've brought you a couple of her paintings and some of mine.' She looked proud. The girls walked over to a barbecue table and Mandy took out the paintings.

'Grandma started to teach me and I always watched her when she sat with her brush and paints.' Mandy unfurled two of her grandmother's paintings. 'My grandma gave me these. This one's called *Frog Dreaming* and this orange one is *Witchetty Grub Land*.'

Louise studied the bright colours. Hesitatingly she said, 'It's all dots.'

'That's right, it's called dot painting. That's what I'm learning.'

'Show me *your* paintings. I want to see your paintings too.'

'Sure.' Mandy placed two paintings side-by-side on the table. She appeared embarrassed. Perhaps Louise was just being kind.

34

Louise gazed at Mandy's dot paintings of desert tracks and totem symbols of a mob of kangaroos.

'They're beautiful. I love the bright colours. Have you shown them to other kids, or teachers at school?'

'Nah, they think I'm a troublemaker.'

As she spoke, Louise noticed how Mandy seemed dejected. Louise remembered her grandmother saying, 'Only in silence may you hear.' She decided not to question Mandy any more.

'Let's walk into town and have some lemonade, and if we have time, go back to the pond and look for more frogs,' Louise said finally.

As they walked Louise said naively, 'Tell me about your dad.'

There was a long pause. 'I don't know much about my dad. I don't know if he's dead, but then I don't know if he's alive either.'

Louise thought that was strange. Mandy's dark onyx eyes clouded over. When they reached the deli shop, Louise bought a couple of cans of Solo. They walked across the road to a small park, sat on a bench and drank their lemonade. Two youths, about sixteen, saw them sitting there. They swaggered over and leered at Mandy.

'What's going on, Mandy?' the taller blond-haired boy said.

'Nothing, just sitting with my friend.' Louise looked away nervously.

'Hey blondie, what's going on with you, don't you want to look at us?' Louise froze. She couldn't tell them that she wished they would go away.

'Give us some of your lemonade,' the shorter, dark-skinned boy said.

'Yeah, come on blondie, give us a kiss.' The taller boy smirked and made out to stroke Louise's hair. She didn't know what to say or do and felt herself shaking, her heart racing.

'Why don't you just piss off and leave us alone,' Mandy said as she got up as if to walk away.

'What's wrong with you, Mandy? You could always give us what we want, and you know you does,' the taller one said menacingly.

Mandy took a deep breath and looked him straight in the eye.

Walking towards him she said, 'You listen to me, Jason, listen to what I say. You touch my friend and you'll pay for it. I've got cousins who could clean you up real proper. You'll soon learn what their fists are made of.'

'Okay, you black tart, don't get pissy with us,' Jason said as he turned and walked away. His friend followed him out of the park. Mandy picked up her satchel and, with a flash of triumph, led Louise out of the park.

Encouraged by Mandy's presence, she felt a surge of confidence. 'Wow, even when you are threatened you stay calm.'

It was two-thirty, over an hour to go before Louise was due to be picked up. She looked nervously at the boys as they disappeared down a side street.

'Don't worry, they won't come back and we won't see them again. They're all talk. They say things like that because they're dumb, they don't know what else to say.'

Louise liked Mandy's response. 'There's plenty of boys around like them – but there are others. You just gotta pick 'em carefully,' continued Mandy.

'Thanks, I just wasn't sure what to do.'

'You'll soon learn. Just think about your inside world, how you believe in yourself and then you won't have to give two hoots about those boys – then you'll see that your outside world is not so important, that's what my grandma taught me.'

Louise was intrigued; she'd never thought like that.

'You have to choose your boyfriends carefully. Come on, I'll drop these paintings off at my place and then we can go back to the pond.'

They walked three blocks away from the town centre to a street lined with boxy fibro cottages. 'Wait here and I'll dump the satchel.' Mandy walked up the weed-strewn path of the third house. In a couple of minutes she emerged.

'This is my sister's place. She's twenty-five and she's got four kids as well as me living with her.'

There was an old beaten-up car in the driveway. Two Aboriginal men came out. They stood near the front door and waved to them.

'I told them about you. They won't say anything when they first meet you, but they're okay.'

The girls walked back to the pond. Louise tried to clear her mind from the experience with the boys. She was still thinking about the way Mandy handled the situation and about her advice to believe in yourself. She's so strong, thought Louise. They talked as they walked, mostly about their grandmothers. To Louise's surprise, Mandy said she'd like to come to the farm.

Louise wasn't sure how to respond, although she wanted to be encouraging. 'I'm here for the rest of the week. My grandma says it would be okay. When would you like to come?'

'Whenever.'

'What about Thursday. Thursday morning? You could stay for lunch.'

Mandy looked apprehensive. The tough girl in the park had disappeared. She had never been invited out before by someone like Louise.

She shrugged. 'Okay.'

'Good. And you can tell me more about dot painting.' Louise was confident her grandmother would make Mandy welcome. She knew Margaret Davitt thought that Crystal Brook was more interesting with Aboriginal people in the population.

'I thought I was only going to say hello to you at the football and now it's all turned out so good,' said Louise.

'Yep, sure has.'

Sunlight jagged through the trees. The girls spent an hour chatting, paddling in the pond and watching fingers of light penetrate the water.

'Here, chew this grass till your spit turns green,' said Mandy. 'That's how we learn to live off the land.'

'I'll try.' Louise chewed fronds of grass into a bitter mash and then spat it out. 'This is fun, we should do this again.'

'If you want to.'

They wandered back to the oval. Louise thought about Mandy, with her eyes full of devilry and love. She loved her dot paintings and sketches of kangaroos, and had noticed her notebook – probably full of stories about Aboriginal camps and cooking fires. The girls sat on the grass, chatting until they heard the sound of a car pulling up.

Margaret Davitt waved and got out. Louise walked over and hugged her. 'Can Mandy come to the farm on Thursday morning and stay for lunch?'

'Yes, I don't see why not.' Margaret turned to Mandy. 'You'll be most welcome.'

Mandy pushed her hair away from her face and smiled.

'Thursday morning then,' said Louise.

Farm Visit

MANDY ARRIVED AT the farm at ten o'clock on Thursday, earlier than expected. She was dropped off by one of the men Louise had seen, an uncle, in the battered Datsun that she'd seen in their driveway. Mandy looked hesitant.

'Thanks for coming' Louise said warmly. 'I'm so glad you're here.'

Inside the farmhouse, Mandy gazed at the well-ordered kitchen. They talked about life on the farm and who originally lived there. Margaret Davitt spoke modestly about her home and then produced fruit juice and brownies. Mandy looked at the family photographs and recognised Louise as a small child. How happy she looked with her brothers. They finished their drinks.

'Come on, let's go,' Louise said, 'I'll show you the farm.'

'You girls take some chocolate and wear raincoats, it's going to rain today,' Margaret said.

'Okay, thanks ,Grandma,' Louise said, pocketing a bar of chocolate.

They set off, thick clouds hanging low across the yellow-green contours of surrounding hills. A steady breeze blew and sodden leaves lay in clumps under rugged old gum trees. They walked across an empty paddock studded with huge red gum trees, some with blackened trunks from lightning strikes, others gnarled and twisted as if contorted with pain. Branches moved in the breeze and, in the dull light, lorikeets, rosellas, magpies and some honeyeaters darted and flew.

'Rivers once flowed across this land, in the Dreaming,' Mandy said suddenly.

'What's the Dreaming?'

'It's about how we once lived, about our ancestors, about our closeness to the land and how we imagine what the land was like a long time ago.'

'That's amazing.'

'See this land, where that road runs between the hills in long curves? I reckon a river once flowed there.' Mandy pointed.

Louise looked towards the denuded hills and tried to imagine a flowing river once being there. What on earth was all this about, she wondered.

She sensed that Mandy knew the land at a deep level. She had not heard anything like this before and couldn't make much sense of it, but it left its mark. A mould of loving and learning from indigenous people was being set. Her mind began to fill with ideas about living on the land thousands of years before.

'I'll think differently about this land now. It must have been someone else's land before my grandpa and his dad came here,' Louise said, shifting and staring ahead.

'Come on. We need to reach those hills. And taste them,' Mandy said.

Louise wondered what Mandy meant by 'tasting' the hills.

They walked from paddock to paddock, opening and closing gates, moving briskly in the slight drizzle. They finally reached the limits of the farm and moved onto a track that led to a winding road. Above them was a solid grey curtain of drifting clouds. Below, on the side of the track, was wet brown earth and mossy rocks.

'You need to be as close to your land as possible,' Mandy said. 'That's what we're taught.'

Fascinated, Louise wanted to understand more about Mandy's thinking.

'As soon as us kids are able to sit up, we're taught to look at the animals and birds and draw them in the sand. My grandma taught me, so I learned all about the animals in the bush. This makes us smart and strong. They don't teach you this at school.'

Mandy's talk about drawing animals in the sand making you smart and strong didn't make much sense to Louise, but Mandy spoke with great feeling and Louise felt inspired.

'This earth is part of our past,' Mandy continued as they looked down on the quilted field. On this grey day the landscape was fascinating to look at because the greens and yellows glowed.

As rain fell on her friend's face, Louise noticed the velvet sheen of her skin. The girls exchanged shy glances. It was now one o'clock.

It would take over an hour to get back to the farmhouse. But Louise was keen to reach the hills that she'd only ever seen from a distance so returning in time for lunch didn't matter. Sheep grazed under drizzly rain. The girls ate their chocolate beneath a big red gum tree.

'It's amazing, but I've never been to these hills before,' said Louise. 'I feel different now I'm here. You're right, this land is special– it's kind of strange.' She thought about Mandy's people, once living there – people whose land Louise's grandfather and great-grandfather had stripped of trees.

At the top of the hill, Mandy pointed out scant creeks and leeward-leaning windswept trees in a gully below. 'These trees have sour berries that my people eat,' she said proudly.

'I can't understand, I really can't … why we haven't been taught all this about your people at school?'

'Because nobody wants to know us.'

'But why not? Tell me why not?'

'Because they don't like us, I s'pose … But let's not talk about it, we don't have much time left.'

Louise pictured the hills, inhabited, and the dry creek rippling and flowing to the sea.

Eventually, they turned and walked back to the farm. It was almost 2.30. Margaret was glad to see them as she'd begun to worry. Louise wanted to meet Mandy again, learn more about a person's inner world, about camp fires, the bush and people sitting on the ground telling stories or dancing.

But the meeting was not to be. Louise heard, on her next visit to her grandparents' farm, that Mandy had gone back to Oodnadatta. No one was sure when, or if, she would return.

3: Exploring and Learning

Bada Ridge Camp Site

AFTER ZENO'S ROADSIDE stop, the next stage southwards was expected to take about four hours, depending on the state of the roads. Louise and Carmen leaned back on their pillows in the 4WD and made themselves as comfortable as possible in the cramped conditions. Beyond them now, lay the pastoral and arable lands of the south where sudden torrential rains would turn pastures into a sea of mud and where a day or two later burning sun would shrivel flowing streams into stagnant pools. In low gear, they struggled up a steep gravel track shaded by straggly acacia and eucalyptus.

After almost four hours along a bumpy pot-holed road with Abebe wrestling the steering wheel, they turned sharply, drove up an even steeper track, and parked on a plateau area on which were erected a dozen substantial tents, each with a wooden platform base. Degu parked alongside. An unpainted breeze-block, drop-toilet ablutions block and simple kitchen were the only permanent buildings.

A deep wide valley spread below them, dotted with distant villages. Louise looked across a spur of the plateau. It had been raining and from the plateau's edge runnels scoured the slopes.

'I'll bet you haven't seen anything quite like this,' Zeno said proudly to his students, as he stood alongside Louise and Carmen.

Louise walked to the edge of the plateau and gazed on a distant village, a sensation of wonder spreading from the back of her head into her eyes and then into the pit of her stomach. She breathed in the fragrance of acacia and eucalypt. She saw streams carving out little ravines and spreading silt on the flood plain floor, where fields and gardens were cultivated.

'It's like falling in love – we'll never forget this,' she said to Carmen, as she contemplated her first encounter with Oromo village people.

Meanwhile Abebe and Degu collected wood and arranged the fireplace. Water and food were carried in from the vehicles. A petrol generator provided limited lighting and some power for refrigeration. Abebe cooked expertly over three gas rings and prepared the evening meal of vegetable and goat meat stew. The atmosphere was intoxicating, a compelling mixture of people: experienced and inexperienced, black and white, Ethiopian, American, Australian, Arab, English and German – an exciting collision of values and cultures. Watching Abebe, Degu and Zeno, Louise realised how these different men were very much at home. She stared at them, aware she was beginning a new life.

'*Enebla, enebla!*' Abebe called to tell them that food was ready. The cool air hung in stillness over their site and after such a long day they were all hungry. They sat in two groups. In the centre of each was a single large bowl containing the thick stew. Before each person was a thin *injera* pancake. Louise watched Zeno and Abebe as they scooped food from the central bowl with their pancakes. The students did likewise, gingerly. Louise enjoyed the slight sour taste of the soft *injera* as she mopped up the stew's rich juices. Zeno looked at her and smiled.

Zeno sat next to Carmen, opposite Louise and Rick the American. Eating and drinking while talking to students about Ethiopia was natural for Zeno. He and Rick spoke of people practising permaculture on terraced fields; of small boys keeping birds away from crops of sorghum; of women walking great distances to collect water for their village and of nomadic herdsmen protecting goat and cattle herds from hyenas, cheetahs or sometimes leopards.

'And so there it is, our first fieldwork site,' said Zeno pointing to the valley below. 'Villagers will talk to you about their work, their family life. We'll get a picture of a community's health, particularly of women and children. The more you listen to the women, the more information you'll uncover.'

The students murmured acknowledgement as they sat at the meal table on packing cases and a few old canvas-backed captain's chairs.

'Surviving in this country is what these people do every day. They are strong, never forget that. They are one thread in a vast tapestry.' Louise couldn't help gazing at Zeno. Distracted and silent, she imagined spending time alone with him. She made herself look away.

Zeno continued, 'Remember also, people subsist, there is no safety net for them.' Louise wondered what this land was like during the big drought and what happened to the people.

Zeno spoke softly as if reading Louise's thoughts. 'In the droughts the land forgot itself and because I was well fed, I felt like a foreigner in my own country. Pasture land broke into huge cracks and then came the dust, the endless dust … During the recent famine, everywhere, and particularly in the north, people hoped, but sank in the dust of their starving world.' Zeno grasped his hands and lowered his head as paraffin table lamps flickered and early moonlight filtered through the clouds.

'Mothers carried their children great distances to food centres. And, of course, there were deaths, thousands of them. Despite the drought, these deaths need not have happened. I knew some of these people … they tumbled wasted bodies into a thousand stony graves – and that's how it was. Humble, beautiful people brutalised by poverty – individuals lost among so many dead.' Zeno paused. 'To be or not to be … that is what life is like for Ethiopia's rural poor.'

Louise sensed his mood and felt for him.

'What's the answer, Zeno?' Rick asked. 'Is there an answer?'

'Education to improve literacy levels, and the desire to change people's thinking so that famine is not considered inevitable. It's difficult.'

As the temperature fell each person's breath floated up into the night sky. Abebe cleared the table and the students retired to their tents. In her sleeping bag, holding her torch, Louise tried to read but found it difficult to concentrate. Carmen was already dozing. Louise thought of the village people and tried to imagine their lives. She was eager to begin writing about them but she drifted to sleep.

A Village below the Bada Ridge

THE FOLLOWING MORNING Abebe was up early and had kettles boiling away. He put cups, plates with *injera* and jars of *mari* (honey) on the camp table. 'Gotta look after you people with all you're going to do today with Dr Wolde,' he said to the early risers who were clustering around him. 'Anyone doesn't like *mari* and *buna* (coffee)?' He smiled broadly.

The group assembled, some yawning. Abebe measured water and coffee into each cup. They sat chatting and drinking.

'We'll leave in about half an hour and take the track down into the valley where we can meet village people,' Zeno said to Abebe.

Zeno wanted to introduce students to this little-known group of Oromo-speaking villages below the Bada Ridge. They would provide a contrast with the subsisting nomadic people of the Omo Valley region, the final destination on this trip. He hoped the progress in these villages could be adopted elsewhere, a beacon of progress, he thought, like a lighthouse light flickering on, off, on – with a message guiding and telling people what to do and what to avoid.

'It'll take a good hour to get to the bottom of the valley. Three of you have already walked in this valley so you can go with Abebe to the market in Asela,' Zeno said.

Abebe brought a large earthenware water jug and filled the students' water bottles. Zeno laid his map on the table and the students gathered round. 'We'll start our walk from the track head on the edge of the plateau. It's easy walking from here to the beginning of the descent, but over an hour to the bottom of the valley. It could take longer. It's not an easy walk, but you'll see how spectacular it is. I'll give you fifteen minutes to get ready,' Zeno said. 'Make sure your water bottles are full and you've packed enough bananas and chocolate and anything else you need to keep going. Bring some warm clothing as we might stay the night in the valley, but don't worry about sleeping bags. If necessary, villagers will provide you with goatskins and cowhides. You'll be warm enough.'

Zeno led the party off the edge of their tented plateau site and slowly down the steep gravelly track which wound its way along the valley side. Sometimes they were climbing as their narrow path took the safest route before descending again. Skirting rock outcrops, they saw goats grazing on precipitous slopes. Zeno stopped on a lip of the path with a sheer drop. The valley far below was yellow, brown and purple. He took a step back and asked the students to do the same in order to avoid any rush of vertigo.

The track ahead became broken as they climbed again until they reached slabs of rock and a bend in the track leading down. The early sun was not yet hot, but the students were bathed in sweat. Zeno paused on a flat spur to wait for those at the back. There was just sufficient room for them to stand above the sheer drop and see the tilled land near to a village below.

'These tracks are the shortest way into the valley. The road we were on yesterday skirts the valley but is well away from the villages. When we get closer to the bottom you will see how, despite its rocky nature, many sides of the valley have been terraced for cultivation. The people use every inch of arable land.'

'When did the terraces first appear?' asked Louise.

'Good question. In this region, probably as far back as the fourteenth century there were terraces here in some form or another or perhaps even earlier. Not exactly these same terraces, of course.'

'That's incredible.'

The students stood about staring at the landscape, reluctant to move. The morning light was brighter and the dry air was heating up.

'Another half hour and we'll be on the valley floor,' Zeno said, while turning to see if all the students were safe on the steep incline. Louise walked behind Zeno. He turned again to check the students and caught her eye. 'You're doing well,' he said. He met her gaze and did not avert his eyes.

Finally they walked off the track onto the undulating valley floor. Ahead of them was the first evidence of tilled land. As they approached the settlement of a dozen huts above a dry creek bed, a young woman appeared, carrying a baby. She walked slowly from a hut towards a *gwaro* (garden). Noticing the approaching party she turned, stared and waved. Zeno waved back. A girl of eight or nine joined her. She was a slight child, thin at ankle and wrist. Her skin was dark brown, her thick black hair curly and cropped, showing the fine structure of her face. Her feet were bare, her dress torn. Despite her thinness, Louise thought she had rarely seen a prettier child. Zeno knew the girl from a year ago. 'She's a beautiful child, bright but also subdued,' said Zeno. 'She's interested in going to school but out here, that's impossible, especially for a girl.'

Louise wished the girl could grow beyond a woman's narrow, burdened back-breaking life. She hoped the traditional opposition to a girl being educated would soon fall away. The little girl stood close to the young woman with the baby, who gently directed her to pick up a bucket and collect water from the distant stream. Louise was sad as she watched the girl lug her bucket and disappear beyond the gardens. The battered bucket in the girl's hand seemed like a betrayal of her life.

Zeno introduced the students and, with a welcoming gesture, the young woman, Biftu. invited them to walk around the settlement. She took them alongside the tilled garden on which some ten women were working, mainly weeding and breaking the earth with hoes around their corn plants, leafy vegetables and what looked like bok choy. The women wore brightly-coloured cotton skirts, thin and faded so that the patterns could just be discerned; their skin could be seen through the fabric. To begin with, they ignored the students and continued working. Zeno asked the woman with the baby if her mother was in the village.

She pointed to the track to the village.

Zeno explained to the students that her mother was Kaboue, a respected village elder. 'She is sharp as a razor,' he said, 'and never in a hurry. Everyone agrees she is wise. You will enjoy meeting her.'

After staying for an hour, observing the women working in the gardens, Zeno told Biftu, who was now putting vegetables in a reed basket, that they would walk to the main village to meet her mother. Zeno beckoned to the students and they walked on across rough pasture and broken, sandy land.

Kaboue's village was on a tributary flood plain another mile away. Her hut was in the centre of the village compound, well above the creek in which there was a trickle of water and a few pools. Stunted trees grew alongside the creek. Dogs, chickens and the odd goat wandered around the compound which was almost empty of people because, as with the outlier settlement, women were working in the gardens.

'We'll take our time,' Zeno said. 'Kaboue is probably somewhere nearby solving a dispute or giving advice.'

'What sort of advice?' asked Carmen.

'Child rearing, crop planning, grain storage, bereavement, and dealing with the men when they return.'

'Where are the men?'

'Most likely looking after cattle on pastures alongside the main river. They'll return when plots closer to the village regenerate.'

'How long will they stay away?'

'Who knows – a few days, a week or two, sometimes months at a time.'

Zeno set about finding the sage. He asked an older woman sitting outside her hut where Kaboue could be found. The woman stared and did not reply. She was bent over trying to catch her breath.

'How old is she?' Carmen whispered to Zeno as she looked at the woman's lined, drawn face, her crinkly hair thin as spooled cotton.

The old woman ignored them and stared at the ground.

'I have no idea, but her working days are certainly over and she'll be cared for in the village.' The old lady didn't move. From time to time, she turned a knobbly walking stick handle over and over in her hands.

Kaboue could not be located, so Zeno took the students beyond the village down the creek bank, past more tilled land and onto scrubby pasture country. They walked above the pasture for another mile, climbing towards a prominent rock ledge. Louise wondered why Zeno was taking them further away from the village and the gardens where Kaboue would be found. Then he stopped and looked back towards the village.

'Look across this pasture towards the village and you will see the cycle of these people's lives at a glance – pasture, water supply, cultivation and settlement; and it has been like this for centuries.'

The students looked across a scattering of tree tops and boulders towards the village. Now they could understand why Zeno had brought them here: for the completeness of the picture before them.

'The village would have begun its life as a nomadic resting place and then taken root,' Zeno said. 'The outlier settlement is a good example. Initially it was within easy walking distance of the main village and then gradually huts and permanent life were established. Here you can see progress from nomadic life to cultivation and pastoral settlement.'

'Is it like this in every village in the valley?' asked Horst.

'Yes and no,' Zeno replied. 'What develops in one place may not be appropriate in another, but they buy and sell alongside each other at local markets.'

The students took photos of the nearby village, the creek, gardens and the distant outlier settlement.

'Okay, we'll walk back to the village and find Kaboue.' Zeno stepped off the ledge and, sure of foot, began the descent. In half an hour they were again on the outskirts of the village. The word had got around and Kaboue was waiting for them outside her hut. She was a neat, compact woman who remembered Zeno and spoke in a gentle but commanding voice. She shook hands and greeted each student.

Louise estimated Kaboue was probably fifty years of age. Her walk was elegant and she carried herself with quiet assurance; her directions seemed to convey a kind of code which the village women understood, as if Kaboue's gentle gestures were a secret language. Her grasp of the essentials of village life was based on a bedrock of deep, non-judgemental wisdom. Kaboue simply knew her duty, her guidance, so necessary in this isolated settlement – the principal elder on whom they relied.

'Of course we must feed you,' she said to Zeno, who translated for the students.

'She wishes to provide us all with a traditional village meal. That is their custom towards visitors who spend time with them. We should accept. Cherish the moment. We won't get to another village today but there's plenty to see here. Kaboue will answer your questions. She is well acquainted with the community and its customs.'

'Isn't their main meal taken in the evening?' Louise asked.

'That's right, but it's too dangerous for us to take the track out of the valley in the dark and we don't plan to spend the night here. We'll share a small meal with them around one o'clock and leave by mid-afternoon.'

Although it was a busy time in the garden and fields, with women looking after children as they weeded and gathered baskets of vegetables, they were aware of visitors. They soon left the fields and returned to the village to help prepare food. Kaboue had summoned them. She was like a friendly but uncompromising hen with her chicks as she rounded up women from the fields, gesturing and giving specific instructions. They responded with smiles and laughter.

With children playing around them, the women cut up vegetables, and killed and plucked three chickens. Younger women watched Kaboue carefully as she gave instructions, pointing, insisting and smiling as she emphasised how the meal was to be prepared.

As the party of village women and students sat in a tightly knit circle, Louise found herself face to face with Kaboue. Zeno translated.

'I am glad to see you,' Kaboue said, holding out her hand to Louise.

'Thank you for your hospitality,' Louise said. Zeno addressed Kaboue and spoke in Oromo.

'You will always be welcome to share with us,' replied Kaboue.

Share with them when they have so few resources, thought Louise. What a privilege.

Preparation of the food happened quickly. Over the meal, only Kaboue spoke to Zeno's students. The other women just listened. Her eyes sparkled and she smiled constantly. Louise learnt that the villagers traded their grain and vegetables in the local market for hoes and small ploughs, implements not used in other regions. She also learned that, if age-old customs were not passed on by significant elders such as Kaboue, the likelihood of starvation and famine was enhanced. Louise admired the timeless wisdom of this Oromo woman as she related her knowledge of the seasons, of the harvesting of sorghum and millet, of storing seeds for the next planting. This was effective husbandry of the most fundamental kind – a practical village strategy, determined by Kaboue. She would have spent a lifetime collecting seeds, comparing soils and conserving water.

Zeno's party spent almost three hours sitting, talking, drinking *tella*, their beer made from sorghum, eating roasted corn, with chicken and vegetable hot-pot spooned onto the biscuit-coloured *injera* and *kocho*. Louise listened carefully, grasping the sense of the conversations, even when Zeno did not translate. She relaxed and let the gestures and voices wash over her.

Louise felt like she was being entertained at the court of a queen – the intriguing Kaboue. Yet she sensed an undertone, especially among the younger women, almost as if they were imprisoned by her influence.

At the end of the meal Kaboue thanked Zeno and his students for visiting her village. He replied thanking her and the women and promised to return at the first opportunity. Louise realised that he needed to court her support if the changes he had in mind were to be introduced. At this moment she recognised how similar to Kaboue was her grandmother's calmness, and belief that hardship can be endured.

Zeno's party said their farewells and began their walk out of the valley and back up the steep gravelly track to their plateau camp. Just after dusk he led the students safely to their camp site. They slept well that night.

'Consider a Man's Background'

THE NEXT MORNING Zeno announced they would visit the Thursday market at Asela. Everyone thought they were in for another long day's trekking and meeting Oromo people, but Zeno said that he had no intention of exhausting them.

'Maybe that's his way, one full day and when at the end we're exhausted he provides something easier just to keep us interested,' Louise said to Carmen as they sipped coffee over a later-than-usual breakfast.

'He sure doesn't want us to lead a retired life.'

'I think he imagines that something spectacular will happen and we'll fall in love with Ethiopia forever.'

Louise noticed Zeno looking directly at her. She wanted to ask him what it might be like for a Western woman to live in Ethiopia.

'What part of Ethiopia do you think he wants us to fall in love with?' asked Carmen, interrupting Louise's thoughts.

'The people, wherever they are.'

'Do you think so?'

'Yes, of course. Didn't you notice his respect and admiration for the Oromo women in that village?'

'Yes I did, but I suspect his charm factor is like that with any woman he meets.' Carmen raised her eyebrows.

'I think he just wants to generate interest in Ethiopia's people so there is momentum to support his ideas. He believes famine can be eliminated and that better education and improved health facilities are the answer. I don't think he'll rest until his goals are accomplished.'

Louise blushed as she spoke. Carmen noticed her pensive look.

'I suggest we find out more about him, who exactly he is, who he lives with, whether he has children and whether he wants to go on living in Ethiopia, or take up opportunities overseas, like many highly qualified Ethiopians do,' said Carmen.

'That's good advice.'

'Yes. When all else fails consider a man's background.'

Louise changed the subject. 'I'll ask him about his plans for change in Ethiopia.'

'Louise, you've got the talent and will to alter lives for the better – you're what he's looking for.'

'Do you think so?' Louise smiled.

'Of course, of course.' Carmen rubbed her hands together in the chill morning air and Louise imagined being alone with Zeno with him kissing her, running his fingers down between her breasts ...

'Louise, are you okay?'

'Yes, of course. I was thinking about what Zeno will want us to see at the Asela market and when we reach the Omo valley!'

Mid-morning Abebe drove to the Asela market on a tarmac road which ran along a high plateau overlooking a steep valley. Around the horizon were distant mountains that with the rising sun glowed like honey. A warm, dry wind blew down from nearby etched hills. Abebe, followed by Degu driving the second vehicle, left the road and approached the market along a cracked, sandy-coloured track. They parked under an acacia and, with the sun raking across the track, Louise, Carmen, Horst, Bassam, Zeno and the others left the 4WDs and joined farmers, merchants and villagers in the open-air market.

They wove their way among highly spirited groups with men laughing in open *tella bet* (beer houses). There were rows of trestle stalls displaying jars of acacia honey, sugar and tea, and then fruit stalls with women selling rather battered sweet bananas, pineapples, mango, papaya, avocado and grapes. Beyond that, vegetable stalls were piled with tomatoes, green beans, snow peas, broccoli, asparagus, cabbages and green chilli. On the ground were sacks of potatoes and onions. Further on, women sat on coloured mats alongside sacks of millet, sorghum, maize, rapeseed and coffee beans. People were bartering. Two men purchased a sack of millet and loaded it onto a mule.

'Did the famine reach this region? Carmen asked Zeno. 'There seems plenty of food here.'

'There were pockets here around Asela where the famine was not as bad,' replied Zeno.

He shrugged. 'Now, with a little rain, farmers are again producing food for the markets.'

Beyond the vegetable stalls there were women sitting on the ground selling large earthenware pots, saucepans and kettles. Beside them other women wove baskets. Louise and Carmen watched and admired the women's skill.

'We must buy something, just a keepsake. The jewellery table over there looks a good bet,' said Carmen.

Louise smiled. 'Good idea, perhaps some cowrie shell necklaces for friends back home.'

They walked to a group of trestles laden with local made jewellery. Smiling women encouraged them to try on necklaces made of beads, metal bracelets, cowrie-shell rings, earrings, ornamental neckbands and shell chokers.

'Trying on these necklaces and chokers is the easy part,' said Louise. 'I'm not sure what to choose.'

'These women seem patient so we can take our time. I sense they know we'll buy something.'

When Louise tried on different threaded shell necklaces the stall owner rose from her chair and gently fixed the clasps.

'*Ameuseugnallo* (thank you),' said Louise. The woman smiled and nodded.

'That's it, these three necklaces.' Louise gestured to the

jewel-bedecked Oromo woman and, guided by her, counted out the appropriate *birr* (Ethiopian currency).

'Okay, Carmen, what have you chosen?'

'Metal bracelets with a matching pendant. That'll do me.'

'Louise looked around to see where Zeno had gone. At the outer limit of the market, cattle, goats, a few sheep and the highly prized donkeys were tethered, standing in dunged straw. The cattle's pungent excrement was cooked by the morning sun. Zeno had walked over to talk to a man he knew. They seemed to be old friends. They discussed the man's bartering for two goats. Eventually when the deal was made there was hand slapping and congratulations all round.

Louise and Carmen joined Zeno and observed the endless debates about the quality of livestock and whether prices paid were fair. Zeno explained how there was endless scrutiny about the bartering which he explained was part of the joy of coming to this market. He was enthusiastic as he described the market's origin and central role. 'If you lived here this is where you'd come to buy all you need. In Ethiopia, buying and selling almost everything is practised in markets like this. Coming to this market is a necessity for these people and it's an important day out.' Zeno's burning love for the market and its people was apparent. 'Markets like this lost much of their zest and many declined during the famine, but they didn't disappear,' he added.

They wandered from stall to stall and came across two young men selling multicoloured plastic sandals. Next to them were older men sitting alongside piles of spades, hoes and trowels.

'In poorer regions in the far south people still dig and plough with sticks and become exhausted, so obtaining these tools here is evidence of improved agriculture,' said Zeno. 'But we've still a long way to go.' He stood by Louise and followed the line of her gaze across the market. 'We could spend more time here but we have a long day tomorrow and we should find the others and a *migib bet* (small café). There's one with umbrella-shaded tables at the entrance to the market.' In a brief second their eyes met. 'Are you hungry?' Zeno asked.

'I sure am, and thirsty.'

At the entrance to the market they found the café tables behind which were some ironwood trees and a corrugated kitchen shed. There were ten people in their party, and Zeno and Abebe arranged tables so they could eat together. A man brought two jugs of *tella*, *some* bottles of water, and a woman brought a tray of *buna* and a basket of *injera*. Bassam and Carmen ordered bottles of *bishaan amo* (mineral water). Abebe passed the *tella* jugs around and filled plastic mugs. Zeno recommended that they order the traditional spicy meat and vegetable *wot* with *injera*, supplemented with a lamb (*bege*) fried meat dish (*signa tibs*) along with a mild yellow sauce (*alicha*). Abebe and Zeno ordered *berberi* (chilli) to give more heat and flavour to their food.

Bowls of the meat and vegetarian dishes were placed in the middle of the table. Everyone was now very lively. Zeno, Abebe and Degu tore off corners of *injera*, scooped up the meat and vegetables. Watching them carefully, the others scooped out the *wot*, *signa tibs* and *alicha*.

Over an hour passed. It was time to leave. Zeno settled the account and after thanking the staff, they stepped out from the umbrella shade and walked back to the parked vehicles. The market-day crowds were returning home. Many men flush with *tella* drove their donkeys while their women carried baskets laden with eggs, fruit, meat, vegetables and assortments of pots and pans.

Abebe and Degu drove back along the tarmac road to the campsite which they reached by late afternoon. Heavy clouds were building and replacing the clear blue sky of the warm day. When they reached the camp site, Zeno set the next morning's departure for 9 am.

The Omo River Valley

ON THEIR THIRD night at the camp it did not stop raining. In the morning there was a persistent drizzle when they left for the Lower Omo Valley. The roads were awash as they drove on rubble-strewn gravel through low hills in an alternating thick, and then clearing mist. Louise felt she was driving into clouds. She could only just discern the plains below and the peaks of hills. From time to time as the road became steeper Degu's lead 4WD disappeared into the mist. A rough signpost pointed their way to the Lower Omo and eventually to the towns of Arba Minch, Key Afar and Jinka. The drivers were struggling to see, so both vehicles stopped until the mist cleared.

Alongside them the leaves of wild-olive bush, eucalypt, tough acacia and long grass dripped. They sat in the vehicle, talking for an hour until there were just slivers of mist hanging ahead.

The further off the beaten track I go, the more I'll experience the real Ethiopia, Louise thought as she stared at the scant, veiled eucalyptus trees. It stopped raining. 'Zenabu no more,' called out Zeno. He explained that *zenabu* meant *it's raining*. Abebe switched on the engine, and they rode on through the valley's seeping damp.

With the windows down they enjoyed the scent of flowering acacias. Rain had brought freshness to the landscape, and mist now gave way to bright light. Louise thought about the ebb, flow and stress of Ethiopian weather. She savoured this moment of dripping trees steaming in the warming sun.

On the drive to Arba Minch, Zeno took them to visit the Dorze tribe, famous for their weaving. He told them how the division of labour in this ancient tribe was well established – the women spun and the men wove bright multicoloured fabrics. Louise and Carmen watched Dorze women concentrating on their spinning, occasionally glancing at their visitors.

Zeno's program was so full that every time Louise wanted to spend more time on what she was observing, the group had to move on. Her fingers tapped on a vacant loom as she gazed at the hunched weavers in this unlit room where for centuries they had practised their art. The effects of long hours bent in one position were taking their toll. Again and again, sitting in one position, they lifted the loom's harness, inserted yarn into the fabric and, maintaining necessary loom tension, mumbled among themselves. The finished colourful weavings in red, blue and yellow were hung on racks on the hillside outside the village. Does anything change here, she wondered, or are they now just tourist attractions that will soon be dispensed with, become unemployed, die young and be forgotten?

On the journey to Jinka and Turmi in the heart of Hamar tribal country they visited the rival Banna tribe and their market at Key Afar. They saw goats and cattle being bought and sold, and bags of different grains being bartered.

Ten minutes from the market they passed a village and could hear loud music. Then, swirling women in bright cotton skirts called, rejoiced and sang as they danced. Spinning flamenco-like, with hands aloft, leaping with lightness and control, their bodies glistened with perspiration. Louise watched the spectacle, incredulous at the dancers' energy, feather-light, and women rejoicing, despite drought, destructive storms and famine. Zeno told her they were celebrating a village woman's successful birth.

Louise loved exploring the Lower Omo tribal lands from her first sight of the Omo River Valley. The early morning light on eucalyptus reminded her of home. She was fascinated by the children tending goats, by the different Banna, Hamar, Mursi and Karo tribal people, by women cooking over open fires, the village gardens and the tribal markets in animist Key Afar and Jinka. She thought endlessly about the complexities of tribal life, of disaster and salvation and of the people's resilience, and thought then of her grandmother's optimistic view about there being nothing to fear in life.

'You're in your dreams again,' Carmen said. 'Would you ever come and work here?'

'Oh, I don't know. I may return one day to finish what I've started on this trip.'

'And I'll come back with you, if the timing is right.'

'Carmen, really! What a brilliant idea! I'll have to come back if I'm to understand the way of life of the Hamar women. I want to focus my research on them.'

'You'd return for no other reason…?'

Beside the River Omo

ON THE LAST day before returning to Addis, Carmen and Louise stood on the banks of the Omo River. The slow-flowing tributaries across the sandy hinterland, in places no more than a trickle, surpassed all that Louise had anticipated. She had thought of the Omo as a non-descript, muddy crocodile river – just a series of temporary puddles that sometimes swelled and overflowed. Now, in a southerly Karo village she watched the river gather momentum, and realised how thousands of people depended on it. Would this land that they loved be taken from them if development such as sugar and cotton mills, and in particular, widespread tourism, with five-star hotels, came to the valley? She pictured these vibrant villages becoming ghost towns.

Louise felt minuscule in the valley which seemed to wrap itself around her. She heard faint distant thunder and realised this was the 'rain-song swagger' which, apparently, told the people that drought was behind them and that ample harvests ensued. Louise gazed towards the catchment zone, imagining the River Omo infiltrating the gardens and fields.

At this moment Zeno walked over and joined them. Sensing Louise's awe, he talked enthusiastically about the different tribes that inhabited the valley. 'I'm sure you'll find out what inspires tribal people and what is injurious to their spirit,' he said to Louise. 'Observe these people's dance of life because, despite hardships, it is rich, believe me.' Then he asked, 'And who are the people, young and old, who avoid a too early death?'

Louise thought this a strange and rather pessimistic question.

What exactly does he mean? she wondered.

Zeno continued, 'Remember, like us, they don't want to die young, although as you know, throughout Ethiopia, and certainly here in the south, infant mortality rates are far too high.'

The group listened.

'Finally, to be practical,' he continued, looking directly at Louise but addressing his question to the group, 'ask yourselves which young people in each tribe are most likely to go away, to escape to the city from what they think is rural drudgery.'

'You mean drinking, parties and personal freedom?' Louise ventured.

'Those, of course – they can easily be caught up in an adventure and disown the family and tribe that have nurtured them. And if they become sick, as many of them do, they are isolated and cannot return to the haven of the tribe.'

'Do some of them succeed when they leave the tribe? And who is most likely to succeed?' Louise was intrigued.

'Your answer is probably as good as mine. What do you think?'

Somewhat taken aback, Louise tried to provide an answer. 'I suppose only the most resolute are likely to succeed and even they would need support.'

'And what are their characteristics?' Zeno asked her.

'I don't know enough about the young people who might leave their tribe, but I imagine the lure of bright lights and town life is attractive.'

'Yes, that's true, Louise. We can discuss this more fully later.'

Louise thought he suddenly appeared unnecessarily formal and perhaps even dismissive. Yet at that moment she suddenly felt his gaze was fiercely sexy; she sensed hi virility and found him irresistible. On occasions in front of the other students, Louise was embarrassed at his obvious interest in her while secretly she was flattered by it.

This was very different from her first teenage love at home in the Adelaide Hills with Rob, the undergraduate medical student.

4: Sex and Love

Lomiwen teqebelech –
'She accepted the lemon'

BACK IN ADDIS following their fieldwork with Zeno Wolde and before returning to London, Louise and Carmen made plans to fly north and visit the rock-hewn churches of Lalibella. On the hot afternoon before they left, Louise was wearing slip-on shoes with a slight heel, and a blue, thin-strapped summer dress that lit up her face and complemented her eyes. It fitted snuggly around her breasts and waist and showed off her lithe, tanned figure. She sat alone, enjoying coffee in the umbrella-covered university campus canteen, reading the essayist, poet and short story writer Abbe Gubennya. Then Zeno appeared. She wondered if he had been tracking her.

'I've been hoping to catch up with you before you leave. If you have time, would you come to my office so I can give you a memento of your visit?'

It was a tantalising invitation, one that Louise had half expected and would not turn down. An inner voice urged her to go with Zeno. She would return to Ethiopia to complete fieldwork, so it would be good to build her professional relationship with him. Nothing could come of their friendship because as soon as she returned from Lalibella, she and Carmen would fly back to London.

She left the campus refectory with Zeno and took a leisurely walk to his office. He opened the door, sat down at his polished wooden desk and invited Louise to take an adjacent chair. She felt comfortable with Zeno and knew, given his respect, she could easily leave without drama. Although she had no intention of leaving in a hurry.

She glanced round the room and looked over his lean muscular figure as she scanned the books on his shelves: *Politics of the Ethiopian Famine 1974-75, Paediatrics and Infant Mortality, Black Lions: Lives of Ethiopia's Literary Giants, The Poems of Dr Zhivago*, and *South Africa's Anti Apartheid Poetry*.

Zeno told her that he'd collected books on overseas study or conference trips, in London, New York, Rome, Paris and Cape Town. She pictured him thumbing through books in overseas bookshops. He talked enthusiastically about his books and travel.

Suddenly she sensed his mood change and found herself looking directly at him. Two of the poppers at the top of her dress were undone. There was a lull in the Addis traffic and briefly the room was silent. Zeno broke his gaze and said he would like to help her acquire a collection of significant books about the health anthropology of Ethiopia and that, in his view, it should also include literary works, poetry as well as prose. He produced a small book.

'I would like you to accept this first edition of the Ivo Strecker fieldwork book about the symbolism and life of the Hamar, Banna, and Karo tribes of the Lower Omo Valley. It's one of the few published – I'm sure you will find it useful.'

She wondered why he was giving her this precious book. Does he want me to work with him?

As he handed her the book, she eyed him flirtatiously. Then he whispered, 'This, Louise, is for you.'

'Thank you, Zeno, I will cherish this. I will read it carefully and hope that I can repay you in some way.'

'Repay me by returning to study here.'

Zeno leant forward, kissed her on the forehead, ran his hand through her hair and wrapped his arms around her. She closed her eyes and felt him taste her skin as he kissed her lips.

Had there been a plan for any of this, Louise wondered, as Zeno kissed her again. As she lifted her arms around him he lifted the straps from her shoulders, reached behind, unzipped her dress and let it slide over her hips to the floor. Currents of excitement and desire flooded in her. He touched her skin gently but intently. She undid his shirt and ran her fingers over his hairy chest and across his groin. He left her momentarily and quickly locked the door. Stripped to the waist now, he kissed her, licked her earlobes and neck, stroked her buttocks and buried his face between her breasts. As he pushed against her she felt his hard bulge. For Louise, the urgency of what she knew was their limited time together removed all inhibitions …

Finally he withdrew and, lying on his side, gazed at Louise. There was perspiration on her forehead and in her hair. They relaxed, gently touched each other's faces, and kissed.

Their breathing slowed. They lay in each other's arms for a long time, before getting up to dress.

'I'll drive you home to my place and you can have a shower, and then we'll find a restaurant.'

'I'd like that, but what about Carmen and our flight to Lalibella?'

'I can phone the student apartments and you can leave a message for her. I'll take you back after dinner.'

Instinctively she knew that truly he wanted her and had planned this moment.

After a short drive across the city they entered Zeno's apartment. He left a message for Carmen saying that Louise would return well in time for their trip.

Louise's breasts felt tender as she stood and soaked in the shower. She shampooed her hair and carefully soaped and washed away the last traces of Zeno from her body.

When she had dried and dressed, she went into the lounge to be embraced by Zeno. He had already booked a table at a secluded restaurant in a new Addis hotel.

Over dinner he raised the prospect of Louise returning to Addis Ababa to undertake fieldwork within a few months, much earlier than she had originally planned. She was enthusiastic and told him that her university in London could arrange for scholarship support when she studied in Ethiopia. Zeno talked about his research in anthropology and Louise wondered how she might navigate her way through preliminary thesis preparation in London and arrive back much earlier. Life makes an offer like this only once, she thought.

He settled himself in his chair opposite, reflected on this new reality and said in a measured voice, 'And you, Louise, have the talent to produce original work which will contribute greatly to the understanding of Ethiopian life. You remind me of the Ethiopian jazz song '*Lomiwen teqebelech*' ('She accepted the lemon') sung by the 1970s Ethiopian jazz star Mahmoud Ahmed in which a lemon is thrown at his girlfriend's feet and, if she picks it up, it means she will marry him.

'And you know,' he whispered, 'the girl in the song is like you, as beautiful as Makda Queen of Sheba ... and she picked up the lemon.'

'That's a beautiful story.'

5: A Fervent Soul

Zeno's Childhood and Youth

In May 1952, on a hot, steamy early morning in a crowded maternity ward of Addis Ababa's old Black Lion Hospital, a twenty-year-old Kenyan woman, Gabriella Wolde, stared in pain at the flaking ceiling. Then, squeezing her nurse's hand as hard as she could, she gave birth to her second child, a son she named Zeno Negash Wolde.

As Gabriella Wolde fed her newborn son for the first time she sensed that he was different. While still in the hospital, she told her older sister her prediction that he might be a leader one day. Her sister looked pained. 'Your prediction – as you call it – could cause you much trouble.'

Gabriella said that Zeno had a direct gaze, very much like his father. 'Sometimes it's almost as if he's looking into the future.'

'I hope you're wrong,' said her sister.

Zeno's father, Amare Wolde, born and bred in Amhara country near Bahir Dar, was a lifelong advocate of political and social reform. He met his wife on a visit to Nairobi when they were both training to be teachers. Zeno's older brother and two younger sisters were different from him in that they generally conformed, and were certainly less inquiring. Amare always hoped his children would follow his example. 'The opportunity is yours,' he would say. It was no surprise when Zeno grew to manhood and acquired many of his father's beliefs and aspirations.

'That boy has a mind of his own,' said Amare when Zeno was only four.

'He's so much like you,' said Gabriella.

'Hmm, well, it looks like Zeno and I will be in this together.' Amare was pleased.

Zeno's family would often visit his father's relatives who lived and farmed in villages in the provinces of Amhara and Tigray. There Zeno joined village boys in tending their goats and came to enjoy their songs, stories and walks to the goat kraal. It was usually late autumn when he was there. He remembered it being dry and warm all day but cold at night, sleeping in the open air alongside the animals. On cold nights his breath was visible and before sleep his friends' eyes seemed polished by moonlight. These were exciting times for a young city boy and he always wanted to stay longer. His mother listened attentively to his stories about herding goats and sometimes seeing leopards in the distance.

'Did you know,' said twelve-year-old Zeno, 'when, dik-diks are grazing at night and I stand with my friends at the scrub's edge, look-ing into the darkness and listening to the stillness, it is sometimes broken by the howl of hyenas or the chirping of small birds ... those goatherd boys are so lucky, to feel this every night.'

Gabriella noticed the detail in his stories and the forthrightness of his views.

'Tell me why you like the goatherd boys.'

'They are kind and tough.'

'That's a good reason, but you know, they are poor and illiter-ate and it will take a lifetime, or much longer, to improve their lot.' Zeno was saddened and, for this reason, always remembered her comment.

Testing himself to the limit and taking risks were natural for him. 'Adventure, always adventure, is Zeno's thing,' a high school teacher said to his parents. Gabriella knew this already. At sixteen, in the school holidays, Zeno caught a train to Nairobi and to Khartoum to explore the countryside around these growing cities. His mother agreed reluctantly to his wanderings although she soon realised that, headstrong as he was, she really had no choice. On these trips Zeno learnt different languages, particularly Arabic when in Khartoum, and began to establish a network of friends and contacts, as well as to enjoy his first sexual experiences.

Zeno grew into a strong and handsome young man whom women found attractive and he was stirred by the presence of young, beautiful women. He told his friends about his experiences, including the story about the frenzy that erupted when police raided the house of a Khartoum student friend where he was staying, because they believed it was an illegal brothel. He was troubled because they had narrowly escaped arrest. He said he loved the young woman he was with, and did not know what had happened to her after police took her away. Zeno met many young women and was invited to their homes, whether in Addis, Nairobi or even Khartoum. Due to his language fluency and charm, he was accepted and well liked. He spoke Amharic, knew Oromo and had a good command of written and spoken English. He also had a basic knowledge of Italian and by the time he was ready to enter university he could also converse, at a basic level, in Arabic.

Zeno's parents were committed and sometimes uncompromising in their Orthodox Coptic Christian beliefs, but never fanatical. Gabriella had embraced Amare's religion. Education was a priority.

Zeno's connection to his mother was very strong. 'Much of the Arabian Peninsula as well as East Africa contributed to the making of my son. That of course, is what his father would say too,' enthused Gabriella to her sister one day after Zeno had returned from Nairobi. She was devoted to him, perhaps to the point of indulgence.

When Zeno was twenty-three his outspoken father disappeared. One evening he went to a political meeting and never returned. It was assumed by his family and colleagues that he'd been murdered by a hit man, hired by members of the Derg. A month later, his mutilated body was found in a ditch outside Addis. Zeno went, with his mother, to identify him. As they stood and stared at his father's corpse, Zeno put his arm round his weeping mother's shoulders and vowed, not revenge, but a commitment to work for Ethiopia's poor.

'That's it,' he said to Gabriella as they left the morgue. 'That is what I have to do, work tirelessly for the people of Ethiopia.'

Amare Wolde's body was taken to his home village near Bahir Dar for a funeral in the presence of his immediate family and a few relatives. Gabriella wouldn't allow her family to see her crying and grieving and while she certainly shed tears, she walked in dignified silence beside her husband's coffin. Her calm face betrayed nothing of her sorrow. Zeno also maintained his poise and, at the end of the ritual, embraced his mother tenderly and kissed her, vowing to be always worthy of his father.

‘

'An Impetuous Genius'

AT THE END of formal schooling Zeno entered university to study medicine and anthropology. He made plenty of friends at Addis Ababa University and many of his contemporaries regarded him as brilliant and inventive, if rather wayward. An admiring but some-times ironic response often followed the mention of his name: 'Oh, that impetuous genius, Zeno Wolde!'

Zeno matched hard work and self-discipline with dedication. Like his father, he married a Kenyan woman while at university. He was just twenty and his wife nineteen. He and his wife Makena had two daughters; they were aged fourteen and twelve when Louise Davitt and Carmen Smith first arrived in Addis Ababa. Zeno had separated from Makena four years before their arrival. Makena told friends that Zeno's focus on his research, endless time away from home supporting his students, along with time spent on advocacy and lobbying for health and agricultural reform, contributed to the breakdown of their marriage. His work always came first. 'You stand by the front door, hoping, waiting for the old Zeno to arrive, to enjoy his kisses, his smiles and laughter, and for him to play with his daughters, but that gift of his love has disappeared.'

After the divorce, his wife and daughters moved back to Nairobi and, since Zeno continued to live in Addis, he had little contact with them. His friends queried this situation. It did not occur to him that he had abandoned them. He admitted there were occasions when he felt sorry for what had happened. It wasn't as if Zeno did not love his daughters but, as his wife's visits to her family in Kenya became more frequent, Zeno started to lose interest. At the time he was surprised by how little he cared when, after one long visit, Makena did not return. He made no attempt to persuade her otherwise. 'Mostly I had no idea what fermented in Zeno's brain,' Makeno wrote in a letter to her mother. 'Probably something revolutionary.' When disappointment inevitably set in regarding separation from his daughters, he threw himself more than ever into his work. Zeno Wolde said he had a duty to Ethiopia and he could live and work nowhere else.

During his undergraduate university years Zeno had received a UNESCO scholarship to complete his medical training in London. 'Heaven knows why I was given the scholarship,' he said with a certain modesty. Yet, while he had the talent to pass the medical exams, he already had an alternative career in mind. Zeno remembered the goatherd boys and the poverty of the villages, and imagined he could influence the economic, if not the political, life of his country. He would fight for poor village and tribal people, although against the national government Zeno realised it would often be an unequal match. Then he remembered his father and reflected again on the injustice of rural poverty.

Imprisonment

As a young man with a wife and a baby, Zeno often disagreed with local politicians. He wrote pamphlets criticising their decisions. In one he wrote: *They have no consistent policy other than one of post-poning decisions and wasting people's time. It's always tomorrow, or next week, next month, or next year, but never today.*

Accusing politicians of postponing decisions became a repeated theme in Zeno's writing and generated debate in coffee houses and *tella bet* where ordinary people could hear his views. He self-published a small book of short stories about the poor of Ethiopia. His assertions about the causes of poverty made local governments consider him a threat to their power. He wrote: *As in Selassie's time, nothing has changed – it is the government's view that famine reminds ordinary people of their duty to be humble. It also keeps them too weak to rebel.*

Zeno was tracked down one night in the town of Gonder in the north of the country and arrested. He was incensed at being taken away but soon grasped the reality of imprisonment. He should not have been surprised. His goading of authority, his pamphlets and speeches about Ethiopia's poor being harnessed to unrewarding labour, and whose dire circumstances were ignored by successive regional governments, had prompted his arrest. Zeno knew how Ethiopia's rich and influential politicians, and certainly the Derg, upheld the values of money and power.

With a rope around his neck and tied to his manacled wrists, he was thrown into the back of a truck and driven away. He remembered hearing a prison door close behind him. He met emaciated men, picking at scabs on their faces and arms, sitting in overcrowded dark grimy cells. He heard the crack of a whip across a man's back and his cry for mercy.

It was a week before his family and friends learned about his imprisonment. They hoped he would survive the onerous conditions and help other prisoners to do likewise. He would help them as much as he could, and knew he would never forget the stench in the cell he shared with eight other men. It was believed to be situated where the old Emperor once housed lions. It was a hellhole at night, with men lying close to each other as swarms of insects buzzed around them. Each morning, one by one, the prisoners were let out for brief ablutions.

Zeno studied the conglomeration of men that filled the low-ceilinged cage with its rusting, stained walls. Somehow he managed to shake off his fear but he kept wondering how long he would be incarcerated. On his third night, he recognised a young Tigrayan man named Meffara, with whom he'd conversed a month before in a Bahir Dar *tella bet*. Meffara's eyes were sunken and his hair dirty; grime and filth stiffened his clothes.

'This place,' said Meffara, 'I can't stand it. I feel I'll never leave.'

'Meffara, I don't want to hear about how you are feeling, or see you trembling. I only want to know about your determination to survive. You will be released, believe me.'

Meffara looked startled at Zeno's reprimand. He moved closer to him. 'Help me,' he whispered. 'I've no idea when I'll be released. Please help me!'

'I will, if you help yourself. Remember we're in this hellhole together.'

On cold nights, even Zeno felt as chilled as he had ever been. As Meffara and the others shivered, he tried to get them thinking and talking about how they might best survive. He had to work with grey faces, grey thinking and the nervous terror enveloping them. He badgered them, recited Amharic classical *qine* (love poems) to them, helped them plan each day. 'Think ahead,' he said. 'Think what could bring you great rewards when you leave here.' From the first, he willed himself to adjust to life in prison, setting out to convince broken men, each in their personal abyss, that their spirit could rise above humiliation. 'Continue to love yourselves,' he exhorted.

The men asked themselves, who is this man? Why is he fearless?

During nights amid the chaos, Meffara prayed for a miracle – that he would walk home across fields to join his wife and child. This was the sort of miracle he and others needed. For Meffara, thin and morose, Zeno's attitude was the one thing that lifted his spirit.

One morning after Meffara was abused by the guards, Zeno spoke to him directly. 'Meffara, today is the last time you will feel helpless. No good comes of giving in to bullies. I'm sure you'll be released soon. I've heard they want to clear out this place, knock it down or return it to the old Emperor's lions.'

They both laughed.

Like Meffara, Zeno had never been imprisoned before. Physical punishment by local police and prison guards was meted out for no other reason than resentment of Zeno's confidence. With their sticks and *giraf* (hippo-hide whip) they were there to keep order, and at meal times it was not unusual to see guards whip men if they thought they were out of line in the queue. Bribery was rife.

'You have money?' a guard brandishing a *giraf* asked Zeno one morning.

Zeno shook his head. 'No money,' he said, having hidden some *birr* notes in a carefully concealed inside trouser pocket. He anticipated what would follow – the swishing sound of the *giraf* followed by a dull crack as the leather cut across his back and buttocks. Fearful underweight prisoners in threadbare clothing looked on.

As far as the guards were concerned, Zeno was often out of line. He accepted the blows with stillness, considered a mark of distinction by other prisoners. He would not permit his fellow prisoners, let alone the guards, the luxury of seeing him cower.

Over the following weeks he was kicked and beaten but remained calm. Fortunately he was physically strong enough to absorb and survive the blows. With each blow he became more determined to oppose injustice. After a whipping, he could still summon a smile of reassurance for the other prisoners. Zeno inspired fellow prisoners. He soothed and calmed them.

Zeno's biggest challenge for maintaining sanity was not knowing how long he would be imprisoned. No one knew when they would be released; only a few knew why they had been imprisoned. There were no trials, no explanations. Was it just local police, abetted by local politicians, taking the law into their own hands? It was a lottery, not a question of whether an offence had or had not been committed.

'Yes,' he said, looking at his fellow prisoners, 'it's tough luck for us all.' But Zeno kept his spirits up and let his mind wander back to nights of dancing, of caresses, of happiness and tenderness; nights of reciting *qine*. 'Look,' he said to his fellow prisoners, 'poets urge us to create life rather than snuff it out.'

He recited poetry to himself to obliterate the deafening shouts of guards and prisoners, bouncing off the walls. *Love isn't always sweet, sometimes it's bitter and you need to make sacrifices ... and ... mankind has thought himself a superior being, while all day long the tree laughs.* And then he quoted Tsegaye Gabre-Medhin who had taught him at Addis University: *I crave for knowledge, I envy tolerant peaceful folk, I am frightened by ignorance, I loathe violence.*

His fellow prisoners blinked in the half-light of their cell and were soothed by his words.

Release

Two months after Zeno was arrested, he was released. Meffara had already been released. Mid-morning, Zeno was led through passageways and past prisoners' cells and cages. Along the way he cast glances at the dirty cells and the prisoners' unwashed, sore-ridden bodies. In the half-light he could see their sad looks. Then at the prison's outer door, he was told he could go. There was no reason given for his release. Perhaps it was because the old Emperor's regime had collapsed. Many other changes were afoot, evidenced by more than a hint of panic in the guards' behaviour. Perhaps it was just because food was scarce and prisoners were becoming restless; there were fewer guards, as local police had gone away to help with harvests. Or maybe it was just because the guards wanted to be rid of him.

Zeno looked at the sky as he quickly walked away. He sighed as he cleared the compound and set out on a winding broken road downhill into Gonder. He felt in an inner trouser pocket for the *birr* he had managed to hide. It was still there, enough to pay for coffee, some food and a bus journey to Addis. As he walked, he decided that there was no way he would protest in the manner of that fateful night in the *tella bet* or write such accusing pamphlets again. It should be possible to write, negotiate and lobby for change without putting himself at risk of imprisonment. He crossed the street and entered a roadside coffee bar. An incense candle was lit and strong black coffee was served.

He caught the next bus south out of Gonder. In late 1974, on the old overloaded buses, it was a long two- or often three-day journey via Bahir Dar back to Addis. On the crammed, torn seats, Zeno watched the Tana Lake country recede slowly as the bus bumped, creaked and then hauled itself up hills. Zeno tried to sleep but the bus stopped at every village and was sometimes waved down by peasant farmers on their way to and from work. Mostly the bus didn't stop for them, but nevertheless they still waved cheerily at the driver. Zeno's nerves were stilled when they waved, his anxiety swept aside. As the bus trundled on, with images of these poor but cheery farmers in his mind, he closed his eyes, relaxed and slept.

At dawn on the third morning, on the outskirts of Addis, he saw the early signs of the day's activities as farmers drove goats to markets; horse and donkey carts carried produce to local stalls; bakers lit their roadside ovens and cafés served the first coffee and meals of the day. At eight o'clock he left the bus, entered a roadside tent café and ate fried eggs and toast with a mug of coffee – a thousand times better than prison slop.

He walked for half an hour through back streets to his family apartment. His wife and baby daughter were away in Nairobi. He washed and shaved in their small bathroom. He was so used to little sleep that he felt no ill effects from the long bus ride, so made his way to the university library where he passed the morning in fitful expectation that he could be arrested again. By lunchtime he was tired. He walked slowly back to his apartment and slept more deeply than he had done in many months. In the evening he joined friends at a wine and beer hall where musicians, singers and dancers entertained until late.

He told them stories of his prison experiences. After a meal and a few drinks he was in the mood to talk about Amharic poetry to any young woman he was drawn to. He felt as if he was back to his old self. The hall was full of people eating, dancing or sitting back, listening to the music. Zeno danced as well.

At times, however, Zeno failed to recognise the resentment he could arouse by unwittingly presenting himself and his ideas as indispensable. As his friends listened to his ideas on rural poverty and how it could be overcome, they feared his words and beliefs might cause him further trouble.

As the evening wore on, more people arrived and Zeno danced with a waitress. They moved close together. In the dim light he gently stroked her face. She immediately took his hand and placed it between her breasts. Aroused, Zeno did not withdraw his hand as the young woman danced closer to him. When the music ended they sat together talking, touching and kissing, leaving just before the bar closed. The resolute nature of Zeno's behaviour in prison was replaced by his irrepressible sensual desires.

Beauty Born of Despair

WEEKS LATER, WITH imprisonment almost forgotten, Zeno again discussed with close friends how important it was to fight oppression, exploitation, illiteracy and ignorance. He fervently believed, to use one of his favourite expressions, that 'beauty can be born out of despair'. He provoked colleagues by asking them, 'Why should poor people not become rich?' He would also say, 'The cry of the poor distracts my thoughts – and that cry must be answered.'

His close Kenyan friend Amos Oginwa listened to this comment. 'That's an exceptional commitment,' he said. Zeno never held back when emphasising the needs of Ethiopia's poor and didn't mince his words about the miserable administrators whom he despised. His anger was acute. At the root was his sense of injustice, along with guilt that he was not doing enough. His father was never far from his mind.

'You're creating opposition when it's not necessary,' Amos said when he became exasperated at Zeno's claims.

Amos regarded Zeno with fondness, but also awe. Amos had married Zeno's beautiful Amharan friend Tana from Bahir Dar.

Zeno often returned to this area or visited other remote villages for weeks on end and no one knew where he was. He witnessed hardship but he was always given shelter and food; young village men and women enjoyed his company. This was his extended family. After being away for long periods, he would return as if nothing

88

much had happened. He never wanted to be pinned down.

'He'll change in time. Someone else might influence him,' said Tana. 'It makes little sense for him to try and lead on so many different issues.' She was sympathetic and aware how Zeno's focus, like acid on zinc, bit deep into the grain of his working life.

'The problem is, he probably thinks he's the only one who can solve other people's problems,' Tana told Amos. 'See if you can get him to be more circumspect. He'll listen to you. After all, you're his closest friend.'

Amos, more than anyone, understood the often blazing candour of Zeno's views. When Zeno was in full flight, Amos said he was 'like an open window on a bright summer morning.' Zeno told Amos that his best days were those in summer when he could leave the city, reach a village and breathe the odours of goats and cattle and the sweat that comes from working in the fields alongside peasant people.

Malaria and Bilharzia

IT WAS HIGH summer in 1976 when Zeno first reached the Southern Tribal Lands. When he arrived he was shocked by what he saw. Naked, dehydrated children in both the Hamar and Banna tribes were lying on cowhides with little shelter from the burning sun. His examination revealed a severe outbreak of malaria. In every village he visited there were fever-ridden infants and young children experiencing severe headaches and sweating profusely. Exhausted mothers, knowing their children were very ill, showed their love even more, but were essentially helpless, their goatskin skirts hanging loosely on thin bodies.

In a seriously affected Hamar settlement, Zeno sat on a cowhide and nursed a child. He stroked her hair, gently touched her swollen stomach and sensed her pain through his fingers. The village sage told him that, following bloodied diarrhoea, three children had died the previous week and that the child he was nursing would certainly die too because no treatment was available. Zeno felt the anguish of the mothers and proud tribal people.

Gently, he laid the child he was nursing back on the cowhide under the spreading acacia and stood looking out across the dusty village, so quiet it was frightening. He felt helpless and angry, and this anger stayed with him as he held in his mind a picture of these beautiful but sick children and their distraught parents. He wanted immediate action for the prevention of malaria. When he acknowledged to himself that, in Hamar or Banna country, this was not possible, he was filled with sorrow. Logic, reason, medical understanding were the proper way to effect appropriate treatment – not fables, myths and legends. It seemed, he thought, that nothing changed here.

Why can't we produce a single person to ensure the health of these beautiful children? he asked himself. He knew the answer: 'Because no one wants to know the tribal people of the south.' He knew that hundreds of the nation's doctors had migrated and were practising and making fortunes in Chicago and Los Angeles. Zeno could not think of any recently graduated Ethiopian doctor who had come to practise in the south.

After three days Zeno said goodbye to the Hamar tribe, walked down the sandy track, climbed into his old diesel Range Rover and drove further south to a Karo fishing village alongside the great Omo River. Here he found more tragedy. For many weeks, to cope with the scorching heat, Karo children had been swimming in the weed-strewn and sometimes crocodile-infested river. There had been an outbreak of the water-borne disease bilharzia. Infected children were lying around listlessly in a village that generally teemed with their play and laughter. Twenty to thirty of them urinated blood and had blotchy raised skin rashes. Zeno could see how the sick children were victims of circumstances over which they had no control.

Before arriving he had expected their lives would be healthy and happy. Outside a hut he saw a child writhing and whimpering with severe abdominal pains. He thought then of his mother's care when he was sick. He thought of the city doctor who prescribed antibiotics. Usually, the sky here made him feel open and confident, made him think of the children going to school and fishermen coming home with a good catch. This time the sky was the same but the village was a different place. The sandy ground was hot beneath his feet. Death was real and lurking.

What is happening to these people, Zeno wondered. He recalled a magazine article he had read about the incidence of bilharzia and how quickly it could be cured. It was depressing for him to realise that no effective treatment was available here and hence children would suffer and die from an easily treatable disease. On hands and knees he crawled into a thatch-roofed sapling hut and crouched alongside a sick child as its family looked on. He knew he could not change their destiny.

When thunder pulsed on the horizon on the second day of his visit and sounds of warblers filled the thickened air, Zeno was delighted. With renewed energy and despite the glaze of summer heat and threatening storm, he knew that the land and people would be renewed, bilharzia would be cured – he would see to that. His optimism had returned with the approaching rain. Furthermore, he wanted to tell the world how, in the future, the health and livelihood of the Karo as well as the Banna and Hamar tribes would improve. He was confident he knew how this could happen without altering their lives too much and, certainly, not by driving them from their lands.

For Zeno, a significant part of the late 1970s was travelling overseas for conferences and study. He met new people, negotiated for research funding and seldom if ever thought of Makena and his daughters, only of Ethiopia.

Makena used to complain that they couldn't persuade him to stay home with them, even if they wanted to. She knew that when an offer came to present at an overseas conference, he would take it. She used to think of him as the 'Ethiopian abroad'.

But even when Zeno was in London or New York, his country remained inside him. He felt a part of the Amharic language and its evolving literature, of the cultural traditions and costumes. 'I can live outside of Ethiopia and still have it in my heart,' he told Amos. The land was indelible for him – the rural hinterland always contained memories of childhood. Like an absent lover, he ached for Ethiopia's physical presence. He missed the Simien Mountains, the land and antiquities of Tigray, the grazing scrublands and villages of the nomadic tribal south, the sound of Amharic and Oromo speech and the web of friendships and associations that inspired him.

Zeno had a grand vision for Ethiopia. Many of his friends thought he was the ultimate rebel because he was highly critical of the Derg and, despite disturbances in the countryside, which could place him at risk, he continued to write and lobby for reform.

Enthusiasm and Confidence

A MAN OF wide reading and philosophical bent, Zeno had great insight into Amharic literature, and wrote thoughtful analyses of Ethiopian history. There was no denying that by the time Louise and Carmen arrived, his output of three anthropology books, many pamphlets and newspaper articles and some thirty research papers, was prolific.

His friends treasured his enthusiasm as he'd say things like: 'We must walk rather than shuffle, dance rather than just stand and stare.' This attitude permeated his work, and what he'd seen in the countryside made him desperate for solutions to the many deaths he observed. The degradation of starving people haunted him.

Village life was his canvas, and in the field, living alongside villagers, he shared his ideas. Yet he experienced a growing loneliness. If he were to fulfil his destiny, he needed companionship. He had a plan which pulsed insistently in his consciousness; he knew what was missing and, deep down, was confident it could happen for him.

Those who did not know him and who talked about his work only from a distance, probably imagined him as a visionary, out of touch with what governments could achieve and how tradition was itself an obstacle to the reforms he envisaged. But those who understood how his passion and intellect operated would have known better.

In April 1986 he looked forward to the return of the young woman who could share his passions, love his country as he did and who would withstand the privations he experienced.

6: A Different Life

Louise's Return

IN OCTOBER 1985, back in London, Louise received the first of many letters and cards from Zeno. He also sent postcards to Carmen and the other fieldworkers, encouraging them to return. He was warm and welcoming in his correspondence. His first letter to Louise was both poetic and explicit. He wrote of the emotions she stirred when he remembered their lovemaking in his office; but enjoying sex with her was only one part of happiness he'd experienced in her company. He praised her as a young woman who never held back, who took great care to respect Ethiopian traditions and ways of life, and who wrote about them with fervour. And again, he conveyed his own bond with Ethiopia. In one card he wrote:

Dear Louise,

As I think you know, I like to sing about my country. Ravaged is its earth, but when the rains come then the land throbs and life changes – bees buzz, pollinate and fruit flourishes, and people are renewed – you will see. I look forward to your return … as soon as possible!

Love, Zeno

On that first field trip Louise had never escaped his notice. He had watched her when, behind dark glasses and a pulled-down wide-brimmed hat, with her open-necked blouse and lithe body, she had walked along dry riverbeds among gaunt cattle. He remembered her nodding to him in the midst of group conversations. 'Her face,' he told Amos, 'captivated me. I have tried to visualise her since she returned to London and maybe also to her Australian home. I remember the sparkle of her quick blue eyes, her lips always shaped into a friendly smile so that I anticipated a passionate kiss.'

Again and again over the next few months Louise appeared in his thoughts. Occasionally, in conversations with colleagues, her name would be mentioned, and Zeno hoped she would suddenly appear. He imagined sharing dinner with her, enjoying her spontaneous laugh and spending long nights together, and then watching her fast asleep in the early morning. But he grew apprehensive when she did not return a phone call or immediately respond to a letter.

Louise returned to Ethiopia in April 1986, earlier than she had originally planned but months later than Zeno had hoped. He met her at the airport mid-morning. His first glimpse of her was at the customs' barrier. His eyes lit up and he waved vigorously.

'Hello, Louise. How marvellous you're back here.' He kissed and embraced her, feeling invigorated.

'What made you come to the airport?' Louise teased, with a cheeky smile.

'I had a free morning.'

'I hoped you'd be here.'

Zeno smiled. 'I'm so happy you're back in Addis. Ethiopia will be a much more exciting and rewarding place with you here.'

'It's good to be back.'

He tried to read her thoughts. He followed her in the terminal, watched her smile and stored these images in his memory. In the airport's hubbub, Louise's beauty and nature struck him – this was the young woman he wanted by his side.

Zeno was confident that with Louise beside him he could bring about reform and change lives. He would tell her about the need for reform and how it could be slow and obstructed by shortage of resources, and ambitious politicians with self-serving alternative plans.

Louise spent her first few days back in Addis exploring. She

wandered among the shops and markets. She sat quietly in Addis'
St George's Cathedral. She walked up and down Intoto Avenue and
King George Street, watching street vendors and uniformed police-
men directing chaotic traffic. She visited the archaeological museum
and did as much as she could to familiarise herself with some of
the astonishing antiquities; the 3.5 million-year-old skull known
as Lucy, stone statues of seated female figures considered fertility
symbols, prehistoric indigenous pottery found around Axum, prehistoric stone tools from the region of Afar, and pictures of ancient
rock art depicting people and wild animals.

Most people came to Ethiopia to visit old palaces, churches and
monasteries richly decorated with Coptic icons. Although this was
important for Louise, she had come to live, hopefully with Zeno,
and then alongside village people in order to be able to tell their
stories. She was as much a storyteller as a research anthropologist.
She vowed that when she lived among villagers, she would do her
best to merge with them and learn about their history.

For the first week Louise stayed in the university student apartment.
Zeno was prepared to take his time before suggesting that they live
together. Louise, for her part, wanted to demonstrate her independence and, although their many meetings together were friendly and
loving, there was none of the compelling intimacy that they had
experienced six months previously.

'I will wait for you forever if need be,' Zeno said to her during a
happy lunchtime meeting.

'Can you bear to wait?' Louise replied, in a jovial, mischievous
mood.

Yet, she also wondered if a relationship with Zeno would be any
different from her fling with her London University supervisor Mike
Boetcher.

Vulnerability

IN EARLY MAY of 1985, before she had first travelled to Ethiopia, Louise attended a three-day anthropology conference at Britain's University of York. It was the time when France had just performed a nuclear test at Mururoa Island in the Pacific; in the coffee lounges this was the topic of heated conversation. Her London doctoral supervisor Mike Boetcher gave the keynote address, while several of his students gave poster presentations. She had always found Mike attractive. He was in his early forties. He had dark, slightly greying curly hair, a rugged face and his hands were large and strong, like the hands, Louise thought, of olive farmers she had seen in the hills of Perugia.

She was caught up in the wave of Mike's enthusiasm for fieldwork research in Ethiopia and Kenya. To cap it all, Louise had just received a letter from Rob in Adelaide telling her about his relationship with a nurse named Teresa who, he implied, was becoming a priority in his life. Louise had thought this could happen, and told herself it really didn't matter, but she felt real heartache. Rob had been her first love and they had been together, in one way or another, for almost six years. She confided in Carmen, who was sympathetic. Together they decided that what they had to do was to enjoy and benefit from the conference.

On the last night there was a dinner followed by dancing. Louise danced with Mike Boetcher, who was particularly attentive. He also danced with Carmen and talked with other university colleagues. Conversation flowed. Mike watched Louise move about the dance floor and wondered about her quietness and what she thought of him. He drank more wine.

'More wine, Louise?' he asked filling her glass when she sat at the table alongside him.

'Why not?'

Louise wondered about Mike's interest in her company. He danced with her again and when they returned to their seats he filled her glass. Louise could feel herself becoming tipsy. At eleven, Carmen decided to leave and Louise wished her goodnight. 'See you in the morning over breakfast,' she called. When the band played their last piece Mike asked her if she would like to join him at the hotel bar for a nightcap. By this time there were only a few hangers-on at the bar. Louise was flattered by his attention. He ordered a bottle of burgundy, poured Louise more wine and suggested they should take their drinks to the terrace overlooking the hotel's small garden.

'We need fresh air,' he said.

To his delight Louise did not resist his taking her hand and guiding her from the bar to the outside terrace. Louise felt his arm round her waist and then, holding her face in his hands, he kissed her on the forehead and then on her lips. She felt she ought to say to him, 'You're a married man,' but she found him attractive and didn't resist. But should she stay where she was or make an excuse and leave?

Before she could decide, Mike began to caress her and he felt her arch and press close to him. Both were aroused and he sensed she was not disinclined. She felt him harden against her.

'We can't make love here,' she said.

'Would you like to go now?' Mike asked.

'To my room?' she whispered. Together they stumbled across the hotel ground floor and took the lift to the second floor. Louise found the card and unlocked her bedroom door.

The next day the conference ended. Louise enjoyed breakfast with other conferees and attended the concluding seminars and address.

Hidden in her briefcase was a card from Mike, thanking her for a beautiful night. He commented on her talent as a researcher and on her elegance. There were ambiguities in his note as he sought to continue as her lover while maintaining a distance with his academic supervisory role.

In London in the months that followed, Louise sensed they might make love again, but in the circumstances it was important that their relationship was a discreet working and professional one rather than a loving and sexual bond. She didn't imagine a future with Mike. After all, he was married with three children. She saw their relationship clearly. He might grow more passionate and demanding if they ever made love again, but she was determined not to make unreasonable demands on him and therefore his family. Long-term, she definitely did not wish to be regarded as his mistress.

When Louise returned to Addis Ababa for the second time, she was affected by a sense of vulnerability should the relationship with Zeno turn sour. She still worried. Could it be just a brief affair like the one she'd had with Mike Boetcher? She concentrated on her studies and museum visits, and bided her time. Ten days after she had arrived back in Addis and before the next extended fieldwork, Zeno invited her to dinner. This was not the first time they had eaten an evening meal together since her return, but his invitation this time was expressed as a command, however genteel, rather than delivered in his often more casual, even take-it-or-leave-it tone.

Generally, Louise took little interest in her clothes, preferring that they be functional. Like her student colleagues Louise dressed casually in slacks. In preparation for this dinner, however, she brushed her hair till it shone and put on a fitted purple dress with the hem line above the knees. She wondered if Zeno might still have those feelings for her that were apparent on her first trip. Since her return she had seen him eyeing her when he thought she was not noticing.

Meanwhile, a mile away, Zeno was deliberating on how he should dress. Casual, he thought, but also neat and fitting. He was never ostentatious but wanted this dinner to be special. After almost two weeks of each of them toying with the other, life separate from her was becoming difficult for him.

At 6 o'clock he collected Louise from her university unit. They kissed each other on the cheek before he drove into the centre of Addis. Rain had fallen unexpectedly and the usually grimy streets were cleansed with the gravel and rubbish washed to the kerbside. They entered the restaurant and sat at a table overlooking a garden. Zeno ordered a bottle of white wine.

'You haven't told me much about yourself,' Louise began.

'I don't think there's much to tell.'

Louise persisted. 'You lead a full social life and enjoy plenty of travel.'

'That's true.'

'Is it an ideal life?'

Zeno was taken aback. Louise's question was direct and delivered with an unexpected commanding tone. His surprise was obvious. They both laughed as Zeno gathered himself.

'Yes and no. I don't think I'm leading a life that's so different from the kind I'd like to have. Of course, I don't see much of my daughters. They live in Nairobi with their mother, but are more or less independent. I visit them when I can but it's not very often. Ethiopia and my work are central and, I suppose, consume me.'

'What's this *central* part of your life that, as you say, consumes you?'

Zeno avoided answering the question directly. 'I think of life as a tangle of interests, all interacting. And, as I think you know, I have many interests, which I embrace and share. That's the way I think.'

Louise noticed the change in his face, from a pensive look to one of determination in the thrust of his jaw.

'You're a very philosophical person. Tell me more about your friends.'

'Friendship is important – you know that. Amos is a close friend.

He now teaches in Nairobi. Often I have to make choices in my life and give up some things, or give up some friends who I have met overseas because it is no longer possible to see them. I have friends here in Addis, in Nairobi and, of course, a very close friend from Adelaide and London. Do you want me to tell you about her?'

He smiled and looked directly over his wine glass at Louise. She put her hand on his, encouraging him to continue, and he in turn stroked it.

'I know I can't have everything I want in life. That's not possible.' Zeno smiled again and raised his open hands. He intended to say, 'And I want you,' but held back.

Louise looked into his eyes. 'Zeno, what's a priority for you?'

'Goodness, what a question. You put me on the spot.'

'Go on, tell me, have a go.'

'Working with people I love and admire. They are my source of inspiration. Is that a reasonable answer?'

Louise reflected for a moment and, then picked up the bottle of wine and topped up his glass. 'Tell me about your parents. Are they still alive?'

He realised he'd not told Louise about his family. Now she was seeking some details. Louise wondered if she had spoken too directly, but Zeno leaned slightly forward and, with his hands clasped and elbows on the table, appreciated the opportunity to talk about his parents.

'My mother is alive and well and now lives in Nairobi. She's a warm person. She's generous to a fault, quietly confident but also optimistic and resilient. You would like her.'

'I would like to meet her. How do you get on with her?'

'I love and respect her. She's not had an easy life, largely because of my father. Like his father before him, my father experienced sadness and depression. Then he could be wayward and was often angry – usually about politics. He would disappear for days on end just to be on his own, usually in the north. "I'm going for a few days to beautiful Tigray," he would say.'

Louise was moved. When he paused she encouraged him to continue.

'My parents had just separated before he died. My father was one of those people born with a sense of responsibility. He was very conscientious. He believed in Ethiopia as a strong independent country. But he was a difficult person. He argued too much about politics. We think he was murdered, but no one knows for sure.'

Louise said softly, 'I'm so sorry about your father. That must have been an awful shock.'

'It was at the time, but we now know what to expect if we challenge those in power, or their henchmen.'

He sighed and gazed at her with the same loving look that Louise had first experienced when they had made love on his office floor. Then all at once a smile spread across his face which obliterated the sad look.

The waiter took their main course orders and topped up each glass. Zeno felt heartened by Louise's obvious interest in his father and mother; he thought that, in this frame of mind, she might agree to live with him. He had thought of every contingency as to why she might prefer to stay in her university unit.

'When could you move in and live with me?'

'I thought you'd never ask.'

Zeno stood. The very thing that had bothered him so much these past weeks was now expunged. He walked around the table, hugged Louise and kissed her on the lips. He was excited but also at peace with himself, and saw many opportunities with her at his side. So much could now be achieved. The loving manner in which she responded stirred and gave him confidence.

'When would you be able to move in? I'll have my flat ready for you.'

'Why not tonight? It seems as good a time as any.'

'Fantastic!'

Oblivious to the other diners and his surroundings, Zeno hugged and kissed her again.

They gave scant thought to the food in front of them until Zeno laughed and pointed to Louise's dinner. 'We'd better eat before we get thrown out.'

They resumed eating and as they talked, he complimented her. With all the noise in the restaurant they had difficulty hearing, so they leant towards each other, their foreheads almost touching, stirring the senses. They knew they would make love this night.

Zeno drove Louise back to his flat. She had no nightwear.

'You can wear a shirt of mine as a nightdress. I think you'd look best in the blue-and-white striped one.'

'At least I'll need it in the morning.'

The square bedroom with uncarpeted floor was neatly furnished with a small double bed and two bedside tables. A thick, cream-coloured doona and matching pillows looked as if they had never been used. The wonder of it, to Louise, was that this man, whose working life was such a frenzy of activity, slept in this soft creamy room. Presumably, here he was replenished.

They both undressed. They moved with the poetry of experienced lovers. They hugged and touched each other. Louise pulled back the doona and they lay together and whispered about their love. Zeno talked about her hair, her breasts, her lips, her eyes and her face that he said he had kept in his heart these last six months. When he stroked her thighs, fingered, licked and slipped inside her, their bodies grasped, arched and twisted.

At dawn, after a night of repeated lovemaking, Zeno lay back, smitten. Louise, now wearing his shirt, stepped from the bed. He sat up, turned and watched her.

'I have to go to the bathroom,' she said, 'otherwise I'll burst.'

As she stepped from the bed, the tails of his shirt lifted slightly and he glimpsed the glimmering flesh of her buttocks. He longed to grasp them, spin her round, bury his face in her firm warm breasts and make love again. She turned and stroked his head. He seized her hand, pressed it to his mouth and covered it with kisses, then pulled her to him.

Famine and Tigrayan Villages

SIX WEEKS LATER Zeno and Louise drove north from Addis to Bahir Dar and then on to Gonder. The drive took three days, mostly over rubble-strewn roads and a few stretches of broken tarmac. On their third night they stayed at a hostel in Gonder and the following morning set off north towards Tigray village country.

Zeno was pleased to be on their way to the northern villages he had told Louise so much about. He said she had to see them if she was to learn about the recent famine. He summarised what they could expect to find, describing the landscape and the effect of starvation on certain villages. Zeno ached when he considered the grinding poverty which these beautiful people endured. Sympathetic and concerned, his magnetism and appeal seemed stronger than ever to Louise. When he speaks about these people, she thought, it's as if his words burn, and sparks fly off the anvil of his being.

All went well on the four-hour drive and the half-hour's walk across rocky terrain to the first village. It was the first time Louise had visited the far north where the famine had been most intense. The general features of the land and the villages displayed poverty and personal trauma. Upon reaching the village, Louise was struck dumb by what she saw. For months it and other villages had been covered by red-yellow dust that had swirled and settled on everything. It was as if an ochre veil had been carefully wrapped around huts and gardens. And this dust-covered Tigrayan border village was where people lived.

Zeno already knew about this *hidmo* (collection of village huts).

He had come here specifically to show Louise a ravaged settlement, so she would be able to give voice to the dimensions of famine.

At the edge of the *hidmo* Louise pulled her wide-brimmed straw hat down to her ears and wiped the sweat from her face. As she walked closer, she noticed a woman crouching alone under an old and withered tree. Beyond her was an empty, windswept, treeless plateau. As the woman sought shade from the sparse tree, her knees were drawn up and her head was buried between them. In silence, hardly moving, she sat there but, aware of Louise's presence, turned slightly to look at her. The drought had gone on for more than a year and, in the second year, hunger had stalked the Amharan and Tigrayan villages. The crouching woman was a symbol of suffering, but Louise saw her as undistracted, unhurried and someone who, despite her gaunt appearance, might blossom again. Such was Louise's hope.

Any rain that had fallen had turned dust to mud, which the sun then baked hard. On the edge of the *hidmo* there was evidence in many sloping cracks that when rain fell it washed over the dry ground and vanished into dry riverbeds. No rain appeared to be conserved at all. With so little rain, the countryside was barren and cracked as far as Louise could see, with yellowing patches of shrivelled grass forming intermittent tenuous islands on the fissured earth. Because there was so little grass to eat, the few goats and cattle looked thin and weak. Oxen were so feeble they were unable to draw the heavy ploughs. It would not be long before these animals died where they stood. Without strong oxen, the villagers would be unable to plant sufficient seed for the next growing season when the rains might return.

'What a tragedy,' she said. 'This is how severe poverty tortures and then kills the poor.'

Louise walked along a track between withered corn and sorghum, and stopped alongside a group of six crumbling mud-walled huts. Inside the huts were bench seats, topped with dry cow dung, all cracked and crumbling. The straw on rooftops was dry and in need of repair, and fences that had once separated each garden were broken so that cattle could wander, trample and eat what few *teff* plants, corn and sorghum stalks were left. Villagers who had survived the famine sat around. Zeno told her they were trying to conserve what energy they had left.

They observed the painfully thin people, their huts, withered gardens, and the background of treeless, distant hills. Zeno said that though he had seen it many times, it was still distressing. Then he added quietly, 'In order to survive, these people have to remember so much. When out in the fields, they have to keep track of the best strips of soil where crops might still grow, know which cattle and goats will most likely survive, keep a close eye on what chickens remain, know where to search, further and further away from the village, in order to find water, and they must remember all useful happenings, such as which nearby village might possibly have a little spare grain. Remembering, particularly by the headmen and sages, is vital for each village's survival.'

Louise thought how terribly ill-suited she was to experience all this, but knew why Zeno had brought her here. Around the perimeter of the village she noticed a woman standing alone, looking at her. Louise walked slowly up to her thinking that, with her high cheekbones, how very lovely she was despite the gaunt protruding shoulders, her bony thinness and dusty hair.

The woman stared at Louise. She said nothing and did not gesture. Her lips were parched as if sand had seeped into her mouth. She appeared full of grief; Louise did not know what to say or do. Then, as the woman moved away to a distant hut, her threadbare skirt rustled with each slow stride and her bracelets rang harmoniously. Despite her poverty and although trembling and weak, the woman appeared proud.

Maybe the woman sensed that when the rains came and summer sun ripened the sorghum, *teff* and passionfruit, then richness could spread itself again over the land. Knowing this may have kept this woman hopeful in the midst of her despair.

Louise followed her to the centre of the settlement and looked around. She learned from Zeno that the woman's name was Petra. She was a beast of burden like the other run-down workhorses in this village. Louise watched Petra walk away and slowly descend the stony track to her hut.

There's no lack of will here, Louise said to herself, just a lack of food. Then she noticed a group of men staring at her. In their faces, she thought, were looks of resignation as they took up painful tasks, like burying more dead; their calloused hands now useless. The abundance the world beyond enjoyed was not for them.

Louise continued her walk among the women of the village, glancing inside their huts. Women stared at her. She waved to them and they smiled. A woman beckoned to her as if to say, 'Don't be frightened; come, talk.' Alongside the older woman who had beckoned, Louise tried her limited Amharic.

She attempted to say, '*Ameuseugnallo* ...' The woman stared, half smiled, and replied. Louise now struggled to understand and looked around for Zeno. He was out of earshot, talking with a group of elderly women outside a hut. Louise touched the woman gently on her shoulder, clasped her hand and realised how much the woman was grateful for being recognised. Louise continued to gesture her appreciation of their meeting and the woman smiled and talked on for a minute or two until Zeno joined them and translated.

'She's telling you how this village once had plenty of food and then she could have invited you to eat with her, but now she has nothing to offer.'

Amidst blistering heat, night-time cold, perpetual hunger and shortage of water, men dug graves, women collected water from far-off temporary wells in dry stream beds, while others planted and cut scant sorghum, made their pancake bread, and milked what few goats had survived.

During the next week they visited four more villages. The scene was much the same. Villagers greeted them, some smiling and showing exaggerated courtesy, while others stared or generally ignored them. Louise noted the conditions, commented to Zeno about levels of poverty and ached for each impoverished and starving person. When she appeared traumatised by what she experienced, Zeno encouraged her.

'Come on, Louise. Don't be too sad. Life will soon improve for these people, and once we are back in Addis you can write about what you have seen. Your writing will identify the villagers' needs and reach significant people, here and overseas, who can help provide necessary resources.'

Louise was confused. It was not her job to save these people, but to observe and write as sensitively and persuasively as possible, immersing herself so she truly appreciated their needs. The task was huge and again she wondered if she was sufficiently able. Recognising her apprehension, Zeno told her she had the talent to advocate for these people.

At the end of six days, moving from village to village, they returned to Gonder and rested before setting off for a week's trek, climbing and camping on the Simien plateau. Zeno's cure for trauma and shattered nerves was to trek in the Simien Mountains.

Family Adventures – Teenage Years

LOUISE HAD ENJOYED the usual rough and tumble with her older brothers, and the fantastic ideas and high risk adventures she read about in books, or watched on television. Her imagination took her on adventures, making family excursions and camping holidays all the more exciting.

'Within safety limits, children should be able to roam,' said Louise's mother. 'That's how they learn self-reliance.'

Along with her brothers, Louise had developed independence through plenty of outdoor activities. She camped on South Australia's Coorong – a mixture of salt and fresh water lagoons sheltered by sand dunes from the Southern Ocean – and collected wild mushrooms and berries. They dug for cockles on the beach and at night over an open fire cooked the wild food. The Coorong never lost its novelty for her. When high winds blew and storm waves pounded the coast, pelicans and cormorants flew inland and the sea changed colour from doll's-eye blue to steel grey.

'I love sleeping among the dunes and listening to the sound of the roaring surf,' she said to her mother. 'The sea is like a symphony.'

Fourteen-year-old Louise proudly recounted her camping stories, telling her parents about canoeing around the bird-filled inlets, with the wavering light and the dwindling smoke of campfires. Now, in addition to her reading and holidays spent at Crystal Brook, she had the wild and remarkable Coorong to fuel her imagination.

At the Davitt family home, weekends were special. Louise loved Sunday mornings when she had her father Gerald to herself as he accompanied her to the Bayside Nippers' Lifesaving Club. Late one Sunday morning, after the lifesaving activities, her father drove down the coast where Louise fossicked on a cliff face.

'Look, there's more old fossils up there,' she said. 'Come on, let's climb the cliff up to the top.'

'You go, I'll watch.'

The sound of the surf below eventually drowned out Louise's excited calls. The track steepened until she was little more than a pin figure to Gerald. She waved to him from the cliff top, and then disappeared. Minutes later she reappeared and began her descent on a different and more hazardous track. An eerie whistling of sea breeze hummed across the cliff face. Stones and gravel tumbled as she descended. Louise zigzagged across the crumbling surface and, as she came closer, Gerald noticed her glowing expression – a look of never-ending enthusiasm. Would her risk-taking one day take a tumble?

The same characteristics appeared in her love of the ocean. She swam well and developed a body and muscles that were strong and pliable. Her lifesaving coach said Louise had a great feel for the water.

'Don't think about it – just do it!' she would shout, laughing at her father and brothers as she paddled her surfboard out to catch a wave. Louise and her brothers learned to jump and dive off the platform of the old Horseshoe Bay jetty at high tide. It was over a three-metre drop. After a jump, with Louise invariably in the lead, they would compete to see who could stay longest beneath the water. They scared and excited each other with this crazy activity and were constantly attracted by the thrill.

'Geoff, what were your last thoughts before you entered the water?' Louise teased as she prepared for another jump.

'I've no idea, what about you?'

'To see how long I could stay under – longer than you and Alex.'

'What can you see down there?' Geoff asked. 'Anything interesting?'

'You'd be surprised. Jump in with me and take a look. If you stay down long enough you'll see seahorses, the odd seal, and maybe a white pointer. Come on, I dare you.'

Her brothers soon learned not to up the challenge, because Louise would never shy away.

'Louise never backs away from anything or anyone,' said Alex to his older brother as they changed in the Horseshoe Bay Lifesavers' Club.

'Yes, that's just how she is,' replied Geoff, 'and I don't reckon she'll ever change.'

The Roof of Africa – Simien Plateau Trek

IN THE NORTH, Zeno showed Louise the rugged high plateau country. He enjoyed hiking in this spectacular and largely virgin country. He had first walked and camped here when he was fifteen and almost every year since. In this country, where there were no newspapers, no radio and no phone, his head cleared and after a few days his priorities became clear-cut. And he found reserves of strength.

The spectacular mountains contrasted with the barren Amharan and Tigrayan villages and with Louise's memories of camping on the windswept Coorong. If Louise was to know Ethiopia she must, Zeno reasoned, experience both the villages and the Simien plateau. Far from the equator, the mountains experienced temperatures which sometimes dropped below freezing; hail and snow could fall on the highest points. On warm days however, there was the likelihood of sunburn.

'Don't worry, I'll keep my hat on and I've brought plenty of sun cream.'

Zeno smiled. 'Yes, too much sun can sap your strength. Preserve your energy, that's what locals will tell you.'

It was late July, in Ethiopia's rainy season on the plateau. Zeno told Louise this was the season known as *keremt*. Together they walked carefully in the mid-morning sun along a narrow track that ran above sheer precipices and past basalt cliffs to their Sankaber camp site a thousand feet below. When it rained in the afternoon, as it often did, rocks became slippery and hazardous.

'It becomes treacherous if heavy rains become a torrent on the tracks and wash gravel and small rocks over the edge, causing further erosion. Don't go too close to the edge. I'll guide you. I've walked this track before so follow me closely.'

'My hands are sweating just thinking about it.'

As they walked on a slim ledge alongside a nearly vertical cliff face, they were confronted by a thirty-foot high tree topped with a red and purple globular flower. 'What's that tree called? It's so tall and majestic.'

'It's the giant lobelia. It's found only in this part of Ethiopia. We're lucky to see this fine specimen.'

Louise was moved by the height and toughness of this colossal flower, as if some invisible hand had nurtured it in these harsh conditions. 'Gosh it's growing in a rocky crevice; you'd think the weather on this plateau would be the death of any flowers. It's magnificent, Zeno. How on earth does it manage to grow here?'

'It adjusts. It's been growing here for centuries, and like you, it's beautiful,' he said, gently pulling her towards him and kissing her forehead. 'When I'm drunk with happiness what else should I do but kiss you?'

They clung briefly together. He ran a loving hand over her shoulder and across her back and buttocks – gentle in his devotion. 'You can touch me like that anytime,' said Louise. The whine of the mountain breeze was now audible as it whipped across the crags above them.

'This wind is a sure sign of rain.'

'Do you think it'll rain before we reach our camp site?'

'It will rain for sure, but the rain clouds could circle and miss us.'

Zeno led the way down the steep slope. Although experienced and sure-footed, he was still cautious. He walked with such an athletic lightness of tread that Louise, at times, struggled to keep up. Concentrating, they lapsed into pleasant silence. Louise looked down and noticed large birds circling in the thermals below. Above, colossal domes of cumulus cloud lifted over the mountain peaks.

It was difficult for her, burdened with a full rucksack, to enjoy the spectacular scenery, watch every step and converse with Zeno. As the day wore on, their eight-hour hike taxed her stamina. She gazed at Zeno ahead of her. He was strikingly handsome, slim and well-muscled; occasionally his gaze was dark and haunted, yet for the most part he was full of warmth and tenderness.

'This Simien plateau is the roof of Africa,' Zeno called through buffeting wind. 'We Ethiopians think it is extraordinary and so I had to bring you here – it's largely unspoiled and little known.'

'I love it. We seem so far away from Addis. And these giant mountain columns that reach to the sky – it's all so stunning.'

'I'm so happy here with you,' said Zeno.

'Me too.' Louise gazed at the mountain peaks. 'But do we have a right to be so happy when all around us, especially in the villages, we see so much poverty and starvation?'

'Eventually, starvation in Ethiopia will be eliminated. And we must enjoy our time together, because in ten days we'll be back in Addis with the demands of work.' Zeno looked at her admiringly. 'I can see the adventurer in you!'

In the sharp mountain light, Zeno was compelling; his bright brown eyes, his alertness and awareness.

'You must be used to a very different life back in Australia.'

'It's different, but it has prepared me for coming here.'

'Do you miss your friends in London and Adelaide?'

'I keep in close contact with my family and friends – mostly by letters. I've always done so. And I'm happy here, you know that.' Zeno was enthralled.

They descended the final mile to their camp site, picking their way over and around boulders and seeking handholds as their path fell away steeply then flattened out on the final stretch to their site.

They pitched their small tent on a wide, grassy ledge, lit a fire using twigs from old acacia shrubs and a small dead juniper tree, and made good use of their canteen. Zeno heated a packet of thick vegetable soup and Louise cut up the false banana *kocho* bread. When they had finished the soup Zeno brewed their coffee and produced a small bottle of liqueur.

'This is my 'holy water', he said. 'It goes well with coffee but you only drink a little at a time. It's nearly pure alcohol. It will warm you.'

'Where do you get your holy water from?' Louise asked as she took a sip. It tasted like a sweet but sharp brandy. She grimaced.

'From the Dorze. I have a friend, Makkone, who is a chief in this tribe and, when on occasions we meet, he supplies me with his holy water. The Dorze live in hills in the south. It's leopard country and a long way from here.'

'You took me there on my first trip.'

'Of course, I remember.'

They sat and watched as stars appeared and, in bright moonlight, their eyes glittered in the flare of their campfire which made orange and black patterns on the surrounding mountain walls.

'The world doesn't know about the magnificence of walks on the Simien plateau,' said Zeno proudly. 'Here we are, all alone, thirty miles from anyone. Only a few people know of this place, know its great canyons and our walia ibex ... and no one knows we are here.'

'What is your walia ibex? Tell me about it.'

'It's a rather large type of wild goat that lives on the narrow ledges below cliff faces. It's a protected species. We might see them in early morning higher up the mountain. If we see one, we'll be lucky. I have friends who have walked these trails many times and never sighted the ibex.'

'I wonder if we'll ever come back to this place. It's magnificent. I'd like to come back here, just the two of us again!'

'Yes, we can. Remember a few weeks ago when I told you about this place and that we might walk and camp here, and you thought I was crazy. So what do you think now?'

'I'm stunned, overwhelmed, by your Simien Mountains.'

Warmed by their fire, they sat leaning on each other. Instead of lapsing into more contemplation, Louise said, 'I know it's difficult for you talk about the famine Ethiopia experienced over the last two years, but I want you to tell me about it. I saw films in London and felt guilty, almost as if my friends and I had stolen food from these Ethiopians.'

'Oh, Louise, no one stole food from the starving. Remember, in the deep south there wasn't much famine at all.'

'Is that because there was no drought there?'

'Yes it was dry, but the tribes there – the Hamar, the Banna, the Mursi and the Karo – had their goats and cattle, generally more per head than the people in Amhara and Tigray where the famine was worst. And being animists, the tribes of the south did not sit back and think that God would provide.'

Louise looked astonished. 'Are you saying that religion played a part in the severity of the famine?'

'Only indirectly. There was little forward planning; grain storage was meagre and, as the drought continued, there was a too easy acceptance of the inevitable. Many probably thought that God would provide, until of course it developed into the famine.'

'Was it really inevitable that hundreds of thousands of people died?'

Zeno looked pained. He cleared his throat. 'That's what it looked like to me. The extent of starvation and the large numbers that died did not, in my view, have to happen. Distribution of grain and cooking oil was not effective and some of it was plundered, but that's a controversial point and not worth pursuing. And often there's too *much* food aid. By that, I mean waiting for handouts can cripple a country.'

Louise wondered how to reply. 'You've studied and lived among these people, and I know you think that the Derg had no idea what to do ... so what's your answer?'

'First of all, demonstrate that a more productive agriculture can occur. You see, much land in Ethiopia is fertile and the people are hardworking so we have to be as self-sufficient as possible. And we know more about our country than foreign NGOs because we live here. Secondly, literacy levels must improve. Literate people are better equipped to avoid famine and infant mortality. And when we have a fully literate population we won't need to be micro-managed by overseas aid agencies.' He sighed.

'Yes, these are massive tasks, Zeno.'

They stopped talking. High above them were sheared-off rock spires, buttresses protruding from thousand-feet-high rock walls and mountainous colonnades, which appeared to support the plateau from which they had descended. Alongside their Sankaber site were boulder gravel tracks, which dropped away to a narrow, shallow gorge and a parched grey riverbed. They could hear the deep wheezing croak of a thick-billed raven searching the campsite for food scraps and garbage, along with the distant cry of hyenas.

'These problems must be tackled. We can't go on as if the famines never occurred. I don't want Ethiopia known as Africa's land of famine.'

Zeno put more juniper twigs on the fire and refilled their coffee pot. The smell of coffee in this mountain air reminded Louise of family camps on the Coorong, when it was lit by bright moonlight, with the background noise of the roaring Southern Ocean surf pounding the beach, and where in the morning the tide would have cast up its wrack. She thought of the Ngarrindjeri Aborigines who had lived successfully on the sandy Coorong for forty thousand years and of Mandy, her Aboriginal friend from Oodnadatta. She reflected on the state of indigenous people in Australia, their dusty isolated camps and the loss for so many of them of their independent hunter-gatherer life. She brushed a tear away and wondered if Zeno's ideas and commitment would work for Australia's Aborigines.

'Do you have other goals too?' she asked.

'Yes, my other goal is more of a feeling, but one which drives me. The feeling I have is an instinctive contempt for those who think that change cannot take place. When I spend time in the villages I am struck by the sheer waste of talent, especially among the women. Despite their bondage, these women are dignified and creative.'

'So what are the obstacles, other than shortage of money?'

'There is not enough passion for change. If people could see what is possible then their passion would develop. We must work closely with the people, help their passion grow.'

'You talk as if I'm already researching and writing alongside you and I haven't even begun.'

'I know, Louise, but I think our passion and commitment are the same.'

Louise smiled. She thought of her grandmother in Crystal Brook saying that everything worthwhile in life takes time.

Although confident about Louise's talent and commitment, Zeno still felt he had to warn her about the difficulties she could face when undertaking fieldwork with isolated tribes. 'Your research won't be easy; despite your commitment you'll have your detractors and will be met with ingratitude, as I have.'

Louise knew she was in for the long haul, fully prepared to commit to working alongside Zeno for many years – knowing her time as a skilled anthropologist would arrive.

As if sensing Louise's thoughts, Zeno continued: 'Our research will see me to retirement and probably you as well, and for decades after that. There must be change, no more famine, and greatly improved levels of literacy. And change must come at least at a canter and not a donkey trot.'

'In fifty years from now, do you think life in Ethiopia will be much different?'

'Ethiopia will change. It's not like a becalmed ship, winds are blowing that will fill its sails.' His eyes glistened. 'The world is ours, we can fashion change, and I like to think of Ethiopia as a seed sprouting because it is watered and loved, like the giant lobelia.'

'You're an optimist, Zeno.'

'You must be if you love this country as I do.'

'How far ahead can you predict?'

'Probably only tomorrow and next week,' he said. 'I've learned that the longer the period for which I predict the more likely I am to be wrong. But we have to begin somewhere.'

She stroked his face and kissed him on the cheek. She felt a powerful surge of desire as she felt the outline of his skull beneath her fingers. This whirlwind of a man, she thought, he intends to change Ethiopia.

'Ah Zeno, you live on mountain passes and high plateaus rather than in the valleys.'

'You flatter me, but remember no one leads from a cellar.'

Light faded quickly as a multitude of stars flickered in the night sky and the temperature fell steeply. Louise stood up, took her torch and disappeared into the acacia and juniper bush. 'I'm ready for bed,' she said as she returned, took off her boots and crawled into their tent. Zeno followed. In the dim torchlight of their tent he watched her undress and climb into their sleeping bag. He peeled off his clothes, caught her eye, recognised their shared feeling and crawled in alongside her. He stroked her hips and breasts, kissed her gently as their bodies folded into each other.

After making love, Louise rested her head on his chest. As she lay listening to his heartbeat, she wondered if the changes he wanted would come quickly enough.

There was sporadic rain during the cold night. In the morning the air was hazy. Refreshed, they continued their hike back along old mule tracks to where they had left their 4WD. They would take the road back to Gonder and then on via Bahir Dar back to Addis.

Setting Up Home Together

TWO MONTHS AFTER returning from the Simien plateau, they set up their home in a more spacious unit allotted to them by the University of Addis Ababa. As a professor, Zeno had status and influence. He was well known and well liked. He was open about his love for Louise and any conservative opposition to them living together as an unmarried couple was easily overcome. He wanted to show her more of the landscape, people and history of his country – that was why she had come to Ethiopia.

At home one evening, Zeno remembered the first photograph of Louise that she'd given him. Strange isn't it, he thought, what swells up from one's memory. He took the photo from his wallet and experienced a strange feeling, as if he was waiting for the arrival of a mythical Greek woman who had landed unexpectedly in Hellas rather than Addis Ababa. He looked at Louise's sparkling blue eyes and her sensual athletic body, and thought, with all the ignorance of a man who too easily puts aside his past, that the only woman he ever wanted to live with was Louise Davitt. He liked the defined protrusion of her breasts, her neat, firm rounded buttocks and the curved sweep of her belly. She warmed and responded to his touch and, in all their conversations, whatever the topic, there was an obvious energy and barely suppressed longing between them.

He told Amos, 'With Louise in my arms I can achieve anything.'

Later when alone, he remembered a vivid dream: he, Zeno Wolde, the agent of change, was addressing the Ethiopian parliament, guaranteeing huge education spending to eliminate illiteracy, along with the comprehensive development of rural health clinics, and then going on a world tour where he garnered overseas investment for his country. He wanted tell Louise about his dream, his fantasy, but for the moment thought better of it. If the predictions in it came to pass, he would tell her then.

When they set up home together they enlarged their circle of friends. Many colleagues and students across the campus enjoyed their hospitality. They even received a surprise phone call from Horst, the German student from Hamburg. He had returned and was engaged to an Ethiopian girl, Bezawit, originally from Bar Dar. They were to live in Addis for the next year before Horst took up an agricultural research position at Arba Minch. Louise immediately made friends with Bezawit and they regularly met on campus and in their respective homes.

They met other Ethiopian women and discussed domestic and local events and decided how they would support each other. They organised bills to be paid for families who had little money and they formed support groups to help people affected by a severe outbreak of influenza. They raised money for the maternity unit at Addis Ababa's overcrowded Black Lion Hospital and collected and distributed children's books in order to promote literacy in schools. Louise gained strength and confidence from these meetings and her friendship with Bezawit.

When Zeno walked with Louise across the university campus and through the Addis markets, he was proud as he watched people turn to look at her. He knew that the loveliness she offered him day after day, and which renewed his energy, also inspired others. He saw how Louise unconsciously provoked desire in other men by their glances of admiration. He loved watching her tall slim figure glide between the trestle tables of market stalls and bend to pick and purchase fruit, vegetables, thyme, ginger and cloves from her favourite vendors.

In these market places, in contrast to what Louise had seen in the villages, there was plenty of food. Carcasses of *bege* (lamb), *yebere siga* (beef) and *fiyel* (goat) hung from butchers' stalls where men in overalls armed with their *bilowa* (sharp butcher's knives) would provide the chosen cut. Women in brightly coloured shawls sat selling breads, eggs, lentils, beetroots, bananas, spinach and flowers. Louise was amazed by the stalls piled high with blankets, multi-coloured fabrics, pots and pans, spades and hoes. Also on display were Ethiopia's famous copper jewelry, coloured beads, brooches and necklaces, wrist bangles and glassware. Men and women sat at foot-pedal sewing machines making umbrella shades; they hammered at crude plough blades and old bicycle frames. It seemed to Louise that the more they hammered, the greater the chance of attracting people who might buy their jewellery, or possibly, even those few who owned the luxury Mercedes and drove around Addis. It appeared that the gap between the struggling poor, working all hours on the land and in the markets, and the few super-rich was widening, irrespective of the policy of the Derg.

As she walked from stall to stall Louise lent a careful ear and watchful eye to learn more about the stallholders. The importance of traditions, once emphasised to her by her friend Mandy, came back to her. She wished Mandy could be here with her, and knew that if she ever met her again, she would tell her about these Ethiopian markets. This way of life had been going on for hundreds of years.

Standing in this hot noisy market she speculated about the possibility of change. Among Ethiopia's leaders, dominated now by the Derg, there appeared no restless thinker, at least none that Zeno and his friends knew about; no one who would advocate for change and challenge the established practices. Could that person be Zeno Wolde?

She didn't want Zeno to challenge the government, but he would, no doubt, challenge the Derg government's desire for maximum control over food distribution and farm management. She knew he would live by his principles even if his life was at risk.

But here in the markets, she was enjoying the present – the

distinctive smells of pineapples, melons, nutmeg, lemon, pepper and cloves and bloodied hanging beef, goat and lamb. Ethiopia is nothing without these markets, she thought; they are where the people meet and engage with each other, and share ideas and cultures.

Zeno loved watching her buying from and encouraging stall-holders as if she had been doing it all her life. She's a trailblazer, he thought, a change agent. He put his arm round her waist. 'Your elegance makes the market sellers' faces light up when you talk to them.'

'Thank you, Zeno, but I think they are just being kind.'

'Never,' Zeno laughed. 'These people are encouraged by you; I see it clearly. When you walk between the stalls they enjoy your radiance and want to talk to you.' In the midst of the milling crowds, they hugged each other.

As far as Zeno was concerned, Louise was in tune with the people. It was the warmest compliment he could give. Louise paused by rolls of colourful fabrics, pretending to look at the patterns, but really recalling the occasion when he gave her Ivor Strecker's book in his office and they first made delicious love.

'The more first-hand experience you have, the better. People will want to hear from you and listen to your stories.'

'Do you think so?'

'I'm sure of it.'

Louise enjoyed his confidence in her and realised that a defining quality of Zeno, when he was truly happy, was his overflowing enthusiasm. She kissed him gently on the cheek and, loaded with their purchases of fruit, vegetables and a piece of yellow-and-red Dorse woven cotton fabric, they walked out of the shaded market, onto streets with dozens of people strolling in twos and threes, shielding themselves from the hot afternoon sun.

Treading Carefully

DESPITE THE POWER and influence of the Derg, Louise and Zeno were active in their enlarged group of scholars from Ethiopia and overseas – anthropologists, doctors, poets, administrators and, occasionally, a few politicians of reformist mind. Horst and his Ethiopian wife Bezawit were often in their company.

In the field Louise met Ethiopia's rural poor. It was challenging and intoxicating, the focus of so much that she had thought about as an undergraduate. She shared her stories on campus with other students, and became a member of international organisations such as Save the Children and Community Aid Abroad. She took an active interest in their work and submitted articles for their publications. She longed for poverty to be reduced in the villages and tribal lands and for greater awareness of the talent of these people, particularly the women. She grieved for these poor people, especially when she recalled the city with richly dressed women from overseas with their male escorts alighting from chauffeured limousines, their luggage carried by uniformed porters as they entered an international hotel.

'Oh, for God's sake, when will this change and the barefoot people of the villages have a better life?' she asked Bezawit and Horst, when remembering this scene. Much personal control was required not to react with anger to the suffering of Ethiopian peasants, compared to the arrogance of the Derg and the display of wealth she observed from a few in the city.

Perhaps she loves Ethiopia and its people as much as I do, Zeno thought. He remembered his childhood friendship with the goat-herd boys of Tigray.

Louise had a growing interest in Ethiopian politics, but was guided by Zeno's advice to 'tread carefully'. His father's tragic early death was probably due to overzealous political involvement. Louise also knew that any foreign criticism of the Derg could jeopardise existing relief programs and, despite the fact that in private Zeno described the Government's forced evacuation of famine-ridden lands as brutal and uneconomic, in public both were vigilant. They studiously avoided political comment, but became heartened by reports that the worst of the Derg's resettlement programs had been suspended and that peasant and village organisations were reasserting themselves. Given this, Louise had greater access to the villages for her research.

Slowly she built her networks, understood more Amharic and Oromo, and gained trust among village people. She had recently heard about the possibility of constructing underground water tanks in villages, so that a regular water supply could improve hygiene. She imagined village children splashing water over each other and mothers bathing their children in clean water.

The more she travelled, the more Louise sought credible explanations about the 1984–85 famine. Night-time cold, harsh winds, drought and soil erosion played their part. She read how people in a holding camp in Wollo were forcibly removed to a remote valley and how they said they were treated there 'like garbage'. She read how outspoken resisters of resettlement were roped up and moved far away from their homes. As a researcher, she asked questions about the causes and extent of famine, but was mindful that no matter how vivid her observations, they had to be written about as neutrally as possible. She must avoid the temptation to write something too provocative, however justified. As a visitor, she was learning how to survive.

Hunger for these people, Louise thought, was not just about need but rather man's inhumanity. The tough and heroic people in these villages still held their heads up high. But how, she asked herself, could they resist for so long? What was their secret? She learned that Petra, the gaunt woman with the almond-shaped eyes and bangles she had met when they entered the village the previous year, had died and was buried following what was apocalyptically said to be 'the hundredth drought'.

It was not like Adelaide or London, where famine does not exist, and if the poor were hungry there were support services providing food and shelter. She wanted to make a difference.

Self-Medication

DURING THE NEXT six months Louise studied and wrote in Addis. She and Zeno also took many trips to Oromo, Amharan and Tigrayan villages, particularly among the Oromo, where conversations turned to wholesale purges by the Derg in which traditional settlements had been displaced and many thousands of people moved, against their will, to 'uninhabited virgin areas'. Louise and Zeno could observe but not interfere.

They enjoyed villagers' hospitality and slept comfortably together on the compacted earthen floors in their straw huts. Zeno walked, gazelle-like, immersed in his own delight at being in this rugged country. When they arrived at a village he talked to the people in a gentle and respectful way, yet had no qualms about being direct. Nothing shocked him – not starvation, infections or death. Their health was his priority, particularly concerning difficult pregnancies and the high level of infant mortality. He discussed these issues with the women. It was always the women who talked; their men were distant, as if they took influenza infections, malaria outbreaks and infant mortality for granted.

Zeno taught sick people to self-medicate, especially using traditional curative practices. He used mixtures of garlic, ginger and rue to treat influenza-type infections, and ground basil to help reduce the effects of malaria. It was hard to look closely at gaunt young women carrying bony children with swollen bellies and crinkly brittle hair that looked more orange than black. Yet he talked to them, nurturing hope. 'Good boy,' he would say to a starving boy as he gave him medicine, 'that's the way.'

Zeno's first step was to keep sick people alive, the second to cure their sickness, the third to teach them how to take precautions and avoid infections. 'How lovely he is,' the women would say. They hadn't seen the likes of Zeno. His tender expertise was extraordinary. They hoped he would return regularly.

'Just think like this,' he explained to Louise. 'If we can influence one village to improve their practices, this will influence others.'

'What do you mean?'

'Once we have established better practice in one village, then there'll be a chain reaction. The example of people in a village with improved healthcare will be talked about by other villagers and encourage them to start up a health clinic.'

Zeno reminded Louise that the villagers were subsistence farmers who had no surpluses and lacked storage facilities – different from the people in the villages below the Bada Ridge.

'So how can their lives improve? Is subsistence farming the only option left for them?'

'The women are the ones who can bring about change.'

Louise was pleased to hear Zeno say it.

'They must be given responsibility,' he said. 'But if women have greater power and independence this goes against age-old customs – and in these villages women have, on average, eight children, so seeing them as managers of smallholdings and negotiating for the effective marketing of crops is still a long way off. And men are often away minding cattle and that's a status they don't consider changing.'

'Can women receive specific UN development grants?'

'Not at the moment. Village women are at the "bottom" with no education.'

A brief pessimism enveloped Louise as she thought of the unmarked graves she had seen – the destiny of poor women.

7: Life with the Hamar

Map of the Southern Tribal Lands

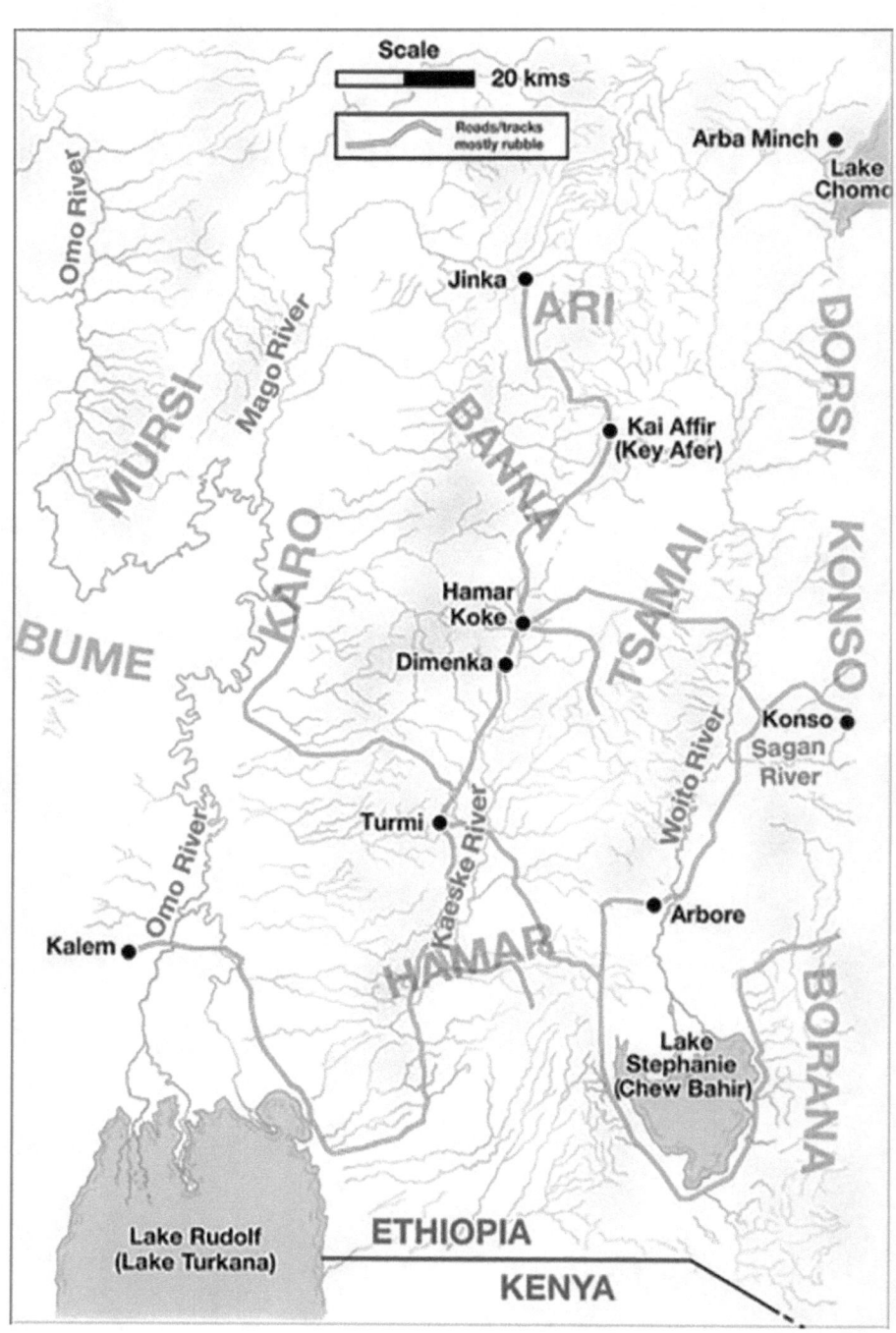

Scale
20 kms

Roads/tracks
mostly rubble

Omo River

Arba Minch
Lake Chomo

Jinka

ARI

Mago River

Kai Affir
(Key Afer)

MURSI

DORSI

BANNA

KARO

TSAMAI

KONSO

BUME

Hamar
Koke

Dimenka

Woito River

Konso
Sagan River

Omo River

Kaeske River

Turmi

Arbore

Kalem

HAMAR

BORANA

Lake
Stephanie
(Chew Bahir)

Lake Rudolf
(Lake Turkana)

ETHIOPIA

KENYA

'... Watch the Older Women'

'I WANT TO live with a Hamar tribe, and write about the influence of their customs,' Louise said to Zeno.

'Are you sure you need to be with the Hamar?'

'Yes. I want their life to be familiar to me. They are a distinct nomadic pastoral tribe with a reputation for independence – it's a long time since anyone has described their life by living with them. And you've told me that the pastoral lifestyle of the Hamar is similar to those of early Egyptian civilisation. Also I want to identify any similarities with Australian Aborigines, particularly the Ngarrindjeri.' Ever since she had spent time as a teenager with her friend Mandy, she dreamed of living with an Aboriginal nomadic tribe.

Zeno knew better than to oppose her. 'You're restless as the driven rain, you are. I'll make arrangements for you.'

It was Zeno's job to be the nurturer, arranger and guide for his students. Conscious of his professional responsibilities, he felt duty-bound to protect Louise from the severe assignment of living alone with the Hamar. Yet, the success of their partnership depended on him encouraging her passion. She knew the experience would be tough.

'I have to do this,' she repeated to Zeno when they met for mid-morning coffee in the university canteen. He reached over the table and held her hand.

'I admire your plan. It almost seems you have sworn an oath of loyalty to the Hamar.' He paused. 'Why are you so determined to go back there?'

'You ask such obvious questions sometimes,' she said, teasing Zeno and squeezing his hand.

'And what makes you think you can live successfully with the Hamar for many months?'

'I know it won't be easy. But I need to get to know them. You've told me how important it is to be an advocate, and to defend people such as the Hamar against threats to their existence.'

'I've never doubted your determination and talent, you know that.' Zeno was worried about Louise being away from their home. He had become used to her always being available for lovemaking and to counsel and share with him; to halt his shadowy secret of feeling depressed, which could take hold when he was lonely. To be with her was to be relieved of the burden of himself.

'Yes, it's possible for you to spend time with the Hamar. I will arrange this through an NGO friend who knows the tribe.'

Louise spoke about the importance of researching the health needs and the high infant mortality rates of the Hamar, the Banna and the Karo. Zeno listened carefully. 'Because of you, Zeno, this project will be successful. You'll see.'

'Thanks, but it's your project. I'll support you as much as possible. But again, I must warn you that it won't be easy. Essentially, for three months of living with the Hamar you will have to live off goat's milk, sorghum porridge, honey, goat meat and *kocho* bread – even ox blood. Can you cope with that? You will walk everywhere with them and sleep alongside the women in their huts; ablutions are in the bush on the treks and perhaps in communal long drops in some villages. And your soap will be the leaves of the *sankara* soap tree. You will be naked except for a slit goatskin skirt, and unless you insist, like the Hamar women you won't be wearing any underwear.' Zeno was direct.

'Yes, I'll dress as they do, and be like them when I'm with them. I'm excited about the experience.'

'You realise,' he continued, 'much of their grazing lands are quite remote, and the distances you'll walk are considerable. You must always carry enough drinking water. The Hamar can walk for days on end, living primarily on *kurkufa*. And if there is too much rain, the villages are cut off and sometimes washed away.'

'I'll survive. I can't think of anything I want to do more.'

'I'm proud of you.' He kissed Louise's forehead, and then pulled her close. 'By the time you finish this trek you won't need me anymore. The Hamar will be your teachers – these resilient people will show you so much.'

Instead of feeling the joy of Louise's likely success and the beneficial effects on her career, anguish ate at Zeno. He sensed that Louise's accomplishments could alter her status and possibly their relationship. This beautiful bright woman would no longer be his student but a colleague, one who could develop her own rewarding and admired career. 'You're brighter than the water of a mountain spring.' he said.

'And you're a darling, always supporting me. I love you, Zeno.'

Zeno contacted a tribal land manager, Samuel Tayennu, to make arrangements for Louise. Samuel was originally from the Banna tribe and familiar with the Hamar groups. He understood their particular mixed Amharic-Hamar language, and knew and respected their customs. He located a Hamar family willing to accept Louise. She would receive guidance and hospitality from an older woman called Koti, a significant Hamar elder and a community healer. Louise would live with members of Koti's extended family and Koti would arrange for a respected warrior called Bashada to guide her on walks and act as protector, if required.

Louise's plans to spend time with the Hamar were now viable. To live and trek with the Hamar would require considerable courage, stamina and good fortune. Louise wasn't fazed. She had no illusions.

A month after Zeno made contact with Samuel Tayennu, Louise met him in his office in Addis. Samuel was slim and very dark-skinned, much darker than Zeno. He greeted Louise warmly.

'Hello, you must be Louise.'

'Yes, hello.'

'I've been looking forward to our meeting. Zeno has told me all about you. Please take a seat. It's most unusual for a young Western woman to spend time out in remote bush country with the Hamar. However, I have contacted a Hamar community and your request has been approved.'

'Thank you, I appreciate it.' Louise's eyes lit up. 'Thank you, Samuel.'

'Next Tuesday I will pick you up from your apartment and we'll drive south to Shashemene. We'll leave early morning and should reach Shashemene by midday, or a little later depending on how many stops we have. It's a good road and I recommend that we stop on the way so that you can see the Rift Valley lakes and the wildlife between Ziway and Negele.'

'How exciting. Yes, I'd like to see as much of the countryside as possible.'

'If you like, we can stay overnight in Ziway before we reach Shashemene. It's a pleasant little town with a few cheap hotels. If we stay I can show you Ziway's birdlife and perhaps we can take a boat ride on the Ziway Lake. We might see hippopotamuses.'

'Yes, I'd enjoy that. Is there any chance of seeing sea eagles or your famous marabou storks?'

'Sure, we can do that. Do you think Zeno will come with us?' Louise sensed that Samuel hoped Zeno could accompany them. Perhaps he felt uncomfortable travelling with a white woman.

'I'll ask him, but he has a heavy workload at the moment.'

'I understand how busy he is,' Samuel replied. 'I have great respect for Zeno and his work.'

'Do we go to the Omo Valley after we reach Shashemene?'

'Yes, we'll make for Sodo and drive on to Arba Minch.' Samuel pushed a road map across his desk. 'We'll try and reach Arba Minch by early evening on our third day. I'm not happy to be on that road after dark. I take every precaution not to be out there at nighttime.'

Samuel and Louise pored over the map, checking roads, tracks and terrain from Sodo to Arba Minch and then as far south as Jinka and Turmi.

Samuel smiled as he said, 'I'm sure the Hamar will like you.'

'Thank you. Zeno has told me how well you know the roads and the people of the Omo Valley.'

'I'm learning all the time. I was born in a Banna village. As a small boy I learned to walk on stilts to watch for the cheetahs that attacked our goats and cattle. I speak languages of the tribal region and understand different dialects. My family left their village and went to Addis when I was eight years old. In recent years I have lived from time to time among the tribal people, like you are going to.'

'I'm not sure exactly what to expect, but I'll observe carefully and do my best to adjust.'

'I know the Hamar groups you'll be with. They will support you. Some of them will remember Zeno.'

'But he was there over ten years ago, wasn't he?'

'Yes, but they'll remember him. They'd love to have him with them again, they told me.'

'And now I'll be learning from them. I don't expect living with them to be easy.'

'True, but you will have an unforgettable glimpse of Hamar paradise – at least when there are good rains.'

'I look forward to experiencing this paradise.'

'If I may, I'd like to give you a piece of advice. Zeno may have told you this,' said Samuel hesitantly. 'I know you're a keen researcher but when you're in the field with the Hamar you will have little time for recorded fieldwork. Most of your time will be spent being sociable, adapting to their rhythms, and keeping as fit and well as possible. You'll walk from village to village, pasture lot to pasture lot, and will have to help search for water on the enormous white sand beds of the Kaeske River. And … you'll need to be patient; just wait for things to happen, watch the Hamar as they solve their problems.'

'Thanks Samuel, I won't rush anything.'

'If you watch the leaders, follow them and, if appropriate, do what they do, you'll soon get to know things.'

'Will the leaders be obvious?'

'Yes, watch the older women. They are wise. Look out for Koti. She will protect you; help you survive and enjoy living with them. You will be welcomed; Koti will make sure of that.'

'I can't wait to start.'

'Zeno has told me that you never give in.'

'I try not to. Do you have you any other advice?'

'Pace yourself, adjust to their food and drink. Make yourself comfortable in their straw-roofed huts, get used to sitting on a cowhide and dressing as they do. And remember, there is still a mystery about these people who have lived for centuries in one of the remotest territories in Ethiopia.'

'What do you think is their mystery?'

'I'm not sure, but they've lived in the Omo Valley for generations and yet have left few traces.'

'Aren't there villages?'

'Of course, at this moment, but when they leave a village, it soon becomes overgrown and goes back to its wild state. You'll get the idea of how the landscape changes when you see the effect of late August rains.'

'Did you observe the Hamar before and after the last famine?'

There was a long silence. 'I walked from Turmi to Jinka and saw the country of the Hamar,' he said. 'Even when there were clouds in the sky, the sun was fierce and the land was parched. But even in the drought the Hamar women were preparing sorghum seeds for the next year's planting. That's their optimism.'

'Yes, I watched it on television back home in Australia, and they said it was difficult to get food to where it was needed.'

'That's true, but there were also political issues. We'll be more prepared if there's another drought. Your partner is not only advocating change but is providing us with examples of how it can take place.'

'Yes, Zeno's certainly committed to reforming peasant agriculture.'

'There is no fire like Zeno's passion for Ethiopia's rural poor, but the change he advocates will come slowly. In the past, political leaders have been too busy plotting against one another to realise that people like Zeno are working for all of Ethiopia, as well as the rural poor. I hope they will eventually listen to him.'

Samuel smiled. 'Would you like a coffee?' he asked. 'We can talk about these issues while we plan your time with the Hamar.'

'Yes, good. I'm ready for a strong one.'

Living with the Hamar

TWO WEEKS LATER, Samuel and Louise spent two nights at Awasa and one at Shashemene where Louise saw black and white sea eagles circling the lakes, and tall grey and pink marabou storks standing in lake shallows. As dawn broke on the third day, Samuel left the road between Jinka and Turmi in the heart of the Southern Nations and Peoples' Region. He drove his old Nissan Patrol south along rutted tracks. Louise saw small herds of cattle and goats. The physical harshness of the scarred, heath-like plateau, with its scattering of acacias and thorn trees, contrasted with lush vegetation alongside the dry stream beds. Eventually Samuel drove onto a track which crossed a small trickling stream fringed with dense acacias and eucalypts, skilfully negotiating the steep track down and then up the bank and onto open grass country. The land was greener here, with more wildflowers, and shrubs with small yellow flowers like the gorse bushes she'd seen in the English countryside. Finally he stopped on the outskirts of a village with sapling huts, reed-matted walls and biscuit-brown terraced garden beds.

'Here we are,' Samuel said. 'A Hamar village. We must first meet the headman.'

Samuel was greeted with smiles and hugs. Louise looked around. Here was a simple life but, by her standards, extreme poverty. People stared and smiled as she stood alongside Samuel. The lean, sandal-clad Hamar headman, Bashada, was waiting to welcome them. He wore faded shorts with a brown shawl draped across his bony shoulders. He carried a thick stick in one hand and a rifle swung from his left shoulder. Bashada shook hands with Samuel, bowed to Louise and in Oromo-Hamar dialect, expressed his welcome.

'He's a very fit and bright man,' Samuel said to Louise. 'I know him well; he's loyal and reliable.'

Bashada, recognising the compliment, wore the air of a proven leader, his brown eyes sharp as a hawk's. His prowess as a warrior with a spear had won him acclaim. He nodded and smiled. His tall, thin body was muscular, and when he walked he reminded Louise of a leopard stalking. He had been walking and running as a herdsman since childhood.

Six Hamar women beckoned. Their hair was braided and decorated with brightly coloured beads. They were wearing cowrie shell necklaces. She knew Hamar women loved decoration and colour and was immediately taken by the way bright red, blue, white and green beads highlighted their butter-and-ochre-braided hair and their smooth, chocolate-brown skin. Then she was introduced to Koti, a respected elder and grandmother figure who wore a worn red and blue cotton skirt and many wristbands and necklaces. As an older woman she wore a light-blue cotton blouse.

'Koti will look after you. She knows you will respect their traditions and is happy to have you join them. You will learn many things from her,' Samuel said.

Koti stepped forward and hugged Louise. She had a calm aura. Louise thanked her in limited Amharic, which seemed to delight the older woman.

Samuel was soon ready to leave. 'If you need to, Koti will arrange for another woman to walk with you to Turmi where you can phone me.' He paused. 'But I'm sure you'll survive and phoning me won't be necessary.'

'Don't worry, I'll be fine. Please tell Zeno how happy I am to be here.'

'Yes, I'll do that. We'll collect you in three months when you reach a village close to the town of Hamar Koke. Koti knows where we will meet you.'

'Thank you, Samuel.'

Samuel kissed her lightly on the cheek and then drove away. Louise felt a pang of loneliness, but Koti hugged her again and bare-breasted young women stood close and smiled reassuringly.

There was a long silence when Louise first entered the hut allotted to her by Koti and put her rucksack and few belongings on the floor. She sat on the ground, stared briefly at the thatched ceiling and looked around. She undressed and, somewhat nervously, put on the slit goatskin skirt provided by Koti. Naked now except for the skirt she felt slightly embarrassed. She need not have worried. The women smiled at her and made welcoming gestures.

The afternoon and early evening passed sociably and quickly as Louise listened to women chatting, and watched them as they weeded and picked vegetables in a village garden. She helped collect water from a well dug into a dry sand stream bed, worked alongside them in their garden and shared some fruit. Late afternoon wind brought the fragrance of eucalyptus, reminding her of the wooded Adelaide Hills.

During the first week Louise was happy in the gardens, and almost enchanted by sleeping on hard baked ground in a small sapling hut with four or five Hamar women and children to whom she could not speak. Yet always there was bonhomie in their gestures. It was a gentle introduction and once again she remembered Mandy's description of Aborigines living successfully in the Australian bush.

On the eighth morning she woke early. For the first time, she wondered whether she'd made a mistake. A sleepless, uncomfortable night brought doubt in its wake. She stared at the women still asleep alongside her, recalling their friendliness of previous days. She completed her ablutions in the bush and, after washing herself, drank brewed tea and ate what looked like passionfruit and dried figs along with *kocho* bread and honey. Afterwards she found Koti with two younger women getting ready to walk to the next village and, hopefully, fresh pasture. The walking eased her doubt.

Louise wasn't sure what to expect as they trekked across stony ground with Hamar herdsmen, women and their children. She walked amid dust, burning heat, and sometimes the cooling shadows cast by large boulders.

As she tired, her romantic images of life with the Hamar faded. After four hours of walking to the *woredu* (another district) she was lost in fatigue. She became anxious. Everyone else seemed to be enjoying their trek along the dry river valley. Louise followed as they climbed a rocky track in a slow line with their cattle and goats stretched out in single file.

Most of the women walked barefoot. Louise was glad to have her sandals. The herdsmen made no concessions for her but strode on, driving the animals. Thanks to a life of barefoot walking, the thorns and sharp stones made little impression on the leathery soles of the villagers' feet. They seemed to float and skip over the bare, rocky tracks.

Louise wondered how long the Hamar people had been living here and why they remained so attached to their isolation and nomadic pastoralism. Do they know about the world beyond? Or am I the prisoner, let out from the routines of the modern world? Louise was to ask herself these questions again and again.

By late afternoon she found her walking rhythm. She thought the Hamar were like dancers – the tall smiling women with their matted hair and scarred backs; the pregnant among them with their curving bellies and thrusting breasts, moving so gracefully. They could easily be killed by another famine, yet as they walked they appeared to Louise to be as bright and happy as anyone could be. As scant grass appeared, Louise sensed how these people were linked to the earth, as if they had front row seats in the universe, absorbing the yellow, gold, brown and evening purple of the landscape.

Women carried children on their backs, others carried water and firewood. Older children walked alongside the herdsmen. Their hardy cattle could go without water for many days and were well suited to the rocky terrain and scarce grazing. The sun was scorching and the breeze blew the heat of the land onto their faces. Louise thought how different her childhood was to the Hamar children's among the ravines, thorny scrub, the cheetahs, hyenas and the distant black-maned lions. She loved how they shouted: 'Wonderful, wonderful, welcome (*merhaba*),' when they came across fresh pasture.

She soon noticed what Zeno had told her: 'They live by sharing.' And in this sharing they were marvellously adapted, spiritually and practically, to their nomadic pastoralism. Louise felt as if she could have been back with the Hamar in the Omo Valley a few hundred years before. Nothing much had changed. These ancient people blended so easily with their environment, much the same as the Australian Aborigines Mandy had described.

For Louise polygamy was an issue, but she put this in the back of her mind and enjoyed the group's happiness as they walked on, now in clouds of dust amidst much shouting, bleating and mooing. Louise kept up with them. She remembered Zeno telling her what could happen to anyone who was left behind in this isolated region; they would be prey for wild animals.

The group walked with steady, easy rhythm. Sweat streamed down Louise's face. She spotted gazelles, a baboon and nearby dik-diks. At one point she thought she saw a lion and became hyper-alert, her eyes peeled for the slightest movement. She knew lions were rare, having been kept at bay or killed off by armed Hamar men. Zeno had assured her that Hamar herdsmen knew how to guard their precious cattle against attacks by packs of wild dogs, hyenas, cheetahs and the occasional lion.

Louise realised how, like the wildlife, these people were survivors. They pressed on through the maze of scorched acacia, over split boulders, dried-up grass and weeds. The herdsmen were the antithesis to the 'soft and genteel' twentieth century people she had lived with in London and Adelaide.

By late afternoon, they reached a village with round wooden sapling-and-straw huts. Cattle and goats were tethered at the outskirts. The village was nothing to speak of – dirt tracks, overgrown gardens, fireplaces, and evidence of burials on the red earth beyond the village.

Preparations for a meal began. The adults drank coffee from wide calabash bowls. Two goats were singled out for the kill. Louise watched as the creatures seemed to give their dumb assent before the cut, and their blood flowed. At that moment the whole village was still; children, Hamar men and women in the prime of life along with old men and women, watched. The goats were quickly skinned and then roasted on an open fire. There was plenty of meat; nothing was wasted. Louise was stunned by the speed and simplicity of the event. She'd heard the saying that everyone becomes the thing they kill. This seemed to be the case when she watched the Hamar children crush a beetle or cattle fly in the dust and rub the juices between their fingers. Their introduction to killing in order to survive began with small creatures.

The moon rose slowly, full and yellow. An eerie night silence fell over the land. Sitting with the Hamar women outside a circle of huts, Louise felt the gravity of life and death, something she'd never experienced before. She already felt an immense debt to them. She would remember this trek forever: the splash of goat blood, the smell of the smoky roasting fire, the sound of children playing in the dust, the sight of the distant lion and the silent, gliding walk of the Hamar herdsmen with their sticks, guns and whips.

Settling down for the night wasn't easy. The simple act of Hamar men sleeping in the open, on cowhides, surrounded by cattle or alongside a goat kraal was, Louise thought, so different from sleeping in an Australian bushman's swag on the dunes of the South Australian Coorong. After the meal, Louise was beckoned by a group of women to join them for the night in their sapling hut. Inside, Louise smelled the beaten earth, the scent of many bodies and animals, the stale, pungent mustiness. Six women and five children clustered and curled on the floor. Louise lay on her cowhide in a curve next to the hut wall, close to the entrance. She wrapped a thin, grey, rough cotton blanket around herself, made a pillow of her small knapsack and settled down under gathering shadows. She observed the women cuddling children and getting comfortable.

No one talked. Communication was by hand movements. Louise inhaled the sticky air. A litter of thoughts scattered through her mind. Who would worry if this unique tribe died out? It was the same feelings she had when, with Zeno, she had observed the effects of famine on the Amharans and Tigrayans of the north.

Louise listened to the rustling night as she tried to clarify her thoughts. She sat up and wrote a short poem titled *Survival*.

Survival

Along sandy, thorn scrub country
a lion prowls, sniffs, finds a scent.
A herdsman drives his cattle,
scans the land, circles his herd, calls them,
sprints, ever wary of the predator. Could it
be hyena, cheetah, or lion?

He's fought them off before, his scars and flesh
marks tell of kills, so the lion too is wary.
A rifle bullet now more deadly than the spear,
they watch each other at a distance; each
knows the other, as if they'd met in earlier combat,
gladiators on this open tree-lined arena.

It's the lion that breaks rank and, close now,
circles the herd. Frightened, they halt, paw the ground.
The herdsman waits. It's his country too, he'll
not lose cattle today. Confident, he cocks his rifle,
fires a warning shot. Sound reverberates, the lion
halts, and even from a distance smells the cordite.

Perhaps an uneven battle – it knows when to retreat
and like the herdsman, must survive, so for the moment
pads away, and cattle and herdsman move on.

Louise had ideas but no solutions to the Hamar's necessary survival of the fittest. She thought of her grandmother's advice about the importance of being happy in the moment. But as the night wore on, she still could not sleep and kept thinking about sickness and early deaths and how the arrival of an urban culture with paved roads and five-star hotels could sever this nomadic community from their ancient ways. It would be traumatic. She curled her body to face the doorway and, snuggling beneath her blanket, finally drifted to sleep.

Maintaining the Vigil

THE ELDERS DECIDED to stay in this village for a month, allowing them to feed their cattle and to collect water from a distant small stream, a tributary of the Woyto River. They could also collect honey from hives left hanging in trees surrounding the village, grind the sorghum, cook their bread and *kurkufa,* and select cows for blooding. Life was satisfying, even if primitive. Louise was learning to enjoy *gorphak,* their fig-like fruit which tolerated drought conditions. She whispered her mantra: 'I must live as they do, eat their food and drink, otherwise I won't survive the coming months.'

Louise looked at the crowded group of women and children in the hut. A few women had already left for morning ablutions, disappearing into scrub beyond the village compound. Louise had eventually slept well. The women smiled at her as the morning's golden light glinted through slits in the sapling walls. Turning towards the narrow opening, Louise breathed the morning air and walked away from the hut's pungent odour. There was no obvious kitchen, only fireplaces and tethered cattle and goats. Louise collected some water and disappeared into the bush, relieved to be able to wash herself. When she returned she was ready for more *shoforo* (coffee). Koti gestured and in pidgin Hamar, which Louise was beginning to understand, told her about plans for the day.

'The gardens are overgrown so we will weed this morning. The soil is good. You will see that since we were last here some vegetables have survived. You can help pick them.'

'Good, I'll do that.'

'You can follow our skilled gardeners. Some are wonderful, you'll see, but there are other women you should ignore; you won't learn anything from them.'

'I understand.'

Koti laughed and shook her head, looking towards the younger women.

After breakfast Louise followed the women to the outskirts of the village. She surveyed the scene and saw the tracks in the straggly gardens and the distant goat kraal. Women guarded their gardens, usually from scavenging monkeys. When a woman moved from her guarding position at the garden's edge, another replaced her. Louise wondered about possible threats – perhaps lions – or a raid by the Mursi or even the Bume or Tsamai. Being vigilant was necessary in the gardens, with women and boys always ready to scare away birds and monkeys or warn their men about a possible raid. Throughout the morning the women weeded, dug with sticks and watered. Some of the gardens' bean pods were so dry that they were of no more value than the blossoms of a weed, yet they checked each one for a skerrick of food.

Louise thought about her ordered way of life; her old habits and maxims seemed redundant, almost false. She thought back to Mandy and her story about how the Ngarrindjeri Aborigines harvested berries in the bush and lived for thousands of years on the sandy Coorong alongside the Southern Ocean.

At the end of her third day in this village, Louise spent an uncomfortable night. She had never felt so ill. It must be the *tella* and the raw meat I tried to swallow yesterday evening, she thought.

She rose before dawn, crept out of the hut, across the compound and into the scrub. No one was about. Stars hung overhead. Aching and feeling weak and sick, she leaned against an acacia, bent over and vomited onto the earth. Holding onto low-lying branches, she took off her skirt and relieved herself beneath the trees. Her stomach pains increased and diarrhoea followed. As Louise crouched in the scrub she felt as if she were emptying what remained of her London and Adelaide life. Her face was set in the pain. She had never imagined she could feel so ill. She wished so much she was back home with Zeno. Her body shook and she gripped the branch as if it was her lifeline.

Then she remembered that in her rucksack were anti-nausea medication and Noroxin pills to cure diarrhoea. She put on her skirt and, step by careful step, trudged back across the compound's beaten earth to her hut. She took the medication, sat down, didn't move, and waited for her companions to stir. There was no *hakim* (doctor) available. Zeno was unreachable. She didn't want to admit how much she missed him; his smile, his holding her. Anyway, if asked she resolved to tell him she was fine. She had to adjust, and be more careful about what she ate and drank.

Louise ignored coffee and breakfast. She would repeat the dose of Noroxin later in the day. In a few days she was sure she would be well again.

Meanwhile, women hummed and sang as they cleaned their huts, prepared food and looked after children. Louise sensed the ancient and mythical nature of their singing. Perhaps these songs had been sung since earliest times. She sat on her cowhide and listened. Her lips formed the same sounds and words the women were singing. This sublime picture of the women's reverence for their history inspired Louise to want to search for more evidence of the Hamar's origins. She began to forget her illness.

Louise could now interpret much of Koti's Oromo-Hamar pidgin, supplemented by her gestures. Other women chatted too and the conversation was lively. An older woman named Vadju, considered a traditionalist, explained how singing was used to greet men and their *misso* (hunting friends) returning from a hunt, to remind people of ancestors, to greet the day, welcome the achievement of manhood, celebrate a birth and mourn a death.

Vadju said that singing told of the roles of men and women, with men at the top and women at the bottom. There was mumbling and some disagreement. Louise realised that Vadju didn't agree with women having a leadership role. A younger woman spoke about how singing is used for comfort when husbands punish them, sometimes cruelly. Vadju appeared dismissive and tension rose within the group.

'What about the use of the *giraf*?' a vibrant young recently married woman asked. It was a word Louise recognised. 'Men use the *giraf* on us too much.'

'Yes,' said another young woman holding a baby, 'the *giraf* is used here for donkeys, goats, cattle and women.'

'If you have done wrong you probably deserve to be whipped,' grumbled Vadju.

The younger women were still discussing being whipped by their husbands when Koti said it was time for them to complete their gardening before the midday meal. They understood it was wise to follow Koti's direction.

The mood in the gardens was relaxed and happy. Women chatted as they weeded, called and waved to each other. They picked a type of spinach and dug up what looked like sweet potatoes. Sorghum, although withered, was still surviving. It seemed a miracle that anything could grow in such thin, sandy soil.

Noticing Louise, an older woman said, 'We can grow anything here.' Her face demonstrated her belief, convincing Louise that the Hamar would always survive and make the most of their land, although she hoped for something better for them: improved soil, hoes instead of sticks, selling spare vegetables in the Turmi market.

Gardening belonged to the women. They believed their vegetables were of greater value to the Hamar than goats or cattle. And so, aware of the significance of gardening for the women, Louise loved working alongside them. She thought she would eat more beans, vegetables and sorghum, after her bout of gastro.

Later Louise became aware of how the gardening women chatted admiringly about a young woman, fifteen or sixteen years old, who had walked away, ostensibly to collect water from a pool in a nearby stream bed. They knew she had gone to meet her lover in the bush. The older women had seen it all before. Sexual encounters among the Hamar were generally unromantic, rarely tender and sometimes brutish. Louise was astonished at how the women accepted brutality when they engaged in sexual relations. The sexually active men were always looking for opportunities and would not be denied. And this young woman left the garden willingly.

In the distant scrub Louise could just see her and her older man lie under the shelter of a flat-topped acacia tree. The naked young woman's face was buried in the man's chest as he thrust and bore down on her. It seemed she was being crushed and Louise heard her utter a momentary, muffled, breathy cry. Louise imagined sand and grit being imbedded in her back and buttocks.

Louise and the women continued cultivating the sparse legumes and root vegetables. The sexual encounter in the bush ended and the young bare-breasted girl returned with sand sticking to her skirt, back and shoulders. She walked slowly with poise back to the garden. The women nodded to her, conveying familiar gestures of female inclusion.

Ultimately the leaders of opinion were men. Louise hoped she could observe men's activities without engaging directly with them. Koti said if Louise wanted to be in harmony with the men, she could walk with them but must wait for them to tell her about their wives, their cattle and their conflicts. Women, Louise understood, had to learn to be silent, forget their sorrows and get on with life. For the moment, given Hamar traditions, a closer understanding of men's roles and relationships was out of her reach.

Her thoughts wandered back to Mandy. She wondered what she would advise. No doubt Mandy would appreciate the Hamar and be comfortable with them. 'Be bold, Louise,' she heard the spirited Mandy say. 'Be independent and respect yourself, whatever happens – that's important.' Louise remembered Mandy's response to the boys who harassed them in the Crystal Brook park when they were thirteen. She wondered if the wise Koti would accept Mandy's point of view about the importance of women being independent. Probably not; Hamar men would continue to be dominant.

The Hamar stayed in this village for over a month. The bustling Koti continued to take a motherly interest in Louise. She explained that menstruating women could live in a hut at the edge of the village and they contained their blood flow with a wad of leaves fashioned into a crude pad.

Koti called her after breakfast one morning as they walked to the gardens. 'Louise, life will be good if you follow me, you cannot change things overnight.' She smiled and sqeezed Louise's hand. Louise thought about the things Koti had said, about everyday activities she could follow, like walking in line when carrying water, accepting Hamar traditions. If Louise was unsure, then Koti would explain. Koti's strong hands enfolded hers. 'Let's see, Louise, how our vegetables are growing. Despite poor soils, you will always find food in the gardens, believe me.'

Constantly careful now about what she ate and drank, Louise would not allow old habits to return, such as her habit of initiating conversations, particularly with Bashada. She wanted to make suggestions about the management of children, and even to remonstrate with a husband when he punished his wife, but Koti let her know this was not acceptable.

'You understand our ways better now,' said Koti. 'People who follow our traditions succeed.' Louise nodded her approval. Practise fitting in, mirror them, she said to herself.

Mirages and Carrying Water

AT THE END of Louise's sixth week the group set out for another village. As the group walked they merged with Hamar people from an adjoining settlement. Ahead of her, in the bend of a riverbed, moved a line of brightly adorned women chatting happily, carrying children, water and belongings. Tall men with smooth, well-used canes, and some with old rifles, walked separately and ahead of the women. Men and boys drove some forty cattle and twenty goats, and strode easily as they controlled their animals and kept watch for cheetahs, hyenas and wild dogs. Women sometimes stopped to collect wildflowers to decorate their hair. Louise noticed how the men avoided unnecessary exertion, even when they rounded up straying cattle.

By mid-afternoon the group was beginning to tire. They stopped at a shallow well. Louise took off her floppy hat, undid the red cotton scarf tied lightly round her neck and wiped sweat from her forehead. She soaked the scarf, retied it and, along with the women, drank water from a bowl. 'Drink as much as you need,' said a woman in broken Oromo. The woman's words and gestures were clear, and she spoke with concern. 'When you walk, don't be thirsty. Drink water, always drink.' She gazed at Louise. They grasped hands freely, and Louise felt a fresh level of acceptance.

That evening another goat was slaughtered and its meat mixed with vegetables and ox blood. Six women supervised the cooking-pots. As evening fell, people chatted and laughed and sat in a half-moon with pots of food in their midst. The long day of trekking left few traces of tiredness among the Hamar. Louise, however, felt exhausted. Men organised the tethering and guarding of cattle and goats, and women moved to the shelter of the huts, some with babies on their backs or holding the hands of toddlers. The air was motionless and flies clung to hut walls, clothing and blankets. Louise stared across the compound to where cattle and goats were tethered; the dust they kicked up seemed to hang in the air and drift to the ground as slowly as dandelion fluff.

The women spoke of a thunderstorm mounting as the sky grew blacker. They put out water jugs. A strong wind shook the sapling huts. A fork of lightning lit the village. Trees and bushes bent before the onslaught. Huge raindrops belted down. Louise saw men running to ensure their cattle were secure. The air was filled with a fury she had never experienced. She found the roaring wind, the reverberations of thunder and the violent lightning flashes exhilarating. In half an hour, the rain turned to a drizzle and the wind slackened. The cattle tossed their heads and shook off the rain. Small wells and many water jugs were filled as nearby streams swelled.

In the morning Louise saw how the storm had battered the sorghum stalks. Women rounded up their few chickens, collected eggs and replanted vegetables. An atmosphere of delight pervaded the village and stayed there for the next few days. The rain had come at just the right time.

Since the beginning, Louise was impressed with the Hamars' dignity and the way everyone knew their role and responsibilities. She likened it to being on a racing yacht on South Australia's St Vincent's Gulf, where there was little talk as each crew member performed essential tasks and only acknowledged other crew with gestures.

On their treks the group leader Bashada was, as usual, out in front, directing and maintaining an appropriate pace. *Is he always so optimistic, so self-assured?* Louise wondered. *Or is his memory of the route so embedded, so much a part of his life since childhood that he never makes mistakes?* Koti advised that Bashada's behaviour leading a trek was not much different from the behaviour of his ancestors. 'There is coming and going between us.' Louise learned that a Hamar man's life from birth to death was considered to be a series of events which brought the man closer to his ancestors.

The nearer the group came to a familiar, shaded watering place, the more at ease they became. A few women, knowing that a rest break was not far away, broke into a flow of cheerful chatter. Had Louise met these women in Adelaide or London, she was sure she would have become friends with many of them. She enjoyed their friendly earthiness.

By late afternoon on a day at the end of Louise's second month, the group moved purposefully over stubble grass-country, soft under-foot. Murmurs of thankfulness rippled among them. Louise had difficulty containing her enthusiasm, feeling as if she could touch the daylight moon. She admired the young Hamar women, walking with their breasts so firm, their taut thighs, their sensual grace; it made her smile and think of her own loving with Zeno.

She had told Koti how much she loved the sun. Yet by mid-afternoon as the heat made mirages that changed the look of the plains, she changed her mind. She heard whispered consultations and wondered what the Hamar were talking about.

The burning afternoon heat made voices brittle. Then she saw what the Hamar had seen. In the distance, mirages of lakes, of silvery water, appeared between the thorn trees and across the grassy plains, shimmering. They could easily deceive walkers. Even though the Hamar had seen these mirages many times they still looked real.

In the swirling heat the landscape changed. Everyone was silent, preserving energy until sunset and waiting for a drop in temperature.

'You look as if you are worried,' a woman named Mactu said to Louise. Mactu knew she was tired. Then she added, 'Don't be afraid, we won't let you fail.'

Louise reassured her she wasn't worried, just thinking. She wasn't sure how much Mactu understood but as they looked at each other a smile of friendship was shared.

Louise watched Bashada. She knew he was a thinker. There was nothing casual in his behaviour; his focus never wavered. Replaying history, he followed the same track his forebears had trodden, told the same tales they had told. He was the group's guarantor of daily survival.

Even in the silence the women urged Louise to keep going, to see and appreciate their life. 'Please stay; don't turn away from us,' their eyes seemed to say. She was growing in confidence and beginning to feel part of the landscape – elemental, constant. Stories about her commitment were circulating among the Hamar. That night, in praise of the women, Louise wrote a prose poem she titled *Hamar Woman Walking*:

Hamar Woman Walking

She knows each stone, ridge and valley well,
corrects her stride; mistakes are costly.
she proves her ancestors' tread was song-like,
music floating on air, imitation handed down,
mother, daughter, granddaughter,
precise sand-lines.
Barefoot over and across land she walks unaided,
feather-light, descending to earth,
hearing its beat, smooth as a silk sarong.
Her poetry of motion is recited
as I follow, enthralled at such even pace.
Her reservoir of rhythm springs from a heartbeat
similar to ours, yet more in tune with the earth.
This morning as the night wind fades,
her slender body seems a shaft of light,
her tread like blossom falling from a bough,
in a finely balanced, lissom unhurried air.
Pent breath, striding, she utters not a word.

She's given legs for gliding well.
But has she ever walked on other ground?
On icy mountain tops, on wind-swept dunes,
trenched runnels or ribbed sea shores?
Each day she sets out with a smiling face,
toughened by rites of passage.
She trades expertise with chiefs, tribal sages,
those with the knack of surviving this country.
She's a compound, fashioned by survival needs.

She finds waterholes on a dry riverbed,
fills goatskin bags, carries them aloft,
bears huge weight with straight back, unerring stride.
Reason says she should fall and spill
her precious load in stony wastes,
but with ancestral tread she dispels doubt,
fatigue mitigates thirst and pangs of hunger.
In equal measure she weighs sun and rain,
delighting in each.
Her earthy wisdom, freely shared
guides me, sets my feet and mind to her land
in silent appreciation of this privilege.

Rites of Passage

LOUISE MADE CASUAL friends with some Hamar women of her own age, all of whom had children. She supported them, on occasions, by carrying an exhausted child or by collecting water and clearing up after a meal. She also knew how not to offend. She thought she was getting the balance about right. She noticed how the women accepted painful and ruinous events such as whippings, shortage of food, and infant mortality.

Louise wished she knew more about Hamar traditions. Zeno had told her about the bull jumping, the whipping ceremony, and the *evangadi* (Hamar love dance) which followed the whipping. One morning she asked Koti, in broken Oromic mixed with Amharic if she could learn more about these traditions. Koti responded warmly.

'These come down from my grandparents and great-grandparents who lived in this valley many years ago. What we do today, they did too.'

'What about the traditions of betrothal and marriage?'

'This is a ceremony unique to the Hamar. Not many people from outside the tribe ever see our ceremony of courage and betrothal.'

'Would I be allowed to watch?'

'Yes, of course. Some people think it is a cruel ceremony, but it demonstrates loyalty of the woman to the man and the man shows his courage to commit himself to the Hamar.'

'Doesn't it demonstrate the courage of women rather than men?' Louise recalled Zeno telling her about the caning of young women.

'Perhaps,' Koti replied, 'but the fact is, young men and women look forward to this initiation ceremony. A small ceremony will take place in two days' time. Young men have already begun to prepare. It's an essential ceremony for a young man to prove his courage so he will be able to marry his chosen woman.'

Throughout the next day, as the ceremony approached, the young women laughed, teased each other and made plans. They envied the long raised scars on the backs of older women which held sensual value for their men.

On the eve of the ceremony, women curled their hair with butter and ochre, and put on fresh jewellery. Men selected castrated bulls. Five young men had disappeared days before to rub cow dung on their chests and charcoal and butter over their faces as part of their preparation for jumping the cattle. Louise thought this was a scene ready-made for an artist to depict a primitive scene.

Next morning, the young women chatted excitedly. There was usually a break of a few days after the bull jumping but Koti advised that on this occasion the whipping would follow. There was tension but also humour and happiness. Older women who had suffered much in their lives, been whipped, given birth to seven or eight children only to see as many as five or six of them die in infancy, nevertheless were enthusiastic about the ceremony. This was a woman's path to marriage and motherhood.

'The ceremony will begin this afternoon,' said Koti proudly, as she walked past Louise.

By mid-afternoon, the group left the village and walked a short distance into a sandy clearing shaded by a few eucalypts. The late sun glowed burnt orange. Women stood on the edge of the clearing, clapping and dancing. Men with canes, the *maza*, wandered in and around the group telling people they were ready.

Cattle were lined up. Older men held them by the head or tail. The young men would soon be summoned. Louise was anxious about seeing these rituals.

Koti sensed her worry. 'This tradition is important,' she said. 'It links us to our ancestors and to all the other women who wear these scars.'

A line of twenty cattle was herded into the clearing and the crowd began to chant. Five naked, barefoot young men leapt onto the backs of obedient beasts and began jumping, backwards and forwards from one animal's back to another. To fall was failure, with manhood postponed. Each man was prepared, focused and determined to avoid falling and injuring himself. As the men leapt, they were admonished, jeered or cheered. Some stood briefly, naked and still on a bull's back before leaping to safety.

Chanting echoed across the clearing. Koti explained the chant's meaning to Louise: 'Farewell to youth and welcome blessed manhood – leap, leap, and let our cheers feed you with courage, desire and the magnificence of Hamar manhood.' When one young man slipped and fell, he was jeered and eliminated. Humiliated, he would have to try again at a future initiation in a year's time. But generally the tall, slender young men remain unscathed.

Suddenly, just as quickly as it began, the bull jumping was over. The cattle were driven away and an hour later the women's challenging horn blowing began.

When the whipping commenced Louise at times had to look away. Some of the women were pregnant. Many of them were sisters and close friends of the rewarded, agile young men. Naked except for their skirts, the women presented themselves, voluntarily, to be beaten by older men wielding long flexible canes. Each stroke across their bare backs cut into soft flesh till the blood ran. Levels of excitement, if not hysteria, drove the young women on. They presented themselves again and again to show their loyalty to their men, brothers and lovers by being whipped. With each stroke across their backs and shoulders the chanting, stamping and hysteria mounted.

Opposed to violence of any sort, Louise had never witnessed anything like this. She kept a damp handkerchief pressed over her face, sometimes just to avoid seeing a cane split bare flesh. But she saw no anger demonstrated in the whipping. The young women's acceptance, and what appeared at times to be delight, was so intense that Louise was stunned.

Men and women elders insisted the whipping was not cruelty but an act of devotion demonstrating total loyalty by women to their men. Each woman's expressions of joy were, it seemed, to counteract the severe, stinging pain inflicted on her. The women didn't cry out and there were no entreaties for the whipping to stop. Butter and dirt were rubbed into the bleeding wounds. Eventually, when healed, they would leave raised stained scars – everlasting symbols of loyalty.

Finally the whipped women crouched in devotion, and again and again taunted the men that their cane strokes were too weak. To admit pain was to dishonour generations of scarred Hamar women. And, so fated, the torrent of brutality continued.

Is this another way for the Hamar tribe to develop resilience? Louise wondered. Are friendship and loyalty born in this ceremony? Do young women who are caned eventually experience a tingling glow of satisfaction because of their courage and indifference to pain? She had no answers. It was difficult to analyse; things seemed so mixed up – women being caned to demonstrate loyalty; women not wanting revenge; naked young men repeatedly leaping across bulls' backs in order to be able to marry; sensual, teasing love dances that lasted for hours following the whipping.

And does chanting counteract pain? Her thoughts were racing. Does the hysteria of the ceremony enable the women to get in touch with some inner world of the Hamar spirit? And they don't even use *woyna tombo* to deaden the pain. Perhaps the ceremony is a symbol of the harshness of Ethiopia where opposites of tenderness and brutality clash.

She would talk to Zeno about the ceremony when she returned. While she would like to advocate the emancipation of Hamar women, she would not debunk the ceremony and its meaning. Koti was right. It was not wise for anyone to ignore the influence of rituals. Even their one-line chanting, accompanied to the rhythm of the *evangadi*, which, for hours followed the whipping, represented the tribe's uniqueness.

With Koti and the other women, she walked back to the village. Men who had cheered and been responsible for the whipping were now drinking *buna* and *tella* and talking matter of factly about cattle and the food being prepared, as if the initiation ceremony had never happened.

Louise hated to think that these noble people might, one day, disappear. Will governments ever appreciate the uniqueness of the Hamar? she wondered. Even if tarmac roads, cotton and sugar mills, housing and hotels appear in these tribal lands, the Hamar will still be there. And when development occurs and land is confiscated, will discord and fighting break out among the Hamar and other tribes as they fight for survival? She wiped perspiration off her forehead and pulled her floppy hat down to shield her eyes. Developers and government will confiscate tribal land, that's what they'll do, she thought.

Pregnancy and Stillbirth

THE HAMAR STAYED for two more weeks in the village close to the valley clearing. One morning, in the distance, Louise heard the cry of ravens, which reminded her of crows at home. Water was collected. Women were singing. A huge pot of *shoforo* was on one fire and another pot of water was ready to make large bowls of *debarda* (sorghum porridge) on another fire. When the *debarda* was ready it was spooned into separate bowls to cool off and then mixed with sour milk. Across the compound a young pregnant girl, whom Louise had seen in the crowd at the initiation, stood at the entrance to her hut. She smiled and beckoned Louise to join her.

'*Selam*,' said Louise.

'Ah,' the girl replied, '*Ameuseugnallo*.'

She was wearing a neck band indicating she could be a second wife. Her husband was nowhere to be seen. Louise sat on a cowhide mat alongside the pregnant girl. She said her name was Hamine. The girl spoke rapidly in short, simple sentences with gestures that Louise could barely follow. She kept talking as if she were emptying herself of all that was bothering her.

Louise wondered when her baby was due – seemingly very soon. She guessed Hamine was about sixteen years old, possibly younger. Close up, she was thin and Louise could see her rib bones clearly. Her full breasts hung over her protruding belly below which was tied a worn, stained goatskin skirt. Her cheeks were sunken but her dark brown eyes glowed when she smiled. Hamine told Louise about the impending birth, only a week if not days away. Together they talked and gestured, nodded and shook heads, developing rudimentary but effective communication.

Hamine counted on her fingers, telling Louise she was sixteen years old. But since the Hamar didn't celebrate birthdays, and there were no records, she could have lost count of the years.

Hamine seemed surprised at Louise's interest; at times, in the silences, she simply stared. After the birth Hamine would be a different woman from the one who had made love to her warrior husband. Louise wondered what it was like to be her.

Hamine smiled and suddenly said, 'It's beautiful, my country, isn't it?'

'*Ow* (yes).' Louise wondered if Hamine knew what her future would hold. Hamine had given her heart and soul to her philandering husband who, Louise suspected, would not be around for long.

With her large belly, Hamine could be carrying twins. The impending birth could be a wonderful time or one of suffering and despair. She would give birth on her own. Her prospects depended on a straightforward birth. Louise leant towards her and stroked her hair, then kissed her on the cheek. Hamine snuggled into Louise and briefly lay her head on her chest. Although Louise knew she wouldn't understand, she said, 'I love you, the way a mother loves a daughter.'

The Hamar generally put any birth complications down to mysticism; like wind on water where shadows move, bright one moment and dark the next; nature was full of examples of the play between life and death. This fatalism helped them accept infant mortality. Great moments, happy events, great suffering. Everything here is determined by fate, thought Louise.

Louise became aware of another young woman, a teenager, whose infant son had been born dead a few days earlier. The fact that this round-bellied teenager, probably even younger than Hamine, had a stillbirth appeared to be taken for granted. Louise felt sad for the young woman, seeing in the droop of her head a sense of trauma and loss. How does anyone respond to having the delight of impending birth dashed in an instant?

The girl, Oyta, appeared to have received little support from her family or friends. They knew nothing about Western medical procedures that would be available in Addis Ababa and Bahir Dar, that might possibly have prevented the stillbirth. Overcome with grief, Oyta was experiencing *woilem kaba* (depression). She was fragile and temporarily mute. She still sought her child, who lay now in a sandy grave surrounded by dry grass and thorn bush. Older women had buried her dead newborn in the bush beyond the village. Oyta, barely watching, had submitted dutifully when the infant was taken from her for burial. She sat near the grave when she could.

Young Oyta had so little life experience, yet so much was expected of her. She ignored children playing and, with head bowed, fiddled with her hands or scratched at her skin. She stared fixedly at the beaten earth, hour after hour without moving. This weak slip of a teenage girl would exist on the fringes of the group, perhaps even be left behind and, like her infant newborn, die before her time.

Louise wanted to say to Oyta, 'You have to be strong, otherwise you will die.' And then, as if from nowhere, the very pregnant Hamine sidled up and sat on the ground next to Oyta. She kissed her hands and then her forehead and, briefly, the depressed young woman stopped staring at the earth.

They talked quietly. Hamine consoled Oyta and, it seemed, told a funny story, because sitting close by Louise heard laughter. After an hour, Oyta stood and walked with Hamine towards the gardens, holding her head higher than before. She stopped and looked back at Louise, who waved. Oyta waved back. Louise sensed a catharsis taking place. She would tell Zeno and her family the story of these two Hamar teenagers.

A Big Mistake

LATE ONE AFTERNOON, when work in the gardens had finished for the day, Louise decided on impulse to follow a track to a garden more distant from the village. After a brisk ten-minute walk she felt relaxed and happy to find herself alone, knowing there were only a few weeks left before she would be back with Zeno. Deeply buried in thought, she took the track that veered to the right, away from the gardens, as the track to the left was obstructed by a log and a small thorn bush. She didn't notice her mistake.

After twenty minute's walking she found herself in open scrub country and realised she must return. Suddenly on the path ahead of her was a young, muscular Hamar man. Instantly, she recognised him as the same young man who had previously stared at her when she was in the gardens and when she returned from morning ablutions. They had locked eyes. At the time she was amused at his obvious interest but sensed there was nothing to be frightened of. After a few days when he no longer appeared she forgot about him.

'*Salem*,' he said. He had watched her leave the village and followed, overtaking her by scrambling through the scrub alongside her track.

'*Salem*,' she said. Frowning, she turned to walk away. He jumped in front of her and, barring the way, grabbed her hand. She felt his strength as he pulled her under an acacia tree and motioned to her to lie down. Fearful, she stood still as he ran his hand over the fabric of her goatskin skirt and along her thighs. She was frightened of what he might do if she resisted. He fondled her breasts, licked her nipples and tried to kiss her lips. He then pulled her into a clearing behind the acacia which hid them from the track. She felt the roughness of his hands as he lifted her skirt, stroked her inner thigh and, erect now, thrust himself upon her.

'*Aykonen* (no), *aykonen, bejaka* (please), *bejaka!*' she screamed, struggling and trying to push him away. But nothing would stop him. On the sand beneath the acacia he ripped off her skirt. Naked, huge and strong, he wrestled her to the ground. Louise sensed she should not resist, just become limp, and forget who she was for the duration. She tried to speak as shudders of fear and helplessness passed through her. Then she screamed, a horrible wailing cry that came from her but did not belong to her. It was an agony, out of control within Louise as she cried out for help; the epitome of every woman's terror at being violated.

At this moment, Bashada and another man appeared with the woman Mactu who had seen Louise leave the village, and when she did not return had raised her concern with Koti. Louise's assailant stood, grabbed his shorts and sprinted off into the scrub. Louise sobbed as her body shook uncontrollably. Bashada did not give chase but stood quietly by as Mactu consoled Louise, helped her put on her skirt and held her closely, soothing and caressing her. Louise gathered herself and slowly, with Bashada in the lead, they walked back to the village.

Louise remained with the Hamar for another two weeks, developing her friendship with Mactu. Louise was counselled by Koti about the mistake she had made. The young man would be severely punished, probably sent to live with the Mursi if he ever tried to return. Embarrassed, but grateful for Bashada's rescue, she worked in the gardens, and felt increasingly close to their way of life. One morning, Hamine squatted on the earthen floor of her hut and gave birth to twins, a boy and a girl. Louise heard her piercing cries and saw the midwife arrive with razor in hand to cut the umbilical cord.

Successful multiple births were rare and an occasion for rejoicing. Hamine and both her babies had survived. Louise observed the matter-of-fact way in which the women, and the remarkable Hamine, coped. Louise shared in the rejoicing. Women came to cuddle the babies, to hum to them; others danced around her hut and all congratulated the smiling mother. The gift of a new cowhide for Hamine acknowledged her achievement. Sadly, there was no cowhide for Oyta.

That evening, Louise lay on her blanket just inside her hut's entrance, watching the sky turn dark blue then a translucent black. Her thoughts turned to Zeno. She admitted to herself how much she missed him as she listened to whispers of a hot wind that had troubled her during her first weeks with the Hamar; the wind dried the land and, in a few days, could ruin the few lush crops. Now she felt comforted by the dry wind and its sighs.

Louise understood that often when Hamar people are chronically ill and close to dying they disappear. Only the fit are left. No questions are asked. An old, shrivelled and stooped man with a chronic cough, who could no longer walk from village to village, hobbled away at dawn one morning accompanied by a strapping man who, Louise noticed, had previously befriended him. Louise's whole being was gripped by what she sensed was going to happen. She was convinced the old man knew his time had come. He would be killed and left to leopards or hyenas. Four hours later the old man's friend returned, alone.

Days later came endless torrential rain, the first for many months. Louise leaned against the entrance to her hut, taking shelter. There was consternation among the men. They had driven their cattle and goats to pastures many miles away across the other side of the dangerous Kaeske River. It had been a dry riverbed two days earlier and now it was a roaring, flood-swollen river fed by frothing tributaries, and the men and their cattle were not able to return. Their cattle, dispersed to the faraway bush, could become easy prey for leopards and hyenas or possibly a lion. More men were required to help round up the cattle but could not because they were cut off by the floods. Even if they could cross the river and reach higher ground, continuous drumming rain drowned out the cattle and goats' bells. Louise pitied the men for their helplessness in the face of the flooding rains.

After two days there was blue sky again, but the rain had washed away parts of the gardens and left recently ripened sorghum so damp that it could only be used to make beer. There was now a huge clean-up and retrieval task.

Some cattle, perhaps as many as twelve, had disappeared. There were no easy remedies, but only endless hard work in the weeks ahead. So goes the tale of Hamar life, thought Louise, as she worked alongside them in the gardens, observing the diligence with which they set about rebuilding, rounding up remaining cattle, retrieving crops that had survived and accepting what had been washed away.

Last Day with the Hamar

ON HER LAST day, after a short trek and a brief visit to an outlying satellite village, Louise would be picked up by Samuel. The women finished collecting necessary belongings and looked anxiously around the village that, a week before, had been smashed by days of torrential rain. Nothing useful was left behind. The gardens would become overgrown until the next visit, perhaps in a few months' time. The Hamar were leaving behind weeks of labour. When they returned they would start ploughing, planting anew and salvaging what plants had survived.

'I can hardly believe it,' Louise said to Koti as they walked away. 'You take great care of these gardens as if they were your children and then suddenly you leave them.'

'Yes, it seems that way, but like our children they are tough and we have to care for the gardens in the next village. We know how long a garden and pasture can survive, and we can tend them when we return.' After a long pause, she looked at Louise and added, 'And we have always been able to do this.'

Louise wanted to reply, 'Except in the famine,' but she nodded.

She walked alongside Koti and other women. Turning back, she saw Hamine carrying her twins and marvelled at her resilience and maturity. She was breastfeeding both babies.

By mid-afternoon the group arrived at the satellite village on the eastern bank of a small Omo tributary. Tired as she was, Louise entered into the spirit of this homecoming celebration. Excited, she thought of how close she was to seeing Zeno again. Her life would be renewed when she was back with him. She also knew how her three months of living and trekking with the tough and dignified Hamar tribe would mark her for the rest of her life. It was not just about spending time with an ancient Ethiopian tribe but of living, as Mandy had said, 'close to the earth'.

The rendezvous point with Samuel was ten miles west of the small town of Hamar Koke. If Samuel didn't come that day, as arranged, he would arrive at the village within a day or two. Her heart beat fast as she waited on the edge of the village compound. Koti, Hamine and some other women came to see her off. Louise saw children waving. She had won their affection by her commitment and friendliness, and the women did not want her to leave.

When Koti spoke enthusiastically about Louise's stay, the other women nodded approvingly. Louise felt blunted by the afternoon heat and a hot wind that blew relentlessly, whistling through big acacias and eucalypts. Yet, she was excited at the prospect of her reunion with Zeno. She imagined being back in her home in Addis alone with him. In the distance she thought she heard the rumble of a Nissan Patrol diesel engine. It seemed a long time coming. She knew Samuel's Nissan had to make its own track over the rough and dusty acacia-studded terrain. The dry season had just arrived and the Omo Valley would become a parched wilderness of scrubby grasses, withered acacia and brittle brown thorn bushes.

An hour later, through the deserted scrub, Louise saw a cloud of dust. She suddenly experienced a brief flash of self-doubt about her future with Zeno and cursed herself for it. Then she heard three long blasts of a horn and Samuel's Nissan powered through the distant scrub, pulling up some two hundred metres away. She looked up and, to her surprise, saw Zeno climb down from the passenger seat and stride across the tracks towards her.

'Well, what a survivor you are,' he said, hugging her and smiling broadly.

To Zeno, Louise looked thin and tired. Gone was the carefree full-cheeked woman he remembered when she left Addis. She was tanned and weathered and apparently strong, but he had not expected to find physical signs of hunger in her appearance. But her smiling eyes, close embrace and the feel of her breasts against him made him put aside this impression. As they waved goodbye, Zeno picked up her small rucksack and hand in hand they walked across the rock-strewn field to the track where Samuel was waiting with the Nissan. While she had felt at home with the Hamar, she also knew she would always be a stranger, no matter how long she lived with them.

They drove on winding sandy tracks and stayed the night at a small, recently built bush lodge three miles beyond Turmi. Zeno ran a tub bath with lukewarm water. Louise lay soaking, and when she returned to the bedroom Zeno had laid out her clean underwear, slacks and Louise's favourite cream blouse which he loved to see her in.

'My God, I'll have to get used to wearing a bra and knickers again.'

Zeno looked at her lovingly as she dressed.

After supper they went for a stroll. Zeno thought Louise seemed different, tired perhaps, a little remote, probably preoccupied with what she had experienced these past months. She was strangely quiet and there seemed to be unusually long silences. There was a moment of utter stillness which Zeno hoped would last forever: the gentle evening sunlight flickered through the eucalypts and at the centre of his picture was Louise. While she was not a stranger, he reasoned it could be a while before they felt at ease together again. Their silence was broken by an outburst of distant bird song.

'Bush crows and rare white-tailed swallows,' said Zeno.

Louise smiled but she was not in the moment. It was an evening when everything seemed jumbled, overwhelming. It was impossible to adjust and take in what was happening now and what had happened with the Hamar during the last three months. She would find a way to tell Zeno about the attempted rape, but not now.

They returned to the lodge and sat in the flower-filled garden.

'I've been bowled over by what I've experienced. It's been life-changing,' she said.

'I told you that would happen.'

'It's going to take a while to assimilate what I've seen and heard. I *do* want to return.'

'Take your time. You've a lifetime's work ahead of you. I'm so thrilled you're back safe and sound.'

'I've had some astonishing experiences and I'll tell you about them before long. But I'm very tired now so let's have an early night.'

Together they returned to their room. 'I can't wait to sleep between sheets, but it could take some getting used to after three months with only a cowhide between me and the ground.'

'We'll get used to everything together,' whispered Zeno as they undressed and, naked, climbed into bed alongside each other. He was very gentle and they made love easily.

During the first month back in Addis, Louise passed each day expanding her notes, recalling significant experiences she'd had living with the Hamar. As she wrote, she did her best to anchor herself in the details of Hamar life and in her friendship with Koti, Mactu and Hamine.

Once again, Zeno was preoccupied with work, although their relationship and his fondness for her appeared as strong as ever. She wondered if he had any idea of how she had longed to be back with him. His continued desire to make passionate love she read as undeniable proof of his feelings towards her.

8: Exploring Options

Inaugural Lecture

WHEN ADDIS ABABA University's department of anthropology received UN development funds to supplement a substantial Wellcome Trust grant, it was decided to preface extensive fieldwork with an inaugural lecture titled: *No More Famine: Dispelling Ethiopia's Demon.* Zeno was invited to give the lecture. Government ministers, politicians, administrators, a few foreign diplomats and other academics, along with journalists and many students, were invited.

On previous occasions, when Zeno had spoken at Addis Ababa University and at the University of Nairobi, he had filled lecture theatres. But this occasion stood out. Every place in the auditorium was taken while students sat or stood in gangways. The Minister for Health and regional health administrators, appointed by the Derg, were present, along with the University Vice-Chancellor and his wife, colleagues, friends and guests from industry and politics. The Vice-Chancellor chaired the lecture.

Zeno's recent radio broadcasts, television appearances on nightly news programs and coverage in the *Addis Tribune* and *Ethiopian Herald* had raised his profile. People were keen to hear what he had to say. Politicians and senior bureaucrats as well as leading academics were now courting him.

While praising Zeno's work, the Vice-Chancellor's introduction drew parallels between the quality of the keynote speaker and his institution. He was looking for sponsorship, perhaps from the few alumni present, but also from the national government and international funding sources.

'Dr Zeno Wolde has an international reputation for his work in medical anthropology,' he began. 'The influence of his research and writing is acknowledged by us all. He has played a crucial role in identifying the needs, as well as the talents, of Ethiopia's rural poor. He has initiated applied research projects, attracted international support and supervised young Ethiopian and overseas anthropology researchers. He has a reputation for innovation.' The Vice-Chancellor became more effusive. 'And his multidisciplinary approach – he is also a qualified doctor as well as a renowned anthropologist – has established new procedures, particularly as his research findings can be quickly applied. Please welcome Dr Zeno Wolde.'

At the end of his detailed, hour-long presentation, Zeno received a standing ovation. He had pulled off a major coup. By attracting influential political figures, along with the promise that his address would be published as a supplement in the Ethiopian press, he was recognised as a significant advocate for health and agricultural reform.

'His interpretation of rural needs is to be treasured,' visiting US Professor Jim Stroman from Johns Hopkins University confided to Louise during the reception that followed.

'There is no doubt he is the best medical anthropologist we possess,' boasted the Vice-Chancellor to the Health Minister. 'He's inspirational for students, and a leader in our university. Journal editors, as well as our own press, say that his writing is compelling.'

'Our government will be keen to help you promote Dr Wolde's work,' said the Health Minister. The Vice-Chancellor raised his eyebrows and looked directly at the Minister, who nodded in such a way as to make him want to continue his compliments and foster his involvement with Zeno Wolde and the university.

'You have a golden opinion of Dr Wolde, Vice-Chancellor, and after listening to him today I agree with you. My government will be keen to hear from him directly.'

The audience at the reception congratulated Zeno. Louise, delighted, listened to the accolades. Meanwhile, the Minister of

Health, amid the lively conversation and the clinking of glasses, moved to talk directly with Zeno.

'Everyone's interest was sustained by your eloquence and your personal stories, which I greatly appreciated. It's time for change and your ideas for regional health clinics and improved agriculture management must be implemented.'

Zeno wondered about the compliments, especially since this was the first time they had met; certainly it was the first time the Minister had heard about Zeno's ideas, let alone read any of his writings.

'Come and see me. I'll get the government to back your ideas. I know I'll get support in the cabinet.' The Minister puffed himself up and smiled, believing he'd achieved a coup. Louise, standing within earshot, did not fully understand why the Minister was so keen to support Zeno, and felt misgivings.

'Thank you, I appreciate your support,' Zeno replied humbly. Later he whispered to Louise, 'I'll tell you later what I think of this Minister's claims of support. I've heard all this before.'

Zeno's scepticism was carefully disguised. He recognised that the Minister was carefully assembling a political agenda. He imagined him telling his allies about the lecture. He would make claims, some grandiose, momentarily impressive, soaring but unrealistic, but Zeno knew from experience that ministers only carried through any program if it was to their advantage. And this offer of support, in the heightened and exciting atmosphere of the university's reception, though tempting, was no different. There was no obligation on the Minister's part to find resources to build more antenatal clinics in the rural communities, or to seek support from a fellow minister to initiate simple agricultural reforms of the sort Zeno had advocated.

Servility not Advice

A MONTH LATER, to Zeno's surprise, the Minister of Health was as good as his word and invited him to address members of his department in the Parliament building. The meeting was to be an open forum discussion with a focus on antenatal care in rural Ethiopia. Zeno could present his research and be questioned about his case evidence.

Twenty people sat round a table in a conference room. Another fifteen, all men in Derg army uniform, sat behind the front row. The Minister welcomed participants and explained the reason for the seminar.

The strategies Zeno advocated included the provision of well-funded and resourced regional rural clinics with a focus on antenatal services. When Zeno repeated this proposal, some senior bureaucrats showed their lack of interest with bowed heads. It was pointed out to Zeno, as if he were unaware, that in rural Ethiopia there was limited transport on unmade roads. He was told that for the most part, usable roads were non-existent in the high Simien plateau country; furthermore, in the Southern Tribal Lands, gravel-and-rubble-strewn roads were impossible to use in the wet season.

The Minister suddenly intervened. A flash of irritation darkened his face.

'Only well-funded researchers like yourself can visit these places, let alone build and service rural health clinics. We have to be realistic. At the moment what you are proposing is not possible.'

Zeno had foreseen the challenge. He paused, thinking of the

starving but resolute village people he knew. Skilfully, he turned the discussion to specific needs of women during childbirth. It was obvious that most of those around the table had little knowledge of the conditions that rural women experienced.

'If a woman's labour is complicated, and it often is, she may have to walk or be carried to the nearest nursing facility which, at a minimum, is generally three or four hours' walk away. And for many tribal people it's a half-day walk away – often much longer. That's what has to change.'

Despite his passion and the detail Zeno presented, the participants, with a few exceptions, seemed bored. He told the meeting that it was estimated that the maternal death rate was at least one in every thirty women, and every woman in a village knew someone who had died in childbirth. Zeno recognised that this meeting had not been organised for him to give advice, especially when the Derg perceived much of what he said to be unwelcome. They expected servility, not advice.

'But don't women accept this – these maternal death rates? It's their way of life,' stated a plumpish, greying man dressed in an army officer's uniform dripping with medals. He looked openly annoyed.

What Zeno had said about maternal death rates was perfectly true, and what's more, it was information to which the Derg surely had access. Zeno's voice then rang out more loudly than he had intended.

'At the moment they've no option. They are courageous, but also, for the most part, as meek as lambs.' Zeno paused. He realised where the meeting was heading, especially when the audience was unmoved by his information about the high death rate of women during childbirth. After an hour the Minister decided he had heard enough.

'It's very good of you to tell us about your research so that we now know more about what is going on in the villages, especially those that experienced the famine. We would like to support your work.' The Minister was trying to sound interested, but with an apologetic smile and a shrug to his colleagues he ended the meeting.

After the usual courtesies, Zeno and Louise left the building. Zeno had a way of ignoring what he didn't want to hear, even from Louise. But those who understood how power operated knew better than Zeno that if he was perceived to oppose them, even just a little, he would not be allowed to continue on his way unchallenged. Or, if he was perceived to genuinely challenge the Derg, he could be expunged from the face of the earth.

'People in high places are beginning to know you very well, Zeno, and the media want your time,' Louise consoled. 'Cultivating the media is necessary to obtain resources and begin to achieve change. But despite popularity you must be wary of the government.'

'I'm not sure why I should cultivate the media, let alone the government. I don't need any gilding.'

'I know you are not seeking publicity for its own sake, but that's not how others see you. Success creates rivals, if not enemies. Publicity and more demands on your time inevitably will follow.' She had noticed, especially at the meeting, his increasing indifference to conventional ideas of dignity in public along with his ability to, as she put it, 'flout reality'.

'My dear Louise, we must never let ourselves be dragged away from the poverty we are not supposed to see, the death cries we are not supposed to hear and the stories we are not supposed to write.'

Louise realised that, as ever, he had no wish to be silenced.

'Yes, but I don't want you to be seen in obvious opposition to the government. That spells trouble.'

Over lunch, two days after the antenatal seminar, Zeno promised Louise he would never say or write anything extreme that could cause trouble. 'Only a considered and balanced view will be in my writing; that's my goal.' He raised his eyebrows and smiled.

'I'll believe that when it happens,' Louise said.

Gabriella

LIVING WITH ZENO was full of twists and turns: he worked long hours, travelled the country and regularly took on overseas conference keynote addresses. There was little time for relaxation. He changed the subject whenever Louise suggested they take a break or have a holiday. After initially looking on and admiring Zeno's capacity for work, Louise felt she was now part of his schedule. Their work together gathered momentum, so it appeared useless to resist the hectic pace or try to develop a more leisurely home life.

In the evening, often after returning home from a full day of teaching and researching, he went straight to his study and continued working.

One evening, she broached the subject that he knew was on her mind. 'Will you ever consider having a sabbatical overseas, in London, or New York or even in Adelaide? Refresh yourself, travel and meet colleagues overseas?'

'Darling, I have my life here,' he replied. 'And I have my copies of Achebe's and Camus' novels right at my fingertips. What more do I need?' Zeno was fond of quoting to Louise from Achebe's novel, *A Man of the People*: 'I sat on my bed and tried to think … I soon realised that what was needed was action; quick sharp action.'

Louise sensed his commitment to Ethiopia pulsing inside him: action, action for his country. And even when he appeared exhausted he could will himself to carry on. Inaction was anathema.

Louise hosted dinners at their small home with close friends or visiting overseas scholars and, whenever opportunities arose, she and Zeno dined together at their favourite Addis restaurants. At those times, recollections about his father and his untimely death seemed to burn even more freshly than when Amare was killed. It seemed that no thought or event – no matter how compelling – had the power to exclude his father's influence unless, Zeno admitted, he was with his mother.

Louise had spoken to Zeno's mother by phone and although they had never met, they enjoyed chatting to each other. Louise's two brief visits to Nairobi were early in her relationship with Zeno and he had not suggested visiting his mother. One evening, he surprised Louise by telling her they should fly to Nairobi and stay with his mother.

'It will provide an opportunity for you to see something of Kenya, and for me to show you the region where my mother grew up. We can walk some of the tracks around her home village close to Mount Kenya – perhaps even climb the mountain.'

She wondered if he really wanted to do this, to climb that mountain, especially as she thought he looked tired and certainly needed cheering up. But she said, 'I would like that very much. When do we leave?' She had to pin him down and fix the date, otherwise something to do with his work would crop up and the trip would be cancelled.

'If it's okay with you, we can fly to Nairobi at the end of next week. Leave on the last flight on Friday afternoon.'

'Shall I book our seats?'

'Please do and I'll let my mother know when we'll arrive.'

The thought of the two women meeting delighted him. Introducing his beloved mother to this intelligent and sensuous blonde woman, his loving partner, was an event he had dreamed about. He imagined them meeting in Gabriella's Nairobi home and embracing, women of different generations from separate continents and cultures. He was confident they would bond and that Gabriella and Louise would come to love each other. Why had he not introduced them earlier?

Ten days later, on a cool Friday evening, they arrived at Addis airport. Meanwhile, for the last week, Louise had been the topic of conversation between Gabriella and her friends. In a phone call to Zeno, Gabriella told him they had talked of little else and wondered if he was serious about her.

Zeno's mother had only seen one photograph, a head shot of Louise, published some years before in an anthropology magazine. Zeno had told his mother very little about her, other than she came from Australia, was blonde and had blue eyes.

He knew that, as in the past, Gabriella would be anxious about his conversations of a radical political or religious nature. But she was loving and genial, and never said anything that was coldly stinging. She could turn water into wine. She always welcomed and loved him, and gave thanks.

During the flight, Zeno told Louise about Gabriella's home and village birthplace north of Mt Kenya, saying jocularly that, while his mother encouraged him, she also let him know when he needed to come back to earth. Louise agreed; she too had difficulty reining in Zeno's life when, one moment he was floating on air, climbing irresistibly, and in another he had, through some mischance, missed a foothold and lost control.

When the plane landed they collected their cases and slipped quickly through customs. Zeno booked a taxi straight from the airport to his mother's home.

While Louise was curious to learn about Zeno's childhood she would not probe. During the taxi ride they were both in good spirits and Zeno was more relaxed than she had ever known.

'Mother, this is Louise.'

Zeno put his arm around his mother. Gabriella smiled, held out her arms to Louise and hugged her closely. She captivated Louise with her openness and in the way she wore her long, brightly coloured Kenyan motif dress and fine circular copper earrings. Louise saw a gracious and loving woman. At the same time, she was aware that during her marriage, this intelligent woman had experienced hurt and disappointment, and for the most part had always lived in her strict husband's wake. Original high expectations for her own career had never come to fruition yet, Zeno said, she had never uttered a word of regret.

She ushered them into her comfortably furnished lounge. Louise glanced at the family photos in identical light-brown wooden frames, religious symbols of Christ the Saviour, small pieces of pottery and two African landscape paintings on the walls.

'You have a beautiful home.'

'Thank you. I hope you'll be comfortable here. You sit with Zeno and I'll put on the kettle. Are you hungry after your journey? I think you might like a piece of my homemade cake – what do you think?'

'Mother's a genius with food, aren't you, Mother?'

'Not really, Zeno, I just like to cook.'

'You certainly do, and we always enjoy your cooking,' he said proudly.

'You know, Louise, I'm so pleased Zeno has brought you with him.' She flashed a broad smile at her son and entered the kitchen.

The warmth of Gabriella's welcome relaxed Louise and Zeno. They stayed four nights and slept in Gabriella's spare bedroom with its small double bed. They took her to shop and eat in Nairobi and planned their trip to the region of her home village. Walking with them around her suburb, Gabriella was proud to introduce them to neighbours and friends. She took them to her local church. As they moved around, Louise felt something uncanny. Alongside the soft and enthusiastic Gabriella was her stirring and intense son, often lost in thoughts, in his planning, his opposition to the Derg, his sense that he rarely achieved the reforms he advocated. He was preoccupied. Louise could almost hear the machinery of Zeno's mind churning inside his skull. She looked at him, engrossed, gazing ahead and walking separately from them.

She caught up with him. 'Are you okay?' she whispered. Her hand was on his shoulder as he walked on.

'Yes, I'm fine.' A sinking feeling passed over her, like a dark cloud passing momentarily across the morning sun.

Gabriella's hospitality and simple acts of kindness were a pleasure, although Louise was unlikely to see much of her in the years ahead because of her life in Addis and occasionally London. She consoled herself with the belief that she could become a lifelong friend. When they left, Louise promised Gabriella she would return.

Mt Kenya

'WE'LL CIRCLE THE city to the east and then join Park Road, which will take us on the main road to Thika and Mount Kenya,' Zeno explained. 'There's a small safari park in the foothills of Mt Kenya with comfortable accommodation.'

'Have you booked or are we taking a chance?'

'It may surprise you, but I've booked for three nights before we drive to Nanuki.'

On the first morning, while Zeno slept, Louise was up before sunrise. At that hour she could observe the stir of wild animals across the sculptured plains of the Lorogi Plateau country where hundreds of plovers and crested cranes wandered in the sprouting grass. In the distance, she noticed the strange, sooty-coloured hornbills. Above the grey half-lit plains below, the early morning clouds and birds of prey hovered. With its halcyon calm, this was a moment of life-gratitude which she would write about for family and friends.

It wasn't long before Zeno joined her. He hugged her, then pointed to a just-emerging range of hills about ten miles away. 'That's the edge of the Great Rift Valley. There are plenty of monkeys, rhinoceros, zebras, gazelles, jackals and lions there.'

'Can we go to the Rift Valley?'

'Of course. There's a two-day trip run by the safari centre. They'll drive us there and we'll stay a couple of nights on the edge of the valley. We'll see enough to leave you spellbound.'

They spent their three days trekking with guides around the ancient volcanic Mount Kenya. At the foot of the mountain, Louise visited villages where women walked barefoot, carrying children, firewood or water. Vegetable gardens were tended by women, with goats wandering in yards and pigs penned. Louise realised how these gardens were more productive than anything she had observed among the nomadic Hamar.

Zeno was enthusiastic. 'All of this is much the same as when Gabriella was a child.'

They decided they were fit enough to climb to Mt Kenya's summit.

'I recommend the Sirimon route,' the centre's receptionist explained, 'with Jodo – he's our most experienced guide. It will take you a minimum of two nights to the peak. We're developing this route and at the moment you'll have to sleep in what we call wilderness camp sites. Depending on how you feel when you reach the summit, it's possible to descend in one day.'

Louise dealt effectively with the onset of altitude sickness, but a thousand feet below the summit camp Zeno was very quiet. Until this moment, he'd never considered he would have any trouble, but a painful throbbing headache left him disoriented. He didn't mention to Louise or the guide that, during the previous day's walking, he had felt unusually tired. His work regime was catching up with him and he had ignored symptoms of shortness of breath experienced days before. Louise assumed his silence was because he was concentrating on his footsteps. Jodo ordered a halt and told Zeno to rest and drink.

'You're probably dehydrated,' he said sympathetically. 'Don't worry, this can happen on the mountain.'

Jodo confirmed with Louise that she was fit, and then observed Zeno as he sat on a rock with his head between his knees. They rested for an hour as Zeno sipped water. He was dumbfounded by his nausea and struggled to speak. Loss of energy distressed him.

'Darling, you look exhausted.' Louise did not want to undermine Zeno but was worried about him.

Zeno tried to smile. 'What's a man like me doing collapsing

before he's finished the task? I'm alright, it's just this headache,' he murmured. He desisted from accepting sympathy.

'I'm keeping you back from reaching the summit,' he said apologetically. He wanted to sound jovial, but did not.

'Man, you rest for another hour if necessary and then we'll set a slower pace. It's not safe to take people to the summit when they feel unwell,' Jodo said, 'and you must let me know if you are ready to carry on.'

'Another ten minutes and I'll be fine.' Jodo looked intently at him.

In just over an hour Zeno had recovered sufficiently and, saying how ashamed he was of his physical weakness, set out to reach the summit camp. 'I'm sorry I've held you back.'

'Not at all,' Jodo reassured. 'You've recovered well and can rest when we reach our camp.'

Louise put a hand on Zeno's shoulder. 'You look better now; just take it easy, we've plenty of time.'

This time Jodo set a more moderate pace and checked Zeno regularly. He was still experiencing discomfort but was determined to keep pace with Louise and Jodo. Less than two hours later they reached the wilderness summit camp. Zeno sank to the ground, drank deeply from his flask and let Louise and Jodo set up camp and prepare their evening meal.

Lying with Zeno under a small awning tent that night, Louise stroked his forehead and consoled him.

'Well, I'm not as fit as I thought I was. That puts paid to my plan to be a world-class mountaineer.' With this self-deprecating remark, Louise realised his confidence was returning.

'I doubt you could ever be a mountaineer with the workload you have. Your workload is like climbing Mount Kenya every week, with just one day for the ascent and one for the descent. You need to slow down, even just a little.'

Zeno could not envisage eliminating any of the projects in which he was engaged. Louise realised he believed he would look foolish if he withdrew from any of them.

The morning was very cold. After a breakfast of thick porridge, they set off for the summit. Louise avoided discussing Zeno's state of health until she was sure he had recovered. Besides, she was too weary herself to deal with the emotions she had experienced yesterday on the mountain. And Zeno would not admit to how ill he had felt.

They trekked across a moorland-type plateau and then across ridges and arêtes, and after three hours they reached the twin peaks of Batian and Nelion.

'Here you can appreciate the beauty of Mount Kenya,' said Jodo as he pointed to the wide plains below. Scarcely were the words out of his mouth than, through binoculars, Louise discerned clusters of Kenya's grazing exotic wildlife. She stared and stared. Jodo was right. The dots on the plains far below were gazelles, zebras, elephants, buffalo and there were probably leopards in the thorn trees, and a lion pride or two. She felt the stirrings of an even deeper passion for Africa and, with it, a longing for a fulfilled life with Zeno. She wondered if they might they have a child together. And if they were to be together, could Australia be included in their life in Ethiopia and Kenya?

They stood for a long while before beginning the descent. They took photos of each other and the spectacular mountain peaks. Jodo chose the fast and easy descent route which he was confident Zeno could endure. By late afternoon they reached the bamboo-forested hillside track within easy reach of the safari wilderness centre.

After showering, they sat down for their evening meal and discussed their days on Mount Kenya. They recalled the minutiae of the fauna, flora, geological details and the spectacular views. Gone was Zeno's vague half smile, the trembling hands, his confusion and disorientation below the summit camp.

'The centre has a two-day 4WD trip to the edge of the Great Rift Valley. It's approximately forty miles to the edge. We can leave tomorrow,' Zeno said over their dinner. Louise yearned to reach the Rift Valley and see the wildlife up close.

'I can't wait. I would have begged you to take me if you had not made the arrangement.'

'Tomorrow when we reach the Rift Valley you will see more wildlife than you have ever thought possible.'

The Great Rift Valley

THE KENYAN RIFT Valley, that giant crack in the earth's surface, was completely different from the country around the foothills of Mount Kenya. The grass covering its rich alluvial soil was a type of low-creeping knotted couch. As Zeno and Louise watched from their 4WD, innumerable gazelles and zebras grazed nearby, and enormous ostriches tiptoed their way between low acacia bushes. They noticed a warthog sow leading her young, and baboons bouncing around among mimosas at the edge of a lake.

'In just this small area, you can understand what is meant by the uniqueness of the Rift Valley,' said Zeno. 'The colourful lakes you see in the distance are the home of gigantic hippopotamuses. They come ashore at night and are huge feeders on the grasses that stretch away from the lake's edge. So, fix your eyes on the valley floor and you should be able to see traces of where they crush and chew the grasses.'

Louise leant her head on his shoulder and gazed at the wildlife, grasslands and distant lakes. This view was among the finest gifts Zeno could bestow. High in the sky, keen winds scattered the clouds as they climbed out of the 4WD and stood among the mimosas.

'How can I capture this moment in writing?' she asked.

'Just record what you see and feel: grasslands, gazelles, zebras, lakes and mimosas.'

They spent that night at a hostel on the edge of the Rift Valley. Lying in bed with Zeno, Louise imagined future holiday trips, driving and trekking together along the lengths of the papyrus-lined silver-white shores of Lakes Nakuru and Elmenteita. She told Zeno she wanted to listen again to the cries of the long-legged, long-beaked waterbirds and photograph them as they waded and fed. Ecstatic, Louise listened to gentle rain on the hostel's tin roof as the mists of night rolled in across the valley.

After the steady rain of the night, their last day was an example of how rapidly life could change in the valley. The sun rose in a blinding light and a gusty burning wind blew across the veldt. Well supplied and with plenty of water in their 4WD, Louise and Zeno searched the plains for lions and leopards. They noticed colossal hippo tracks in the sands at the lake's margin. Zeno was right, of course – lions and leopards lay in the heat alongside waterholes. Beyond them was a group of hyenas and gazelles that, days before, had grazed on the plains and now sought cool retreats under thorn trees. She tried to imagine the valley and plains when dinosaurs might have walked there. The animals she had in mind were early carnivores, similar, she thought, to present-day lions and leopards but much bigger. She wondered how early white settlers adjusted to living here.

'I can't imagine what this valley was like a hundred years ago, let alone when early man first walked and hunted here.' For Louise, the surprises and contrasts in the Great Rift Valley were inexhaustible.

'The Rift Valley has many secrets and like our lives, Louise, its aspect changes from year to year. Sometimes the Rift Valley is placid and amazingly lovely, and at other times it is threatening and eerie. The climate can be severe. It changes very quickly from one day to the next, and it's never sympathetic; wildlife is at its mercy.'

Louise listened and stared at animals standing in the withering heat by the shrinking waterholes.

Zeno noticed her concern. 'It's very hot now but when dark clouds cover the valley and rain falls, the grasses, trees and animals are happy again. Don't worry – wild animals adjust to the weather.'

It was late afternoon. Maniki, their driver and guide, drove them back slowly along a dirt track. 'I've a final treat in store for you, if we're lucky,' he said. 'There's a waterhole I know away from the track. It's surrounded by many flat rocks and on a hot day in the late afternoon many different butterflies gather there to enjoy the heat.'

Twenty minutes later Maniki drove off the track, parked and beckoned Louise and Zeno to follow him. After a ten-minute walk, Maniki waved, indicating that the butterfly rocks were just ahead. Cautiously they approached.

On the edges of a large rock pool was a series of flat rocks; the surfaces were covered with a quivering veil of butterflies of every colour – yellow, red, orange, black and bright blue. The butterflies opened and shut their colourful wings in the intense heat. Louise gazed at the fragile spectacle, so impossibly lovely.

'This is another of Kenya's beautiful secrets,' Maniki said proudly.

On their last night in their Rift Valley hostel, Louise envisaged returning with Zeno for a safari holiday, or indeed inviting her parents to accompany them.

Zeno was keen to return to his work in Addis. While Louise had commitments there and in London, she wanted to have more time to appreciate the landscape and history of Kenya. She remained intrigued by Zeno's Kenyan heritage. She noticed how he appeared relaxed and at home in Kenya – perhaps more so than in Ethiopia. Would he want them to move from Addis and set up home in Nairobi? Over coffee she raised the possibility. Given the tumult of his life in Ethiopia, would he be less driven in Kenya? 'I didn't anticipate you being so happy back in Kenya; it's been delightful to see.'

'My darling, I love Nairobi and the countryside, it's in my blood, but no more so than Ethiopia.'

'No one is as devoted to Ethiopia as you are. But if you want to live and do similar work in Kenya then I'd be happy with that.'

'Where has this idea come from?'

'I just thought how extraordinarily happy you've been, spending time here.'

'Yes, I've been very happy on this trip, not least because you have enjoyed it so much. But I've no intention of applying for a position at the university here. My commitment is to Ethiopia and always has been.'

Louise knew that it was one thing for Zeno to reinvent himself and be less outspoken in Ethiopia but another for him to live in another country. It required reserves of commitment that Zeno felt would take him away from Ethiopia.

'Oh, that's fine by me. I know how much you're respected in Ethiopia. I'm happy in Addis and we certainly have plenty of research to complete. And new projects to be developed.'

'Yes, we've got a lot to do back home and there's probably some overseas trips coming up.'

'Overseas trips?'

'The San Francisco medical anthropology conference in May is one.'

'But that's months away and I haven't heard if my paper has been accepted,' Louise said.

'We should plan to go anyway. Your paper will be accepted, mark my words.'

To Louise's surprise, Zeno told her that when the conference was over they could fly from San Francisco to Adelaide. 'Just for a short trip,' he said. 'Don't you think that's a great idea? I'd enjoy being in Australia and meeting your family.'

Louise felt her heart race. She was delighted but had not expected this late-night casual conversation to turn out this way. She looked straight at Zeno. 'What a beautiful conclusion to our time in Kenya, first with your mum and then in the Great Rift Valley.'

With a man like Zeno, Louise knew that what was required were not precipitous demands but gentle suggestions at regular intervals.

Examiners

ZENO SUPPORTED LOUISE'S writing and research, just as she supported his. True, his renown gave him an advantage which, Louise thought, she could not match. Yet, he always treated her as his intellectual equal.

After admiring the outline of her thesis, he made suggestions one evening as to who might review or, indeed, examine it. 'Perhaps Haawkon Davos. He works for Médecins Sans Frontières. I think he'd be pleased to read your work. I'm just speculating, of course, but I know him and he's highly regarded.'

She had heard him mention Haawkon, a Norwegian medical anthropologist, and had read a paper or two of his on health priorities in sub-Saharan Africa, but she didn't associate him with her interests.

'He'd be ideal. He wants to find talented, hands-on researchers like you. Who wouldn't?'

'Really? Why would he want to read my work?'

Louise thought Zeno's suggestion about Davos was fantasy. And yet, she was excited that someone working on the front line might be willing to respond to her. 'Tell me more about him.'

'He has visiting fellowships at London University and in New York. His work on reducing rates of infant mortality in the developing world reflects your interests. He has wide experience, and the poet in him will enjoy being with you.'

'What has poetry got to do with examining my thesis?'

'Poets, my dear Louise, and I really don't need to tell you this, are both expressive and evocative. Poetry can affect your thinking.'

'What do you mean?'

'Their language helps you to be sensitive to what you observe. Haawkon has that reputation. His writings and behaviour are gentle, but expressive. He's also persuasive. And he lures me with descriptions and stories of dispossessed people, many of which have deeply affected me.'

'You're also a poet in the way you quest for truth and then persuade people, with you words, me in particular, to your way of thinking.'

'And why not? Do you never persuade me to accept your point of view?' They laughed.

If Zeno ever wrote a memoir, Louise knew it would be lucid, encouraging and poetic. It would include his passion for metaphor, self-scrutiny and political awareness. He advised his students to write like Chinua Achebe. 'Achebe,' he told them, 'writes simply and with restraint.'

Zeno brought her back to the present. 'Now you are nearing completion, it's important to consider who might examine your thesis.'

'In addition to Haawkon Davos?'

'Yes, of course. Many leading anthropologists would be privileged to examine your work.' He imagined her on the international conference circuit, with Ethiopia and himself gaining recognition as a consequence.

The fading evening light filtered across the room behind Zeno, fixing him briefly in silhouette so that, for a moment, with the sun in her eyes, she could just observe an outline that could be any native Ethiopian. She experienced a fleeting wave of panic. She remembered the Hamar man who almost had his way with her. And then Zeno moved to one side and was there again. His gaze was full of love.

Zeno knew some might believe that Louise's thesis was written by him. Academia in Addis Ababa, as in London or New York or anywhere, was a competitive business. No suspicions should be aroused concerning the originality of her writing. Nevertheless, he would read her thesis before its submission.

'Well, Zeno, I'll be finished soon, so be ready. And even if you are working away from Addis I'll be expecting a quick response. In fact, I'll probably pester you to take the thing with you,' Louise laughed.

Louise, with Zeno's help, had her first research paper, 'Health Needs of Remote People of the Lower Omo Valley', published in the *International Journal of Anthropology.* It was received by academic colleagues with considerable interest and subsequently acknowledged for its originality. This was followed by an invitation to present at the international Anthropology Symposium at San Francisco State University later that year. It was early 1988, a time in her life when one success was followed by another. Louise was thrilled, but also apprehensive. She would need to accurately portray the Hamar and other tribes of the Lower Omo Valley, and be ready to provide fine details for conference delegates.

Zeno had anticipated the acceptance of her submitted paper. Her presentation would help establish her and bring Ethiopia to the attention of other young anthropologists.

Next day, before Louise was up, Zeno had been in touch with university friends in San Francisco. He wanted her to have significant contacts before she arrived. He had read the conference program and discovered that the keynote speaker was to be the prominent anthropologist, Haawkon Davos. He had worked in East Africa alongside Zeno and would probably, despite his busy schedule, respond to Louise's paper. Zeno had also met Haawkon in London and invited him to give a series of lectures in Addis. They had maintained contact and, although Zeno hadn't seen him for some time, he was sure Haawkon would be an influential supporter of Louise's research.

Over breakfast, Zeno told Louise about Haawkon's role in San Francisco. His enthusiasm for the Norwegian appealed to her.

'What's he like?'

'Tall, suntanned from skiing, athletic, and I guess in his late thirties.'

'Sounds more like a ski instructor than an academic.'

'He's academic alright, but very practical and influential.'

San Francisco

THEY FLEW TO San Francisco, with a three-day stopover in London where they had a brief meeting with her old London University supervisor, Mike Boetcher, and time with Carmen who, despite their short stay, was determined to provide hospitality for her friend and partner.

During a walk together across Russell Square, when Zeno was out of earshot, Carmen said, 'I sensed on our first Ethiopian field trip you two were set for each other.'

They enjoyed the warm spring weather in San Francisco. On their second evening in the city they walked with fellow conferees to a restaurant just off Lombard Street.

'What do you think of San Francisco?' Ted Fordman, the joint State University conference convenor, asked Louise. 'We're proud of San Francisco. You must visit Fisherman's Wharf and take a tram ride up and down Lombard Street. There's no street in the world like it.'

They walked on. Zeno took her arm as they passed a young man lying in a doorway. Along the street other men were curled up along the pavement. Some coughed and groaned. Louise noticed how gaunt and unwell they looked and how some were shivering. A thin, bearded young man pulled his blanket tighter around his shoulders as a gust of wind blew down the street. His doorway barely had space for him to curl up in. At the corner of an alleyway, a young woman comforted a breathless man with a thin face and stick-like arms. She stroked his face and Louise heard her say, 'I still love you. I always will.' She stood, and slowly walked away.

'Come back tomorrow, please come back,' the man said. Vacant-eyed, he watched her disappear. It seemed so out of keeping in this prosperous part of the city – sick men on pavements and in shadowy doorways.

Zeno whispered to Louise that he had heard of this condition but not come face-to-face with anyone who was suffering from it. Louise realised what it was and recalled that in Australia it was originally known as GRID – Gay Related Immune Disease – because, in the beginning it was considered a disease limited to homosexuals. Seeing men lying in the street was, however, unexpected and shocking. Zeno and the other conferees ignored the young men. He sensed Louise's growing unease.

'They've been on our streets for some time now,' said Ted. 'At least there are fewer of them than a year ago. Just ignore them, they'll eventually disappear.'

'Disappear? Zeno, what does he mean?' Louise whispered.

'I have no idea. Maybe they'll leave in a few months or even die within a year. I've never seen anything like this before.'

As they overtook a sick young man shuffling down the street, the conference group again looked away. They came to the end of the street and paused to check their way. There was a lull in the noise of traffic and the only sound was the dry, rattling cough from the man they had just passed. Louise looked back. She wanted to return and comfort him. 'Good God, they're so young.'

'Are you alright?' Zeno took her arm.

'Yes, but what can we do to help these men?'

'Nothing at the moment, and anyway it's none of our business.'

'Should we pretend we haven't noticed them? Some of these men are struggling to breathe. Surely they should be in hospital.'

Zeno ignored her. She shrugged and looked past him towards another man on the pavement.

'It makes me sad when I see people who are rejected. If some of them have pneumonia, why are they here? I want to know more about them.'

Zeno clutched her arm tighter as they crossed the road leading to the restaurant. He wondered how to quell her concern. He too was amazed at the sight of these emaciated, sore-ridden young men. But his primary aim now was, without further distractions, to usher Louise to the restaurant.

'You can raise your concerns with Haawkon. He'll listen to you, I'm sure.'

It was almost seven o'clock when the group sighted the restaurant sign.

'There it is, the Giovanni,' said Ted. It was a familiar sanctuary and he told his party how it always pleased him to bring guests to the Giovanni.

'I'm glad we're here,' said Zeno, feeling relieved. He knew that if the opportunity arose during the dinner, Louise was bound to pursue the GRID issue. There was nothing he could do to divert her.

'Not everyone is here yet.

The restaurant began to fill. The noise level rose so she leant close to Zeno to make herself heard. 'Why did we ignore those sick men? Can good people really abandon others in obvious distress?' He watched her reach in her sleeve for a handkerchief to wipe her eyes. She wondered who to believe about the men's condition, how to find out what the truth was about their illness.

'Their illness is not easy to talk about, Louise, and not really appropriate this evening.'

'I'll be discreet.'

Zeno knew then that Louise's concern could become a principal topic of conversation. Moved by her compassion, he wondered what she would say. Four more people entered the restaurant, one of whom was the tall, tanned Haawkon Davos. People turned to him. He noticed Zeno.

'So here you are, looking as bright as ever,' he said as he shook

Zeno's hand and hugged him. 'I heard you were attending. Marvellous that you are here, Zeno, we have much to discuss.'

'Haawkon, this is Louise Davitt, originally from Australia but now living and working with me in Addis,' said Zeno proudly.

Louise looked at this tall man with thick blond hair and an easy smile. She wondered if she had met him before.

Sixteen people took their seats. Louise, with Zeno next to her, deliberately moved to sit opposite Haawkon. He talked to Ted next to him, but smiled at them often.

'Haawkon, I think you should spend more time in the US. We would welcome you as a member of staff. You would only have to put your name on the application and grants would become available,' Bob Schutt from Berkely impressed on Haawkon. But Haawkon let the compliment pass with just a smile and a quiet, 'Thank you, Bob.'

Ted tapped his wine glass and waited for silence.

'Welcome, everyone, and in particular a warm welcome to our overseas visitors and of course to our keynote speaker, Haawkon Davos. Let's drink to a successful conference and to the many friendships and collaborations we will make here this week in beautiful San Francisco.'

Haawkon nodded towards Ted and gestured his thanks to others at the table. Zeno leant across the table. 'You'll have to get used to these compliments. Many of us have registered just because you are presenting.'

'I cannot imagine why. You've already heard and read much of my stuff.'

'That's true, but you always have something new to present and most people here will not have heard you before.'

Conversation was spirited and enquiring, and ranged, as far as the GRID epidemic was concerned, from those who believed it was a homosexual disease, to others who thought it was more complex.

'What is the origin of GRID?' Louise asked Haawkon when there was a brief lull in the conversation.

'It's not entirely clear. I believe the virus was originally isolated in

1984. Careful observation, talking to people who have the condition and of course clinical details which we share will provide answers. We know that people who eventually become very sick probably have weak immune systems. When they catch the infection their illness progresses and becomes a most serious if not a terminal illness.'

Louise sensed he would not think the sick men on San Francisco's streets should be ignored or abandoned to their fate.

'We'll have to share ideas about the condition. It's now called human immunodeficiency virus, or HIV for short, which can progress to acquired immunodeficiency syndrome, known as AIDS, although early on, at least in the media, I understand the term GRID was used. We have much research to undertake to improve our understanding. That's how I see it.'

Conferees turned to listen to Haawkon. They talked about story-telling and the recounting of primitive songs in Africa and Australia. Haawkon's emphasis on the relationship between songs and tribal health showed the importance of history to understand contemporary health events.

'Are the primitive songs you are talking about much like the song lines in Bruce Chatwin's novel about Australian Aborigines? ' Louise asked.

'Not exactly. The song lines, as I understand them, are Dreaming tracks which wander over Australia and where, in the Dreamtime, the name of everything they met was sung. Aboriginal songs tell us much about the environment, people's lives and how they dealt with birth, sickness and death. We have much to learn from these people. We must talk more about Aboriginal songs.'

'I'd like that.' Louise envisaged Mandy, now merged with her Aranda Aboriginal tribe, conversing and sharing with the Hamar.

Encouraged by Zeno, the conversation soon focused on Haawkon. 'Life, for all primitive peoples, is pretty much the same, in so far as it forces them to think unremittingly about how to survive. And then they celebrate their survival. Primitive songs spring from their survival.'

Then conferees once again spoke about the possible causes of the disease infecting so many young men in San Francisco. 'Isn't this disease only found among homosexuals?' someone asked.

'It's bound to be much more complex,' Haawkon replied. 'I know people in the heterosexual population in South Africa and Mozambique who have similar symptoms. And it's most likely there are people in the heterosexual population in the UK and US also with the disease, but at the moment it suits some sections of the media to refer to the disease as GRID. But they could be so wrong. Isn't that true, Bob ?'

'Yes, I know what you mean. In time we'll learn the exact cause of the disease, but at least, at the moment, we think it only seems to affect the homosexual population.'

'I think it's too simple to claim this disease is limited to homo-sexuals,' said Haawkon. 'Many of these men have also been drug users, and I've heard of a case where an American member of the Peace Corps has the disease. He's a fellow doctor working in Angola, who is a haemophiliac and not a homosexual. He must have caught the disease during a blood transfusion. It is certainly going to take time to understand the causes and find a cure.'

Opportunities

THE FOLLOWING MORNING Haawkon Davos delivered his keynote address. Sometimes he was grave, sometimes humorous, but always realistic and engaging. His case examples of the effect of tradition in the developing world, and his emphasis on the need to improve health and education from the ground up, were descriptive and compelling.

Louise's presentation was in the late afternoon. She told of walking with the Hamar. She described the effects of a stillbirth and the high rates of infant mortality. She displayed her photographs of the brightly adorned Hamar women working in their gardens. The audience was entranced as if they had been transported to the Omo Valley. The forcefulness of her presentation was balanced by the delicate way in which she demonstrated her respect for the Hamar and other tribes. Skilfully handling compliments and requests for copies of her paper, she also showed a keen interest in other delegates' research. Afterwards she joined Zeno and Haawkon in the conference hotel café.

'You'll have to present to my colleagues in New York,' Haawkon said. 'They will appreciate hearing from you.' Zeno and Haawkon had already discussed the possibility of a short trip to New York following the conference.

'You mean now, while we're in the US?'

'Why not?' said Zeno. 'You'll enjoy New York.'

'If you are interested I can make arrangements – that's no problem,' Haawkon said enthusiastically. 'There are cut-price fares and it's only a six-hour flight. We can leave on the 6 am flight from San Francisco and be in New York by mid-afternoon. My research stipend will cover your airfare and both of you can stay in my apartment.'

Louise had not expected this. There had been arrangements going on that she had not been privy to and she had heard conference delegates talking about plans for activities in San Francisco. She was not sure how to respond … whether to go to New York or stay in San Francisco.

'I should enjoy that, but I don't think we have the time.'

'Yes, you do. We still have a full week after the conference before we leave for Australia, and I'm going to spend a couple of days at Berkeley with former colleagues,' said Zeno. 'So while I'm with them, you can go with Haawkon to New York.' Zeno was enthusiastic. He thought a couple of days in New York with Haawkon would further her career and, since Haawkon was no romantic, Louise would be perfectly safe in his company.

'I'm flattered,' said Louise, somewhat taken aback by both Haawkon's offer and Zeno's enthusiasm that she should fly to New York. It was clear that Zeno attached great importance to Louise being with Haawkon in New York while he had more free time in San Francisco.

She wondered whether the trip to New York, at a moment's notice, was a way of adopting Zeno's strategy to just keep resources flowing. He liked developing a new project before the current one was complete. She wanted to keep a tight rein on each project and make sure she kept to completion dates. She also wanted to enjoy San Francisco and prepare thoroughly for her trip home to Adelaide. But she had to admit that Haawkon's offer was tempting.

'We can fly to New York two days after conference completion. I'll ask my secretary to arrange flights and a time for your presentation to my colleagues. Bill Weiman, editor of the *American Medical Anthropology* journal, will be there and I'd like you to meet him so he can consider publishing your paper.'

Delighted with Haawkon's support, Louise wondered why Zeno

would not come with her. That evening she discussed staying in Haawkon's apartment with Zeno.

'You can stay in a hotel if you wish but it's perfectly acceptable to me that you stay with Haawkon. Accept his hospitality. Look, Haawkon's crazy about his work, not about you.'

Louise nodded and agreed to fly to New York.

Conference addresses, dinners, seminars and poster displays, along with informal meetings with other conference delegates, filled their time in San Francisco. Two days after the conference ended, Louise packed her bag for the three-day trip to New York. Haawkon picked her up before dawn for the drive to the airport.

'Enjoy yourself,' said Zeno, kissing her and then waving as her cab drove away. He went to Berkeley that morning for his meetings.

New York

ON THE FLIGHT, Haawkon was enthusiastic. 'You're going to enjoy this, especially as so many people are looking forward to meeting you.'

'I hope I can live up to your expectations.'

'You will, I've no doubt about that.'

He told her he wanted her time in New York to be rewarding. 'I've told colleagues about your time with the Hamar and how you identified with them and found it difficult to leave.'

'That's true. But I was just learning to talk with them when I left and returned with Zeno to Addis. Every day I was with the Hamar I learned more about their language.'

'Something you'll never forget … it must have been a unique experience.'

Haawkon did not disguise his interest, but Louise considered that this was more professional than romantic, and anyway Zeno had told her how Haawkon always took a nurturing interest in colleagues and fellow researchers, of whatever sex, especially if he perceived them to be potential trailblazers.

They landed at JFK airport at 4 pm and took a cab to Haawkon's apartment on the East Side. He had been away for three weeks but his housekeeper had prepared the bedrooms and purchased basic food. He carried her case and showed her to a smart bedroom with its own ensuite. 'Don't be nervous, Louise, many of my friends, male and female, have stayed with me in this apartment. Decent New York hotels are expensive and you're only here for a few nights.'

Louise smiled, and relaxed.

'I'll leave you to freshen up and when you're ready, join me in the living room. In the meantime I'll make some phone calls and book a restaurant. We'll be joined by Bill Weiman and his wife.'

'Thanks, that's great. I'll join you shortly.'

Louise's room had a large curtained window overlooking an internal courtyard. There was a small desk and a couple of arm-chairs, rather like a quality hotel bedroom but without television. She unpacked, wondered whether she should wear cream slacks or a favourite purple dress. She chose the slacks. 'My God,' she said out loud as she dressed after her shower, 'this is very different from living with the Hamar.' She joined Haawkon in the living room.

'Coffee or wine?'

'Thanks, Haawkon, a dry white would be lovely. But I'd like to phone Zeno first.'

'Of course, but while it's almost six o'clock here it's only three in San Francisco. I suggest you phone his hotel and leave a message for him to call you here. Here, have the wine while you make your call.'

She felt his gaze pass momentarily over her body. She raised her eyes and looked towards him but he had already turned away and walked into his kitchen, leaving her free to make her call out of earshot.

'Dr Wolde is not here at the moment. Would you like me to record a message?' said the San Francisco hotel operator.

'Yes please.' She waited for the signal. 'Hi Zeno. It's me. We had a great flight and we're out to dinner tonight with Haawkon's friends. Wish you could join us. Hope your day went well. Will phone in the morning. I love you.'

Dinner at a smart Italian restaurant went well. Bill Weiman was friendly and offered to publish some of Louise's writing, especially if she could produce a series of articles. His journal was prestigious, and having articles published in it would facilitate access to sought-after grants.

When they arrived back at the apartment Haawkon was quite formal, wished her goodnight and retired immediately to his own bedroom.

Haawkon seemed to have accounted for every minute of the next day. She met a range of colleagues over early morning breakfast at New York University as they discussed the design and funding of different research projects. The competitive drive of the Americans left her spellbound. They were brilliant talkers. At mid-morning Louise gave her seminar, which was more of a discourse with her audience than the full-blown presentation she had delivered in San Francisco. Fellow researchers, particularly young post-graduate anthropologists, asked about her work in Ethiopia. She explained the vagaries and attractions of different tribal groups, the need for improved antenatal care and the influence of tradition on agricultural practice.

Haawkon took her and two visiting colleagues from his native Norway to the Lincoln Centre for a Chopin piano recital followed by a late lunch. Louise was enjoying every minute but, fit and young as she was, she wondered if she could keep up the pace Haawkon set, and the day was only half over.

He was the perfect host. He should be called Cool Haawkon, she thought – always in control.

At 4 pm there was a meeting in the paediatrics department to discuss antenatal conditions and needs in Ethiopia. She felt the inadequacy of her experience, but again Haawkon promoted her and gave her leads to which she could respond.

There were twelve other people at dinner that night in the fashionable restaurant. Louise found herself between the visiting Norwegian anthropologist and a French paediatrician who had attended the afternoon's seminar. The wine flowed and Haawkon moved assiduously from person to person to make sure they all knew about Louise.

'Could I have your attention? This is the Australian, Louise Davitt, from Adelaide and London Universities and the University of Addis Ababa. She's already completed pioneering work with isolated tribes in southern Ethiopia. I have benefited much from listening to her, so please make yourself known to Louise and share some of your experiences with her.'

A constant stream of diners came to her table to talk. Addresses, phone numbers, invitations and references to articles and books were shared. By ten o'clock everyone was ready to leave. Louise had made many contacts and received more invitations to present at future conferences. Haawkon had achieved his aim.

The next morning Haawkon was up and out before Louise was dressed. She valued the quiet time. He left a note saying he had been called to an emergency meeting at the infectious diseases hospital, with a patient who had just returned from Angola. He would be back by 9.30, in time to take her to Columbia University for a presentation similar to the previous day's. She wondered if the patient's condition was like the disease she'd noticed on San Francisco's streets. Louise was still concerned about the sick young men and would not write about her time in San Francisco without reference to them – remembering their emaciated bodies, racking coughs and staggering walks.

Haawkon returned a little later than planned.

'I'm sorry I'm late, but it's alright, I've phoned the people at Columbia. When you've presented we'll have a light lunch and then do some sightseeing,' he said.

Louise was weary and keen to be back with Zeno to prepare for the trip home to Adelaide. But she was caught up in Haawkon's slipstream.

After the presentation and lunch in the Columbia University staff club, they set off to the UN building and then on to some art galleries on the Lower East side. Haawkon took her to the Sculpture Centre and the recently opened Baumgold Gallery's exhibition of twentieth century artists. Louise, although reaching saturation point at the never-ending activity, felt an inner radiance at being with this 'Scandinavian tornado'. Haawkon's gentle humour and enthusiasm were like a stream flowing powerfully over and around any obstacles.

They stopped briefly for late afternoon tea and then took a cab back to his apartment. Haawkon said he wanted her to have a break and that dinner would not be a late one in view of her early flight the next morning.

'Have a good hour's rest. We'll leave by 6.15 at the latest.'

'Are you going to rest? Do you ever get tired?'

'Yes, of course, but I recover quickly. It's in the genes, I suppose.'

Looking at his athletic body, his clear, unwrinkled skin and sparkling blue eyes, Louise speculated that he could be a teenager rather than a man approaching forty. She retired to her bedroom. As she lay on the bed she thought about the hectic day and the fact that it wasn't over yet. After half an hour dozing, she showered and dressed in her purple dress.

Haawkon had been preoccupied with phone calls but when she walked into the living room it was clear that he was struck by her radiance. His obligation to Zeno had been to give Louise a rewarding professional experience. He had done that.

'Okay,' he said. 'We're both ready, so let's go.' Louise wondered about his clipped tone but reasoned he was tired and had been on the go for twelve hours. She saw him pick up a package as they left the apartment.

At a small restaurant with French cuisine, they sat opposite each other, next to the window. Haawkon ordered a bottle of white wine and sparkling mineral water. Louise thought he was being unduly formal in his tone. She determined to break the ice.

'I've watched you today and talked to your friends. You've already done enough for two lifetimes. I think of you as a tornado. A Scandinavian tornado, if there is such a thing.'

'Thank you, but I don't think so.'

Haawkon sipped his wine and stared at her.

'I'm wondering whether you have ever been married or had a partner. You've never mentioned anyone and everyone just talks about you in relation to your work. So, Haawkon, who are you? Is there anything other than medicine, anthropology and MSF that drives you?'

'That's the hardest thing in the world for me to answer. I'm thirty-nine and for sixteen years I've been working around the world for international aid programs, including of course MSF.'

Louise wanted to interrupt and say, 'There you are, talking about your work again.' But she let him continue.

'Women are very mysterious. I married a young Norwegian woman when I was twenty-one and she was eighteen. In Norway they used to joke that people made love for their health. That wasn't my experience. My marriage didn't last; we were too young. She went away to Britain as an au pair and then to the US and I believe remarried. I loved her, as one does when one is young, but I soon learned there was no good in looking for her. I decided I didn't want to get involved again and have spent my life focusing on my work. And that's been very rewarding.'

And then, looking rather sheepish, he added, 'And that's how I came to meet you.'

'And that's my good fortune, Haawkon.'

He stretched under the table and produced the gift-wrapped package she had noticed as they left his apartment.

'I bought this for you. This can be a reminder of our time together in New York.'

'Oh Haawkon, thank you. You are very generous. You've already done so much for me. Can I open it now?'

'Of course.' Haawkon looked briefly out of the window as if wanting to appear disinterested but then switched his gaze to her face.

It was a hardback copy of selected poems of William Carlos Williams. Inside was a card with a portrait of a pensive young Japanese woman titled 'Beauty Looking Back'. On it Haawkon had copied out lines from one of the poems. *The rain falls upon the earth and grass and flowers come perfectly into form.* Underneath he had written: *Thanks for coming to New York. I shall always remember our time together. Cheers, Haawkon.*

'This is beautiful, Haawkon. I'll cherish it. I see that Carlos Willams is a bit like you, a qualified doctor who also pursued another career. Being a poet, no less?'

'I'd never thought of him like that, but I enjoy his poetry.'

217

'Read me a poem before we eat.'

'If you insist.'

Louise handed him the book.

'I'll read a short piece from the poem 'At Night' … *The stars that are small lights [...] I walk by their sparkle relieved and comforted.*

What comforts you, Haawkon? she wondered. 'You read beautifully. I look forward to you reading more poetry to me.'

He nodded. 'When the time is right.'

As they ate, they talked about Zeno's work and how he was advocating change while facing ingrained Ethiopian traditions. 'Your eyes light up whenever you talk about Zeno's work,' Louise said.

'He's a pioneer who is inspirational. He bridges different disciplines and, above all, maintains his close contacts in the field. Only someone as committed as Zeno could survive his workload.'

'Yes, but Ethiopian politicians are wary of his association with isolated rural tribes and villages. Many are afraid of change, and certainly on the scale that Zeno is advocating.'

There was silence. They said nothing for a minute until eventually Louise said, 'Some claim he's one-eyed. But change is necessary in order to prevent future famines and high rates of infant mortality.'

'I agree, but I'm worried he could be overreaching himself, and we all want him to have this level of energy and inspiration in ten years time.'

'I hope he will.'

They finished their coffee and prepared to leave. Louise could not think ahead ten minutes let alone ten years. Haawkon's gift, his poetry reading and gaze were fixed in her mind. She glowed. He pretended not to notice, paid the bill, and they caught a cab back to his apartment.

'You'll need an early night,' he said. Louise wondered if giving her the poetry book had somehow changed their relationship.

'Thanks for a great time Haawkon. You are so generous.'

She glanced to where he was standing by his drink cabinet. Impulsively she walked across, kissed him on the cheek, said,

'Thanks again,' and hugged him goodnight. She felt him relax, become aroused and begin to caress her. She wondered if he would lead her to the sofa but instead he released his grip, kissed her gently on the forehead and turned away.

Louise was amazed. What control, she thought.

Haawkon cleared his throat. 'We'll leave at 4.30 am; I'll set my alarm and have a cab ready to take us to the airport. Come and stay with me again when you're in New York.'

'Of course I will,' she said as she entered her bedroom.

In bed she wondered whether he would come to her room and make love to her. She was sure it was what he desired and, although worried about this attraction, she had to admit that, in her bedroom's half light, she would enjoy it too, if she wasn't with Zeno. As she lay thinking about the last three days and then, wondering about the morning flight back to Zeno and San Francisco, she fell asleep.

The cab arrived on time and thirty minutes later dropped them off at the JFK. They walked through the departures hall. Louise checked her bag and lined up in the security queue. Haawkon kissed her gently on the cheek.

9: *Irreconcilable Desires*

Adelaide

LOUISE WANTED ZENO to feel comfortable during their stay with her family in Australia. While waiting in the customs queue at Sydney airport, she thought she could sing for her family the Gershwin songs: 'Love Walked In' and 'The Man I Love is Here to Stay'. She chuckled at the thought. Wouldn't that be something?

Having cleared customs, they boarded the flight bound for Adelaide. Louise looked forward to seeing her family. Zeno appeared apprehensive. Her parents could be wondering when he and Louise might marry. A de-facto partner might not be considered a long-term proposition for their daughter. Louise noticed his tension. She told him not to worry and that she would always be there for him. Zeno relaxed, and sat back in his seat.

Louise's parents stared across the runway and watched the aircraft come in over the sea, land smoothly and taxi to its bay. Through the glass they could see Louise and Zeno leave the aircraft and walk across the open tarmac of the old airport.

Gerald Davitt peered through the arrivals hall window. It was three years since he had last seen Louise and he only knew Zeno from what she had written in her recent letters. He braced himself.

'There they are,' Monica said excitedly as the couple walked through the swing doors. Zeno was the focus of attention, which would hardly diminish for the next three weeks.

All through that waiting time the previous day and now at the airport, Gerald had been contemplative. Now Louise was home at last. He collected himself and waved enthusiastically.

Louise held Zeno's arm as they pushed their luggage-laden trolley through the crowd to greet her parents. 'You are the most beautiful person,' Louise whispered to Zeno, anticipating his apprehension. 'This is Zeno,' Louise said thrusting him forward to embrace Monica and shake Gerald's hand.

'Hello Zeno. Welcome,' said Gerald, giving him a quick handshake.

'He's usually very confident but he's nervous about meeting you,' Louise said and winked at Zeno. He grinned broadly.

'That's true enough but I'm very happy to be here at last. It's been a long wait.'

While Louise and Zeno were distracted by luggage and airport noise, Monica whispered to Gerald, 'Relax, they're okay. Look at her, she's so happy.'

'Zeno, Louise has told us so much about you – all good.' Gerald smiled. He was determined to like his prospective son-in-law. He knew nothing much about Africa except the huge and wretched legacy of the slave trade, and South Africa's iniquitous apartheid regime. But he was keen to learn more and certainly, within his own circle of friends, to promote Zeno. He would respect Zeno Wolde and allow closeness to develop through their mutual love for his daughter.

'This is it,' said Gerald when they located his car in the airport car park. As he started the engine with Zeno sitting alongside him in the passenger seat, Monica said, 'I've tried to persuade your father to buy a new car but he insists this one will do.'

'Commodores are pretty good – it'll do us for another ten years,' joked Gerald.

'Well, if it's still drivable, why change it?' asked Zeno. 'We drive cars in Ethiopia till they fall apart.'

'Darling, that's only partly true,' said Louise. 'There are some people in Addis who regularly buy new cars.'

'Just corrupt politicians and the few very rich.'

Gerald's Commodore sped past the city and on through the Adelaide Hills towards the family home in the small town of Stirling.

Geoff and Alex were there with their wives and Geoff and Sophie's baby son, Sam. They greeted Zeno and their sister with smiles and laughter. Louise was close to tears.

'How well you look, baby sister,' said Geoff as they embraced.

'You look younger than ever,' said the usually reticent Alex as he kissed and hugged his sister.

Louise put her arm round Zeno. How secure she felt with him. She was proud of her family and confident that Zeno would be happy in their company.

The Davitts' four-bedroom house was in colonial style, with floor-to-ceiling windows looking on to wide verandahs and carefully clipped lawns, laden fruit trees and brick paved paths. Louise and Zeno soon settled in with the family in the large warm kitchen with a wood-fire stove.

The nearby town had walking tracks through the hills and a winding road twenty kilometres down to the coast. Louise introduced Zeno to the walking trails where, from different viewing platforms, the spectacular coastline could be seen. There had been heavy winter rain so the landscape was green and lush, but when they first arrived a warm anticyclone spell enveloped the southern part of the South Australian state so they walked in sunshine.

In the first week, every morning before breakfast, Louise and Zeno enjoyed a brisk ten-kilometre walk. Louise loved being back home with her family and walking with Zeno in gentle winter sunshine. So much was in her favour, she thought she might suggest they have a child. They had flirted with the idea before, but their heavy schedules had, at that time, made it almost unthinkable.

Zeno was not surprised when Louise suggested she wanted to conceive. He was happy to be in the Davitts' home, enjoying the company of her parents and brothers; glad to be away from the demanding schedule that, for so long, had been his way of life. Louise's happiness made her yet more beautiful in his eyes. His natural impulse was to agree. Previously, given the nature of his working life, he would have provided reasons as to why they were not ready for a family of their own. But now he was carried along in the happiness of the Davitt family.

Zeno's passion was comparable to when they had first made love. When they met family friends they were like teenage lovers. They touched and fondled each other no matter what the company.

'Sometimes it's embarrassing; I have to hold myself back from saying anything to Louise,' Monica said to her husband in a quiet moment. 'You are so discreet,' she continued. 'Bless you. Last night when we were in the restaurant I understood something I haven't realised before.'

'What?'

'That Louise's love for Zeno says something about her love for Ethiopia's people.'

'Has she told you that?'

'Not in so many words. But you know she has wide horizons. She sees immense opportunities in her life with Zeno. And she's always been determined to accomplish whatever she sets her mind to.'

'What exactly are you telling me?'

'It's my roundabout way of saying that she's wedded to living in East Africa and overall she sees Africa as exciting.'

Monica paused. Her husband looked bemused.

'She's intent on promoting Ethiopia, and that's borne out in her love for Zeno.'

'Has she told you that she's going to live in Ethiopia permanently?' Gerald asked.

'Not exactly, but she did say she regards it as a garden that must be tended.'

'Did she say that?'

'Yes. Although of course she didn't tell me everything. But you know what she's like. She said that, in the past, Ethiopia has been trampled on and crushed, and unless it's nurtured, famines will continue and its potential won't be realised. Her passion for what she's doing seems ingrained.'

'That's our Louise, she's always committed.' Gerald tried to swallow the lump in his throat. 'I suppose she could put down roots there.'

Monica put her arm round him. 'We can always visit her.'

She spoke about Zeno's virtues: his manliness and kindness, his intellect, his love for Louise. 'The most we can ask for is that he loves her.'

'Yes, I can understand why she loves Zeno,' said Gerald. 'He must be a man of some consequence, otherwise Louise wouldn't choose to live with him.'

'Perhaps one day Louise will write a story about life in Ethiopia with Zeno – like Karen Blixen's *Out of Africa*. Remember how she used to write stories when she was a girl? They were often about exotic places and people. Places she'd read about.'

'Louise writing about Africa wouldn't surprise me. She takes her responsibilities seriously.' But Gerald still looked worried.

Aboriginal Art

LOUISE AND ZENO's Australian visit was passing quickly. Monica noticed an advertisement for an exhibition of Aboriginal art at an indigenous art gallery in central Adelaide and suggested a visit. Louise recalled Mandy Watson from Oodnadatta and her dot paintings.

They entered the gallery and collected a brochure for the exhibition. And there it was: *Dot Paintings* by Mandy Watson. Then she saw Mandy. She was standing alongside a bright white witchetty-grub painting with its green tracks to waterholes set against an orange, earthy brown-and-black dot background. Louise walked up to her. Mandy was much plumper than before. A loose-fitting blue blouse hung over her belly.

Recognition was instant and they kissed and hugged. Louise introduced Zeno, Gerald and Monica. Mandy told them about her exhibition and volunteered to take them around the gallery. On every wall were her spectacular dot-art works of people, camps, yellow-grass landscapes, dry riverbeds, waterholes, gum trees, frogs, lizards, kangaroos, wallabies, koalas and insects.

Mandy and Louise reminisced about the events of that day at the Crystal Brook farm as if they had been burned into their memory. They even remembered some of the words they had exchanged. Louise realised that Mandy's perception of the land had shaped her own thinking and been with her in Ethiopia.

'Let's exchange addresses so that we can keep in touch, and I'll contact you next time I'm in Adelaide,' Louise said, smiling at Mandy.

'Great, and if we have time perhaps we could go back to Crystal Brook,' said Mandy. 'Relive old times.'

'Of course, of course, when I next get the chance.'

Mandy told Louise how she lived in a suburb on the outskirts of the city, although her husband wanted them to return to his tribal lands in the desert, north of the state. Yet Mandy wanted to stay in Adelaide, continue painting and have her five children go to their local school. Louise soon realised Mandy had no other option than to conform to her husband's plan. She was pregnant again, expecting her sixth in five months' time. Louise wanted to whisper, 'Stay here and go on painting. Choose what *you* want to do.' But she didn't.

Suddenly, Mandy was in a hurry to bring their viewing and discussion to a close and leave with her children as quickly as possible, almost as though Mandy's life was a camp site that had to be cleared. Apparently her husband was waiting in the car. Louise remembered how Mandy had told her that her father's father and his father before him hunted kangaroos in the bush, drank water from creeks and ate sour berries from trees in gullies and how free they were; but with her ancestors' passing how life had changed.

During lunch Louise, Zeno and her parents discussed the exhibition. Zeno was enthralled. He saw in Mandy's art not only evidence of a unique talent, but a message about Australian indigenous life, one he thought comparable to Ethiopia's. Zeno appreciated the boldness of her paintings. He hoped they would meet Mandy again. 'Could there be a better example of indigenous art than this?' he asked.

Conception

LOUISE AND ZENO enjoyed family barbecues in the hills, visited vineyards in McLaren Vale, walked on Southern Ocean beaches and visited Port Elliot's Horseshoe Bay with its old jetty that Louise had jumped from as a child. Louise told Zeno how, on family holidays, they swam across the bay and learned to bodysurf.

'I've never heard of bodysurfing,' admitted Zeno. 'Darling, you'll have to teach me.'

'If it was warmer I'd teach you now,' laughed Louise.

As they strolled Louise told Zeno the history of the bay with its many shipwrecks. 'Nineteenth century square-rigged sailing ships tried to establish anchorage in the bay, but storms swept them onto the granite cliffs.'

'How awful.'

'Yes, it was awful. People drowned trying to get ashore. You can read about it on the history displays that are set up all along the cliff.'

They stopped by a new colourful display board and read about shipwrecks and then some information about 'Southern Right Whales, sighted off the Southern Ocean coast from late May to October'.

They stood on the observation platform and looked for a breaching whale. As the cold breeze bit into them they scanned the ocean, but saw nothing. Zeno's eyes fixed on Louise's with warmth and love. He hugged and kissed her.

❖

They spent a couple of days visiting one of Louise's girlfriends and her husband in the crayfish fishing village of Robe. Zeno communicated easily and her friends soon understood what had attracted Louise to him. Everyone assumed that this highly personable and handsome man was her life partner … even Gerald was now confident that Louise had chosen well.

On their second day in Robe, after breakfast, Zeno and Louise drove east in their hired Suzuki along soft sand tracks above and between wild dunes that fringed the shoreline of pounding waves. They parked their vehicle and walked towards the shore. Holding hands, they climbed steep dunes and tumbled into a hollow. Bliss and winter's morning sun, kisses and peals of laughter escaped their entangled bodies.

'We'll always be together,' said Zeno.

'Yes, and we're all alone here,' said Louise, taking off her sweater and jeans.

'All alone except for that beautiful yacht on the horizon,' joked Zeno.

'If I'm on top I can watch the yacht and you at the same time,' said Louise as she took off her blouse and knickers. Zeno stripped. He lifted her as she clasped her legs around his waist and covered his face with kisses. 'I love you,' she whispered. He lay down; she sat astride him and felt his hardness enter her. Excited, they grasped and pressed their moist bodies as close to each other as possible and ignored the sand and shells sticking to them.

Satisfied, Louise rested her head on Zeno's chest. Then, after half an hour in their dune hideaway, they rubbed the sand off their bodies, dressed and walked hand in hand back across the dunes to their parked vehicle. Louise would always remember that place where she was sure she conceived their child. She also thought fleetingly of Rob and their love in the dunes those years ago.

'One day,' Zeno said, 'we'll come back to these dunes, watch the moon come up and remind ourselves that this is where we made love and vowed to be together forever.'

As their departure loomed, Zeno was invited to give a talk at Louise's Alma Mater, Adelaide University. He was charming and willing to answer questions. He had an instinctive storyteller's knack that was profusely visual, treating his audience to details of Ethiopia's fauna, flora, languages, history and culture, as well as its poverty and potential. His presentation was richly detailed, often humorous.

The news spread that this well-known scholar was briefly in Australia and he received an invitation to address the anthropology and medical faculties in Sydney. Next day they flew to Sydney where Zeno was warmly received. His talk touched upon a variety of health and agricultural needs in isolated rural areas of Ethiopia; it was presented with his usual vigour, interesting anecdotes and without a hint of presenting his people as victims of harsh conditions.

He painted word pictures of Ethiopian people, their huts and living conditions, their resilience and charm. Afterwards, in a meeting with staff, the head of department wondered if he would be willing to return on a visiting fellowship position. Zeno was intrigued but acknowledged his responsibility to his colleagues back home and to his fieldwork centres in Oromia, Amhara, Tigray and the Southern Tribal Lands. His priority, he said, was to give effective voice to a noble people, Ethiopia's rural poor.

Their work together would, she knew, forever bind their relationship. On holiday, surrounded by her family, Zeno had smiled and laughed with ease, enjoying the welcome he felt within the comfortable Davitt home. In Australia his thoughts and dreams were not complicated by his responsibilities and career in Ethiopia. He was stress-free. But he could still hear a voice from inside, perhaps his father's as much as his, reminding him of his responsibilities to his country.

Life Change

SIX WEEKS AFTER their return from Australia they were sitting at their kitchen table late on a Friday morning. Louise had just come back from a visit to the university health centre and Zeno had returned from his university office with papers to work on during the coming weekend.

'I've got something to tell you,' Louise said. 'Prepare yourself.'

'I'm prepared for anything.'

'It's confirmed. I'm pregnant!'

'Well, what have I done to deserve such beautiful news?'

'I think you know.' Louise laughed.

'It's too good to be true ... how wonderful,' he said and walked round the table to embrace her.

'This calls for a celebration. Shall we phone your parents?'

'Not yet, give me another month. And you are the only one who knows, except of course me and the doctor.'

'A child will change our lives. We're seriously united now.' He smiled. 'I'll finish what I'm writing and then I'll take you out for lunch.'

Zeno went to his study. Louise sat at the kitchen table surrounded by her books. She wanted to write and tell her parents her news straight away and also tell Carmen. Sipping coffee and looking out of the kitchen window at their small back garden, she contemplated her place in Ethiopia, and back in London. Her university teaching positions were on her mind. Yet she was thrilled about being pregnant no matter whether she was in Addis Ababa, London or Adelaide. She had dreamed about becoming a mother and now it was real. She thought of Mandy and their children meeting one day. She wondered how the birth of a child might alter their lives.

The most she knew about Zeno's attitude to being a father came from his mother Gabriella, who was silent when she had asked her about Zeno's daughters. Louise tried to picture Zeno as a father in a few months' time, and then the same Zeno five and ten years ahead. They were on an unknown and certainly exciting journey.

In fact, it has been exciting ever since I met Zeno Wolde, she thought, and not just because he's a great lover, or because of our travels and what he has helped me to see and do in Ethiopia. She wondered again about their future. She thought of his fecundity … of the child growing inside her and of Zeno's passion for his country. And she and their child would be there to support him, always.

Soon, another invitation for Zeno to address conferences in Nairobi and Johannesburg arrived. Louise agreed he had to accept. It would be difficult for them to change their routines, especially now their work was so highly regarded, with research grants and conference invitations arriving regularly. Louise continued to have ideas about living in London or San Francisco. But she knew Zeno's commitment to Ethiopia, and prepared for a period of intense activity across East Africa.

Zeno was particularly tender to Louise after their return. She was very fit and her pregnancy proceeded normally. She contemplated flying back to Adelaide for a few weeks but decided that that was out of the question. Zeno was delighted to see how well she was. He paid her many compliments, brought home flowers and bought her tribal icons from markets. He loved the fact that she was collecting these icons and identifying with Ethiopia. Here in their home, the pictures, ornaments and fabrics she had chosen created warmth that Zeno had not previously known.

'I know you're pregnant, but your pace hasn't slackened,' he said one early evening before dinner. 'I can't keep up with you.'

'That's a joke. I always think I have to run and keep infinite hours otherwise I won't keep up with *you*.'

Four years after she began the research, topped off by her time with the Hamar, Louise submitted her thesis. Her doctorate was awarded and her thesis was with a London publisher. Her international reputation was growing. Zeno told her it was an exceptional piece of work and fully deserved the recognition it attracted. A permanent part-time position was offered to her at the University of Addis Ababa with a visiting fellowship in London. She was in high spirits.

At the start of the fourth month of her pregnancy, Louise phoned and told her parents, assuring them she was well. Her parents were delighted and Monica suggested that she would come to Ethiopia for the birth. Louise was pleased, but said it would be preferable for her mother to arrive when the baby was a few weeks old and they had settled into a routine. Zeno told Gabriella that they planned to fly to Nairobi well before the birth. Louise knew his mother was pleased to be informed, although Gabriella probably realised the initiative came from Louise.

Louise had regular check-ups. Her blood pressure and glucose levels were normal, and she had no oedema. She maintained her exercise regime. The child's heartbeat was strong. By the sixth month, just before they flew to Nairobi, Louise saw that people were turning to look at her. Her protruding belly was now attracting attention.

At home she looked at herself in the large bathroom mirror and noticed vigorous movement in her belly. She placed her hand on it and then undid the top button of her blouse and felt her swelling breasts. She imagined she could still walk with the Hamar and climb in the Simien Mountains. If Hamine, the pregnant Hamar girl she had met, could carry twins successfully throughout treks in the Omo and Kaeske valleys, she thought, then I can surely travel to Nairobi and Cape Town, or possibly even make a quick trip to London, and go on working at my usual pace.

Zeno became concerned about her 'no-time-to-lose' attitude which seemed to contribute to an increase in her work rate. There were fresh grant applications to complete, papers for international refereed journals to write, as well as responses to conference invitations. With less than three months to go until the birth, he stood behind her at their kitchen table where she was reading and making notes. He put his hand tenderly on her shoulder.

'Don't you think you should ease up on the pressure you are putting on yourself?

'I'm fine, Zeno, there's nothing to be worried about.' He wasn't convinced.

He had seen so many miscarriages and stillbirths in the rural population. Louise's hectic pace could end that way. For her part, Louise was anxious to allay his fears and convince him that pregnancy didn't reduce her energy and was not a health risk.

Zeno kissed her on the cheek. 'You know how much I love you,' he said. She was ready to receive his full-on-the-mouth kisses. She took his hand and pulled him towards her.

'Okay, you win,' she said, teasing. 'Let's go to bed before making love becomes more than a trifle difficult.'

Needing no more encouragement, he followed her to their bedroom. Zeno stroked the smooth and undulating landscape of her body and they gently made love.

Zeno told Louise that of all the women he had known, she was the one who had all the qualities which, for so long, he had desired in a woman. Their lovemaking, well into her pregnancy, had left him wanting more of her. She treasured his presence. They knew that no differences in their origins or busy and often separate travel would ever set them apart.

Another Project

LOUISE WAS AWARE of how stretched Zeno was but she also knew he did not like to be reminded of it. A few days later, on impulse she asked, 'Do you really think you can take on any more projects?'

'What do you mean?'

'Well, you know the phone message from the Vice-Chancellor's office asking you to meet him to discuss some joint project with the University of Nairobi.'

'Did I tell you about that?'

'You mentioned it briefly, a sort of throwaway line the other morning when you were leaving.'

'We haven't had the meeting yet.'

'Has a date been arranged?'

'Yes, it's tomorrow morning at ten o'clock in the VC's office.'

'Do you know what the agenda is?'

'I'm not exactly sure: it's something to do with a joint research project on agricultural reform and rural health in Ethiopia and Kenya, with our university combining with the University of Nairobi.'

'And what's your role?'

'I've no idea. That's what I'll find out tomorrow. I expect it could be some sort of advisory job, probably based on some of my recent work.'

Louise was silent. This would be another project that could consume him. She wanted him to succeed but didn't want him to spread himself too thinly; she worried he'd get a reputation for not being fully committed to any one project, simply because he was overloaded. But she knew he would reject any consideration that he could not take on more.

◈

Zeno should have felt satisfied with his comprehensive research portfolio. On the morning of his meeting with the Vice-Chancellor he arrived early at his own office to meet two Ethiopian students to discuss their projects, one in the Gambela Province and another up on the Tigray border. He was in a buoyant mood.

'Here we live and here we die,' he exclaimed lightheartedly to his students. 'Ethiopia needs to be open to the world. You will need to find out what's going on in Britain, France, Australia, Canada and of course the US, and bring their best practices here. That is what we need.' They nodded in agreement.

'Have you seen the latest statistics on infant mortality in Ethiopia?' he asked, handing them a copy of a recently published paper in *Anthropology International* and a *Guardian* newspaper article. The articles were wide-ranging but were full of condemnation of the Derg for ignoring the health and education needs of Ethiopians living in remote rural areas.

'The scenes in the lower Omo Valley, in the Simien plateau region and around Korem in southern Tigray are a lot worse than what is described here. And when you see this for yourselves you'll want to secure funding to carry out necessary reforms.'

The students watched him as he leaned forward and, gesturing, said, 'There is one golden rule. When you design aid projects in these rural areas you have to walk before you can run.'

The students showed him their initial plans for setting up joint health and education centres.

'Your ideas are good.' Zeno was enthusiastic. 'But remember this, when you reach your sites in Gambela and Simien, you'll have native people there who know more than you or I will ever know. Even though you are Ethiopians, you will be hurled into a strange world. Tell them about your ideas, but listen carefully to what they tell you, and be ready to modify your plans. Above all, make sure the leaders in their communities are closely identified with your projects.'

'Welcome, Dr Wolde,' the Vice-Chancellor said, his stern demeanour not revealing his intention. 'Please sit down. You know Haimanil, my personal assistant.' She smiled at Zeno.

'I'm pleased to meet you,' Zeno said, smiling back. He sat down in an easy chair across from the Vice-Chancellor.

'How are you keeping, Dr Wolde?'

'I'm well. And you, Vice-Chancellor?'

'Just fine, Zeno.' The Vice-Chancellor was now smiling. It was unusual for him to address a member of his staff by their given name. 'I've some excellent news for you.'

The differences in these two men lay between them like a chasm: the experimenting nonconformist adventurer, sitting opposite his powerful and conformist Derg-appointed Vice-Chancellor. Zeno wondered what the VC's 'excellent news' could be, and whether they might ever bridge their political differences. He did his best to be courteous.

The Vice-Chancellor opened a folder on his desk and pulled out a two-page letter. 'We've had a significant offer of a very well-funded joint project with the University of Nairobi.' He spoke with the controlled air of a bureaucrat who was impressed by his own power.

'That's interesting,' said Zeno. 'I like the idea of joint university projects. It's extraordinary how shared projects can have greater influence on all concerned.'

'This one is to trial and evaluate health and education centres, and initiate reform of agricultural production at a local level,' said the Vice-Chancellor, enunciating carefully. 'What is truly exciting for you is that it is a multidisciplinary project. I am sure you knew that it was being considered, so it won't come to you as a complete surprise.' The Vice-Chancellor was in full swing, almost as if he had designed the project himself.

'Initially the project will be funded for five years. The finance amounts to half a million dollars, and will come from our respective governments, along with significant international aid and a grant from an overseas trust. I'm sure you know about the overseas grant since you helped write the initial application.' The Vice-Chancellor smiled broadly. A flicker of delight passed over Zeno's face.

'Our Minister of Health recalled your fine lecture last year and recommended you to his Kenyan counterpart. They want you to be the project director. And since you are the connoisseur ...' The Vice-Chancellor paused, obviously pleased with his description of Zeno. 'This makes you the obvious choice for the project director.' Zeno wanted to say there were plenty of able people in his field but remained silent. 'You will receive introductions across this country and also in Kenya. Nothing will be put in your way.' He shut the folder slowly as if caressing something precious.

Zeno was stunned. He had dreamed about a project of this nature. He wanted to ask, 'When do I start?' But instead, like a prodigal son, he felt himself welcomed into the university's inner sanctuary and wanted to show his respect for the Vice-Chancellor's evident belief that he could direct such a project.

Zeno's life at this point was already very full and, with Louise's guidance, well ordered. A project of this magnitude would take him away from home. Yet he could not refuse.

'Of course I'm interested and flattered by the suggestion that I be the project leader.'

But before Zeno had a chance to explain his personal situation, the Vice-Chancellor continued. 'I could see your eyes light up when I mentioned the multidisciplinary nature of the project and the fact that it will include Kenyan researchers as well. You will have a chance to influence policy at the highest level.' The Vice-Chancellor paused and smiled at Zeno. 'Don't be afraid of directing the project how you see fit. You will receive additional resources when you believe they are needed. We all want the project to succeed.'

Zeno's was tempted to joke and say, 'So now you expect me to be the university's golden boy,' but he thought better of it.

'You will be expected to finalise the design, choose your research team and the specific sites here in Ethiopia as well as in Kenya.'

'I'd be honoured to do that, but ... I'm already fully committed.' Zeno showed his apprehension. The Vice-Chancellor ignored him.

'There are no buts, Zeno. The government is expecting you to lead this project and give it impetus. Few other anthropologists have your grasp of the issues. This will be a feather in your cap and of course for our university. I'm sure you will blossom as the project gets under way. And please feel free to involve your partner, Dr Davitt. I'm aware she has an excellent reputation in the relevant research areas.'

Zeno suppressed a smile. He was surprised and delighted at the possible inclusion of Louise. The Vice-Chancellor's staff had done their homework. He wanted to rush home to tell her. He had no alternative but to accept the Vice-Chancellor's and the Derg government's offer. It was more of a command than an offer.

'We want you to convene a meeting as soon as possible of your chosen Ethiopian and Kenyan researchers, and indeed anyone else you believe could contribute. Give me an answer in a week so that our minister can announce the project. The government wants you to organise the first meeting with your colleagues here in Addis Ababa and then in Nairobi; the respective government representatives will be invited to attend. The initial funding will last until at least late 1994. My staff will help you with the arrangements. You will need to fly to Nairobi almost immediately to help select their researchers. Their respective departments will be advised as soon as you agree to accept leadership of the project.'

Zeno sat with thoughts teeming through his brain. For him, there was the indescribable pull of the Simien plateau, of Amhara and Tigray and Africa's Great Rift Valley, the nomadic lives of the Masai, Hamar and Banna tribes; the beautiful and seductive women of Ethiopia, along with Kenya's Kikuyu and Luo women. He thought of the books he would devour to give authenticity to the project;

the agricultural and medical reforms he could initiate; the travel he would undertake and the people he would meet. He could not squander this opportunity.

He left the office like a released cage bird and walked to the small café on the edge of the campus to consider his options. Louise was expecting their first child in six weeks and now he would be expected to commute between Addis Ababa and Nairobi and probably Cape Town, Johannesburg and even London. And he already had a full research, supervision and teaching load. He was worried as well as excited. He knew the Vice-Chancellor would not accept any explanation as to why he couldn't lead the project. But he also understood it could alter his life. His physical and intellectual energy would be tested to their limits. There would be no turning back. What would Louise say and how would this project alter her career and their home life? He thought of her smiling eyes and remembered the great flush of delight in her face whenever he returned home or when they met during their working day for time together. In her company Zeno felt invincible.

He considered the offer and the imperative to decide by the end of the week. The VC, he reminded himself, would have left our meeting thinking that I have already accepted. What on earth would happen if I turned it down? I'll have to accept, and promptly. And Louise and I will plan our lives accordingly. He finished his wine, left the café and walked home.

Zeno sat down in his usual chair in their living room.

'You're home early. So what did the VC have to say?'

'You'll never guess. I've been invited to direct a joint Ethiopian-Kenyan project on agricultural and health reform in isolated rural regions.'

'How marvellous! Darling, I'm thrilled for you. That's wonderful. You've worked so hard to achieve this, and project director is what you deserve. No one could direct a project like this as well as you.

We must phone Gabriella and I'll tell Mum and Dad how proud I am of you.' She smiled and embraced him. He held her as excitement pulsed through him.

'When does this project begin?'

'Almost immediately. As soon as it is announced that I'm the project director, I have to fly to Nairobi and interview potential Kenyan research and administrative staff.'

'Will your office be here in Addis?'

'Half in Addis and the rest in Nairobi, at least until the data collection is well under way.'

'How long will that take?'

'At least two years to begin with, but probably longer. Funding is for five years, but if all goes well, then I'm told more resources will be made available.'

Louise realised that Zeno could be working all hours to negotiate agreements, and to select and motivate staff. She felt thrilled for him but uneasy at how his travel and work schedule could affect their lives.

'Let's have a celebratory lunch together and I can tell our baby what a clever person his or her dad is.'

'You flatter me, but you know I like that. Let's eat at the restaurant on the campus.'

Very pregnant, Louise continued to exercise daily by walking morning and late afternoon around the campus. Instinctively, she prepared for the birth.

The Birth

LOUISE WAS FIT and well in the weeks that preceded the birth. Her doctor was confident her baby would go full term. Confirmed as the international project leader, Zeno had twice visited Nairobi. Louise saw how pressured he was, but her questions about his work and how he was feeling were smoothly deflected.

'I'm fine; it's you we should be concerned about. And don't worry, I'll certainly be here in Addis for the birth.'

They understood that for many months a year he would be living in an apartment in Nairobi, supervising data collection in the field in northern Kenya, chairing meetings, advising politicians and producing interim field reports. However much he loved Louise, it would be difficult to maintain the constant intimacy they had enjoyed for the last four years.

With two weeks to go to their baby's birth, they faced dilemmas. As each day rushed into the next, the once barely noticed differences between them became slightly more acute. Zeno had to travel. Louise had to prepare their home for the child. Zeno had to maintain his work rate so that the project was a success. He believed that home was Louise's territory. She realised, with her usual stoicism, that work and travel were Zeno's priority. As the birth neared, both felt like children, anxious and thrilled to soon open a long-hoped-for birthday present.

'The baby is kicking almost all day now. Another week and we'll be parents.' Louise said one night in bed.

'Let me feel him kick.' Zeno rested his hand on Louise's swollen and lumpy belly. 'Oh, that sure is a kick! It must be a boy.'

'It's a lively baby, whatever sex it is,' said Louise.

Zeno's fascination grew as he stroked Louise's bulging belly.

There was always lightness to the way Louise moved even though she was heavily pregnant. He, on the other hand, even when trying to be useful, seemed preoccupied and at times uncharacteristically clumsy. Louise wondered whether he was depressed. She said nothing. On the evening before her final check-up with the midwife, they had their evening meal at home.

'I'll see to dinner; you sit still and rest. You'll have to use all your energy when I'm away for a few days, so conserve it now,' she said smiling.

'Yes, okay, but I'll probably eat out when I'm not visiting you.'

'What a doer you are … always on the move. Only at home when you have to be.'

Zeno, who a minute before had been in the happiest frame of mind, now looked bewildered. He was never easily roused but was irritated by Louise's comment. He glanced at her, and was ready to walk away.

'Sorry darling, I was only teasing. I know that you'll do all that's necessary to be with us when our baby is born.'

Ten days later, at six in the morning, she had her first strong contractions. Zeno drove her to Besegun's Hospital annexe. As she lay in the delivery room with Zeno at her side, she said, 'I hope our baby will be perfect.' Her worried face alerted Zeno.

'Everything is going to be fine,' the midwife said, stroking her forehead. Under mild sedation, Louise slid in and out of dreams about camping on the Coorong, listening to Mandy talking about Aboriginal Dreamtime stories, walking with the Hamar, adopting orphan Ethiopian children. An hour later her waters broke and the birthing began.

'Things are going well,' the midwife said to Zeno, who was silently holding Louise's hand. She thought he looked liked a fish out of water. He flinched as Louise let out a series of groans. She gritted her teeth and her eyes were wild. Zeno looked at her sympathetically. He glanced at his watch. 'We've been here eight hours now and the marathon has only just begun.'

'It's the start of a new life for us,' whispered Louise, between waves of pain.

Zeno saw from the midwife's demeanour that the labour was proceeding safely. In isolated rural villages he had witnessed many deaths of women in childbirth.

'We're doing well; the baby is looking forward to meeting you,' said Louise.

Hour after hour, the midwife checked the baby's heartbeat and assured Louise this new life was almost ready to emerge. Finally, she announced, 'The head is crowning.' Louise, as determined as ever and now in a half-sitting position, drew her knees as wide apart and as close to her chest as possible, hoping to observe the moment of her child's birth. In twenty minutes it was over as Louise felt the baby slip from her.

'It's a boy, a beautiful strong boy,' exclaimed the midwife. Louise watched her as she cut the cord, sponged and wrapped the infant and placed him in the crook of her arm. Louise kissed him, stroked his damp black hair, checked the number of fingers on his hands and lay there happy that he was so perfect. Hearing the baby's strong cry, Zeno kissed Louise and his newborn son.

'He's beautiful, just like you. And we'll now tell him his name.'

They clasped each other as Louise nestled her little boy, her greatest triumph. She had given birth to Joshua – a strong son for Zeno.

Zeno phoned Gabriella with the news and also spoke to his daughters to tell them they had a half-brother.

With Joshua's birth, life for Louise and Zeno changed. Louise took maternity leave from the university, but in six months would return to part-time teaching.

Louise breastfed Josh for the first year. Zeno arranged for Dorolieu, an Ethiopian mother, well known to the university crèche, to look after Josh when Louise was teaching. Often Dorolieu accompanied Louise and Josh when she undertook fieldwork in northern Amhara and in the Southern Nations Region. Besides Louise's travel within Ethiopia, there were two London trips with Zeno in the first years of Josh's life.

Louise wrote to Mandy about Joshua, and two weeks later received a small dot painting canvas for him depicting kangaroos and koalas. 'What a wonderful and generous friend Mandy is,' Louise said to Zeno when they opened the parcel. Zeno, meanwhile, maintained his own travel to and from Nairobi along with presentations in Johannesburg, Cape Town, London and New York. Louise and Josh travelled with him to New York. Josh was a priority; Louise did not want to leave him alone. She took him everywhere with her, saying, 'African mothers carry their children when they work in the fields, when they fetch and carry water, and even when they cook, so I'll do the same.'

When the research project began, Zeno spent little time at home in Addis. When he was home he was like a recovering marathon runner, resting as much as possible, or reading in his study or the university library, or driving to Ethiopian research sites before returning to Nairobi.

10: Infatuation and Crisis

Fashna

IN NAIROBI, IT was customary in Amos' department on Friday nights for Zeno and another colleague, Lewis, to go downtown to a beer and wine bar with a dance floor and lithe Kenyan waitresses. It had an inviting ambience and was a popular venue. One Friday night, four months after Zeno had commenced the project's Kenyan stage, they arrived at the bar to find it was already packed out. They jostled their way in and found some empty seats on the edge of the dance floor. Zeno drank his first beer, sat back and relaxed.

At the next table, an attractive young woman sat alone. She glanced over and then looked directly at Zeno. He returned her smile and invited her to join them.

Zeno smelled her perfume and admired her slim, curved body. Her name was Fashna. He bought her a drink and, heads close together, they talked. After a couple of drinks she suggested they dance. He felt her body press close. One hand shaped the slimness of her waist while the other found the wondrous roundness of her firm buttocks. Dance after dance they held each other, jived and glided.

Zeno had courted Louise with a long-term relationship in mind. This young woman on the dance floor was different; just a night of fun, he told himself.

Fashna told him she had been to university but dropped out and now earned money as a nightclub dancer. She was nineteen years old and from the Luo tribe. When they finally sat down, Zeno gazed at her beautiful, half-exposed breasts. He felt a jolt whenever he caught her smiling or staring at him.

The sudden attraction of Fashna was like shock treatment. His passion for her spread over him every few minutes. He wanted intimacy with her.

'You're drinking rather a lot this evening,' said Amos, aware of how animated his friend had become. 'Slow down a little, it's a long night.'

Zeno ignored the comment. His friends understood that when he'd had a few drinks he could, sometimes, become irrational, and could enjoy having fun with dancers and bar girls – taking what was on offer. He had seen this happen before, but not since Zeno had been with Louise.

'When he drinks too much he's foolhardy, like a different man,' whispered Amos to Lewis. Initially Zeno was too engrossed with Fashna to overhear the comment. But a raised-eyebrow look from Amos brought a response.

'Don't worry about me, I'm fine.' And for the next half hour he talked to his friends as well as to Fashna.

'Don't do anything crazy tonight, will you?'

Now, head to head, Zeno and Fashna talked, hugged and kissed. Zeno lifted his glass and clinked with Fashna's, then winked at Amos.

Amos said nothing more until he was ready to leave. 'Look after him, Fashna,' he said.

'Don't worry, I'll take care of him,' Fashna replied as Zeno fondled her.

'Goodnight Zeno,' Amos said and then stood close to his friend, bent down and whispered, 'Don't be a jerk, Zeno, too much alcohol provokes stupidity.'

'I take your point, but I'm fine,' Zeno drawled.

Amos smiled and gave him an open-handed 'well-it's-up-to-you' gesture, which Zeno ignored.

When his friends left, he and Fashna talked on, sharing a whisky. She asked him what he did and he talked a little about his work.

'At the moment I'm working on improved grain storage and better preparation for severe drought.' Fashna seemed really interested.

As he told her about his work he felt alive and clear-headed. She stroked his hand and he felt her touch through his entire body. They kissed each other gently while his hand rested on her firm breasts.

'Why are you in Nairobi?' Fashna asked.

'I'm on leave from the University of Addis Ababa. I've just started working on a joint university project.'

'I thought you said you were a doctor.'

'I am, so you'll be in good hands.' He grinned.

'That's good to know.' She rested her head on his shoulder.

'Come and keep me company,' he said.

'What, tonight, is that what you're suggesting?'

'Yes, tonight.'

'You're cute,' she said kissing him full on the lips.

'You're beautiful,' he whispered.

They took a cab to Zeno's apartment. In bed that night he entered her from behind, stroking her hair and licking her ears. At that instant their joy was profound and Zeno didn't want it to end. He felt his twenty-year-old youthfulness again.

'Stay close to me,' the naked Fashna whispered as she climbed on top of him, pressing her hips down and arousing him again. They came together, the forty-year-old Ethiopian and the teenage Kenyan. The pleasure and joy they gave each other surpassed anything Zeno believed he had previously experienced – he, an ecstatic, experienced lover, enjoying the body of this lithe young woman.

Breathing heavily, they stroked each other, not wanting to separate. Fashna linked her fingers in his as he gently licked her lips as if their moisture was honey sweetness giving him renewed energy.

A part of Zeno was convinced he loved her. He had been tender with her and such tenderness by a man was a rare experience for Fashna. She loved the way he stroked her buttocks and fondled her breasts. She was wilful and hungry for his penetration and, though only nineteen, was street-wise. For Zeno, this experience was a sexual roller-coaster.

The next morning, they showered, dressed, embraced, drank

coffee and then left for breakfast in a nearby café.

Fashna stayed on in his apartment. She had collected some clothes from her downtown flat and moved in. Zeno reasoned that this move was only temporary. Conscious she had achieved something extraordinary, Fashna revelled in her new life. In the first three weeks she bought their food, cleaned and cooked excellent dinners, chose clothes for him, and ignored his occasional ambivalent feelings towards her. She filled the apartment with flowers. They lived in a state of sexual euphoria. Zeno loved her streetwise magnetism and her youthful and exotic Luo beauty.

His friends worried about his recklessness. There was nothing restrained in Zeno's hyper-erotic view of his relationship with Fashna. He didn't ask about her family and friends. He didn't bother to ask about her previous lovers, and how long they had lasted. He believed their impermanence promised him success, such was his narcissism. Unable to stand back and evaluate what was happening, he could not take stock. He knew the relationship had to end, but not how or when.

Initially, Zeno was secretly if not crazily proud of the fact that he had attracted such a beautiful young woman, one who satisfied him and looked after him while he was away from home. They made love each night. 'I love the way you fuck me,' she would whisper as she kissed and licked his ears and Zeno, lying in damp delight, became her conspirator, eagerly anticipating his next penetration. Fashna, with her considerable stamina, knew how to sustain the act and enhance the thrill of their intimacy.

Yet, eventually, she started to bore him. There was a price to pay. She wasn't capable of the challenging conversations he had with Louise. Fashna said very little that interested him, other than to tell him about her other men, those who were often violent and sometimes left without paying; none, she told him, were as respectful and affectionate as him. He felt trapped.

Zeno asked himself … does she love me or all men who enjoy her body? But Zeno still marvelled at her naked beauty: sensuous, beautiful Fashna. In close proximity, he knew his desire for her could well up like a spring that never ran dry. Yet if Fashna stays here, he surmised, she will smile, wink, press herself against me and I will give in. While I feel a strong desire for her, I must not abandon Louise and Josh. I've made a dreadful mistake. I'll tell Fashna to leave and I'll return to Louise and Josh for a few weeks. Fashna will understand. I'll never do that again … But perhaps, later on, perhaps I could still meet her occasionally? This was Zeno, man of paradox, man of kindness, hope and ambiguity, man of passion and friend-ship, man of grace and vehement dreams, who never wanted to hurt anyone, least of all a woman.

Louise phoned during the third week of his liaison with Fashna. She suggested she and Josh come and stay for a few weeks. He told her it was not necessary, as in another week's time he would return home for at least two weeks. By then Fashna, devoid of his company, would have left. He would arrange that.

Zeno returned to Addis and stayed for three weeks, spending time at home, playing with Josh and having family outings. Louise was thrilled. Zeno was apprehensive. He had to think about hug-ging her – nothing seemed spontaneous. The memory of Fashna lingered. He concentrated on being as positive and loving as possible in his relationship with Louise. They made love. Yet, he felt a degree of shame surrounding sex with her, something he'd never before experienced. In time, he told himself, he would quell the memory of Fashna along with the raft of his own underlying guilty feelings about his affair.

Advised by Amos that Fashna had left his apartment, he won-dered why he had become involved in a relationship that could have changed his life. He realised that when he first saw Fashna's beauty, he had lost all control.

A Compromise and a Dream

IT WAS SPRING. There had been presentations for Zeno and Louise back in London and New York and they met Haawkon again, this time in London. Louise spent a month in Adelaide with Joshua and enjoyed another happy meeting with Mandy and her children.

The following year Louise's parents visited when she and Zeno were in London. Her brother Geoff was now an international banker expecting a contract posting to London. Louise wondered if Zeno could also get a permanent position there. She did not expect he would agree to work full-time back in Australia but a London appointment was surely a possibility. And then perhaps Haawkon could get him a London, Geneva or Paris position with Médecins Sans Frontières. Zeno was well qualified for such a position.

Louise had to admit she would like to live away from Africa for a while She wasn't bored with Ethiopia. In fact she loved the country and its people. She had many friends there. But time in London or Paris would, she thought, give her access to old friends and therefore to a version of herself which she felt she had suppressed lately. She missed the freedom of life on the family farm at Crystal Brook which she'd loved as a child. Then there were long walks in the English coun-tryside which ended with a pub meal with old friends. In London she could meet former colleagues and, she thought, would be able to enjoy easier access to Paris, with its landmarks and galleries.

It was all tempting. She longed to take a break. Everything is my responsibility here, she thought. Then she reasoned, I'm being unfair to Zeno – so, it's easier for me to keep quiet. After all, he wants to stay in East Africa. Being in Ethiopia and Kenya was what drove Zeno, gave him identity. An overseas position, however prestigious, would not satisfy him. Occasionally he would discuss the idea but then argue, 'There's nothing overseas that I cannot achieve here.'

So in early 1994 they adopted a temporary compromise: Zeno would stay on for one more year at the University in Nairobi to finish the Kenyan aspect of the project; he would give presentations in Cape Town, Johannesburg and Kampala and would travel regularly back to stay at home in Addis Ababa. And Louise and Joshua would visit him in Nairobi. At the end of that year they would then decide whether to remain working in Addis or seek an overseas appointment.

One night, before Zeno left to begin his last year in Nairobi, Louise had a despairing dream. She was following a tall dark man, who could be Zeno, down a grey-green corridor through room after room and then out into warm night air, into wild savannah country. Then the man's image dwindled and he was out of sight and she was being comforted by her mother stroking her hair to calm her against visions of the circling savannah's lions, leopards and hyenas. She woke suddenly, wanting to scream with fear. Zeno was still asleep.

She got up, walked around the house, showered and dressed, brooding on the mysterious territory of her dream. She told Zeno but he said it was probably a momentary fantasy and she should forget it.

But at night, alone in bed, for weeks to come, she was sure she could hear padding feet and a lion's roar. Stuck fast with terror, she would bury her head in her pillow. She remembered the dream vividly, but as her anguish diminished she would wake in the morning and the walls of her bedroom were as familiar and homely as before. And Zeno was still with her, travelling and achieving, which was his way of telling her that everything was fine, that the project would end and their family life would be happier than ever.

'Woe to the man when all men speak well of him'

IT WAS 1994, the fifth and final year of Zeno's Ethiopia-Kenya reform project. The Derg had been deposed in May 1991 and a reformist government led by the Tigrayan Meles Zenawi was established. Zeno's life continued as if nothing had changed. He was a respected high-flyer, impressing all before him. Praise, invitations and awards rained on him. And this, in part, started his troubles. Amos, on one occasion, quoted to him the remark, 'Woe to the man when all men speak well of him.' He tried to make Zeno analyse what was happening in his life. But Zeno would not listen.

At times, when events were out of his control, he behaved inexplicably, as in his relationship with Fashna. He was tormented by the thought he might never have sufficient time to complete this project to different ministers' satisfaction, not to mention his own. As demands on his time piled up, any sense of joy disappeared.

Initially, total project responsibility was what he wanted, believing he was the only one who fully understood how the project's aims could be achieved. He felt he could never be too far away from his desk and fieldwork sites.

In the latter years of his relationship with Louise, and certainly since the beginning of the Ethiopia-Kenya Project, Zeno had begun to fret. His coming and going, largely between Addis and Nairobi but also Cape Town and Johannesburg, depended on no one but himself. He chose his own timetable. His days were full to overflowing. He felt his father alongside him, bearing witness to his mission.

When addressing seminars, research teams and conferences, Zeno could easily pull himself together, but he became increasingly stressed as acclaim drove him on. Louise and Josh appeared less and less significant. All the travelling affected his relationship with them; he would sort it all out one day, he thought, but not now.

At times he was like a crazed man on a runaway horse. He often worked sixteen or more hours a day. He became obsessed with thoughts of future acclaim because his initiatives would eventually feed a million souls who had previously starved. Amos' warnings still niggled but Louise had said she didn't mind him spending so much of his time in Nairobi, if it was necessary. She wanted him 'to fulfil his dreams'. Neither Amos, nor Louise, knew exactly what was on his mind.

Zeno thought of the time left to achieve his goals, counted years against his age. He researched other anthropologists and worried that he might not have sufficient time to emulate them. He thought he was the only one who could prevent famine and eliminate high rates of infant mortality. Sometimes he verged on euphoria. But in quiet moments, tiring under the heavy load, he experienced darkness.

As his disillusionment grew, the prospect of failure became unbearable. He contemplated entering the houses of the rich in Addis Ababa and Nairobi and haranguing them about wealth earned on the backs of the poor. He bemoaned that there was no justice, and politicians were only interested in their own glory. He brooded.

At home, Louise thought Zeno looked exhausted. One evening she took his hand to lead him to see Josh asleep. But he held back. 'Perhaps it would be better in the morning,' he said. 'I'm very tired … Just a brief look then.'

'Poor Zeno,' she whispered, 'you've had an exhausting day.'

'Not really. I've just had a long day.' He thought how Louise had changed, quite unlike the young woman he had first met. Yet physically she had changed little. Often, when they had first lived together, he had told himself that to be loved by Louise Davitt was happiness itself.

'What's wrong, Zeno? I'm not sure I like what is happening to us – being separated so much and me wondering if you are well and wishing I could be with you.'

'What would you prefer? That I give up my work and tell the Vice-Chancellor and governments I'm incapable of completing the project and that someone else should take over?'

'You're not incapable. I'd never, ever say that.'

'Wake up, Louise. This is a life's work. This is the cutting edge for influencing change in my country. Nothing less!'

This sudden aggressiveness was unknown to Louise. In the past she had been very good at taking him out of his black moods and gently nurturing his self-confidence. Her usual response to his agitation would have been to discuss his work with him, but now she withdrew in silence. They were like strangers in the same house.

Louise told herself she must be patient; that Zeno was tired, overworked, stressed and living with huge responsibilities. In time, he would be his old self again. But what if she was wrong? Perhaps, there was a more sinister explanation for his aggressiveness, his withdrawal.

'Zeno,' she asked, 'perhaps you have malaria, and you don't know about it?'

Angrily, he replied, 'Have you gone mad? I don't have a disease.'

Louise, did not respond. She wanted to say, 'Don't torment me, for God's sake. I beg you, tell me what's happened.' Instead, she asked, 'Why don't you have a break? Take a rest from all your travel and lobbying. Stay at home with us for a few months. You know Josh would love that. Perhaps we could have a few weeks together back in Australia. Mum and Dad would be thrilled. We could find a few weeks, couldn't we? You enjoyed it so much last time.'

Wide-eyed, he stared at her. 'What are you talking about?'

Louise continued, 'You said how you enjoyed your early morning walks, the sound of the surf and seeing the flocks of cormorants. We could be together and do all that again. Let's have a break back in

Australia. We can afford the fares and Josh could spend time with his grandparents and cousins.'

'No, Louise. I must go back to Nairobi, at least for a short while, to finish the project.'

'Why go back when you're so tired? Stay here with us, rest and gain strength. And you have good friends in the medical profession in Addis. You might consult them.'

'No, I have to return. How many times must I tell you, I'm not ill.'

Every emotion he'd withheld from her since the start of the Kenyan arm of the project, every grimace, brooding look, every turning away, every denial was across his face. It was as if he'd been cornered and further withdrawal was his only escape.

'And we are meant to continue to live our lives here separate from you?'

He did not respond. 'Zeno, we miss you. Terribly.'

'And I,' he muttered, 'miss you.'

'You do … or perhaps you don't.' Louise was anxious. It was not like him to avoid questions about their life together. He fingered a book on the table and glanced vacantly at her.

'Zeno, why are you withdrawing from us? You must know how much we love you.'

Even after many years, he wondered if she knew something about Fashna.

A silence fell. Louise saw a nervousness, an agitation, as if he was in a desperate hurry. He looked ill. Was Zeno on the edge of breakdown and disintegration? she wondered. Had she really cornered him? Was he feeling he had no escape? 'Please, Zeno, answer me. It's not like you to ignore me.' Zeno moved from the table and looked out of the window.

'Do you have a better idea than us having a short trip back to Australia? Your tiredness would disappear.'

Zeno continued to stare out the window. Louise felt she now didn't know him at all. Yet she persisted.

'Australian universities would like to hear from you again.'

He wished he was back in Nairobi, away from her questions about his health.

Louise's once sparkling eyes were sad. In the evening light, she looked strained, older than she was. She gazed at him, recalling their tender love. At that moment Zeno thought about what he'd done with Fashna in his first months in Nairobi, down to the very last detail. He was a man, so why should he regret his sudden infatuation, that brief fling?

No memories of his once tender and fulfilling sex with Louise entered his mind. His body ached and his feelings were paralysed. He had no energy. He couldn't find his voice. He needed to escape.

She was tempted to ask him, 'Do you remember on my first trip to Addis – how you invited me to your office and gave me that treasured book?' She wondered if she had taken him for granted, changed in appearance, developed faults in herself. Had he found another woman?

A week later Zeno was still silent. When I'm back in Nairobi, he thought, I can get my mind off my constant tiredness. He would return to Louise and Josh when he felt well again. He was too embarrassed to admit how unwell he felt. He had lost weight and his clothes were beginning to hang off him. People noticed.

He strongly believed that natural medicines could cure his lethargy and reduce the increasing pain in his joints. In Kenya's Nyambene Hills there was an alternative natural medicine centre, with a fine record of restoring people to good health. They will treat me, and no one there will know me, he thought.

In the weeks that followed, Zeno was distant but tried to be cordial. He worked in the university library, supervised surveys in Ethiopian sites, often disappearing for a few days then, thoroughly exhausted, returned home for meals and sleep.

Even when Zeno came home again Louise's days became longer

and lonelier. She struggled to deal with his depressive behaviour. Over a late-night cognac, on an evening before he was due to return again to Nairobi, she said, in the most cheerful voice she could muster, 'I'm sorry, Zeno, but I think that part of your not feeling well is that you take on too much. You must know you are depressed, even if just a little.' And then very quietly she said, 'You're wearing yourself out. You must get help. Please, please get help.'

He ignored her.

'Zeno, are you listening to me? Without knowing the cause of why you feel unwell, you can't come up with a cure. Why don't you see a doctor? I'll make an appointment for you while you're here in Addis.'

Not wanting to cause more friction between them, he replied, 'I promise you, I'll see a doctor as soon as I get back to Nairobi. And anyway, in three months this arm of research will be over and I'll be back here fit and well.'

'I'll certainly look forward to that. Remember, I care very much what you're doing and how your health is.'

He cast a quick glance at her – the briefest tender moment. She looked at him, absorbed and apprehensive.

'Listen, Louise, I'm not sick, just very tired.' He changed the subject. 'When do you expect to get a response for your last paper? The one about the health needs of people living on the Simien plateau? I thought it was really good and would be well received.'

'Zeno, you're a lovable zombie. Are you ignoring my questions by asking for a progress report on my work?' Louise smiled and leaned forward for a kiss. Zeno pretended not to notice.

'We don't need to talk anymore about my health,' he said coldly.

'Okay, then have a break from your endless commitments. You never turn down a request and then become everyone's servant and, in the process, you're exhausted.'

'How am I supposed to run an internationally funded research program and try to have our findings applied if I'm not present? And what's more, when I'm not guiding the projects, then mistakes are made and the funding bodies, as well as the politicians, will doubt my credibility. And then funding will cease.' Zeno had raised his voice.

Louise wanted to say, your credibility is never at stake, it's your health that's at stake. But she said instead, 'Let's kiss Josh goodnight and then get some sleep. I don't want to clash with you, you should know that.'

'I'm sorry, Louise, I don't want to clash with you either.' In silence they went to bed.

Perhaps, wondered Louise as she undressed, Zeno's falling asleep is his way of protecting himself against the unbearable.

Crisis

IN BED, LOUISE listened to Zeno's breathing and reached to touch him. She whispered, 'I will always be with you.' He didn't respond. She assumed he was asleep.

As dawn broke, she stretched and, moving close to him, locked her legs in his, noticing some unusual faint red blotches on his skin. Zeno rolled over and grasped her.

'I love you,' whispered Louise. 'I love you, Zeno.'

He did not reply but mumbled dully and then buried himself in her flesh, a brief return to their once tender lovemaking.

Despite their nakedness, Zeno's will for loving Louise seemed burned out. He stared owlishly at her and thought he had appeased her. The exquisite pleasure they once both enjoyed had faded. Louise realised he was very tired; his mind and body were not in unison. She thought back to when she first gazed at his smooth-skinned, beautiful, tight-muscled body. She remembered his vigour, passion and youthfulness – something she no longer sensed. She wanted to hear him say he loved her. The man she once knew had become someone else.

Louise thought about the old Zeno: the forthright weaver of stories and dreams for a new Ethiopia; Zeno the profound thinker, whose idealism and fortitude had enabled him to navigate the precarious balance between tradition and current day politics, between famine and plenty, dreams and reality. Zeno the caring partner who continued to counsel her so gently and constructively regarding her near rape by the Hamar man. *That* Zeno must return to her.

Louise walked on eggshells but she persisted, reminding him of what a successful team they were. But as always now, the air was heavy with tension. It might have been better if they had openly quarrelled and a victor was declared.

Does Zeno now feel suffocated in his relationship with me? she asked herself. Why won't he talk about how unwell he is? The Hamar women don't seem to have these problems. Perhaps I'll join the Hamar tribe again. After all, she thought, the women's whippings are a demonstration of their love and commitment, and once the bloodied whipping is over they get on with life. Louise detested these whippings, but for a moment she wondered if Hamar women avoided the torment she was experiencing. She had no way of knowing how to resolve her relationship with Zeno.

She was still wondering what to do as she prepared breakfast and packed Josh's schoolbag. In the street she heard a dog barking, the call to morning prayers at a nearby mosque, and the sound of traffic. Louise needed time and a place to think, so after she dropped Josh off at his school she did not return home immediately.

A month later, back in Nairobi, Zeno knew he was seriously ill. He decided to seek traditional herbal medicine far away, where he could be anonymous. Prior to this he had continued to hope that his immune system would conquer his illness. After all, he was Zeno Wolde, fit adventurer and change-maker. Now, he had no choice, and the stigma, that mark of disgrace and condemnation, weighed on him. In his depressive mood he believed that Louise and Josh didn't need him anymore.

He left that morning for the university and then a visit to Gabriella, sensing that, at the alternative medicine health camp he would be being hurled into a different world.

11: Premonition

Agitation

AFTER THREE DAYS back in Nairobi, Zeno went see his mother. He was feverish and she told him he did not look well. He tried to reassure her, but his self-confidence and thoughts did not cohere. His mother wanted to know about Louise and Josh, and more pertinently what might 'let light back through his mind'. She was gentle but quite direct. He sensed she understood more than she knew.

'Zeno, where are Louise and Josh? Why are they not here with you? You must know I like to see them. What have you been doing? What has happened?'

'Do you want to quarrel with me?' he asked sharply. He was agitated. His mother was amazed. Never had he looked like this or spoken to her in this manner.

Zeno knew she was hurt by his agitation. She kept her eyes and words under control. A stab of pain passed through him; he felt acutely alone. Gabriella gave him a sad smile.

'I'll get our dinner,' she said. 'We'll eat in the kitchen; we can have a little time to ourselves, just the two of us.' She spoke in a hopeful voice and set the table while Zeno sat silently. She stroked his head as she served their meal which they ate in near silence. Gabriella decided to take the focus off him.

'This suburb's not as peaceful as it used to be. It seems to be changing for the worse in so many ways. My neighbours have had cars stolen; our church garden has been damaged. And people just don't seem to care.'

'I believe you, Mother,' he said, but again fell silent.

'And the worst of all,' said Gabriella, 'is that the police are never around when we need them and then some people think that even petty crime is all the government's fault. Blame the government, that's what they do, and that's not the answer. It's all very confusing.'

Gabriella really wanted to ask her son why he appeared so sad and unwell, but she continued talking about her own life. She wanted to bridge the distance between them.

'My friends,' she continued, becoming agitated herself, 'my friends at the church are all worried about that horrid disease which they tell me is spreading. Do you know much about it?'

Perspiring now, Zeno appeared distraught and could not bring himself to respond.

'But what I do know,' Gabriella continued, feeling a deep pang of sorrow for her son, 'is that it's up to your medical people to find a cure for it, just as they have for my asthma. In time they will cure you, I know that.' Her efforts to get him to talk about his illness were futile. She realised a significant power had hold of his mind.

His once strong voice was no longer the same and, she thought, he keeps giving me wild looks and seems oddly absent. It was as if he were listening not to her words but to a tragic event coming from far, far away, menacing and inevitable.

Zeno recognised that Gabriella was an ideal mother who would sacrifice everything for him. He breathed heavily and gripped the arms of the carver chair to control his trembling hands. He would control his trembling if he could, and try to curb his increasing anxiety. Even in the warmth of Gabriella's home he felt cold and experienced spasms of shivering which he did his best to disguise.

'I can't say anything at the moment, I'm just very tired. Very tired.'

'Well, go to bed, Zeno, have a good sleep and tell me about Louise and Josh in the morning.'

'I will.'

She wondered if he'd lost his mind as she looked again at the wretched shell of him.

Zeno slept that night in his mother's small back bedroom. He lay on his back staring anxiously in the darkness, stark images and humiliating scenes whirling through his thoughts. He was hot and sweating now. He threw back his blanket but soon was cold again. He could die of the condition. For the first time he recognised the symptoms but didn't want anyone to know about his illness. The stigma was shameful. He must keep it secret. He worried about Louise. He would deal with the fallout. This disgrace, this indignity, would have to be dealt with and must not be associated with his mother's home, as she too would be condemned.

It's a sad and sordid affair, he thought. I was led on, fooled by Fashna the dancer. He wondered also about the Masai masseuse he'd met before, and others as well. Was he just another victim of the disease sweeping the continent? Was he, Dr Zeno Wolde, part of the now rampant epidemic? Was Fashna to blame? Not really. If it was from her, she did not infect him on purpose. And for years since he'd slept with her he'd been well. He wondered about tracking her down to find out if she was well.

If he met her he would be furious. Yet he realised he had courted this disaster. He was the weak one, the imbecile. He wanted to punish himself.

He tried to disentangle his thoughts. Is Louise unwell? He resolved to deal with his illness and when he'd recovered, return to Louise and Josh and his friends, and spend time with his family back in Australia. He would do that. After all, the disease did not belong in his body. He thought of how their life together could still be happy – perhaps they could even have a brother or a sister for Josh. When he had beaten the disease he would be ready for anything.

Zeno made up his mind to leave before dawn and go to the Revival Health Centre (RHC) in the Nyambene Hills. He hoped they would cure him. He had already made tentative arrangements and would put his faith in this place. Their medicines would invigorate him and no one would know. There were discriminatory laws and policies which alienated and excluded people living with the condition. Stigma existed, even in healthcare settings. Could he outrun the stigma? He must not be known as a SLIM, that early term used across Africa for the wasting disease of HIV/AIDS. People so identified were denounced. He did not want Louise and Gabriella to ever know. Society, especially in Ethiopia and Kenya, could shut its doors to his family, should it become known he had the virus. Zeno also knew that people across Africa, particularly women sex workers, had been killed when it was known they had the virus. When I am cured, he thought, I will put my knowledge to good use; I will write a book describing how my disease was cured.

He arose just before dawn and left Gabriella's house with no farewell kiss or comment for his mother. He knew she sensed he was very ill and would have liked to look after him, but he wanted to protect her. My presence will only arouse disgust, he thought.

As he walked to the bus depot, the dark outline of houses enclosed him in shadows. He felt disoriented, dizzy. He thought of Louise and Josh, and brought his hands to his lips and then limply lifted them in the air as if to send a kiss over the land north to them at home in Addis.

The ascending sun gradually brought colour to the buildings and emerging traffic, but in his depressed stupor he hardly noticed. I have made up my mind to get well. I'm going to win this battle on my own. No one must know, no one must know, no one, he told himself as he stumbled on.

His anxiety increased as he approached the depot. Exhausted and riven with fear, he felt stranded, alone, helpless and shivering on this mild spring Nairobi morning.

Realisation and Confession

Zeno had been gone for over a month. A search by the Nairobi police had failed to find him and no one had responded to recent missing persons' notices. Sometimes at night, when Louise turned off the light, she thought he was alongside and turned to kiss him. There were moments when she gave way to grief and perpetual uncertainty. Is he is a ghost? A starving villager? Was he mauled by a lion? Does he have a lover? She rehearsed his arrival: 'Darling, I'm so glad you're home. I won't let you go away again.'

Louise needed wise counsel from a close and trusted friend, someone who could provide compassion and guidance. She phoned Gabriella who was worried but said that she expected Zeno would return, like he always did. That was also her hope. Louise remembered her grandmother Margaret's advice that 'resilience is a quality created by difficulty'. Her grandmother had told her before she left for Ethiopia how she admired people who were *disciplined by hardship*. 'I find them realistic,' she had said. 'They are not easily daunted and they make few claims.' Louise wished Margaret could appear right now. 'Do not complain,' she would say. 'Learn how to deal with your loss.' How do I do this? Louise wondered.

She thought of sharing her feelings with Bezawit, but she was pregnant again and living in Arba Minch. She wished her parents, her grandmother, or even Haawkon could be with her at this moment. She decided to phone Zeno's close Kenyan friend, Amos Oginwa, in Nairobi.

'Amos, its Louise.'

'Louise, good to hear you. Sorry, I still haven't heard from Zeno. How are you?'

'Not good, Amos. I need your help.'

'I'll help you anytime.'

'Amos, it's a month since Zeno disappeared. To begin with, you told me you thought he was still in Kenya. Since then I've heard nothing and I feel abandoned. Not by you, because I know you've made enquiries. But I need to know what's happened to him and how he was when he lived in Nairobi.'

'Louise, we need to talk face to face. It's no good over the phone.'

'Can we meet here in Addis ... or in Nairobi?'

'Yes, of course. I'll come to Addis this coming Friday afternoon. That's easy for me. We should have discussed Zeno much earlier but we both thought, knowing how tough and determined he is, that he would be back before now. And although the university and police have undertaken a wide-ranging search, unfortunately there has been no news.'

'At the moment, Amos, I don't think he's going to come back to Josh and me. But that doesn't mean we don't still love him. We're missing him terribly.'

After his flight from Nairobi, dusk was falling when Amos reached her apartment. They sat facing each other over coffee at her kitchen table. Louise almost cried but controlled herself as well as she could.

'I'm so glad you're here.' She stared at him, tense and frowning.

Amos gazed across the table. He reached out and touched her hand. 'Please ask me anything about Zeno, although I really don't know any more than you since he disappeared.'

'I've had my suspicions, Amos, about what might have been happening while Zeno was living in Nairobi. When he returned each time, it was as if he didn't want to be near me. And he barely showed any interest in Josh.'

Louise knew Amos had a deep-seated kindness, especially when

274

it came to being with someone in distress. Would he share what he knew?

'Amos, I have imagined Zeno sleeping with prostitutes.' She heard her voice trembling. Her body ached. She felt emptier than she had ever felt. In ceasing to be loved as intimately as she had been with Zeno, she felt the loss immensely and with it came an inescapable, vacant loneliness.

'You see, Louise,' said Amos, frowning, 'it's a difficult thing you are saying, that Zeno slept with prostitutes. That wasn't his habit, although, very briefly, he did have a lover in Nairobi. And it's embarrassing for me to tell you this.'

Why would Zeno have another woman? Louise appeared in a trance, momentarily oblivious of Amos' presence. She felt the humility of being betrayed by the man she loved, as if she were just a conduit to another woman. She stared at Amos, then at the table, then back again to Amos.

'Take your time, Louise,' he said as he sat on the edge of his chair, placed his hands on the table and leant towards her.

When preparing for Amos' arrival, Louise had wondered whether she should reproach him for keeping matters about Zeno's life in Nairobi from her. Confused, her thoughts wandered; somewhere out there, Zeno could be fighting for his life. Or, perhaps he's still in Nairobi and sleeping with this other woman. Round and round her thoughts ran.

'You know Zeno well, don't you?' she asked.

'I think I know him as well as it is possible for one man to know another.'

'Do you admire him?'

'It is impossible to know him as well as I do and not to admire him. Zeno is a remarkable man.'

Louise fixed her gaze on Amos. 'Where is he now?'

'I don't know, I really don't know. He has not confided in me since he left to stay with you back here in Addis. The university has told the police about his disappearance, and I understand they have contacted his former wife, Makena. Also, I had a call from Haawkon Davos in London, wondering why he had not heard from Zeno.'

'Yes, Haawkon is a good friend and must be worried about Zeno.' After a brief pause Louise asked, 'Did Zeno want a permanent relationship with this woman?'

'Louise,' he replied, looking at her steadily, 'I am guilty of not confiding in you, or even raising alarm bells. Yes, Zeno lived with this other woman but only briefly – a matter of a few weeks when, almost five years ago, he first commenced the project. I tried to reason with him and hoped his infatuation would be temporary, so that the old Zeno we know and love would return. The relationship didn't last.'

Louise sighed and hung her head. 'I had thought of flying to Nairobi, so we could be with him …'

'Zeno was not the same the night he met this woman. He had had too much to drink, and …'

'Don't worry Amos. It's not your fault. It's Zeno who has caused this – you must have been as helpless as I am.' Louise felt hurt. Yet she was not prepared to abandon him. He was her partner, the father of their son. She needed to know more.

'When did it start and how long did this relationship last?'

'I don't know the fine details. All I know is that for a few weeks in Nairobi in about December 1989, a young Kenyan woman moved in with him. Her name I believe was Fashna. She did not stay long, three weeks or maybe a month at most.'

'Was she studying at the university? Did he see her again, sleep with her again after she left his apartment?'

'I have no idea – I don't think so.'

He put his hand in his pocket, took out his handkerchief and wiped his brow, then covered his eyes as if at that brief moment he didn't want to look at her.

'From what I understood she wasn't a student,' he said quietly with a slightly embarrassed look. He didn't want to say anything against Zeno, but also he didn't want to hurt Louise. And she did not want to put further pressure on Amos – he was her only possible link to Zeno.

'Amos,' she said timidly, looking at him as he gazed sympathetically at her, 'I am hurt. I cannot ignore what has happened but I still love Zeno and will do my best to rebuild our life together, even though our relationship cannot be the same as before.' He nodded. 'Amos, can you find Zeno for me?'

'I'll certainly try. I'm not sure I'll find him, but I'll try.'

'I understand from his mother that he stayed one night with her before he disappeared. Do you want his mother's address?'

'I think I have it, but give it to me again and I'll contact her.'

'Thanks.'

'Why don't you phone her? I'm sure she'd want to hear from you.' Amos was persuasive.

'I phoned her a week ago. She told me he was ill when he stayed with her. I didn't press her because Zeno could suddenly return and my account of his disappearance would look stupid.'

'When I get back, I'll check again with the university administration and with his colleagues to see if they have any news. When I left Nairobi this afternoon, Zeno had been listed by the police as a missing person. I'll talk to them again.'

'And I'll keep in contact with Gabriella and will visit her.' She leaned towards Amos, her fears now unrestrained. She began to cry. 'Zeno wouldn't tell me, but when he left us to return to Nairobi I could see from his face that he was very ill.'

Amos grimaced and wanted to say that he'd known too, but how could he? He didn't want to increase the sense of unease, and the truth was they had no clear evidence that something terrible had happened to Zeno. And what if he suddenly returned?

'I must go. We could meet tomorrow morning after you take Josh to school, if you want to.'

'Yes, let's do that. In the café at the western end of the university campus, you know the one? Would nine o'clock suit you?'

'Yes, I know it. See you at nine.'

Disappearance – 'It's never too late to build bridges'

After Amos left, Louise's sleep was intermittent. She felt a strange pain in her knees and hips and had a sore throat which was most unusual for her. All night she asked herself: where is Zeno, why has he disappeared, who is he with, is he dead? Why has he suddenly become invisible, and nobody knows what has become of him? If he's dead, where and how has he died? Has anyone seen his grave? Please, please give me some answers.

She dreamt. In a dream, she was walking home late one afternoon through the Addis university precincts and she saw Zeno. He was walking ahead of her and was exquisitely dressed. She hurried to catch up with him. He turned and faced her.

'What's all this for? Why are you here?' he asked, his cold gaze sweeping over her. 'What do you want?'

Louise stood closer. 'Talk to me, Zeno', she said, pleading. He said nothing and just stared. She told him of her suspicions, that he had a liaison with another woman in Nairobi – a prostitute. But he denied her accusation. 'It's fanciful,' he said. 'Don't you know how much I love you?'

Then he disappeared as in a fading film. Her state changed from brief but confused bliss to incomprehensible sorrow. She cried. It seemed that the whole of her former life had been like the unrealistic kingdom of Amhara's isolated and inaccessible Garden of Peace, replete with every luxury. She shook herself, and then, distressed, she woke. One moment she was mournful, the next hurt and angry.

Had Zeno disappeared in order to live a different life with the young Kenyan woman? Had he abandoned her and, if so, should she, could she, give up looking for him? She wanted desperately to continue being loved by Zeno, and to have Joshua loved too by his father.

Early morning, before dawn, she rose and, knowing that Zeno had stayed with his mother before he went missing, she decided to write to him there. He'll respond to a letter, she thought, he always has done. Seated at the kitchen table she wrote:

Dear Zeno,

Yesterday evening I sat in our small backyard garden under the old gum tree and gazed at our fruit trees in bloom. They seemed to quiver and breathe in the quiet evening air. I so wished you were here with us.

But at night, I lie alone in an empty bed in a house that is strange for Josh and me without you. When the morning sun pours its brightness through the windows, I'm reminded of the inescapable fact that without you, loneliness surrounds me, and no warming sun brings you here, although you should know I still imagine you with me.

Please send me news of how and where you are. You must know how much I love you. It's never too late, never too late, Zeno, to build bridges if something has come between us – something that you need to tell me about but are fearful of my response. You know me well enough to realise that despite the inevitable pain, I can ride the torment, knowing that, when we overcome whatever has happened, we shall together be stronger and closer than ever. I know in my heart this can happen.

As ever, I still want to be your life partner. I'm the mother of your beautiful son, always your friend, colleague and lover. That is how we have fashioned our lives. You were and are unique to me – such a source of love, and inspiration. Please write to me soon and tell me how and where you are.

Sending my love as ever, your Louise

Louise put down her pen. Perhaps, she thought, the time hasn't yet arrived for Zeno to return and show himself to us again. But for the moment there was little to be gained by staying in Addis; her older brother Geoff and his wife Sophie were in London now and urged her to visit, if only for a short while until Zeno returned. She would tell Amos and Gabriella where she and Josh would be staying in London.

Three weeks later in early November she flew to London to see Geoff and Sophie. Their children, Josh's cousins, would be marvellous company for him. Carmen was in London and, as Amos had advised, Haawkon Davos, while still working for Médecins Sans Frontières, now had a permanent position at the London School of Tropical Medicine.

Return to London

Geoff had insisted she take a break, however brief, from her hectic professional and personal life. But, despite her delight at reunion with him and Sophie, and the warmth and love she received, she was now, more than ever, confronted by the reality of Zeno's disappearance and the anxiety of not knowing when she would see him again.

Rarely given to tears, Louise had cried most nights back in Addis, fretfully hoping he was safe. Her thoughts swung between hope for his return to family life with her and Josh, and the vision of his corpse, the victim of a depraved murderer somewhere in Ethiopia or Kenya. So when she decided to fly to London, an incredible feeling of relief filled her.

When Geoff met them at Heathrow, Louise felt tired and ill; her body ached – probably, she thought, due to the long flight.

'How was your flight, Louise?' Geoff asked over coffee at the airport.

'Fine. And Josh was spoiled by the hostesses – typical Josh, he soon made friends with everyone, didn't you? Just like your father.'

Was she expected to talk about Zeno, she wondered.

Geoff asked if she was unwell. She felt uneasy, blushed and, after a brief silence, she admitted things weren't very good for her, but she expected that after a decent rest her life would return to normal.

'I'm sure Zeno will return soon,' Geoff said. Louise sensed he wanted to comfort her; he'd always been protective.

Never before had they spoken about her personal life. She wanted to talk to him about her life in Ethiopia with Zeno, but this restaurant was not the place. They finished their coffee and drove to Geoff and Sophie's St John's Wood home in West London.

As they drove, Louise remembered her first fieldwork experiences with Zeno, when they hiked in Ethiopia's Simien Mountains and through the famine-ridden villages of Amhara and Tigray. Zeno's plans for the elimination of famine and infant mortality in Ethiopia were now her own. She recalled the first photograph of them, alongside starving village people – and Zeno asking her if she was okay.

'I'm not sure,' she'd answered. 'I've never seen poverty like this.'

Later Zeno explained how they could initiate change in small ways by beginning in one village, so when people saw better harvests because of improved agriculture and well-funded health clinics, other would strive to have the same. 'We can prevent starvation and lift people out of poverty. So, are you interested in working here?' he had asked.

Louise was thrilled by the thought of working alongside Zeno, and undertaking anthropological fieldwork in remote villages of Ethiopia. But now, back in London, she felt strained and full of sadness. She was unable to express what was taking place in her mind, other than she wished that Zeno was with them.

She told Geoff how Zeno had been gone for two months and was officially missing for one. How he had left their home in Addis Ababa and flown to Nairobi, ostensibly to complete the last part of a major Ethiopian–Kenyan fieldwork project. When he did not return, his colleagues at Nairobi University assumed he had travelled to an isolated fieldwork site in northern Kenya and was delayed by weather or work. Ethiopia and Kenya are vast countries and it would not be difficult to get lost and then, unannounced, reappear weeks, if not months, later.

'Geoff, I've tried to find Zeno – placed notices in newspapers: the *Ethiopian Herald*, *Kenyan Star* and Kenya's *Daily Nation*, asking if anyone knows his whereabouts.'

'What response did you get?'

'None at all, not one email or letter, not even a phone call.'

'Eventually you're bound to hear from him. He's so resilient.'

'That's what I hope. I've phoned Zeno's mother, Gabriella in Nairobi, to check if she's heard from him.'

'What did she say?'

'Nothing much, except she thought he was unwell when he stayed with her.'

Geoff rented a two-bedroom ground floor flat for Louise, which was close to his and Sophie's home. Being an independent woman, Louise set up her temporary home quickly and enrolled Joshua in the same primary school as his cousin Sam.

Yet as soon as Louise was alone in the flat, she felt apprehensive. Thoughts of Zeno swirled in her mind. She could not pretend she wasn't frightened, stressed and unwell. On the other hand, she was thrilled to see Geoff and Sophie, their children Sam and Nicole, and was uplifted by their cheerfulness and goodwill. This helped her to think positively about Zeno.

Originally a city boy from Addis Ababa, Zeno had cherished time spent is isolated rural regions of Ethiopia. Louise took heart that village people warmed to him. He could hold them in thrall with his talk. He was never happier than when living among them, sharing their food, listening to their stories. He told her how he was spiritually strengthened by the happy voices of children playing in the bush and from spending nights by a village fire, hearing tales told by old men and women.

During the weeks before she departed for London, Amos had advised her that Zeno was well known in villages across Ethiopia and Kenya's Rift Valley country, and could be in one of these places. Besides, Zeno was a great survivor. Amos told Louise how Zeno had been in many hazardous physical situations, yet he always came through.

Zeno's friend, Haawkon, now lived in London. In the late 1970s and early 1980s they had worked together as young doctors and researchers for the Save the Children organisation across East Africa. Before Louise left Ethiopia, Haawkon had phoned and assured her that after a few weeks in London, he was sure she would receive good news, and when she returned to Addis, Zeno would be waiting, because he was driven by his deep love for her.

Amos and Haawkon's reassurances were soothing, like the dreams she had of waking up alongside Zeno, or watching him cuddle Josh and read to him in Amharic, or play with him in their small back garden. Yes, she thought, Zeno's homecoming will be memorable.

Natural Medicines

Zeno's bus ride to reach the Nyambene Hills was a bumpy four-hour epic. Every hour there was a stop at a village. On the journey he repeated his resolution not to submit to his illness. The bus trundled over pockmarked gravel roads, past green hills and small villages surrounded by plots of corn and sorghum and brown fields waiting for rain. He paid little attention. What villages the bus passed, he could not say. But on the journey he thought wretchedly about Fashna.

When he eventually got off the bus he began his slow walk up the signposted track to the Revival Health Centre. Half an hour into the trek he sat down under an acacia tree. He felt defeated as he pulled his shirt collar round his neck when a fresh breeze sprang up. Then he looked down at his hands, clasped them together and prayed for a successful return to Louise and Josh. He sobbed. Fear consumed him; the worn and winding track seemed to lead to doom rather than salvation.

As he walked, a vision appeared of Josh's brightly coloured, toy-strewn nursery bedroom. 'Josh, Josh,' he whimpered, and then cursed himself for his weakness. Although still determined, self-doubt, like a heavy cloak, wrapped itself around him.

After an hour he emerged quite suddenly into a clearing. There was a warren of brick and timber huts in the midst of clipped buffalo grass lawns separated by gravel paths. A small brick building was marked RECEPTION. Here he found two Kenyan women and a European man in charge of the health centre. Bernard Wilson, the director, was tall and lean. Zeno judged him to be in his late fifties. He was a self-taught natural medicine man who advertised widely and called himself Dr Bernard Wilson RHC. He had been a public servant in Nairobi before developing his interest in health foods, natural medicines and the promotion of wellness.

'Just call me Bernard, or Dr Bernard if you like,' he said jovially. Whenever the opportunity arose, he professed intimacy with distinguished members of the medical profession in Kenya and overseas. Yet there were those who doubted his credibility. He had no medical qualifications and no professional registration. He often displayed sarcastic scorn for registered doctors. He never examined clients; he wouldn't know how to. Yet the RHC advertised stories about how Dr Wilson helped people lose or put on weight and get fit, as well as how, without fail, his herbal medicines and regime cured seriously sick people, and how the life balance counselling he offered eliminated stress.

'A month's treatment and I'll return home,' Zeno told Elizabeth Makula, the centre's administrator, when he registered. He looked at her with a wild stare and gave a false name and address. His shirt was sweat-soaked. He paid the registration fee and was not asked about his medical history, let alone if he was ill, but was told about the benefits of the RHC. Around him were a few overweight and out of condition men and women, while others were hollow-eyed and somewhat emaciated like him. All were there to improve their health. He was given a key to a small single bedroom on the edge of the compound.

Martha, Bernard Wilson's Kenyan assistant, had trained as a nurse in Nairobi. She was short with a beaming smile. She doled out the 'natural' medication Dr Bernard prescribed. The third person, in charge of reception and general administration, was a Kikuyu woman, Elizabeth Makula. She administered the twenty-bed centre and, with the help of a personal trainer hired from a Nairobi gymnasium, organised daily activities, including walks in the adjacent hills, the use of two rowing machines, a treadmill, cross-country trainer along with weight training in a small gym. Counselling was available each day and the centre had a well furnished reading room. Swedish massage was available three days a week from a therapist who visited from Nairobi and stayed over.

It was reputed that Elizabeth was 'very close' to Dr Bernard. He spoke perfect English and some Kikuyu, and wrote prescriptions in beautiful cursive writing with one of the many fountain pens in a holder on his L-shaped desk. His wife was pale-skinned, red-haired, large and noisy. She lived in Nairobi, drove to the centre every two weeks with supplies and ignored Bernard's flirtations with Elizabeth Makula. When Elizabeth was away, which was rare, the red-haired wife took over administration. Women from the nearby village cooked, cleaned and laundered for the centre and village men maintained the property under the supervision of the resident caretaker, Grant Mboya.

During his first weeks at the centre, although Zeno's disease really took hold, Dr Bernard Wilson ignored him. Zeno was suffering. He had not anticipated this. In bed at night, he had to sit up so he could breathe. As the days passed his breathing deteriorated, his fingers and toes began to lose circulation and he had difficulty getting out of bed. There were no drugs to relieve his torture. He wondered if Louise and those who knew him thought he had died. He thought about the people of the villages, admiring students and lovers who might have once sworn to protect him. I have food and shelter here, he thought, but my illness holds me in its trap. A fly on the wall might mistake me for an impoverished beggar, an escaped convict who is only worthy of the hangman's noose.

By the third week he was desperately ill. A constant high fever was accompanied by bouts of shivering. Ulcers appeared on his body, face and legs. He experienced severe pain, like red hot knives and swords piercing his back and stomach. He began to lose control of his bodily functions and found himself lying in urine-soaked clothing. The RHC, contrary to its self-proclaimed purposes, provided no appropriate nursing care but instead a seemingly never-ending supply of garlic and lemon juice, combinations of raw vegetables and a succession of Dr Wilson's concoctions. 'Dr Wilson's organic juices return people to good health,' advised Elizabeth Makula. Bernard Wilson, on his rare contact with Zeno, insisted that wellness and robust health would eventually follow. This was a transition period.

'You'll be well soon,' Martha beamed. 'It's always difficult till you get used to your medicine, soon you'll be well.'

Despite great sadness, Zeno still retained his passion for life, a passion which had always been part of him. He grieved. His body shook with emotion as he remembered Louise. Then came the terrible realisation that his life could be slipping away. The disease was robbing him of his rightful life. Louise Davitt, he thought; I loved her with all my heart and body. Zeno remembered her slim elegance, her open-hearted love for him and his people, her intelligence and courage when she lived with the Hamar. He thought only of her. He was exhausted, but still hoped to be cured.

Despite the pills he swallowed so readily, the bitter leaves he chewed and the many herbal mixtures he drank, his condition worsened. No one cheered or comforted him. By the fourth week his illness was critical. Martha and Elizabeth, along with village staff, became wary of any contact. He cursed and struggled, but on orders from Dr Bernard, he complied with the medication despite knowing he was getting worse. He sensed now that the Revival Health Centre was a mockery and Bernard Wilson, who offered hope when there was none, was engaged in a massive deceit.

When the staff avoided Zeno due to his emaciated sore-ridden state, he decided to leave. But it was too late. He could barely stagger across the compound and no one at the RHC could do anything to change the course of his illness. He had one brief hopeful thought. At any moment Amos could be making his way up the rutted track to save him. But the stigma of his illness prevented Zeno from communicating with Amos and Louise, let alone with the local police.

In the past, when talking about the starving poor, particularly those he had observed in 1984 at Korem on the Tigray Amhara border, Zeno had continually reminded his colleagues, readers and politicians that it was essential for these people to have someone by their side to help in times of trouble. That is what they need most of all, he would say; a continual network of support is essential. But during the last great Ethiopian famine there was no food, so hundreds of thousands in the north starved and died. Zeno now recognised the signs in himself.

At night he thought about Fashna's full lips and naked body. When he woke in the early morning he imagined Louise was by his side and he had been saved. But the advocate of the importance of friends to help cope with illness and isolation was now alone. He spent fever-wracked sleepless nights thinking of Louise and Josh. In a few tranquil moments he still believed he'd see them again, although these thoughts became increasingly rare. 'Ah!' he cried in one delirious state, 'If only I had not been so foolish, I could have built a fence around myself to ward off the diseases.' What he said now made little sense.

At the end of the fourth week the rain poured relentlessly and the air was saturated. The nights were cold in this upland country and a freezing damp blanket enveloped him. There was to be no miracle. The RHC wanted him to leave but didn't know exactly who he was and where he came from, and communicating with the medical profession about clients was avoided. Despite the respect and tenderness of some of the village staff, everyone was at a loss about what to do.

Zeno thought of the lizard that drops its tail to save its life, and wished he had a similar strategy, but there was nothing he could sacrifice to escape the virus' grip. Suffering agonies in his cramped room, he saw no glimpse or salvation from a benevolent God. Dr Bernard Wilson's natural medicines were of no benefit. These people, the smooth-talking Dr Bernard in particular, were shonks, snake-oil salesmen with no understanding of his condition. He had no escape.

It was four weeks since he had shaved, and his face was stained with food and drink that had dribbled down through his whiskers. After five weeks he was close to the end of his suffering. Through the hut's half-opened window he could hear branches of trees shifting, then stillness and no sound. Nothing.

'This stillness, is this death?' he whimpered. In his life Zeno had been celebrated but now, alone, he felt utterly scorned.

'Don't be afraid,' he used to say to Louise and Josh and his colleagues. He was fighting desperately now for every painful breath and it seemed impossible that his struggle could continue much longer. He faced what he feared: being alone and unable to speak, unreachable. Zeno Wolde drifted in and out of consciousness. On his last night it took him forever to stagger out of his bedroom, across the grassy compound towards the forest. His weakened heart struggled to deliver oxygenated blood as his mind unravelled.

The villagers found his body early the next morning on the edge of a small shallow ditch in rough open ground at the edge of a Nyambene Hills forest. He lay in the dirt where he had fallen. He was dressed in a loose T-shirt and jeans; his feet were bare. It seemed he had lurched away from the hut in delirium, in one last desperate bid to find help, then collapsed and died where he fell.

Three days later the centre's staff buried him at the edge of the compound in an unmarked shallow grave. They shovelled damp earth over his canvas coffin. No one knew his nature, his quality – only his helplessness.

12: Friends

Threshold

Louise was determined to make the most of her short stay in London. A week after they arrived, Josh went off to school with his usual bounce and enthusiasm. Like most children, he took everything in his stride, finding delight in new friends, new toys and games, the first conkers, and the splash of winter puddles.

On his first morning, Louise returned home where she lay down on the couch intending to rest for just a few minutes but quickly fell asleep. When she woke it was almost midday. She stood, felt cold and ached in every muscle. Even the lounge radiator this November day felt icy. She shook herself, made coffee and a thick honey sandwich. Sugar levels must be low, she thought. Honey should do the trick.

Finishing the sandwich and coffee, she walked to the nearby tube station. She felt an unusual pain in her knees and hips. Tiredness, or perhaps a wave of despair, enveloped her. On the train to Russell Square, the disappearance of Zeno was again on her mind. She felt listless and remembered walking with him on the Simien plateau, and being in his arms at night in their tent as they listened to hyenas' cries. She could almost smell Hamar people cooking on an open fire and hear Zeno breathing as he slept alongside her. Her confused thoughts ended when she reached Russell Square Station, and as she walked towards the university she felt an unusual heaviness. The pressure of months of concealing her feelings made her feel desperate.

❖

Her friend Carmen was back in London. When Louise met her in the university refectory she was with Carole Byrne, the college deputy medical officer. They beckoned, glad to see her. Carmen knew Zeno had disappeared although this was the first time that Louise had faced her with the news.

Carmen hugged Louise closely and introduced her to Carole.

'I'm so sorry to hear your news,' Carole said.

Louise sensed that Carole and Carmen would understand the loss and torment she was experiencing, but she did not want to burden them. She had to concentrate to control her emotions. Alongside these women, Louise felt safe. In this place, away from anxiety and loss, Louise recounted the significant events of Zeno's disappearance and gradually felt some confidence return.

'Tell me, Carole,' Louise asked as calmly as she could, 'should I have stayed on in Addis despite Zeno's disappearance? If you could put yourself in my position, what would you have done?'

'I'd have sought as much support and love as possible from my family and closest friends,' Carole answered.

'Exactly. That's what I have come to do.' But her defiance was a facade. She started to cry. Carole and Carmen hugged her. After a few minutes she apologised. Carmen told her that crying was natural and there was no need to apologise.

'Do you really need to go back to Ethiopia now that you are here with Josh?' asked Carmen.

'I must. I want to know what has become of Zeno, for Josh's sake as well as mine. Zeno has been my partner for almost ten years. He's been my great love. I ask myself over and over, where is he now, what remains of him? Is he dying somewhere in Kenya and if so, where has he gone to die – and if he is dead, where is he buried?'

'Could you receive advice from friends in Ethiopia or Kenya who might know where Zeno is? Could Amos find out?' Carmen asked.

'I've already asked Amos. Zeno's university has made enquiries. He surely can't completely disappear, forever.'

Louise tried to rein in her fear. It was important not to assume the worst. She envisaged being in London only for a short while and certainly if she received news, she would return immediately to Addis Ababa or Nairobi.

'I'm sure you'll find out what has happened. In a few weeks' time you'll know more and can then plan your return.' They stood to leave.

'Yes, as soon as it's possible ...' Louise began. Suddenly she became pale. Swaying on her feet, she remembered the emaciated frame of Zeno's face during their last time together.

'Sit down, sit down!' Carmen insisted, holding her gently.

Carmen arranged for Louise to come to her university office the next day to discuss possible publications and applications for future research grants. They wanted to discuss the extent to which, just as wild animals in Africa were under threat from human settlement, the great traditions of ancient tribes were also endangered. Both women had worked with poor people, illiterate, primitive – in improving their lives.

Carmen's small office was on the second floor of the health sciences building. Louise stepped into the office and hugged her friend.

'Are you okay? If you don't mind my saying so, you look tired.' Carmen was her usual direct north-country self. Louise felt exhausted, had a sore throat and was again experiencing unusual pain in her hips and knees.

'Louise, you and Josh should come and stay with me, for a weekend at least. It will be like old times.'

'I should like that, but you don't want me staying with you when I'm such a misery.'

'Louise, you're never a misery, never; and I want to support you.'

Louise repeated, almost word for word, what she had shared the previous day, confessing how she had felt exhausted before returning to London ... How her body felt heavy, her legs burdened. She described her emotional pain and the night-time without Zeno ... and about her recurring bouts of chill, sore throats and fever that she had never before experienced.

'Do you think you could have glandular fever?'

'I've never thought of that. I suppose it's possible. I'm certainly run down.'

'Louise, do you think you could be pregnant?'

'No, no, I'm not pregnant.'

'Make an appointment to see Carole professionally. Have a blood test and clear your mind. I'm sure you'll be fine. Just call in at her surgery, then come and have a meal with me at my flat and bring Josh – I want to meet him.'

Carole Byrne

Louise had a brief appointment with Carole, who signed a request for the blood test. On the following day Louise's blood was drawn at the pathology department at the university medical centre. She made her appointment to see Carole for an early afternoon appointment four days later and arranged to meet Haawkon Davos later that afternoon.

As she walked towards the medical centre, the street was crowded with tourists. They were visiting the British Museum to see the 'Inside Africa' exhibition. How ironic, she thought. Zeno's absence caused her momentary shame; every step seemed like one more step away from Zeno, as if she were leaving her life behind.

This is crazy, she thought. I must remain strong. Her grandmother's words echoed. Sympathetic she might have been, but Margaret Davitt had little patience for soft spines even in the most difficult of circumstances.

Louise arrived at the surgery and sat in the waiting room. She picked up a weekly newspaper and read how the Space Shuttle Columbia had conducted the longest mission of the space shuttle program, and that an Ethiopian Airlines flight had been hijacked and then crashed into the Indian Ocean after running out of fuel, killing 125 people.

'Louise?' Carole Byrne walked over and greeted her. She ushered Louise into her consulting room. 'How are you?'

'Not brilliant, but I'll recover.'

'I'm sure you will. I'll need to get a brief case history, and then we can discuss the results of your blood test.'

Louise looked around the room as London's gritty winter light spilled through the ground-floor window. Carole enquired about Louise's life, her relationship with Zeno and her health since she lived in Ethiopia. She was sympathetic in her questioning and quietly identified with Louise's anxiety.

Louise told Carole about her life in Ethiopia, the birth of Joshua, her travels with Zeno and her anthropological work across the country. Carole already knew about Zeno's disappearance. Louise then told her about her unusual pains in the knees and hips and the recurrence of sore throats and general lethargy.

'Now we can discuss the results of your blood test. I assume you fasted for twelve hours before the test?'

'Yes, I certainly did.'

'These are the results,' Carole said pointing to her screen. 'You are not anaemic and you don't have glandular fever. Your kidneys and liver are fine and your cholesterol level is low, well within safety limits.'

'That's good news.'

'When did these joint pains first occur?'

'At least four months ago. I was tired and assumed they would disappear but they've continued and if anything they are worse. And I get colds that keep coming back.'

'It may well be that you've picked up some unusual virus which won't go away, and it's possible we may need to treat you with an extended dose of antibiotics.' Carole paused and readied herself. 'Have you ever been a drug user?'

'Never. Why do you ask?'

'I'm just checking in case we might have to test for serum drug levels.'

'Why? I'm not a drug user and never have been.'

'It's routine when I'm presented with such symptoms. I'm concerned about your joint pains. Do you mind if I examine your throat?'

Louise leaned forward, mouth wide open.

'It's looks raw. Is it tender?'

'You can say that again.'

'What was Zeno's health like before he disappeared?'

'I though he was quite ill, for the last six months anyway.'

'What did his doctor in Ethiopia advise?'

'Zeno avoided going to a doctor although he promised me when he left for Nairobi – before he disappeared, that is – that he would make an appointment to discuss his health. I haven't heard from him since.'

'When did you last have sex together?'

'Oh! Well, probably a month or more before he left. He'd become uninterested, and when he was home he seemed exhausted.' Louise grimaced and closed her eyes.

'And you had regular sex before that?'

'We did, but over the last few years he was often away.' Louise wondered where this questioning was leading. 'Do you have any ideas as to why I'm so tired, especially since I don't have glandular fever?' Suddenly she thought of the sick men she'd seen in San Francisco, winced, put the thought out of her mind and looked straight at Carole.

'I'm not sure.' Carole paused and in the silence, Louise thought how unwell Zeno had been when he left. 'This is a difficult question, although I have to ask you this. When Zeno was away from home, could he ever have had sex with another woman, or indeed with a man?'

Louise felt confused and exhausted, and was reluctant to admit that Zeno could have been promiscuous. In light of all she felt about her life with Zeno she wanted to protect him. And then there was Joshua. He only needed to know good things about his father ... but she had to be truthful.

'Zeno was as heterosexual as they come. There was no man in his life, but I was told by a close friend of Zeno's that he had a liaison with a young Luo woman when he began the Kenyan part of his research … But that was almost five years ago.' She realised what Carole could be thinking. This line of questions was exposing Zeno, but what could she do?

Carole reached over and put her hand on Louise's as she turned away to hide her sudden tearfulness. 'It's necessary to ask you these personal questions.' She squeezed Louise's hand.

Louise stared and remained perfectly still. She tried to put into the back of her mind what she thought the diagnosis might be.

'Would it be acceptable to you if I ordered a test for HIV? The pains that you are experiencing, and the colds that recur, lead me to think that at the very least we need to screen for HIV.'

Louise was dazed, her gaze blank, her face set and wooden. Screen for HIV. It's a kind of death, she thought. For a brief moment she felt utterly depressed. She imagined she was lying destroyed on the ground like a shot animal. She gazed around the room, registering nothing. She thought back to the men on the streets in San Francisco.

'It may not be HIV at all, but in view of what you've told me about Zeno I must eliminate that possibility.'

Louise clenched her hands and again closed her eyes. 'A test for HIV. I guess it's okay with me, but I'm shocked. What can I say? Who should I tell?'

'Just a close and trusted friend or family member at this stage, because there's no certainty you have been infected with HIV. If the test is positive, I'll give you an immediate referral to an infectious diseases specialist – Dr Ted West at the infectious diseases centre at University College Hospital. He also has private rooms in Harley Street. He's easy to talk to and very thorough.'

Louise summoned all her courage in order not to break down again. Why tell me about Dr Ted West? She took time to allow the meaning of a test for HIV to sink in. Carole already thinks I could have the disease, she thought. Memories of Zeno's condition loomed. Her mind was elsewhere as she stared at Carole. Immersed in her thoughts, she was encouraged only by the fact that she could talk to Haawkon after she left the surgery.

'If there's any way I can help, phone me immediately.'

I'm sure, Louise, you can handle this. I have great confidence in you.'

Could I by some miracle *not* have HIV? Louise thought. Could I survive such a disease?

Carole stood, hugged Louise and walked with her to the surgery's exit.

Haawkon's Counsel

Louise crossed the road, walked slowly to Russell Square and sat on a secluded bench. Her mind scrambled as she tried to unravel her situation. She took out her phone and dialled her sister-in law. 'Sophie, it's Louise.'

'Hi Louise, where are you? Did you get good news?'

Louise, taken aback, wished Sophie hadn't been so direct. 'Not really, but I'll tell you about it when I get home. Could you pick Josh up when you collect Sam and Nicole?'

'Of course – no trouble. The children will love Josh coming home with them.'

Sitting on the bench, Louise felt fixed to the spot. Suddenly her shoulders shook as if she had been sobbing. She leaned forward with her head in her hands and stayed in that position for many minutes until she became aware that passers-by were staring at her.

She sat up and picked up the phone. 'Oh, Haawkon, it's me, Louise,' she said in a faltering voice. 'I'm free to meet now.'

He caught the intonation in her voice which sounded far off and plaintive, rather like an echo. 'Hi, Louise. How lovely to hear from you. Where are you?'

'I'm sitting on a bench in Russell Square.'

'Let's meet in that café in the park close to the square. You know the one? It's called Park Café, I think, off Bedford Place. I'll meet you there in twenty minutes.'

Louise walked to the park and sat at an outside table. She watched Haawkon stride across the park. As he approached, he sensed something serious had happened. 'How's my Louise?'

When he stepped close he saw she had been crying. At that moment he remembered her warmth when they'd been together in New York and how, when he gazed at her, he was jolted by a passion which overcame all his rules about how, at that time, he should feel towards her. Compassion came naturally to him. He would offer her tender reassurances and sympathy.

Haawkon bent down and gently hugged her. He strove to find words of comfort but she was too distressed to notice or respond. He took her hand and then gently kissed her forehead. Momentarily she recovered herself but then slumped in the chair beside him. She sobbed and shook for some minutes. He knew from experience how traumatic news could make a person shudder and cry. Haawkon thought how frightened she looked but also how beautiful.

'It's okay, cry on me, Louise,' he whispered. 'It always helps at moments like this. You don't have to tell me what's happened, not yet. There's no hurry.'

When at last Louise grew still, Haawkon continued to hold her hand. Initially she found it impossible to accept his assurances.

Run away! I'll run away, she thought, without looking up at Haawkon.

He wondered if it was bad news about Zeno causing her distress.

She looked at him and blinked through tear-swollen eyes. Then she confessed with a heaving sigh, 'Carole Byrne has recommended that I have a test for HIV. I'm sure that's her diagnosis, though she was very kind and didn't say too much. Haawkon, I'm so ashamed, I'll never forgive myself if that's what I've contracted. What am I going to do? I want to run away, go anywhere, just disappear.'

Haawkon shook his head. 'You're lost at the moment. But even if Carole's hunch is confirmed, we are now able to suppress the virus, so the disease can be controlled. I understand your fear. But you are resilient and I'm sure you will soon overcome this. Believe me.'

He could not deny the immediacy of her fear. Louise glanced at him uneasily. She thought about suicide, but then thought of Josh and was ashamed.

She imagined being wracked by physical pain and was frightened to think of her body scored with sores and unable to breathe like the young men she'd seen in those doorways in San Francisco. A despairing agitation hung like a death shroud over her from which she could see no escape.

'You can't hide, Louise, and I won't let you. The diagnosis hasn't been confirmed and even if you have HIV, this disease is treatable. You are *not* going to die.'

'Treatable, but is it curable?'

'At the moment there is no cure. The goal of treatment for HIV must be to manage the symptoms and suppress the virus. And we are able to do this.'

Haawkon searched for other consoling words. He wanted to quote some favourite lines, *Come live with me and be my love and we will some new pleasures prove,* but for the moment, thought better of it.

She had rarely been far from his mind since they first met. His comment, 'This disease is treatable,' was a stirring command issued with the same optimism he used when treating advanced malaria patients in his MSF clinics. Haawkon had a strong belief in the role that language played in effective treatment and demonstrated how a doctor's language, which was his professional core, could enhance a patient's resilience, as she possibly faced a life-threatening illness.

'Irrespective of a positive diagnosis, you will lead a full life, Louise.'

She felt relief in his comforting embrace. Very briefly, her overwhelming feelings of helplessness and sense of guilt began to fade.

'There are people I know who have HIV,' he went on. 'Their infection is a medical condition, it is not them. Hear me, Louise. We must wait for the test results.' But Haawkon anticipated that Carole Byrne's expectation was valid.

Louise's distress was acute and almost unbearable. She tried to settle her mind, tried to focus on an image of Josh playing and laughing with his cousins, but her heart raced and pulses of fear ran through her.

'But know this, Louise, treatment with the new antiretroviral drugs will soon be a regular feature for people diagnosed with HIV. People take medication on a daily basis to treat high blood pressure, to hold asthma at bay or to treat the different types of diabetes. So if by chance you have HIV, you can take drugs daily to treat your condition.'

Haawkon knew she was afraid. He asked himself, how could he give her access to people and events that would nurture her resilience and quell her anxiety? 'Whatever happens, Louise, make use of your remarkable gifts. Use your talent, I'll insist on that. Believe me, you will not be ignored or rejected, quite the opposite. People will always want your company.'

She could not break out of the numbness and guilt enveloping her. If she had HIV, how would she tell her family and Josh? 'Take drugs for the rest of my life?' she said slowly.

Haawkon continued speaking; with his experience of managing people with life-threatening illnesses he knew he had to reassure her. 'People can live long and effective lives when they take antiretroviral drugs. Even if you have this illness it's not going to destroy you today, tomorrow or in ten years time, let alone destroy who you are, believe me. Pioneering research is going on, so things will only improve.'

But Haawkon knew it would take time before his words would sink in. He was calm, confident he could eventually strip away her anguish and shame. If he could alleviate her pain, even just slightly, she would endure. He also knew that when a person is anxious and depressed, belief in recovery is difficult. The afternoon meeting with her was not at all what he had anticipated.

It was a strain being together in this park as the sun set, no shared laughing conversation against the background hum of London traffic, no walking hand in hand to his office as streetlights glowed, no arrangements to see a play at the National Theatre the following week.

Haawkon decided to be direct. 'I assume, if by chance you have the disease, you know how you could have been infected?'

'By Zeno. Yes, by Zeno.'

'There is a period of time, often some years, when the infected person does not know they have the disease.'

'Early on I'm sure Zeno had no idea he was infected. Haawkon, I feel so helpless. I'm so ashamed of myself … I'm so sorry.'

'At this moment you feel helpless – this feeling is normal. Let it ride. But it will pass. Let's wait for the test results. Now, would you like coffee or shall I take you home?'

'Strong black coffee and then please take me home.'

They drank their coffee almost in silence, with Haawkon allowing Louise space. She felt like crying again. She could neither speak nor turn around and look at children scuffing up leaves as they called and kicked a football to each other nearby. As they walked back towards his office, Haawkon was fully aware of her anguish. She needed a cheerful home filled with loving people. He drove her home to her brother's townhouse in St John's Wood.

'Let me know how your family responds. I'm sure it will be fine. Phone me in the morning and we can arrange to have a meal together. But most important, ring me as soon as you receive the test results.' He leant over and lightly kissed her goodbye.

Edward West

Carole Byrne phoned to tell Louise that the HIV test was positive. A week later Louise met Dr Edward West in his rooms at University College Hospital. He was a fit-looking man with iron-grey hair and bushy eyebrows. Louise thought he was probably in his early fifties, somewhat older than Haawkon. They discussed how Louise could have become infected. West explained how there was a window period when the infected person could pass on the disease. It appeared certain that Zeno was not aware he was infected when they had made love.

Tight-lipped, Louise nodded.

'It's always difficult, Louise, to identify when and how you could have become infected. I understand from your records that you are not an IV drug user and have not had a blood transfusion in Ethiopia when, for example, you gave birth to your son.'

'No, I've never used drugs nor had a blood transfusion.'

'In sub-Saharan Africa, heterosexual intercourse accounts for the vast majority of infections. From what you've told me, that appears to be the cause of your infection.'

West was personable, sympathetic, and Louise felt comfortable with him. He asked her if she knew anyone else who had the disease.

A memory came back: it was the moment when a fellow student at the School of Tropical Medicine had told her he had been diagnosed with HIV. 'I had a good friend who worked as a nurse. He was homosexual and of course many still think HIV is a homosexual's disease. Mark was diagnosed with HIV not long after I met him.

This was before I went to a conference in San Francisco and saw many men with the disease. Mark and I studied the public health course together at the School of Tropical Medicine. It was 1985. He thought that he could fight the disease with natural herbal methods. He said these natural foods belonged in his body and that the virus didn't belong. He believed the natural remedies would kill off the virus. He was convinced. He continued to hide his condition until it was too late.'

West smiled. 'That's a common story. But let me assure you, the drug regime that I'm going to prescribe will help you to live a long life. My recommendation is, acquaint yourself with the drugs and find someone who can help you monitor your health. Now, if you please, I'd like to examine you.'

Louise went to an adjacent examination room, stripped to her underwear and climbed up on the consulting bench. A nurse accompanied Edward West into the room. He tested Louise's reflexes, bent her arms and legs back and forth, probed her stomach, listened to her chest, shone a light in her eyes and ears, and closely examined the skin on her legs, arms and body. He questioned her about her joint pains. He felt the lymph nodes in her groin, neck and under her arms and examined her mouth, then completed an anogenital check for possible other transmitted STDs. 'It's important I check this,' he said. 'It's standard procedure.' Then as she sat on the side of the bench he wrapped a cuff around her left arm and took her blood pressure.

Are you taking any medication at the moment?'

'None at all.'

'Are you still having your periods?'

'Yes, regularly.'

'That's a good sign. I'll need another blood test, and I'll want saliva and urine samples to assess what we call viral load and viral spread.'

Edward West left the room and his nurse then rubbed the inside of Louise's elbow with a swab and slid a needle into her vein. She labelled a small tube of her blood and put it into his out-tray. Louise stared at the tube of blood. She wondered what exactly it contained. Was the virus floating there? It's bad enough when you read in the newspaper about someone being diagnosed with HIV but when it happens to you … She shook her head. This second blood test really brought it home.

West returned. 'We won't need current X-rays or an MRI scan because you don't exhibit any signs of central nervous system involvement, which is a *very* good sign.' Edward West smiled and leant back in his chair. 'Physically you are perfectly well apart, of course, from this infection. And as soon as the drugs I'm prescribing take hold then your joint pains and sore throats should disappear. You realise that there are no protective antibodies for this condition and that the infection persists for life?' He paused to let Louise digest the comment.

Louise nodded. 'Yes, I understand.'

'When people are diagnosed late then there is every likelihood that the virus will have progressed to AIDS. When that happens, treatment is less effective. However, the pathologist is confident that your disease is at a very early stage. The viral load, which is the amount of HIV in a sample of your blood, will be clear to me with this second blood test. I'll keep you informed but I'm confident yours is an infection which can be managed. Naturally, your health will have to be carefully monitored, but Dr Byrne can do that, and I understand from Dr Davos that you have already researched the disease.'

'Hardly, but I want to know as much as possible.'

West assured her again that the disease was manageable. 'This second blood test is also to help me determine the course of therapy.'

'When do I get the drugs for treatment?'

'I'll be prescribing them right now. We'll begin with three types of inhibitor drugs. They must be taken every day; a missed dose increases the risk that the drugs will stop working. There are no food restrictions when taking them. You can drink alcohol but only in moderation. Too much alcohol will impair your immune system.'

'What are the side-effects of the medication?'

'There are a few. They are quite individual. To begin with, patients can experience nausea, some diarrhoea and headaches. Some antiretrovirals can raise a person's cholesterol levels, but not those I'm prescribing. I'll give you a paper indicating the principal side-effects, which should help you deal with them as soon as they arise. But you are healthy and you should be able to cope with them. And you can cuddle and look after your son just as normal. However, you could infect a partner if you have unprotected sex. Condom use is essential. Phone me if you want further advice. I'll review your situation in a month's time.'

'A month? What will you review?'

'We'll start to individualise your treatment.'

'What does that mean?'

'We can find out which drugs best suit you. We may need to adjust the ones I have just prescribed. And remember, research into the condition is ongoing so there's every likelihood that future medication will be more effective and there will be far fewer side-effects. I'll give you an article published this year. It's in *The New England Journal of Medicine*. It's about up-to-the-minute management of HIV/AIDS. The article refers to highly active antiretroviral therapy, known as HAART. It's a form of three-drug therapy which has already shown impressive benefit in the treatment of HIV.'

'Thank you, I'll read it carefully.'

She made the appointment to see Edward West in a month's time and left the hospital. As she walked towards the tube station she saw people doing early Christmas shopping and posters advertising Christmas oratorios at the church of St Martin-in-the-Fields. Would she still be alive to see and enjoy all this by Christmas next year?

Telling

Louise went home that afternoon realising that she had to tell her parents about the diagnosis, about why she was likely to stay in London for many months and what had possibly happened to Zeno. Sophie brought Josh home. After Sophie left, Louise played with him and they talked about why Zeno was not with them.

'You know,' Louise began sadly, 'Daddy's still away. He's not been well ...' Louise sensed that seven-year-old Josh already knew what she was going to tell him.

'I know, Mummy. Sam told me that Daddy's away in Africa, but I'll see him one day. I haven't seen him for a long time.'

'Of course you remember him. You'll always remember him, I know that.' She had gone over many times the same memories and images of the Zeno she had lived with since his disappearance. Memories of love and happiness. She had no wish to immerse Josh in sadness. 'Of course,' Louise repeated, 'Daddy's a long way away, and even if he can't come back we'll remember him together.'

She knew she couldn't trump Josh's questions and ride rough-shod over his confidence. All through this difficult time, Louise had noticed how Josh showed interest in how she was feeling. His playfulness and energy, just like his father, would be encouraging. Sadness and remorse were with her but Josh was a source of strength.

Since her first meeting with West, Louise had spoken to her parents on the phone. They knew she had not been well, probably thinking

311

she had contracted some form of malaria which could be treated by appropriate doses of chloroquine.

A month later, after her second meeting with Ted West, she determined that her parents must now be told the truth. And she could explain what Dr West had told her about the new medication. A letter was better than an email or an alarmist phone call.

Louise was determined to tread carefully, as her parents would be shocked. She didn't want to frighten them with hyperbole, anxiety or any reference to the unpredictability of her condition. They had to be given the details and be reassured. She wrote:

Dear Mum and Dad,

I'm writing to tell you some bad news and some good news. The bad news is serious. I have been diagnosed with the HIV virus. It's rife in Ethiopia and Kenya at the moment. I must have caught the condition from Zeno. I can think of no other cause. I had not been feeling well and had a blood test here in London. I thought that I might have glandular fever. Of course I was shocked and at first very depressed. But having Geoff and Sophie here in London has made such a difference, especially as Joshua is so thrilled to be able to play with Sam and Nicole. And that's a tonic for me, to see him so happy and not apparently missing his father.

I know you will worry about my illness but I'm not going to hide, or live the life of a recluse. The really good news is that recently new drugs called antiretrovirals have become available. I've seen an infectious diseases specialist at University College Hospital who is sure that the disease is in its very early stages and treatable. I'm now on a drug regime taking multiple pills a day and rattling accordingly. The specialist will monitor me for the next few months and then I'll be able to travel. He says I could still live to be a hundred and I am determined to be well and demonstrate that I can live a full life with HIV.

My friend, Haawkon Davos, who I think I have told you about

312

before, convinces me that I can cope with the disease and do much the same as before. Haawkon has been a great support and is very dear to me, and Josh likes him. Haawkon says I have sterling qualities. If I have, then I've got them from you.

As you know, Zeno disappeared. Despite a thorough search by the Kenyan police they've not found him. Sadly, Zeno's friends and I now think he is dead. This won't come as a surprise to you in view of my previous letters but I thought I should confirm that sad news. Josh knows that his dad will not likely return but he's so busy enjoying life here that Zeno's disappearance appears to have hardly registered. I have my old university teaching post back on a short-term contract basis and my colleagues are helping me with grant applications, so all is well on that front. In fact, I'm involved in writing a paper on Ethiopian village life to read to an Oxford conference in a month's time.

I am conscious that you will be bowled over by my news. As soon as you get this letter we can talk on the phone and I will be able to reassure you. I'll fly back to Adelaide for a holiday before too long. You'll be rushed off your feet when Josh and I return. Rest assured I'm in good hands and am not experiencing side-effects from the medication.

Much love as ever, Louise

Advocacy

During the following year Louise had many meetings with Haawkon, Ted West, Carole Byrne and Carmen. Despite continuing searches and requests for information about Zeno, there was still no news of him. In a tentative fashion she discussed her future with Geoff and Sophie, but especially with Haawkon. There was a hardened yet still bright quality to her mood which underpinned her determination to continue her career and live as normal a life as possible.

'I'll control this disease and will never give up believing in the reforms for Ethiopia that Zeno considered so important,' she told her brother. He noted anger in her voice and gestures that he was not used to. Yet this also heralded a welcome impulse for his sister to dispel the burdensome sadness she'd experienced since she returned to London. Now she smiled easily at Josh, Sam and Nicole with her beautiful, brave smile, and played with them with enjoyment. It was as if her blue eyes had summoned up the sun and made her glow again. To Haawkon, she was beginning to look like the old Louise. It seemed that her mind's wilderness was clearing, so that her new life could begin. Haawkon believed there would be an altogether new kind of life which she could inhabit and celebrate, but he was careful not to hurry her.

They went to the theatre together. Haawkon joined Louise and Josh for meals and picnics with the family. They all went on a holiday walking in the Lake District. Haawkon met Louise's parents when, as part of a European holiday, they were briefly in London. However, Louise made it clear he was nothing more than a dear friend. They slept apart.

'I was shipwrecked when I was first diagnosed and I shall always be grateful to Haawkon for guiding and supporting me,' she told her parents. 'He's always there for me, nothing more than that. And after all, he's a confirmed bachelor and leads his own life. But I enjoy his company and Josh likes having him with us.'

'I suppose your disease prevents you from ever having a friend like Haawkon live with you?' That was as direct as Monica Davitt thought she could be.

'Of course, Mum, having HIV obliges me to take extreme care and I would never forgive myself if anyone else became infected because of having sex with me.'

'Louise, I understand, and of course it's difficult to talk about this, but it's good that you have Haawkon as a friend.'

During a lunchtime sandwich together on an unusually sunny November day, almost a year after Louise's diagnosis, Haawkon became more specific about the change of career for her that he had in mind. He offered her glimpses of a role that he was confident she could fill. It would be an adventure-filled career, he said. One that could take her from ravaged regions of the developing world to the private offices of government ministers, from villages across Africa to the UN in New York, and even perhaps the world stage. But Louise was more bemused than excited.

'A career, you say, that is only slightly different from what I have been doing for the last ten years. What is this new career? Aren't you jumping the gun imagining me having a new career? And meeting prime ministers? Why would they want to hear from me?'

Haawkon sensed his opportunity to spell out his idea. 'You will have to travel to Africa and Asia to do this. Australia will be included, but you will be able to leave out the Arctic and Antarctic, especially as you like warm weather.' He grinned. 'And being in the front line will suit you … I'll come with you on some of these trips, if you'll let me.'

'Haawkon, what exactly are you suggesting?'

Haawkon explained how a catastrophe like a diagnosis of HIV and possibly AIDS could bring out the best and the worst in someone.

'What do you mean, the best and worst in someone?'

'I think you know.'

'Tell me – it's your advice I need.'

'HIV, as you know, is a serious condition. The worst situation occurs if someone becomes depressed and then full of fear, believing that HIV is a terminal illness. But you can control the virus, stay well, look after Joshua, develop your career, travel and make friends just as before.'

'What if the virus gets out of control, goes on the rampage?'

'Ignore sensational media stories. More often than not they're wrong. Take your medication every day without fail and the virus will be suppressed.'

Louise tried to rest her mind and not think about being unable to control the disease.

'Apart from a few aches and pains, you are fit and well, and with your experience and skill you can cope with the virus and lead a full life.'

'You mean I can enjoy normal family life, maintain my university career and even write positive articles about living with HIV?'

'That and more.'

'You're being vague. What does *and more* mean?'

'I think you can help change attitudes, reduce stigma and help prevent people from catching HIV … be an ambassador for change and help improve treatment.'

'My God, Haawkon, that's a huge task. I'm not sure I'm ready for that.'

Yet Louise could hear a voice from inside, gently persuading her that Haawkon's plan was impressive and challenging. She knew that in difficult moments like this it was generally a good idea to ask herself what it was she wanted to be doing and then consider how it could be achieved. And I know, she thought, I'll have Haawkon's support.

'Let me think some more about all this, talk to Geoff and discuss again next week when you come back from your conference in Paris.'

'Let's do that. Take your time.'

During the days that Haawkon was in Paris many issues began to surface. Her care for Joshua, the disappearance of Zeno, the shock and implications of the HIV diagnosis, a different life back in London ... as well as her need to travel, manage her condition, develop her career and maintain her friendship with Haawkon. Could the latter be the key to her decision?

Haawkon phoned her from Paris to find out what she and Josh were doing. He didn't mention his idea but said that he'd been in discussions with colleagues concerning how Médecins Sans Frontières and organisations such as Save the Children and World Vision could contribute to the management of HIV/AIDS in the developing world.

'I'll be back in London on Monday night so let's meet for lunch on Tuesday. I've an early morning meeting at Charing Cross Hospital. If it's okay with you, I'll book a table at the Boulevard Brasserie restaurant in Covent Garden, close to the Royal Opera House. You know the one, we've eaten there with Geoff and Sophie. I'll phone you on Monday as soon as I'm home. Take care.'

On Tuesday Louise arrived at the restaurant ten minutes before Haawkon. She'd sorted her priorities. His proposed plan for her was tempting, provided she could take on this advocacy in conjunction with her university position. She sensed Haawkon's plan was well founded. And despite many obstacles, she had to admit she was thrilled by the prospect of trying to bridge the gap between woeful ignorance of the HIV/AIDS condition and helping to establish a positive direction in terms of attitudes, prevention and treatment. Her personal story would be inclusive, and her attitude in managing her condition would make good sense to share.

Upon arriving, Haawkon leant over the table and kissed her on the cheek. 'Marvellous to see you, Louise.'

'You too.' They kissed again.

"I've got something to tell you,' Haawkon said.

'Something good I hope?'

'I'll tell you over lunch.'

They surveyed the menu and ordered the chef's recommendation. Haawkon ordered his usual bottle of mineral water and a bottle of South Australian Riesling. In the restaurant's warmth, he took off his jacket, reached across the table and put his hand on Louise's. Struck by his chiselled features, the sparkling blueness of his eyes and the healthy tan on his smooth face, her memory of his attractiveness when she first met him in San Francisco came back to her. A waiter poured the wine. They clinked glasses.

'Cheers!'

'Now tell me about Paris and what *this something* is you need to tell me.'

'Paris was enjoyable and action-packed as ever. You must come with me next time.'

'I'll come, especially if you take me to bookshops on the Left Bank, to the Louvre and Musée d'Orsay and your favourite, the Pompidou Modern Art Centre.'

'Nothing would be better than having you with me in Paris visiting art galleries. Let's set a date. I suggest some time next month when your term ends – that would suit me. Let me know when you are free and I'll book a flight.'

'Haawkon, that's great – I'd love to fly to Paris with you, provided I can arrange for Sophie and Geoff to look after Josh.'

Louise was pleased with the way their lunch was turning out. She felt a distinctive kind of contentment, a deep sense of happiness at the prospect of spending time in Paris with Haawkon. 'Now tell me about your conference and meeting with colleagues from MSF.'

'I spoke to colleagues from MSF and Save the Children who work across sub-Saharan Africa, about my idea for you to have an advocacy and educational role with regard to the management of HIV.'

'What did they say?'

'If you take on the task, they will arrange introductions and support. They said this type of educational project was needed and they were sure it would gather momentum. And of course, I told them about you.'

'What in particular did you tell them?' Louise raised her eyebrows.

Haawkon looked at her, paused as if struggling to decide how to explain what he had discussed with his colleagues. 'Look at it this way. I explained that, given your communication skills, personal experience in Ethiopia and Kenya, the fact that you have been diagnosed with HIV and understand the condition – and, given your compassion – you can change the lives of people with HIV.'

'Thinking about this project makes me dizzy. But I considered it carefully while you were in Paris and I think it has possibilities for me.'

'I know it will work,' Haawkon said, thrilled with Louise's response. He told her how he thought she could persuade physicians across Africa who initially refused to care for HIV/AIDS patients to change their minds, and also clergy who rejected infected people from their churches or who campaigned against the use of condoms, as well as homophobic politicians and public health officials who needed to learn how the disease was treatable.

'You can help the search for solutions to the HIV/AIDS crisis, and fight for justice for these people, especially those who live in poverty. Given your knowledge and experience, you can save lives.'

'Where would I get the energy to do all this?' In her imagination she was already addressing conferences about effective management of HIV/AIDS, persuading clergy to accept people with the condition, talking to men about the need to wear condoms and discussing with female sex workers the importance of using femidoms when they were having sex with clients.

'Perhaps I'm not explaining the project well enough. But when I first met and heard you present in San Francisco, I realised you had extraordinary energy and commitment, and I don't think that has changed.'

Early afternoon sunlight glided through the restaurant windows to the hum of muted conversation, and the clink of cutlery and glasses. 'I'm doing my best to be as fit as possible and I'm careful not to get overtired.'

'We can plan your program very carefully – arrange for rest days and necessary debriefing sessions with colleagues from MSF. They like the idea of you as a roving ambassador across countries at risk for outbreaks of HIV.'

'Now, Haawkon, what got you thinking about all this, of me as a roving ambassador?'

'My idea for you is not just about the virus; it's also about people and institutions.'

'That's huge … but it's not impossible. Tell me if my understanding is correct – I have a few weeks away, at the moment across Africa, meeting people and advocating the changes you have in mind. Then back home to London to prepare for another conference a few months later.'

'That's it. I can arrange the funding. You will help lives grow rather than diminish. And that's what you were doing well before you were diagnosed.'

'You flatter me, Haawkon.'

'Not a bit. Given your leadership and, together with colleagues, you can help open people's eyes to what has to happen if this disease is to be managed effectively.'

Louise smiled and touched his hand.

'Now, let me order coffee,' Haawkon said. He had been persuasive and reassuring.

'Do you think colleagues and my family will think it strange for me to undertake this project?' she asked. 'Throwing away parts of my university career in order to manage such a huge and probably growing program?'

'Not at all. They will be thrilled for you.'

'Really?'

'My dear Louise, I know you will find this program very rewarding – you will influence people; you'll be highly regarded and this work will also enhance your university career.'

'What a bonus.' They laughed. The heartbeat of their relationship, which had been evolving throughout their lunch, gathered momentum as they left the restaurant, hand in hand.

A different life was beginning for Louise. For a long time she'd been coping with Zeno's disappearance and the diagnosis and management of HIV; now, she was hand in hand with Haawkon, planning to have time with him in Paris and travelling across sub-Saharan Africa promoting rewarding lives for people with a serious illness.

The following week back home at her flat enjoying a Friday sandwich lunch, she read various headlines in the noon edition of the *Evening Standard* about the spacecraft Pathfinder landing on Mars, a small piece about cloned Dolly the sheep doing well, and the latest Mori poll predicting a landslide victory for Tony Blair and the Labour Party. Considering her separateness from this news, she thought about how, apart from family and close friends, she was quite alone in a world, which was wholly indifferent to her existence and fate – and to the fate of millions with the disease.

At three she left to collect Josh from his school. As she walked she felt happy, with a dawning realisation of Haawkon's fondness for her. She experienced a restless sensation, becoming aware of the love she felt for him: Haawkon Davos, Zeno's old friend. Haawkon, she thought, is a kind and interesting man, secure in himself, and one who seems unequivocally convinced that I can enjoy a full life, a life in which he could probably be my loyal companion.

She was thirty-five and she had to admit that now, even in the back of her mind, she was restless for the prospect of a possible family life with Haawkon. She reached the school gates. Her effervescent seven-year-old Joshua ran towards her.

Kindred Spirits

Over an evening meal in Louise's flat they discussed their likely accommodation in Paris during a planned long weekend together.

'Where we sleep always seems to be an issue for us ever since you took me to New York. And this time you don't have your own apartment in Paris,' Louise joked.

'I'll book the hotel and, as we've discussed, two single bedrooms seem appropriate.' Haawkon knew how apprehensive Louise was about any likelihood of passing on her infection. He also wanted to preserve what he and Louise felt for each other. He hoped that this sleeping arrangement would allow them time to enjoy Paris – nurture their feeling for each other as they visited galleries, walked endlessly alongside the Seine and used these opportunities, whenever the mood was appropriate, to talk about ideas for their future.

They flew to Paris three weeks later and touched down at midday. It was the first time since Louise returned to London that they had been away, alone together. Haawkon was a veteran of the journey, spoke reasonable French and knew the city. He'd booked two adjacent bedrooms in the Hotel Albe Saint Michel in the heart of Paris' Latin Quarter close by the Seine.

'I've used this hotel before,' he said as they drove from the airport. 'You'll love its location, it's only five minutes' walk from Notre Dame Cathedral.'

'Sounds fantastic – what a genius you are.'

'Yes, and there are a range of excellent cafés and restaurants nearby.' In the back of the taxi he hugged Louise.

After booking into their hotel and locating their bedrooms, they strolled through nearby streets, Haawkon holding Louise's hand, until they found the Café Latin which served distinctly French cuisine. 'I love the atmosphere of this restaurant,' said an enthusiastic Haawkon. 'They cook everything on the premises, and the food is amazing.'

'And the wine as well?' questioned Louise.

'That as well.'

They were joyous. Louise ordered seafood and Haawkon the marinated chicken breast. Their animated, sometimes whispered conversation during their almost two-hour stay heightened their sexual attraction as they touched, occasionally stroked each other's cheeks and, enjoying red wine, laughed at the passionate personae they presented in the utopian Café Latin. By four they returned to their hotel.

'Let's go and sit in Notre Dame Cathedral before we eat tonight. It's open till eight and we can tour the main hall of the Cathedral and listen to organ music,' Haawkon suggested.

'Yes, let's do that. We can have an hour's rest and then I'll shower and change for this evening.' They linked fingers, kissed each other gently on the cheek and retired to their bedrooms. God, he's easy company, thought Louise. It was not easy for her to maintain this bedroom separateness, she thought. He's respectful and doesn't have the compulsion of most men who, on a second date, want to have sex.

After their Cathedral visit they went to a café for evening refreshments and to plan the next day. Their conversation turned to paintings. Louise had to admit her repertoire was limited. Haawkon said that his wasn't too great either but a morning visit to the Musée d'Orsay followed by an afternoon at the gallery of modern art in the Pompidou Centre would immerse them in some of the finest art Paris had to offer.

'What do you think of Van Gogh's paintings?' asked Haawkon.

'They are different. I like them. From what I know about him he painted with energy and sensitivity. But at the moment I don't think I could name more than two of his paintings.'

'Go on, have a go.'

'Oh, *Sunflowers* would be one and, then there's *Café Terrace at Night*, and of course self-portraits and yes, *The Yellow House*.'

'Well done. Van Gogh called *The Yellow House* an artist's house.'

'I'll remember that.'

'Who was it told me she couldn't name more than one Van Gogh painting?'

'After our visit tomorrow I'll be able to name a few more.'

'Of course you will, and you'll remind me of the paintings you particularly liked.'

'Yes, I'll make notes and buy some impressionist postcards.'

Louise admired Haawkon's decisiveness, which contrasted with her uncertainty. Another quality, she thought, was his careful planning. The straightforward Haawkon never felt the need to articulate detail by detail. And she easily understood what he needed, appreciated and intended.

'Well, we can't sit here till the café closes,' said Haawkon.

'Definitely not, though I'll come back here anytime.'

They left the café and walked back to the hotel. Both were equally aware that going to bed in separate bedrooms after such a happy day together would be a genuine test of self-control. It was awkward. Each recognised the hugeness of their responsibility to the other. To have relaxed and eased themselves into a shared bed would have been easy.

'See you early in the morning,' said Louise, winking at Haawkon as she kissed him goodnight and entered her bedroom.

Lying in bed, Louise thought how relationships in life were often fragile. She admitted that her love for Haawkon was something much more than just a feeling of a rewarding friendship. She wondered about the possibility of a domestic life with him and knew that, given her condition, it would always be difficult. What in the long run must he think of me, always needing to sleep separately from him?' she asked herself. She resolved not to adopt any presumption of an easy resolution just because of the good times when they were having together. It was imperative to proceed carefully, otherwise, being too hasty could mean the relationship would fail. At this point she discarded these thoughts and, drifting to sleep, resolved to enjoy the next few days in Paris.

The Musée d'Orsay, the converted railway station on the Left Bank, was within comfortable walking distance of the Latin Quarter. After a croissant and coffee breakfast, they walked to the museum.

'It was only opened in 1986,' said Haawkon as they strolled along, holding hands. Haawkon pointed out landmarks like the Tuileries Gardens, and in the distance the Champs Elysées. Before buying their tickets and entering the gallery, they sat on a municipal bench overlooking the Seine. Haawkon put his arm round Louise and she cuddled up to him.

'This place, the river, it's beautiful, Haawkon.' He drew her closer.

'It's beautiful with you here.'

In the gallery they took the first hour to get their bearings and cursorily survey the vast collection of impressionist paintings. 'Let's focus on Van Gogh's paintings, they are my favourite,' said Haawkon.

'You choose, it's all new and exciting for me.' Louise enjoyed the trove of stories that Haawkon told about his favourite paintings.

'I'm going to buy the print of Van Gogh's portrait of the psychiatrist Paul Gachet,' Haawkon said. 'He was sympathetic to Van Gogh in the tormented last months of his life. You can see how the painting illustrates Gachet's concern.'

'It's a great choice. I like his stance and caring eyes. We all need someone available like Paul Gachet when we are in trouble ... I think he's rather like you, Haawkon.'

'Really, you flatter me.' Yet Haawkon recognised that, given his concern for her welfare, he had to admit she was reading him accurately.

'Okay, Louise, I've made my choice. What print will you choose to remind you of this visit?' They spent the next hour walking through each gallery and past one compelling painting after another.

'I'm finding it difficult to choose. Renoir's paintings of couples dancing appeal to me and I like his portraits of women, but I think I'll choose Monet's painting of *Water Lilies and the Japanese Bridge*. It's a quiet and humbling painting. Its stillness does much for me.' Haawkon appreciated Louise's capacity to match her quiet consideration with the scene in the Monet painting, as he did her calmness and easy spontaneity. It felt as if Louise had granted him access to a version of himself which he'd long forgotten about.'

'Let's buy that Monet print and then find the gallery café for lunch.'

After a light and long lunch with a lot of talking, they took a cab to the Pompidou Centre.

'It's often called the inside-out building because the escalators are on the outside.' They stood quietly for a while and gazed at the building. They looked at each other. 'I'd forgotten how striking this place is,' said Haawkon. 'Now it comes back to me.'

They entered, read the visitors' information guide telling them that the Centre housed fifty thousand paintings, sculpture and architecture exhibits. Sitting close together they looked through a catalogue with photos of paintings and sculptures. 'I like the elongated surrealist portraits by Modigliani,' said Haawkon.

'Me too, but Picasso's cubism and Jackson Pollock's paintings attract me. I wonder what they were thinking when they painted.'

'That's an interesting point, Louise.' His compliment made her feel comfortable and she liked that.

'When I look at these modern art paintings I often wonder what was on the artist's mind at the time. I would love to know.'

They booked a one-hour guided tour, enjoyed coffee in the mezzanine-level café, both inspired and overwhelmed by what they were seeing. By five o'clock they'd seen enough and were ready to leave.

They had their evening meal in the Café Latin and returned to their hotel. What remained largely unspoken between them was their decision to forgo sex – at this moment that was simply what they both sensed was necessary. And Haawkon knew that, given Louise's situation, having sex at this moment was not the proving ground for love.

Two days later they flew back to London. They shared a cab back to their respective flats. When Louise kissed and said goodbye to Haawkon she realised she was caught in a net of longing and knew that being with him in Paris these last three days had helped her rediscover herself.

Careful

Louise and Haawkon met four days after they returned from Paris. Louise had prepared an evening meal. Having Haawkon in her flat was exhilarating. She knew that in part, the purpose of their meeting was to discuss details of her advocacy tour of Africa later in the year. After she put Joshua to bed Louise made coffee. They retired to the front room sofa. She fixed her eyes on him.

'Let's sort out the African advocacy trip that you have in mind. Is that okay?'

'Fine.' He put down his coffee stroked her cheek and kissed her. 'I'll spell out the details,' he said. 'It'll be good for you to begin as soon as arrangements are made and I'll come with you on this first trip. Kill two birds with one stone,' he said, grinning.

'That's a great idea. I've been apprehensive, but I'll feel more confident if you come with me.'

Haawkon provided details of a low-key lecture tour beginning in Addis Ababa and then moving on to Kampala, Nairobi, Johannesburg and Cape Town. Louise would travel there to talk about how people could avoid catching HIV, and if they *had* contracted the disease, how to control its effects. Haawkon told her he had arranged for her to meet a leading South African lawyer who had openly admitted he was HIV positive. 'He will be a significant ally in your ambassadorial role,' Haawkon said.

'And we agree to share the program?'

'Yes, but that wasn't my original intention. For the moment I'll accept the sharing role, although it really is going to be *your* program.' Haawkon suddenly became quiet.

'Of course, I'll want to share this program with you. It's originally your idea. And anyway, how can I get on without you?' Louise asked, reining in her apprehension.

'Very well, I should think. But I want to be with you when you travel.' Haawkon paused. Louise waited. He sensed she knew what he might say next.

'We are both travellers, Louise. We are researchers and writers. We're kindred spirits. We're both trying to build our lives. And we're relatively free to do just that, to make up our own minds. You have compassion and the patience of the undefeated which, Louise, when all is said and done, is who you are.'

Sitting there in Louise's front room, the previously confident Haawkon looked nervous. He paused again. 'Louise, you know what I am going to ask. I cannot put it off any longer.'

'You mean you want come to Addis, Kampala and Nairobi with me?'

'That and more.' A nervous shudder ran through him. He was aware of Louise gazing lovingly at him. He found it difficult ask her directly. 'I'd like to travel with you as your husband.'

Louise paused, then said, 'And I could travel with you as your wife?'

'That's what I'd hope.'

She shook her head. 'But how will you cope with my illness? Have you really considered that and what it might do for your career? How can you ever live with a woman with this disease who could, even if only the slightest mistake occurred, infect you?'

Louise had read that one shouldn't make a huge life-changing decision when recently bereaved. She also knew that when lost in a fog, you use your senses differently. Making the right decision was a balancing act, but she sensed that alongside Haawkon, her fog was dispersing, and she thought of taking every precaution so they could soon enjoy making love.

In such a manner, to and fro till late in the evening, they traded ideas about their future lives but initially came to no definite conclusion. They hugged each other, kissed goodbye and Haawkon drove home to his flat.

Given her situation, Louise was uncertain about marriage. Wasn't it wise to wait, she had asked Haawkon. Yet he would not be dissuaded. Not at all disconcerted by her response, he persisted. They hadn't made love yet but, as before, Haawkon knew not to hurry Louise.

They met many times over the following month. They went to the Leicester Square Odeon cinema to see the film *Titanic*, which they didn't enjoy. 'Far too melodramatic,' said Haawkon. The following week both enjoyed a popular drama film, *Good Will Hunting*, starring Robin Williams.

'Anything starring Robin Williams is a guarantee of a good film,' said Louise. Haawkon agreed.

His conviction about his love for Louise was clear. Whenever the opportunity occurred, and gaining in confidence, he emphasised the certainty of their love for each other. Already taking shape in Louise's mind was the prospect of a full life with Haawkon and a new demanding career. Again they arranged to have a weekend away together in the Sussex seaside village of Rye.

Haawkon and Louise knew that life together was not going to be easy, but were determined to succeed. One thing was clear in both their minds: they would take every precaution and deal with Louise's disease.

In November 1997 they drove to England's south coast and stayed in a Rye seaside cottage. Josh stayed in London with his cousins. With wind in their hair, the smell of seaweed and screams of seagulls, they walked on the pebble beach. They held hands as they walked, smiled at each other and were happy. Haawkon told Louise that few things gave him such a sense of fulfilment as walking with her on that windswept beach. Louise knew how he could deal with the unexpected, and be fearless and in charge, such as in their time together in New York when, chivalrous and beguiling, Haawkon had organised daily activities in fine detail. Now, carefully prepared, he will make love to me tonight, thought Louise, and instinctively she knew she would give him undivided love.

After dinner that first night they sat before an open wood fire, sipped wine, and Haawkon read verses of William Carlos Williams, Whitman and Wordsworth. Louise responded with her favourite Judith Wright poems, 'Beside the Creek' and 'Homecoming'. When the fire burned low they went to bed.

She watched him undress that night – his slender muscular figure, broad shoulders, long legs and strong hands. He explored her body and Louise found herself totally at ease, totally herself, and as desirous of his love as when she had been alone with him in his New York apartment. They made love tenderly and without apprehension, and in the morning lay in each other's arms. For each of them the warm body of the other brought with it a magic, a gift of commitment they both had longed for.

The Davitts in London

Louise's parents flew to London in January 1998. They had been there the previous year when they first met Haawkon. This time they planned to have a longer stay with Geoff and Sophie. Prior to this visit they had spoken at length to Louise by phone. Gerald in particular wanted to spend time with his daughter. The thought of the disease was forever on his mind. Also, he wanted to talk to Haawkon and was concerned about Louise's plans for the African lecture tour.

Louise and Josh were having an evening meal at Geoff and Sophie's home the night her parents first arrived. Before Louise drove home, Monica whispered to Gerald, 'Arrange to have breakfast with her tomorrow, just the two of you, then you can ask her how well she is and about her plans.'

He agreed. He was thinking not just of the virus which could be killing his daughter, but this crazy plan of hers to counsel people across the world about how HIV sufferers could live a normal life. He felt scared and on occasions angry at the scale of the risk of further infection for Louise.

They met the next day in St John's Wood for a late breakfast. Gerald was concerned that she might reproach him during what he suspected would be a sensitive meeting. He wanted to know in detail how badly infected she was, and how he and Monica could help.

Gerald tried to look relaxed but half expected his beautiful daughter to appear unwell, thinking that the evening before she had just put on a brave face. 'How are you?' he asked.

'I'm fine, Dad, just fine.' Louise responded with a smile and a repeated nod. She appreciated his concern, but knew that it would take time for him to understand what had happened. He didn't want to be counselled by her.

'I'm keen to know how I can help you.' He tried to relax, but the ineradicable thoughts about what he originally believed was just a homosexual disease left him confused. HIV was violating his daughter's body and the man responsible for passing on the infection was supposedly dead. But then, Zeno Wolde was not a homosexual or even a bisexual, as far as Gerald knew. Could it also be that HIV/AIDS was mainly an African disease that affected heterosexual and homosexuals alike but did not affect heterosexual people who lived in England, America or Australia? It didn't make sense. Did Louise know what she was doing? How would it all end up? What was her sense of responsibility to his grandson Joshua? Who exactly was this Haawkon Davos? Would she die within a few years?

'This illness is not an easy thing to talk about,' he said. 'It's all so recent, but I'm sure your specialist knows what he's doing.'

'He's very good, I have confidence in him.'

Gerald nodded. 'And are there side-effects of taking the drugs?'

'Of course, but because there are five different classes of drugs for the treatment of the virus and the availability of these drugs is so recent, they are not sure what these side-effects might be.'

He told her he was proud of her and of the way in which, despite her illness, she was courageous and optimistic. 'How long will you have to take these drugs?' He knew the answer but he wanted to hear Louise's response.

'For the rest of my life, Dad, but that's alright because I can still lead a normal life, provided I maintain my physical and mental health. I have to do that for Josh and everyone's sake. And I will.'

Gerald remembered his daughter in her teenage years, the daughter who had scrambled up steep cliffs, camped on the Coorong shore, swum and dived on Southern Ocean beaches and had so many good friends. Yes, she was the same person. 'Louise, you are so courageous. What are your plans?'

'My plans? To talk to people with the disease and about how HIV can be prevented.'

Gerald looked worried.

'Dad, I have the disease and I still have good health.'

'But Louise, isn't that better done by disease specialists and governments? Why do you want to become so involved? Shouldn't your priority be to focus on taking care of yourself?'

'Do you think I'm wrong to want to let people know they can live a full life with HIV? And that it's important to obtain early diagnosis and access to available antiretroviral drugs?'

'Not wrong, but you are surely placing yourself at yet more risk by being close to infected people, aren't you?'

They sat for a moment in silence.

'Dad, the worst, the most cowardly, the *least* effective thing would be to walk away and hide. The real truth of this condition, how it can be prevented and how it can be managed, has to be told. I want to be able to talk to people, particularly in the developing world. I want to see the incidence of HIV/AIDS reduced, if not disappear. I know that's probably a forlorn hope but I have to make a contribution. Given my involvement with people in Ethiopia and Kenya, and certainly in London, my mind is made up. I feel I have no alternative, Dad, and I'm excited at the prospect.'

Gerald looked with sadness but also admiration at Louise, and wondered, who would have thought our lives have come to this? Her happy childhood, successful studies, travel and all our family loving … and now this disease.

Yet, she reminded him how resilient and inventive she had always been and no doubt would be again. And he knew there was a lesson here; something that, at the start of their breakfast, had appeared to be completely unlikely, even ludicrous, would now happen. He pictured her, with her contagious love for people and vivacious personality, spearheading a campaign educating people about her illness, becoming an advocate for women with the disease who were despised and rejected, and teaching people with the illness how they could lead a full life.

'Whatever you decide to do and wherever you are, we'll support you,' he said quietly but emphatically. And hadn't he always advocated the importance of staying the course, whatever happened?

Soothed by his daughter's strength and commitment, Gerald spoke of the events that had brought her to London and Ethiopia, along with the precious gift of a healthy, bright and lively grandson. Louise could see that her disease was no longer a barrier between them.

He felt much more cheerful now, which he had not expected. With his arm around his daughter they left the restaurant.

13: Resolution

The Revival Health Centre

Carrying out Louise's wish to find Zeno's grave presented many difficulties, but she persisted. Success would not only bring some sort of finality to that part of her life; it would allow her to start a new life beyond Zeno. A 'bridge to the future,' she called it.

To begin with, Louise and Amos had no idea that Zeno had had any contact with or had stayed at the Revival Health Centre (RHC). One of the chief difficulties was that the RHC was not registered, and even when functioning, it was only known about by word of mouth. A further stumbling block was the outright opposition of Kenya's medical profession to such establishments, which they called 'witch-doctor-health-centres'. Another obstacle was the by now insurmountable distrust by the village people of Bernard Wilson. As far as they were concerned, Wilson was a con man. There was no publication of information about who had attended the RHC and no details of what happened to sick people after they left. Questions by staff and patients were ignored and Wilson barricaded himself in his room as suspicions about his practice grew.

After the RHC was vacated and then closed down, administrators from the Kenyan Department of Health in Nairobi sought opinions from village people who had worked there. They organised a community meeting with them at the premises.

'Could you please tell us what went on here?' asked the District Department of Health Administrator, who chaired the meeting. 'We have some information as to who registered here for treatment but we would appreciate details about what went on from those of you who worked here. Feel free to tell us what you know. Please tell us anything you can think of.' Staff who had kept quiet for years now told what they knew.

A woman in the front row was rather agitated and keen to talk. She had worked in the RHC kitchen and chatted to patients.

'Bernard Wilson is a fraud,' said the woman without hesitation. 'People who came here were sick, often very sick, yet I don't think Dr Bernard could cure a common cold, that's what I think of him.' She paused. 'And we've found out he had no qualifications to run his so-called health centre and no one in authority asked what he was doing here.'

'Too many people who came here for treatment paid a lot of money, a *lot* of money, and left just as sick as when they arrived,' said another woman who had worked as a cleaner and a laundry hand.

'It's true what she's saying,' added a man who had worked in the RHC gym and assisted on the morning walks. 'And I'm sure that no SLIM people who came here were ever cured. They just left here to die, but they paid Wilson good money.'

'Despite his health food, medicine and life-balance counselling, no one seemed to benefit,' said an older man who had worked in the garden and knew many of the patients Then, pointing to the woman in the front row, he continued, 'It's like my friend here says, Wilson is a fraud – and he called himself a healer. He knew nothing about healing. To begin with we trusted him, but not anymore. He's deceived our community, he let us down and we are very angry.'

'After he prescribed his pills and vitamins, he had nothing more to do with his patients other than to get Nurse Martha to hand out more pills and vitamin drinks,' said a woman who had worked alongside Nurse Martha. 'Guidelines about Wilson's medicine were not written down; they were just in his head. We had to endure his incompetence. And qualified doctors didn't know about this place, or if they did, they ignored what went on until, for many patients, it was too late.'

Staff told how most mornings, Wilson was in his office before

340

anyone was awake, writing instructions for Martha. At midmorning, cigarette in his mouth, he would wander to the lounge, to the gym or chat to a counsellor, and then have coffee and cake with Elizabeth Makula as he masqueraded as the healing doctor with his talk about the uniqueness of his medicines, and his patients' improved physical and psychic health.

Some of Dr Bernard's staff said that he never examined patients, and when they were clearly ill he was certain to ignore them, or just recommend, via Martha or Elizabeth Makula, the need for more of his pills and potions. Staff and patients soon realised he had tricked them, and when asked how the RHC treated sick people, they said, 'He behaved liked an ostrich.'

Unexpected News

To Louise's dismay, she received no response from newspaper and police advertisements that she and the University of Nairobi administration had placed, asking for information about the whereabouts of Dr Zeno Wolde.

She had almost given up when, more than two years after Zeno's disappearance, she received unexpected news via Amos' friend Lewis. He had been given a poetry book, a 1967 edition of *The Poems of Doctor Zhivago* by Boris Pasternak, with Zeno's name on the inside cover. Somehow it had been acquired by a Kenyan woman who was familiar with the former Nyambene Hills Revival Health Centre and had spent a week there not long after Zeno's death. The poetry book had been found in his room. Lewis knew the woman, and in conversation one night, in the same wine bar where Zeno had met Fashna, she told Lewis about the book. She had no idea who Zeno Wolde was, other than he had once been treated at the RHC. According to Lewis, all of Zeno's other possessions left at the RHC had been burnt. Finding his poetry book proved to be the breakthrough Louise needed. Amos located the RHC for her.

It's a strange world, thought Louise, where a poetry book, a lasting symbol of Zeno, is all I have left as a record of his final days.

Confident now that she knew where Zeno had died, she determined to find his grave. She booked a Saturday evening flight to Nairobi. Haawkon insisted on accompanying her. Josh stayed with Geoff and Sophie for the ten days they were away. They would arrive in Nairobi mid-afternoon on the Saturday.

Amos and his wife Tana met Louise and Haawkon at Jomo Kenyatta airport and took them back to their home. Sitting on a couch in their front room, Louise breathed nervously as she waited with a mixture of excitement and apprehension for Amos to tell her about the RHC.

His voice was low and considered. 'I've spoken to the RHC's caretaker, Grant Mboya. He still lives on the property. He's expecting us early Tuesday afternoon. It's a three-hour drive to the foot of the Nyambene Hills. Then we'll take the gravel track that leads to the RHC. I've checked the route.'

Finding the Grave

The air was sticky as Amos left the main road and drove uphill along the rutted track, winding its way between split rocks, random piles of logs at the track-side, and bulldozed flattened saplings. Beyond the track, Louise noticed dark and sombre forest country which contrasted with the distant sunny fertile plain below. As the steep track flattened out they came on the clearing which housed the RHC. It now sported a large *For Sale* sign.

Amos pulled up and parked behind what had been the administration block. The centre looked empty and in need of paint and maintenance. Louise realised with a racing heart that in this spacious forest clearing and in these huts was where Zeno had almost certainly spent his last weeks.

She left Amos and Haawkon and walked slowly and pensively, threading her way among the laurel and acacia bushes on the uneven and now unmown lawns leading to the collection of weathered wooden huts that once were the centre in which Zeno had put his faith. As she approached, a slim middle-aged Kenyan man came out of the first hut and waved. She waved back.

'You are Ms Louise?' he enquired. 'Your friend Amos has told me about you.'

'Yes, and you must be Grant Mboya.'

'That's me.'

Louise shook his outstretched hand.

'You wanna look at your man's grave?' he asked quietly.

'Yes. That's what I've come for.'

Haawkon and Amos watched them from a distance.

'I can show you where it is,' Grant Mboya said.

Together they walked some four hundred metres to the edge of the clearing. Encroaching forest scrub had all but obscured the oblong mound that was Zeno's unmarked grave. Mostly hidden by tall grasses, it was at the foot of a low hill. Grasses merged into the encroaching scrub, and forest and wildflowers grew on the moist ground.

'That's it,' Grant Mboya said, pointing. 'It's been two years since our villagers and staff buried him. No one knew exactly who he was. He gave a false name and address, but I thought he was someone quite different.'

Together they contemplated Zeno's grave. A feeling of tenderness poured through Louise.

'I'll leave you now,' Grant said. 'If there's anything I can do just come back to the centre and knock on my door. I'll be there.'

'Thank you.'

How strange it is, Louise reflected as she looked tearfully at the grassy mound – that in all my time with Zeno, our travelling and fieldwork together, our exciting early years in Addis Ababa, happiness together in San Francisco, London and Adelaide, the acclaim of his teaching and research, the birth of the son he had always wanted and the offers of research fellowships in New York, Oxford and Sydney – how strange that he should be buried in a simple grave on the edge of an isolated forest far from his home.

She stood for a while and then knelt and kissed the earth. She placed her bunch of wildflowers on top of the grassy mound. She had bought a trowel from a garden centre, and a small fern and a cherry tree sapling in pots; the florist in Nairobi had told her they were suitable for the climate and would grow and last a long time. She planted them in the rough grass beside the grave then sat back on her heels. She thought she might say something to Zeno, perhaps strike up a conversation with him.

She knelt there, overwhelmed. She felt waves of hurt, regret and

sadness but also great love as she stared at the grave. For many minutes she remained still. Crying, Louise gave thanks for Zeno's life.

Then she stood, turned and beckoned to Amos and Haawkon to
join her. She would eventually arrange for a plaque to be placed on
the grave expressing not only her personal love for Zeno but also
how people in Ethiopia and around the world admired him.

The three of them gathered around the grave, holding hands.

'Good bye Zeno, my dear,' Louise sobbed. Haawkon and Amos
bent and touched the grave.

Clouds were gathering over the Nyambene Hills when together
they walked slowly back to where Amos' 4WD was parked. Grant
Mboya stood nearby. 'I'll look after your man's grave,' he said. 'That'll
be my pleasure.'

Amos drove on downhill over the potholed track and turned
onto the Meru Road that would take them past Mt Kenya and on via
Embu, back to Nairobi and Louise's meeting the following day with
Gabriella.

Sharing with Gabriella

In Gabriella's home Louise sat on the edge of a comfortable armchair as they talked. They had spoken many times on the phone and Louise had written to her. In this bright small lounge room Zeno's mother said she'd known he was very sick and had died. Then for the next hour, the two women shared their experiences of Zeno.

'Did he die from the virus?' Gabriella asked. Louise nodded. 'I thought he must have,' Gabriella said sadly, and then, looking at Louise, she added, 'You must be very sad too.' She gripped Louise's hands in hers.

'Of course I'm very sad, hurt also, and at times lost, very lost,' Louise replied. She did not disclose that she was HIV positive and that Zeno had infected her. She wanted to remain positive in the presence of the older woman. 'Zeno was such a unique person.'

Gabriella nodded.

'His modesty, given his achievements, was a revelation to so many. He was so talented. And though, on occasions, he was fascinated with notions of genius, which some people called him, he never ever claimed to possess it. But those who read his publications and watched him at work insisted he was quite exceptional.'

'He won't hear that description now, which is very sad,' said Gabriella.

'Yes, but there'll be future scholars who'll recognise his contribution so his work won't be lost. It's possible to recognise his spirit in his books and other works.'

'He was very independent as a child,' Gabriella said. Then she added proudly, 'But he also supported his friends, and he had a lot of them.'

'Yes he had many loving friends. They will never forget him.'

'That's comforting,' said Gabriella. 'I'll always remember what you've just said.' She paused. 'And I'm sure you have a story to tell, but only when you're ready.'

'I'm certain you know he was convinced that every person, even the poorest and most disabled, had enormous potential. He believed he had a responsibility to enable his students and people of the villages to develop and harvest their talents. He was always in harmony with them.'

The intimate and rewarding life Louise had had with him were apparent to Gabriella. 'I understand what you're saying. And you inspired him, but he also took on too much.'

'That's true.'

There was a long silence between the two women, and then Gabriella suddenly asked, 'Do you still love him?'

'How could I not love him? He is Josh's father and he supported me and was my lover and mentor ever since we met. You must know how much we all admired and loved him.'

'Sometimes he could be quite impulsive.'

Louise knew Zeno could be impulsive, but responded, 'You know, Gabriella, we need to remember Zeno as a most loving, inventive and entertaining son and partner, and also in his work, one of the most insightful. and well researched anthropologists of this generation. His pioneering work in Ethiopia and Kenya will not be forgotten.'

'It's lovely to hear you say that,' cried Gabriella, clapping her hands softly together. 'I didn't know much about his work, he was always moving around. What did you call his work?' She knew, but wanted to hear it again from Louise.

'Anthropology.'

'That's it, anthropology. When you have time, then tell me more about Zeno's work.' She paused. 'And how is Joshua? Does he say anything about his father? Does he remember him?'

'Joshua has very fond memories of his dad, and he always asks about him. When he's older he'll know what a remarkable man his father was.' Louise wanted to say more about Joshua, but she couldn't. She wanted to talk about her bright energetic son and how his life might be adventurous, like his father's. But at this moment it was out of place.

She did not touch on Zeno's role as Josh's father, good as it was in those early infant years. To refer to his absent parenting at this time could be disturbing. It was more important to introduce shreds of optimism into their collective memory. She wanted to say that in good times, and there had been many good times, Zeno enlightened people as well as lightening many burdens of their daily lives.

'People need to know how much Zeno meant to us all and just how we miss him and how we will remember him,' said Louise, trying to hold back tears.

Gabriella whispered, 'Thank you, my dear, you are very kind. It's good to know that Zeno's friends are proud of his work.' She added, 'Such a loss.'

14: Epilogue

Joshua's Reflections – Ethiopia 2015

I'm in Addis Ababa where I was born. Mesay Teboya from Oromiya Province is driving me to the Southern Tribal Lands where Mum spent so much time. When I return to Addis I'll meet her and my Italian fiancée, Francesca. We met on an exchange medical school program in 2009, and plan to marry when we return to London.

Mum married Haawkon Davos in May 1998 in Adelaide's Botanic Gardens, just after my eighth birthday. The sun was high and the day was warm. All Mum's family and friends were there. Haawkon's younger sister and her husband and their two teenage daughters flew from Norway. Carmen flew in from London and, to Mum's great delight, Mandy Watson and her eldest son came. It was a memorable occasion. Everything my grandparents, Gerald and Monica Davitt, had hoped for their daughter was represented at the wedding; laughter and happiness overflowed. Memories of Mum's wedding will always be with me, how radiant and beautiful she was that day. And that's how her life is still, with Haawkon.

Mum and Haawkon set up home in Amersham, a small town on the edge of England's Chiltern Hills. They commute to London where Haawkon has his old one-bedroom flat, close to Russell Square. He still works for MSF and, until last year, taught part-time at London University. Life has been full for them, especially since 2000, when they adopted two orphaned Ethiopian children, Hirut and her younger brother Daniel, and brought them to live with us in Amersham. They are loved siblings and we are a close family.

Mum's very well. She manages her disease effectively and with

Haawkon at her side, has created a happy home life for Hirut and Daniel. Daniel is quiet and studious. Hirut can be rebellious, but Mum loves her and they are inseparable. Mum and Haawkon always had time to attend school functions, take us to weekend sport and enjoy family holidays together in Cornwall, back in Australia and, memorably, in Norway with Haawkon's family. Mum's been incredible.

Above all she's introduced the three of us to Ethiopia. It's a country where I've learned how so much comes together: Coptic Christians, Muslims and animists, famine, abundance, poverty and riches, straw-roofed huts and palatial homes, spectacular mountains, deserts and fertile plains, dry riverbeds and rivers overflowing. But above all, resilient people with a unique history.

Mum is currently in Johannesburg with Francesca. She was invited there to address an international conference. She tells people how she contracted her illness. She's up front. When she meets women sex workers, she hands out condoms and femidoms and teaches them how to negotiate safe sex with men. She tells women that femidoms are a symbol of empowerment for women. She demonstrates this practice at conferences, where delegates come from all over the world to hear her. 'Look,' she says, 'femidoms are something that women can put into their own bodies without having to trust the man to use a condom.' The truth is that Mum succeeds because she gets close to these people, genuinely likes them and doesn't believe in failure. More and more, because of her advocacy, the sex workers she meets are unwilling to jeopardise their health for clients' preferences. It's obvious: if being a sex worker is a woman's only means of livelihood, she must all take care of herself. That's Mum's message, although it's a message that, on occasions, has proved difficult for some people to accept. But she's working at it and never gives up.

Plenty of people talk about the management of the disease from their ivory towers, but Louise Davos is out there telling how she personally manages the condition. Sadly, some people are still verbally abusive, or accuse her of being guilty for contracting the disease, and how it is a sin so grave she should 'burn in hell'. She lives with ignorance of that sort. There are examples of the spread of the disease on the one hand and control on the other. Mum says it's like wrestling with a serpent: sometimes you have it well and truly under control, at other times it slips away. But in cities, towns and villages across Ethiopia and Kenya, there are mobile caravans and tents on street corners requesting people to be tested for HIV. And that is a transformation.

I'll be visiting some new clinics in Oromia province where community health workers are at the frontline controlling malaria. Children are still the most vulnerable because their bodies have yet to build up an immune response to the malaria parasite. My father knew how children were at risk when he worked as a young doctor in their villages forty years ago. A breakthrough now is an injectable drug, artesunate. It is being promoted by the government, although, in this vast country, the roll-out is slow. Controlling malaria is a race against time. Haawkon tells me that Médecins Sans Frontières have trialled artesunate and found that it substantially reduces the risk of death and, compared to quinine, there are fewer side-effects. Yet supply sources and high prices make it difficult for the government to scale-up the program. But their commitment to provide an adequate supply of the drug provides much hope for malaria sufferers. My father would have been thrilled to know this.

I need to comment about my dad. As Camus says, *A child is nothing by himself, it is his parents who represent him. It is through them that he defines himself and is defined in the eyes of the world.* My father's life is important for me. He could so easily be maligned because of how he died. Zeno Wolde worked and wrote during difficult times in Ethiopia's political life. Mum tells me how his work was often secretive, underground, just out of reach of censure by the Derg's political police. His language was that of a reformer and dissenter. That, I'm told, is how his friends remember him.

Clearly my dad was a complex man, an inspiring partner and serial lover of women; a passionate campaigner for reform; a man who was confident and fearless – but also a man of self-doubt. He was meticulous in his writing and research and yet casual and often dissolute in his personal behaviour which, sadly, placed him at risk; at times, he could not steer clear of the devil within him. I shudder when I think of his fate.

Given his enthusiasm, there must have been times when Dad thought life was infinite. That was his first mistake. I often wonder what he learnt as a doctor. In the end he didn't take the opportunity to control his disease. That was another mistake. The stigma associated with the disease got to him, and his ability to use his knowledge was crushed. Stigma undermined his reasoning. Looking back, it was perhaps inevitable that he headed for the brink, not to be seen again.

I often wonder what I might do if something so traumatic happened to me as happened to my mother, or indeed to my father. I'm not sure, but in order to try and solve this I would do a number of things to clear my head. I'd walk across the Chiltern Hills of my childhood and enjoy skylark songs and beech trees dappling in bluebell woods. I'd camp again on South Australia's windswept Coorong and marvel at Mandy Watson's Aboriginal dot paintings and hopefully spend time with her. I'd visit friends in San Francisco, as well as the remarkable people of the Omo Valley and, if possible, I'd spend time in villages in Amhara and Tigray. I'd read Pasternak's poetry, as my father must have done, savouring his words: *You are my gift of life when days / Grow baneful, worse than the disease, / Heroic life is the root of beauty, / And it draws together you and me.* These lines would have given Dad hope, something he could hold onto at that difficult time.

And then I'd discuss with friends and colleagues around the world the issues of improved healthcare and food production, and the importance of recognising and managing climate change. And like my mother and father, I'd try to grapple with issues that make for a better life, such as the abolition of female genital mutilation of women and girls across Africa and also in certain communities in the UK, and probably even in Australia and the US. I believe Mum and Francesca will discuss this issue while they are in Johannesburg.

Mum has great faith in people. For her, life is only dark if we make it so. She's a great letter writer and despite text messages, Twitter and emails, she still writes longhand to tell us about what's happening at home, and more often than not, there is a philosophical comment in her letters. She wrote me a reflective letter before I left for Addis. Here it is:

Dear Josh,

How are you? Are you well prepared for your trip? I'm sure you will enjoy yourself. I would love to be with you. You know how I marvel at the inventiveness and toughness to be found in the tribes of the south, the isolated peoples, the Dorze, Banna, Hamar and Karo, who put so much energy into creating their enduring way of life. We can learn so much from them.

I'm sitting in our Amersham garden as I write. Some genius devised this beautiful place and, as you know, from here I can see the distant hills and the road that winds away from our house and rises gradually to the foot of the Chilterns. It reminds me of the track I walked on with Mandy, my Aboriginal friend, some forty years ago. It's the track that wound its way from my grandparents' Crystal Brook farm to distant, bare, brown-yellow hills. It's strange how, on reflection, a scene can remind you of a similar one a long time ago. Birds are flitting about our garden this spring afternoon. Now a crow, with its steel-bright eye has just landed in an old oak tree and has scattered the thrushes with its deep squawk. You'll see crows on your journey but England's Joe Crow is not a vulture like the ones I have seen hovering over starving villages.

Beech trees and bushes are in bud in our garden and in the hedgerows, a sure sign of spring. Last week Haawkon and I went with friends to Hyde Hall in Essex. It's a botanical garden with an Australian section with wattle and eucalyptus trees.

They reminded me of the Adelaide Hills. Eucalypts are every-where in Ethiopia as well as in Australia. In Ethiopia's towns and villages you'll see how they hang over ripple-tin roofs and their endless strings of bark are used to light fires. There's been a fox in our garden these last few days. They're common in and around Amersham just now. This one is tame and, of course, quite different from spotted whooping hyenas that your father and I saw during our time on the Simien plateau.

There were boys of good and bad behaviour at the shops in Amersham this morning. Some reminded me of the goat- and sheep-herding boys of Amhara, Tigray and the Southern Tribal Lands. I've always thought they were the gentlest boys on earth when, on rough hillsides and sandy flood plains, they cared for their animals. I'll be interested to hear what you think.

We've had steady spring rain and everything is very green. England never has hot winds which, in Ethiopia and Australia, can suck water from rivers. In the heat you'll find necessary shade from thorn and acacia trees, as village and tribal people have always done.

On television last night there was a repeat of games of the 2014 Football World Cup played in Brazil. This reminded me of Amharan village boys dribbling a 'sockball' with their thin leathery feet – their feet were football boots without laces. In the World Cup, twenty footballs were kicked around before the match even started.

Life is not a perfect game, Josh, and if it were, how would we play? Before you left you asked me why I maintain a full travel schedule in the developing world in order to talk about diseases such as HIV/AIDS, malaria, measles and now Ebola. I think it's important to continue to remind people, especially at min-isterial level, how such diseases can be prevented and cured. And you asked how, at home in Amersham and London, I still maintain my health, have a rewarding life teaching, writing, meeting and holidaying with friends and family.

I guess that two worlds meet in my thoughts. England and Australia on the one hand, and then there is Ethiopia. There are threads that bind them. I've learned that, given the unusual ways of genius, there is as much talent, passion and creativity to be found in any sample of nomadic Hamar people or Tigrayans, tilling their fields and minding their goats, as there are in our august universities. Perhaps I'm too romantic, but you'll recognise this talent. You laughed when I told you once that even boys and girls in rags in the villages, and the often naked children of the tribal lands, are very bright; real treasures they are, just like Hirut and Daniel.

Ethiopia will change your thinking as it has mine. It still glows for me, despite the spectrum of pain that, one way or another, I meet every day. Those former years were very good and now I have dear Haawkon. I have no illusions. Every day we are tried in the balance: one day we succeed, another day we are found wanting. One day we are well, another sick. I have learned to tolerate whatever cannot be solved or changed but – and it's a big but – I'll always go on trying with the language of respect and passion to create opportunities that renew people's lives, as mine is renewed every day.

Francesca and I look forward to joining you in Addis in three weeks' time. Take care. Give my love to all my dear Ethiopian friends.

My love as ever, Mum

Of course, Mum never planned to work in the disease prevention field. But she's always been stirred by need, and also by indifference, the indifference that ignores problems, often until it's too late to act.

The roads south from Addis to Arba Minch, Jinka and Turmi are better now, but many are still unsealed. Yet this trip is different from what Mum experienced almost thirty years ago. I won't be living with the Hamar, just visiting. And I'll eventually reach Yabello where a lodge, as a place to stay for backpackers and hardy tourists, is being built by the Borana people. Tourism, which should flourish here, has stopped for the moment, largely because of fear of the Ebola virus. But that epidemic will be solved and people will rediscover the magnificence of Ethiopia. I'm sure that, despite hardship and harsh traditional practices, especially those that are cruel and demeaning to women, Ethiopians will progress and never be crushed.

After eight hours driving, Mesay and I have arrived at our first overnight stop. We're at a campsite beside Lake Awasa. The lake is filled with mirrored mountains and when rainstorms pass over Awasa town, they empty themselves on the peaks. There's plenty of fish in the water along with hydras, water bugs and larvae. Men, young and old, are out fishing. As I gaze across the lake, purple dragonflies flit above the reeds, small frogs croak on the bank, marabou storks stand in the shallows and metallic-blue malachite kingfishers with their reddish bills search for crustaceans. As evening comes, hawks circle, thrumming their wings as they dive to catch rodents.

In this immense landscape the here and now of my parents, of Haawkon, Francesca, Hirut and Daniel are visible. I can see them; feel their desires and loves. And then in the midst of all this there is my need to learn more about Ethiopia. This country has rich traditions, great opportunities, much to teach me – and the plenitude of life leaves me giddy. As night falls, widely spaced drops of rain plop on our tent, purple lightning bursts over the distant mountains and the ground smells of wet life.

This is where I'll end my reflections, at least for the time being. I need to sleep. If I went on writing, keeping as much as possible to the sequence of events that I know about, I would have to write of years and circumstances in different parts of the world for Mum, Dad and Haawkon, of people and of destinies within their lives. I'd have to write about aspirations of the rich and poor, the healthy and sick; about problems and achievements previously unknown, and of restraints when poverty, sickness and famine are prevalent. All this is often on my mind. So, naturally, when I look at Ethiopia's children and enjoy their laughter, I think about Hirut and Daniel. Or I imagine having my own children, and I ask myself what sort of a world they will inherit. Only time will tell.

Glossary

Abbe Gubennya	Ethiopian writer of novels, plays, essays, short stories and poetry. He was recognised as a great fighter for freedom and justice. He is honoured with a statue of him erected in Bahir Dar.
aleqa	chief or a significant priest
alicha	a mild yellow-coloured sauce flavoured with onions and garlic
ameuseugnallo	thank you
Amharic	first language of Ethiopia; language of the Amhara people
aykonen	no
ayzore	'be strong', expression of encouragement in battle, travel or women's labour in childbirth
azmari	a traditional itinerant singer
bege	lamb
bejaka/bejakee	(male/female) please
berberi	dried and powdered red chilli pepper
Biftu	Oromo girl's name meaning Dawn
bilowa	butchery knife, prominent at butchers' shops and stalls in Ethiopian town and country markets
birr	Ethiopian currency
bishaan amo	Oromo for mineral water
buna	coffee

Chinua Achebe	Nobel Prize-winning Nigerian novelist, poet and essayist whose most famous book *Things Fall Apart* has been translated into over fifty languages. 'Achebe reveals the inner workings of the human conscience through the predicament of Africa … and his own intellectual life.'
debarda	sorghum porridge
debir	church
doomfata	the recital of heroic deeds
Derg	Socialist military junta that originally deposed Emperor Haile Selassie and ruled Ethiopia 1974–1991. Derg derived from the *Geez* (a forerunner of modern Amharic) word for committee.
evangadi	a Hamar love dance; part of the rites of passage for Hamar men and women
Fekkare Iyesus	The interpretation of Jesus, Ethiopian sacred text
fiyel	goat
giraf	hippo-hide whip
gorphak	fig-like fruit which tolerates drought conditions
gwaro	fields or tilled land: a garden close to the homestead
hakim	doctor
hidmo	homestead; a collection of huts
injera	flat pancake-like bread made from *teff*
Kaeske (or Korcske)	Hamar river; a most dangerous river when in flood, flows from Dimeka
keremt	season of rains roughly late July to September, particularly on the Simien plateau
kiddus	saints or holy men
kocho	bread made from the sap of the 'false' banana tree
kurkufa	a hard nutritious ball made from sorghum and milk and cooked in butter or oil, which would last

	a Hamar person walking all day
mari	Amharic word for honey
maza	male whippers of women in the Hamar rite of passage ceremony
Mengistu Lemma	One of the best known Ethiopian writers both as a playwright and poet. His plays were regarded as 'comedies with a serious purpose', urging people to criticise social evils. He also drew and painted with watercolours and pastels. Mengistu was the youngest of eight children, six boys and two girls. His father was a significant priest (*aleqa*) of an important church (*debir*). In church schools Mengistu studied classical poetry (*qine*). He also studied in England at the Regents Street Polytechnic in London and at the London School of Economics and Political Science (LSE).
merhaba	welcome, wonderful
migib bet	café
misso	hunting friends
Ngarrindjeri	Aboriginal tribe that lived for forty thousand years around South Australia's Coorong and Lower Lakes
Oromo	The largest single ethnic group in Ethiopia at 32 per cent; they inhabit Oromia, Ethiopia's largest province; also language of the Oromo and, in pidgin form, part language of the Hamar tribe.
qine	classical Amharic poetry
sankara	leaves of the 'soap tree' when mixed with water to make soap
selam	hello (literally 'peace be with you')
shoforo	Hamar coffee, similar to tea

signa tibs	a fried meat dish
SLIM	the original local Uganda name for the wasting disease caused by HIV/AIDS; the term SLIM became applied more widely across Africa
sockball	poor village boys in Ethiopia often play football with a tightly tied bundle of rags which is called a *sockball* – few if any of them have soccer balls
teff	indigenous Ethiopian wheat, staple of Tigray and the highlands but increasingly popular in major cities and extending now into the south
tella	native beer brewed from barley and sometimes sorghum
tella bet	beer house
Tsegaye Gabre-Medhin	Ethiopia's poet laureate and 'premier versatile and prolific man of letters … poet, playright, essayist, social critic, dramatist and peace activist, who was shaped by the subcultures, languages and blending of his Oromo and Amharan heritages; he was opposed by the Derg.'
tikur anbessa	black lion, as in Black Lion Hospital, Addis Ababa
woilem kaba	depression, sad mood state
woredu	a district, as in Hamar *woredu*
wot	spicy sauce
woyna tombo	tree leaves when sniffed (usually in Hamar and Banna country) has a potency similar to cocaine, sometimes imbibed to relieve pain
yebere siga	beef
zenabu	it's raining

Acknowledgements

This story has its origins in meetings with people from Adelaide, London, San Francisco, New York, Nairobi and Addis Ababa, Arba Minch and Bahir Dar, Ethiopia. However, my characters, their views, personalities, relationships and circumstances are entirely fictional. I have acknowledged every author whose work is quoted in this book. There are, however, words of other authors which may be paraphrased on these pages. This is not because I have overlooked their contribution, but because their writings have become part of my own language templates, part of my writing and speaking about *No Turning Back*.

This novel has taken many years to write and it could not have been written without the assistance of many people.

My thanks to: my great friend Max Kemp, the poet Jude Aquilina and to Mary Cunnane. Max's ongoing encouragement and editing of the early drafts enabled me to persist with writing *No Turning Back*. Jude brought a poet's touch with her editing. She played a crucial role in not only appreciating the personalities of the principal characters in *No Turning Back* but in enhancing their roles by her understanding what happens when a person experiences love, happiness or hell. Mary Cunnane's advice that 'less is more' was an invaluable lesson. Thanks also to Simon Kneebone who drew the maps of Ethiopia and the Southern Tribal Lands and to Philip Ellison who set the original text.

I am indebted to Arega Hailu Teffera, former Ambassador to Australia of the Federal Democratic Republic of Ethiopia, for his advice and support for my time in Ethiopia. Arega's expertise and encouragement for this project have been invaluable. Arega read and advised on chapters concerning Ethiopia. Particular thanks are due to Adimasu Gabayo and his brother Abe Gabayo from Addis Ababa for guiding me while in Addis Ababa and Ethiopia's Southern Tribal Lands; to David Virgin for his advice concerning contact with Adimasu Gabayo, and for giving me the benefit of his experience in Kenya and Ethiopia; to Daniel Bayene from Bahir Dar and Canberra for his friendship and enthusiasm and in particular for his advice about the work of the *Save the Children* organisation in Ethiopia; to Dr Mahlet Yigeremu, Dean of the School of Medicine, Addis Ababa University and CEO of the Tikur Anbessa Specialised Hospital, Addis Ababa, who provided significant advice regarding health needs, management and professional training, with particular regard to treatment of infectious diseases in Ethiopia; to Dr Ahmed Reja, Director of Addis Ababa University College of Health Sciences; and in Adelaide to Dr John Guy who provided expert advice regarding diagnosis of HIV and judicious assessment of the effective use of antiretroviral drugs. Thanks John.

My thanks to Louis de Vries, Director of Hybrid Publishers who from the outset was encouraging and enormously supportive. I owe a considerable debt to Anna Blay, Hybrid Publishers' principal editor. Anna's editing and understanding was not only most constructive but was incisive in that she recognised the difficulties of bridging cultures along with interpretations of the effects of trauma of people's lives. Anna's sharing of her life and literary experience provided shape and insightful interpretation of difficult relationships. Anna solved problems.

I have been guided and encouraged from the outset by many people. I single them out for thanks. Lelita Baldock, Valerie Crawford, Ryan Hewitt, Liz Hobbs, Cate Millar, Angela Murray, Terrance Osmond, Marisa Paravia, Deborah Pipe, Warren Porter, Adam Rees, Patrick Rees, Andrew Robertson, Pip Robertson, Jane Robinson, John Scholz, Dr Simon Spedding, Peter Strawhan, Sarah

Taylor, Heather Webster, Alex Woods, Maria Zuurmond and the late Dominie Whyntie.

The sustained support of my wife Tricia has made completing this book possible. Her love, encouragement and willingness to comment on draft chapters were integral to my writing *No Turning Back*. I cannot thank her enough.

Select Bibliography

I gratefully acknowledge the use of the following texts:

Achebe, Chinua, *A Man of the People*. Heinemann, London, 1981.

Achebe, Chinua, *Home and Exile*. Canongate, Edinburgh, 2003.

Achebe, Chinua, *Things Fall Apart*. Heinemann, Oxford, 1986.

Briggs, Philip, *Ethiopia, the Bradt Travel Guide*. Chalfont St Peter, Bucks, UK, 2015.

Camus, Albert, *The First Man*, translated from the French by David Hapgood. Penguin Books, London, 1995.

Clay, Jason W. & Bonnie K. Holcomb, *Politics and the Ethiopian Famine 1984–1985*. Cultural Survival Inc., Cambridge Massachusetts, 1986.

Cochrane, Kathie, *Oodgeroo*, with a contribution by Judith Wright and illustrations by Ron Hurley. St Lucia, Queensland, University of Queensland Press, 1994.

Duffy, Carol Ann, *Sylvia Plath Poems*, (chosen by Duffy). Faber & Faber, London, 2012.

Gallmann, Kuki, *I Dreamed of Africa*. Penguin Books, London, 2007.

Kagan, Dion, 'How to Have Memories in an Epidemic: Recent Documentaries about HIV/AIDS', in *Kill Your Darlings*, April 2013.

Kapuscinski, Ryszard, *The Emperor: Downfall of an Autocrat*, translated from the Polish by William R. Brand and Katarzyna Mroczkowska. Brand, Penguin Books, London, 2006.

Lonely Planet Guide Books, *Ethiopia & Eritrea*. London, 2010.

Lydall, Jean & Ivo Strecker, *The Hamar of Southern Ethiopia, Book*

1 Work Journal. University of Gottingen, Hohenschaflarn, Klaus Renner Verlag, 1979.

Malouf, David, *David Malouf: Book 2 The Writing Life.* Knopf – Random House, Sydney 2014.

Marsden, Philip, *Rising Ground: A Search for the Spirit of Place.* Granta, London, 2014.

Marsden, Philip, *The Barefoot Emperor: An Ethiopian Tragedy.* Harper Collins, London, 2008.

Marsden, Philip, *The Chains of Heaven: An Ethiopian Romance.* Harper Collins, London, 2006.

McCooey, David, *Rosemary Dobson Collected,* (introduction), University of Queensland Press, St Lucia, Queensland, 2012.

McKnight, Reginald (editor), *Wisdom of the African World.* New World Library: Novato, California, 1996.

Meredith, Martin, *The Fate of Africa: From the Hopes of Freedom to the Heart of Despair.* Public Affairs, New York, 2005.

Molvaer, Reidulf K., *Black Lions: The Creative Lives of Modern Ethiopia's Literary Giants and Pioneers.* Red Sea Press Inc., Lawrenceville, New Jersey, 1997.

Pasternak, Boris, *The Poems of Doctor Zhivago,* translated from the Russian by Eugene M. Kayden. Hallmark Edition, Kansas City, Missouri, 1967.

Piot, Peter, *No Time to Lose: A Life in Pursuit of Deadly Viruses.* W.W. Norton, New York, 2012.

Strecker, Ivo, *The Social Practice of Economic Symbolisation: An Anthropological Analysis.* New Jersey, Athlone Press, 1988.

The Pulse – bringing medical humanitarian action to you. Médecins Sans Frontières Monthly Magazine, 2012–2016.

Williams, William Carlos, *William Carlos Williams, Collected Poems I 1909–1939,* edited by A. Walton Litz & Christopher MacGowan. Carcanet Press Ltd, Manchester, 1987.

Winton, Tim, *Island Home: A Landscape Memoir*. Hamish Hamilton, Sydney, 2015.

Wright, Judith, *Judith Wright Collected Poems – 1942-1985*. Harper Collins, Sydney, 1994.

Wynhausen, Elisabeth, *On Resilience*. Melbourne University Press, Melbourne, 2009.